The Ocean Between Us

A Special Note from Susan Wiggs

There is sometimes one single defining moment that launches a book, like the spark beneath a firecracker. In the case of my novel, *The Ocean Between Us*, it was a moment few of us ever witness.

I had been working on an idea about an ordinary woman, a wife and mother, who discovers in the middle of her life that she has misplaced herself. This happens to women all the time. We get so caught up in running a household—managing kids and money, helping our husbands—that one day we wake up and wonder: What about me? What about the dreams I put on the shelf ten or twenty years ago?

So this was a story about a woman and her marriage—a good marriage, as it happens. Novels about bad marriages abound, and I wanted this one to be about two good people who love each other, but who, over the course of their long relationship, have lost each other. Writing about a good marriage isn't easy because, by definition, a functional marriage lacks the high level of drama needed to power a novel. Another problem: the idea was *too* general. I wanted to dramatize the journey of one woman—but who was this woman to be?

And then the magic—that elusive defining moment—happened. Real life intersected with fiction. Nearly three years ago I watched my good friend and fellow writer Geri Krotow fix a Command Pin on her husband's chest at a Change of Command ceremony. This was an elaborate event, attended by family, friends, dignitaries, but I thought it was significant that Geri, a former navy intelligence officer, was the one to make the most dramatic gesture of the day. She made it not as a navy official, but as a wife. While her children looked on, she made the ultimate gesture of sacrifice—entrusting him with his command, even while knowing it could take him far away from her and into the heart of danger. On beautiful Whidbey Island, in Puget Sound, we all felt far removed from war and turmoil, but in fact, we weren't. In the wake of 9/11, people in the military understood that war was imminent, and no one was safe. So Geri wasn't just enacting a symbolic ritual; she was willingly giving her blessing to her husband, knowing he'd be gone for months at a time. She was sending him to face dangers no civilian can imagine and perhaps even come back fundamentally changed—or not at all. This family's bravery touched my heart, and I finally realized what I wanted this book to be.

The Ocean Between Us was shaped by the lives and loves of families in the military. They are a special class of women and men who respond instantly to the call of duty, who can pack up and move an entire household halfway around the world at a moment's notice, only to do it again every couple of years. I was privileged to meet a number of navy wives, and I came to admire their sturdy spirit, their sense of commitment, their take-charge attitude and unabashed patriotism. Women who have known each other only a short time learn to bond quickly and deeply, to help each ther through rough times and celebrate the good. There is a sense that this is a secret sisterhood, a sorority. I read *E-mail to the Front* by Alesia Holliday, who fearlessly and hilariously documents the ups and downs of a military marriage in her phenomenally successful book. When Geri and her family were moving to Italy, her farewell party featured a life-size cutout of Fabio, among other fun things. Yet there were dark times as well, even desperate times for some families.

Because there's a horrific mishap (the military term for accident) aboard the aircraft carrier in *The Ocean Between Us*, I had research to do, which proved to be much harder than simply watching reruns of *JAG*. In the first place, navy people don't use plain English. Sometimes my e-mail exchanges with pilots and sailors needed translation. From a Prowler pilot: "I tell the SDO to sh*tcan the REO Speedwagon for the Event 1 Case 3 Launch.... Time to kick the tires, light the fires.... Don't boresight, check six, bingo to mom." In some of the action scenes, I used jargon without quite knowing what I was saying, but my sources say it checks out to an "OK grade for Wire 3." (This pilot asked not to be named for reasons of national security. His wife told me it was for reasons of not wanting to be perceived as a romance reader.)

Still, the heart of this novel is Grace Bennett, an ordinary woman with the additional burden of being a navy wife. She's helping her husband, Steve, on his climb to the very top of the ranks, all the while managing three active kids and a frenetic lifestyle. It's a juggling act that is complicated by the periodic and prolonged absences of her husband. A hairline crack in their marriage becomes a gaping wound when he goes away to sea. As a result, Grace learns to see herself in new ways, reopen a forgotten dream, and craft a new future for herself.

I'm excited about this book, and I'm proud to report that readers are, too. I've had a number of notes from readers about it, but by far the most meaningful was this one, from Kristi W., a real-life navy wife: "Tears came straight to my eyes. THANK YOU for writing a book about navy wives. I myself am one and have for a year now WISHED someone would write a book about it and share with people how hard the life can be. Then for my favorite author to write one, that just hit me hard. Thank you once again. Your books are just the little dose of fantasy that I need to keep me grounded!"

Susan Wiggs
Cafe Trios
Amalfi, Italy
2004

Alesia has launched a successful writing career as Alyssa Day. Geri Krotow's first novel was published in 2007 and her third, *Sasha's Dad*, will be out in June 2010. Currently stationed with her husband in Moscow, Russia, she blogs about life there at www.gerikrotow.com.

SUSAN WIGGS

The Ocean Between Us

MIRA®

Recycling programs
for this product may
not exist in your area.

ISBN-13: 978-0-7783-2863-6

THE OCEAN BETWEEN US

For questions and comments about the quality of this book please contact us at Customer_eCare@Harlequin.ca.

www.MIRABooks.com

Printed in U.S.A.

First Printing: April 2004
10 9 8 7 6 5 4 3 2

To my friend Geri Krotow and her family,
with love and deepest respect.

PART ONE
MISHAP

Mishap: Unplanned or unexpected event causing
personal injury, occupational illness, death,
material loss or damage, or an explosion
of any kind whether damage occurs or not.

(NAVAL AVIATION SAFETY PROGRAM)

CHAPTER ONE

USS Dominion *(CVN-84)*
0037N 17820W
Speed 33
2215 hours (Time Zone YANKEE)

Steve Bennett glanced at the clock on his computer screen. He ought to be in his rack and sleeping soundly. Instead, he sat with his feet propped on the edge of the workstation, hands clasped behind his head while he stared at a scenic Washington State calendar and thought about Grace.

He was ten thousand miles from home, on an aircraft carrier in the middle of an unofficial communications blackout instigated by Grace herself. His wife. The mother of his children. The woman who had not spoken to him willingly since he'd been deployed.

She had maintained radio silence like a wartime spy. He received official communiqués about the children, and sometimes the occasional report that made him regret giving her power of attorney. But never more than that.

The cruise was nearly over, and for the first time in his career

Steve felt apprehensive about going home. He had no idea whether or not they could put their marriage back together again.

"Captain Bennett?" An administrative officer stood in the doorway with a clipboard in one hand and a PDA in the other.

"What is it, Lieutenant Killigrew?"

"Ms. Francine Atwater is here to see you, sir."

Bennett hid a frown. He'd nearly forgotten their appointment. In the belly of a carrier there was no day or night, just an unrelenting fluorescent sameness, stale recycled air and the constant thunder of flight ops rattling through the steel bones of the ship.

"Send her in." He unfolded his long frame and stood, assuming the stiff and wary posture schooled into him by twenty-six years in the Navy. Killigrew left for a moment, then returned with the reporter. Steve would have preferred to use the public affairs office on the 01 deck, but apparently Ms. Atwater was adamant about exploring every facet of carrier life. It was, after all, the era of the embedded reporter.

Francine Atwater. *Francine.* A member of the "new media," eager to take advantage of the military's newly relaxed information policy. According to his briefing notes, she had arrived COD—carrier onboard delivery—and intended to spend the next two weeks in this floating city with its own airport. Both the skipper of the *Dominion* and Captain Mason Crowther, Commander of the Air Group, had welcomed her personally, but they'd quickly handed her off to others, and now it was Steve's turn.

"Ms. Atwater, I'm Captain Steve Bennett, Deputy Commander of the Air Group." He tried not to stare, but she was the first civilian woman he'd seen in months. In a skirt, no less. He silently paid tribute to the genius who had invented nylon stockings and cherry-colored lipstick.

"Thank you, Captain Bennett." Her glossy lips parted in a smile. She was a charmer, all right, the way she tilted her head to one side and looked up at him through long eyelashes. Still, he detected shadows of fatigue under her carefully made-up eyes.

Newcomers to the carrier usually suffered seasickness and insomnia from all the noise.

"Welcome aboard, ma'am."

"I see you've been briefed about me," she said, indicating his notes from the PAO.

"Yes, ma'am."

"What a surprise. Everyone on this ship has. I swear, the U.S. Navy knows more about me than my own mother. My blood type, shoe size, visual acuity, sophomore-year biology grade—"

"Standard procedure, ma'am." Even in lipstick and nylon stockings, the media held no appeal to the military. Still, he respected the way she stood her ground, especially while wearing three-inch heels. Civilians were advised on practical shipboard attire, but apparently no one had wanted Francine to change her shoes.

A tremendous whoosh, followed by a loud thump, rocked the ship. She staggered a little, and he put out a hand to steady her.

"Tell me I'll get used to that," she said.

"You'd better. We're launching and recovering planes around the clock, day and night. It's not going to stop." He slid open a desk drawer and took out a sealed plastic package. "Take these. I always keep plenty on hand."

"Earplugs?" She slipped the package into her briefcase. "Thanks."

He motioned her to a chair and she sat down, setting aside her bag. She took out a palm-size digital recorder, then swept the small space with a glance that shifted like a radar, homing in on the few personal items in evidence. "You have a beautiful family."

"Thank you, ma'am. I think so."

"How old are your children?"

"Brian and Emma are twins. They're seniors this year. Katie's in ninth grade. And that's Grace, my wife." A world of pain and hope underlay his words, but he prayed the reporter wouldn't notice. Every day he looked at that picture and tried to figure out what would fix this. He'd never deceived his wife before, so he didn't know how to undo the damage he'd caused. An ordinary husband would go home, take her out to dinner and say, "Look, honey. The truth is…" But Bennett couldn't do that from the middle of the ocean.

And sometimes he wondered if he even wanted to, damn it. He'd done his best to keep her from being hurt, but she didn't seem to appreciate that.

In the photo, taken at Mustang Island when they were stationed in Corpus Christi, the four of them were laughing into the camera, sunburned faces glowing.

"This is a great shot," said Ms. Atwater. "They look like the kind of people nothing bad ever happens to."

Interesting observation. He would have agreed with her, right up until this deployment. Grace and the kids were part of the all-American family, the kind you saw on minivan commercials or at summer baseball games.

"What's it like, being away from them for months on end?"

What the hell did she think it was like? A damned fraternity party?

"It's rough. I'm sure you'll hear that from a lot of the sailors on board. It's hard seeing your baby's first steps on videotape or getting a picture of a winning soccer goal by e-mail." Steve wished he had prepared himself better for her nosiness. He should have barricaded his private self. He was supposed to be good at that. According to Grace, he was the champ.

Atwater studied another photograph, this one in a slightly warped frame nearly twenty years old. "But the homecomings are sweet," she murmured, gazing down at the fading image.

He couldn't recall who had taken that shot, but he remembered the moment with painful clarity. It was the end of his first cruise after they'd married. The gray steel hull of an aircraft carrier reared in the background. Sailors, officers and civilians all crushed together, hugging with the desperate joy only military families understood. At the center, he and Grace held each other in an embrace he could still feel all these years later. He clasped her so close that her feet came off the ground, one of her dainty high heels dangling off a slender foot. He could still remember what she smelled like.

Since that photo was taken there had been dozens of other partings and reunions. He could picture each homecoming in succession—Grace pregnant with the twins, no high heels that time, just sneakers that wouldn't lace up around her swollen feet. Then Grace pushing a double stroller that wouldn't fit through doorways. By then, her perfume was more likely to be a blend of baby wipes and cough drops. In later years, the kids kept her busy as she shuffled them between music lessons, sports practices, Brownies and Boy Scouts. But she always came to meet him. She never left him standing like some loser whose wife had given him the shaft while he was at sea, who would sling his seabag over his shoulder and pretend it didn't matter, whistling under his breath as he headed straight for the nearest bar.

Yesterday had been Grace's fortieth birthday. He'd phoned and gotten the machine. Lately she was so prickly about her age, anyway. She probably wouldn't thank him for the reminder.

Atwater asked about his background, his career path in the Navy, his role on the carrier. She listened well, occasionally making notes on a small yellow pad as well as recording him. At one point he glanced at his watch and was surprised to see how much time had passed. She'd talked to him about his family for nearly an hour. He wondered if he'd told her too much. Did the American people really need to know his life was coming undone like a slipknot?

He cleared his throat. "Says on my agenda that I'm your tour guide for nighttime flight ops." He was surprised that she'd gained authorization to be on the flight deck at night, but apparently her project was important to Higher Authority.

"I've been looking forward to this, sir." She came alive in that special way of people who were in love with flying, the more high-tech and dangerous, the better. And there was no form of flying more dangerous than carrier operations.

He was dog tired, but he put on a smile because, in spite of everything, he shared her enthusiasm.

"I thought about going into the service and learning to fly," she said, her eyes shining. "Couldn't make the commitment, though."

"Lots of people can't." He said it without condemnation or pride. It was a plain fact. The U.S. Navy demanded half of your life. It was as simple as that. He'd been in the Navy since his eighteenth birthday. And of his twenty-six years of service, he'd been at sea for half of them. That kind of commitment had its rewards, but it also carried a price. He was finally figuring that out.

As he went to the door, the Inbox on his computer screen blinked, but he didn't check to see what had come in. If it was personal, he didn't want a reporter reading over his shoulder.

He led her single file down a narrow passageway tiled in blue, narrating their journey and cautioning her to avoid slamming her shins on the "knee knockers," structural members at the bottom of each hatch. Lining theP-way were dozens of red cabinets containing fire-control gear and protective clothing. The least little spark could take out half the ship if it happened to ignite in the wrong place.

Steve spoke over his shoulder, but he wasn't sure how much she was taking in. The constant din of flight ops intruded—roaring engines, the hiss and grind of the power plant and arresting gear, the whistle and screech of aircraft slamming on deck—drowning out normal conversation. In the enlisted men's mess, they created a small stir. Sailors enjoying MIDRATS—rations for personnel on night duty—stopped what they were doing the minute they saw Francine Atwater. Their jaws dropped as though unhinged. Even the female sailors stared, not with the raw yearning of the males but with wistfulness, and perhaps a flicker of disdain. In the service of their country, they had learned to do without makeup, without hair spray, without vanity.

As they climbed an open steel ladder, Atwater took it in stride, but she was probably wishing she'd worn pants and thick-soled boots. They crossed the hangar bay, where aircraft waited with wings folded like origami cranes.

In the passageway under flight-deck control, the roar of aircraft pounding the steel deck was louder still. "We need to gear up," Steve said, handing her a flight suit and boots.

"I've been briefed on safety procedures." She sat down and slipped off her civilian shoes, flashing a slim foot encased in a nylon stocking. "Hours and hours of briefing."

"The Navy loves to brief people," he admitted, hearing echoes of the endless droning of Navy gouge he'd endured over the years, litanies of instruction and advisories. "In this case, I hope you listened," he added. Then, assuming she hadn't, he reiterated the list of hazards on the flight deck. A sailor could be sucked into an engine intake. Exhaust from a jet engine had the power to blast a person across the deck, or even overboard. He'd seen large men bouncing like basketballs all the way to the deck edge. Or an arresting wire might snap as a tail hook grabbed it, whipping with enough force to sever a person's legs. Taxiing planes, scurrying yellow tractors, breaking launch bars—all were hazards waiting to happen.

His hand wandered to his throat in a habitual gesture, seeking his St. Christopher medal. Then he remembered that he'd lost it, the good-luck charm he'd had since his first deployment. He never went to sea without it. Ah, hell. At least he wasn't flying.

He distracted himself by perusing the bulletin board of one of the squadrons. The postings included items for sale or trade, a movie schedule and an invitation to the upcoming Steel Beach picnic, during which a dozen or so garage bands would perform. Personnel on board were desperate to create a normal existence in a highly abnormal situation.

It didn't always work, Steve thought.

After she finished gearing up for flight ops, Francine Atwater looked totally different. Steel-toed boots, a shiny gray-green jumpsuit and a white visitor's jersey hid all of her charms except those big brown eyes.

Feeling a bit like an airline flight attendant, he showed her how to operate her float coat. The vest was equipped with a beacon light, a packet of chemical dye to mark the water if she found herself in the drink, a flare, a whistle. "This is your MOBI," he said. It was a transmitter the size of a cell phone, with a whip antenna connected to a small box.

"Let me guess. Man Overboard... Indicator."

"You did your homework."

"I told you, I was briefed. But you're forgetting something," she said.

"What's that?"

"I don't intend to go for a midnight swim."

"Then we're on the same page." He slipped the device into the dye pouch of her float coat and closed the Velcro fastening. "But just in case, the transmitter has its own unique identification. That way, the bridge will know identity and location immediately."

"So this one has my name on it?"

"Just the number of the float coat. You want me to show you how to fasten everything?"

"I've got it," she said.

He showed her a status board outlining the night's exercises. The list indicated who was taking off, who was landing, who the crew members were, the purpose of their particular operation.

"Two of the names are in red," Atwater pointed out. "Is that significant?"

"They're nugget pilots. New guys. This is their first cruise."

"Lieutenant junior grade Joshua Lamont," she read from the chart. "Call sign Lamb."

Steve didn't move a muscle, even though the sound of Lamont's name was a punch in the gut. He wondered if he would ever get used to having Lamont under his command. A C-2 Greyhound transport plane had flown the young pilot aboard as a replacement pilot. Lamont was a member of the Sparhawks, the carrier's squadron of EA-6B Prowlers. The reporter probably thought his call sign was sweet, but Steve knew it came from an incident during training in Nevada—Little Angry Man Boy.

"He's flying Prowler six-two-three," she observed. "My cameramen videotaped the aircrew while they were preparing that plane for tonight's flight."

"You're making a video?" The public affairs office hadn't bothered to tell him exactly what was up.

"You bet."

He shouldn't be surprised. A magazine was no longer just a magazine. These days every publication needed a multimedia presence on the Web, with all the attendant bells and whistles. Higher Authority had given their blessing to the article. These were patriotic times and frankly—unexpectedly—the media had been good to the military in recent times. Strange bedfellows, but sometimes you never knew.

"Lamont's been in the air one hour and forty-eight minutes now," he said. "Looks like they'll be landing soon."

"What about the other name in red—Sean Corn?"

"Lieutenant Corn is due to land directly behind the Prowler. He's driving one of the Tomcats."

"And they're new to night carrier landings?"

"Yes, ma'am, but they've had extensive training." Steve quickly switched to the public-affairs spiel. "A carrier landing is basically a crash landing on an area about four hundred feet long. The margin of error on approach is less than eighteen inches," he told her. "The tail hook has to grab an arresting wire, or you have a bolter and the pilot has to come around for another pass. Success depends on every member of the team doing his job right, doing it on time and following orders. So the question isn't why so many accidents happen but why so few."

"But accidents do happen."

He wondered if she had a secret wish to witness one. "Yes, ma'am."

"Do you fly often, Captain Bennett?"

"Enough to stay qualified."

"Do you miss it?"

"Flying used to be my life, but after almost a thousand carrier traps, I can live without it." He tried not to smile at her thunderstruck expression. "Look, ma'am, if you're looking for drama, you're talking to the wrong guy."

"What's wrong with you?"

"I don't make good copy. Not anymore. I used to be a cowboy, turning everything into a competition. I used to look another pilot in the eye, call him my best friend and then wax his ass in training."

"But you don't do that anymore?"

He hesitated. "I'll introduce you to some guys who do."

They put on headsets, goggles and cranials with ear protectors marked across the top with reflective tape. Then Steve stood aside, motioning her ahead.

They climbed several more steel ladders. Steve opened another hatch and they passed a sign: Beware Jet Blast-Props-Rotor Blades. They crossed the platform, mounted a few more steps and finally reached the four-and-a-half-acre flight deck.

A strong, cold wind slapped at them, carrying with it the reek of jet fuel and hydraulic fluid. Cinders flung up from the nonskid surface of the deck needled their faces. Behind the protective goggles, Francine's eyes reflected amazement. This was a strange new world, with the deck humming underfoot, busy personnel in color-coded jerseys and cranials communicating by gesture, planes and tractors scurrying to and fro. Despite the late hour, bright lights and thundering sound burst across the deck in a chaotic but precisely choreographed ballet of landing aircraft. The deafening noise made speech superfluous, so he gave her an expansive gesture: Welcome to the bird farm. She staggered a little as a blast of wind hit her, but then responded with a thumbs-up.

They crossed the roof to the island tower and climbed a series of ladders, passing various control centers. In Flight Deck Control, a chief petty officer kept track of the different aircraft and their positions on the "Ouija board," little game-piece planes on a scale map of the deck. After asking permission to enter the bridge, he led her up another level to the top of the island, where the Air Boss presided over a domain of darkened cubicles encased in shatterproof safety glass. In Primary Flight Control, touch-sensitive glass, glowing control panels and monitors reflected off the intent faces of busy crew members. Another screen showed the positions of the entire battle group and other vessels in the area. Steve pointed out destroyers, cruisers, a supply ship, the oiler.

"And what's that?" she asked, pointing to the screen.

"Probably a Japanese fishing boat," Steve said.

In the tinted glass aerie, Commander Shep Hardin, the Air Boss on duty, barked commands at the flight deck. He paused briefly to greet them. "Aren't you lucky," he said to Atwater. "A guided tour by the gray wolf himself."

"Thanks a lot, pal," Steve said, then turned to the reporter. "Hardin's no fun, anyway. Want to watch from Vultures Row?"

"I thought you'd never ask."

As they headed for the observation balcony overlooking the flight deck, she asked, "Why did he call you the gray wolf?"

He was sort of wishing she hadn't heard that. "A carrier crew is made up of young men and women, most of them under twenty-five. At forty-four, I'm old." He didn't want to go into all the politics and posturing of his climb to the upper ranks. He pointed to a row of three aircraft chained to the deck. "Those are Prowlers, parked down there. They're used for electronic reconnaissance and jamming."

Francine cupped her hands around her eyes, pressed her face to the glass and studied the lighted deck. "The planes look sort of…lived in."

She was right. These deck-weary aircraft hardly resembled the gleaming birds in Navy publicity photos. They looked as though they'd been patched together with duct tape, baling wire and Bondo.

"Ma'am, flight ops are the whole reason a carrier exists, so keeping the planes operational is crucial. Air crews work 24/7 to keep them ready to go," he assured her, but he hoped she didn't notice the drip of hydraulic fluid spattering the black steel deck. "The Prowler squadron has only four aircraft, so they get used a lot. It's late in the cruise, and the concern isn't making them look pretty. It's making them work right."

"And Lamont, the…nugget, is flying the other one."

"Yes, ma'am."

Using her deck-ops manual for a flat surface, she made a note on her yellow pad.

"You ready to see some landings?" he asked.

"In a sec." She scribbled furiously.

Then he instructed her to lower her goggles, slid open the door and they stepped outside. High off the bow, two shooting stars streaked briefly, drawing twin parallel lines down the black sky before disappearing. Steve tried to alert the reporter, but it was over so quickly that she missed it. No big deal. Shooting stars weren't the main attraction tonight. Planes rained from the sky, one after another, slamming down on deck with screams of rubber and metal. Tail hooks searching for an arresting wire threw up rooster tails of sparks.

He handed the reporter a pair of binoculars and pointed out Landing Signal Officer Whitey Love, who stood with the other LSOs on the port side atop a wind-harried platform. From his vantage point under the edge of the flight deck, near the first set of arresting wires, the LSO studied the night sky through a pair of infrared lenses. Over the headset, he talked to his pilots. It was his job to coax each fifty-thousand-pound aircraft, hurtling at a hundred thirty miles per hour, to a three-hundred-foot landing strip.

A luminous amber signal on the port-deck edge aligned with a row of green lights, signaling that the incoming pilot was on the proper glide path for a safe landing. The dainty-looking tail hook had a shot at just five wires. Each cable could be used for a set number of traps before it was retired, compromised by the strain of stopping the speeding jets. If something went wrong, it could mean the loss of a sixty-million-dollar aircraft off the deck, and perhaps the lives of the pilot and crew.

Steve noticed a whiteshirt and three other VIPs loaded with equipment. Atwater saw his look and motioned him inside.

"My photographer and videographer and their assistant," she explained.

He hoped the camera guys had been briefed on safety, too. The videographer appeared clueless as he filmed a turning jet that was on its way to the elevator. He clearly had no idea that the blast might toss him twenty feet in the air. Just in time, the host yanked him out of harm's way and the group headed to the island.

They met up at deck level, where the floor hummed and a water cooler by the base of the elevator vibrated dangerously. As Francine made the introductions, an ordie in a soiled red shirt stepped inside, slapping a smoking glove against his thigh.

Steve recognized Aviation Ordnanceman Airman Michael Rivera behind the smudged goggles. The sailor quickly came to attention. The photographers immediately aimed their cameras at him.

"Everything all right?" Steve asked.

"Yes, sir. Slight problem with the flares, is all," Rivera said, removing his goggles and scuffed red cranial. "It's okay now."

"Go down to the battle-dressing station and get that hand looked at."

"No need, sir. Just wanted to get out of the wind for a minute."

Rivera was Steve's favorite kind of sailor—professional, dedicated, sure of himself. Not likely to let a smart-ass hotshot fighter pilot intimidate him on the flight deck. Besides that, Rivera's winning smile and genuine warmth made him a regular recruiting poster boy. His face was covered in grime from a long shift on the flight deck, but that only made his teeth look whiter.

Atwater loved him instantly. Steve could tell from the soft-eyed expression on her face. Hell, he might as well indulge her. He made the introductions, and Rivera warmed right up, probably grateful for a break from the chaos of the open deck.

"And what do you do?" Atwater asked him, pen poised over her notebook.

"I deal with ordnance, ma'am. The bomb farm's the area between the island and the rail where bombs and missiles are stored during flight operations. From there they're brought to the aircraft."

"And there was trouble with a flare?"

Rivera nodded. "Flares are used with F-14 Tomcats as a decoy for heat-seeking missiles. Each flare contains eighty internal units, and each of those burn at sixteen hundred degrees, so we're real careful with them." He grinned, and an irrepressible happiness shone from him. "I have even more reason to be careful these days. Had an e-mail from my wife this morning. The doctor found out the baby's sex. We're having a boy." He looked ready to burst with pride. "Our first."

"Will you be home for the birth?" Ms. Atwater asked.

"No, ma'am. But she's got a lot of support at home."

"Where's home?"

"Whidbey Island Naval Air Station in Washington State. Captain Bennett's wife has been a real good friend to Patricia," he added with a grateful look at Steve.

Don't look at me, Steve thought. He had no idea what Grace was up to, but it didn't surprise him to hear she was helping out a young airman's wife. Discomfited, he looked through a viewing pane while the PAO who had been escorting the photographers joined in the conversation with Rivera.

Outside, Steve noticed…something. He'd spent too many hours on a carrier deck to not clue in when something was going on. A subtle change came over the crew charged with recovering the next aircraft. It was like a slight shift in the wind or an invisible spurt of adrenaline, something the reporter or even most of the flight-deck ops would never notice.

Steve excused himself. The CAG LSO, Bud Forster, who didn't usually participate in a recovery unless things got ugly, was speaking quickly into his headset. "Prowler six-two-three…" he said, and his face was made of stone. Steve knew that look.

And he knew whose plane Forster was talking about. Lamont was driving the Prowler, and whatever was going on had not been in the plans for tonight's exercises. Forster was handling it, though, and Steve wasn't about to interrupt his work. He would have stuck around, but when he looked at the deck again, he noticed Francine Atwater and the others following Rivera to the bomb farm. The PAO was nowhere in sight.

None of the civilians would sense the mounting tension, he realized, hurrying down to the deck. But Steve felt it buzzing like an electrical current through his whole body. Shit. He'd have to go round them up like a herd of cats. Your ass is grass, Rivera, Steve thought. And I'm John Deere.

But then he reminded himself that he was the one who was supposed to be in charge of Francine Atwater, and he'd walked away. As he headed toward the ordnance, he thought he saw sparks and a stream of smoke from an aircraft flare dispenser on the deck behind Rivera and the civilians.

He blinked and rubbed his glove across his goggles, and saw it again. They were too far away to hear a shouted warning. But he shouted, anyway, at the same time signaling flight-deck control to sound a fire alarm. During flight ops there was always a fire truck and a team of firefighters standing by with nozzles leading to water tanks and aqueous film-forming foam.

Rivera, who was closest to the dispenser, spun around. He cast about, looking for the source of the fire, and for a second Steve thought he might miss the smoke. Then Rivera grabbed the burning cylinder and headed for the edge of the flight deck. There was a crack like a rifle shot. Sparks and rockets ripped apart the night. Rivera rolled on the ground. His entire arm was a glowing torch.

Steve ran. When he reached the burning man, he plunged to his knees and ripped off his float coat. He used the vest to smother the flames on Rivera's arm and back, screaming for a medic even though he knew he wouldn't be heard. It didn't matter. By now, everyone on the bow of the flight deck would have seen, and help would be on its way. He wanted to stay with Rivera, hold and reassure him, but the dispenser was still smoking. In the cylinder, the internal units were burning with an intensity Steve felt even from three feet away.

If it smokes, get rid of it. The most basic rule of fire control.

He grabbed the handle of the dispenser. His glove ignited and he roared in agony but refused to let go. The damned thing felt like it weighed a ton, yet somehow he managed to rush to the deck edge with it.

A blast of heat and light engulfed him. There was nothing under his feet, and he felt as though he'd been sucked into a tornado. Where the hell was the safety net? That was the only coherent thought he had as he was hurled through empty air. Yet curiously, he could distinguish only one sound through the rush of wind—a throaty and frantic baying sound from the navigation bridge.

It was the special alarm reserved for one of the most dreaded incidents of carrier operations—man overboard.

CHAPTER TWO

~⚬~

Prowler 623/BuNo 163530
0015 hours

Landing in the pitch-dark on the moving deck of a carrier was a freaking nightmare. And Josh Lamont loved the fear with a feverish intensity that sometimes worried his flight crew. When he saw his name on the flight schedule, he felt that familiar sizzle of anticipation. Night exercises, multiple aircraft, every second a hairbreadth from death—heaven didn't get any better than this.

The preflight brief and man-up had been as routine as brushing your teeth. The night was clear and a million; you could see forever. Outside the Prowler's bubble canopy, he could see the stars and planets swirling past. Straight on and high, twin shooting stars slid down and disappeared.

Josh grinned inside his mask, knowing he'd seen something rare. The euphoria of flying allowed him to ignore the fact that he'd been strapped to an ejection seat for two hours and was about to come home to the bird farm for a night-arrested landing. He switched his radio frequency and picked up the off-key singing of Ron Hatch, one of the electronic countermeasures officers, who sat on his right and was belting out his third chorus of "Mary Ann Barnes."

"She can shoot green peas from her fundamental orifice," sang Hatch, "do a double somersault and catch 'em on her tits...."

Newman and Turnbull, the other two ECMOs seated behind them, sang along. They were older and more experienced than Josh. Newman, who sat behind Hatch, looked to be as old as Bennett himself, a veteran of the problematic cruise of the *Kennedy* in 1983.

As the junior officer of the crew, Josh added his voice to the noise. The song about the "Queen of All the Acrobats" was known to every Navy pilot, passed like a secret handshake through flight schools and training programs. Their voices were tinny strains through the headsets, crackling with good humor. Being on the carrier was like being trapped at Alcatraz—no escape, no place to hide. Going up on a mission to touch the stars was a two-hour recess.

Josh studied the view outside the Prowler's bubble. The sky wasn't black, but a rich and layered purple, misty with stars. He had dreamed about this all his life. Flying had been his driving passion since he was a boy. And not just any flying. Navy jets. He had done battle with his parents over his obsession and aimed himself like a missile at his goal. Growing up in urban upper-class Atlanta, he wasn't supposed to be pilot material. His childhood had consisted of excruciatingly quiet dinners in a house you tiptoed through. He used to envy big families filled with kids and noise, a chaotic contrast to his own tense and lonely existence. Attending the Naval Academy had actually felt liberating compared to the stiff, invisible confines of his boyhood.

And now here he was, living the future he'd envisioned for himself. And yet, ironically, this cruise brought him face-to-face with the hidden past. With Steve Bennett, a man he never thought he'd meet.

And then there was Lauren, a woman he never thought he'd

deserve. She was more than a passing fancy. She'd taken up residence inside him. She was part of the air he breathed, the dreams he dreamed. The one thing he loved more than flying.

He imagined her waking up, thinking of him, checking her e-mail to read the short, funny messages he sent from the ship. Just before the man-up, he'd checked his e-mail to find a hurried-sounding note from her: *Please call right away. I need to talk to you.* He didn't have time to contact her before the mission. But as soon as he finished up here, he'd call. He couldn't wait. He wanted to hear her voice saying the only thing he wanted to hear from her: *Yes.*

His thumb began to tremble and search the top of the control stick, manipulating the button to ensure that the jet would sail down the glide slope when the time came. Despite his intense concentration, he caught his mind wandering to Lauren again—the way she liked to be touched, the sound of her voice, the taste of her lips.

He should have pressed her for an answer before shipping out. But then he wondered, did he really want an answer from her? Flying Navy jets was a simple matter compared to loving a woman. All the same, he'd picked out a ring in Pattaya, Thailand.

As they neared their final approach, Hatch and company became all business.

"Don't get fancy on us," Hatch said. "Just do what you need to do. Better to be good than lucky."

"Yeah," said Josh. "But if you're lucky, you don't need to be good."

"Be lucky on someone else's watch."

The ship was down there in the dark somewhere, too distant to see yet. He checked the horizon and the climb indicator to make sure he was level. Altitude eight thousand feet. Speed four-hundred-thirty knots. He made a series of other checks around the cockpit. He touched the Velcro fastening of a pocket on his G-suit—that was where he kept Lauren's ring, for luck. Anything loose in the cockpit turned into a runaway missile during landing.

The approach controller gave him his new final bearing. The Prowler thundered down through three thousand feet. Josh's gaze swept the instrument panel. According to the TACAN, the ship was steaming west-northwest at thirty knots. He came to idle, and the aircraft hung for a moment in an eerie, vaguely magical silence. Then he broke hard left to level the Prowler downwind of the ship. It was too dark to see the wake, but his instruments did the work, showing him lined up with the angled deck.

A couple of minutes passed. "Dirty up," said the approach controller.

Josh pulled back on the throttle, lowered the handle, moved a lever down, hanging out his flaps, slats, gear and droops. Air screamed over the ailerons. Then he released the tail hook and scanned the panel again before calling in his landing checklist.

He was on full alert now, breathing hard, aware of everything with a strange clarity of sensation. He could feel the nylon webbing of the straps binding him to the ejection seat, the spongy pads of his earpieces, the jock-strap rim of the mask over his nose and mouth. He darted his gaze in a set pattern, his own way of checking the instrument readings.

"Prowler six-two-three, at five miles, lock on, call your needles."

Josh compared his readings to the controller's. His hands twitched over the stick and throttles. The tiny toy aircraft on the gyro listed to the right. He made a correction. "Boards out," he said. "Landing check complete." Adrenaline roared through him. He ought to be flying better. It was a bad time for doubts to poke at him, but he couldn't help it.

He looked past the instrument panel. All he saw of the carrier was a misty yellow light. Not a damned thing more. He was three-quarters of a mile out and had to shift from scanning blessedly precise, crystal-clear instruments in the cockpit to focusing on the glowing meatball far below, the centerline of the deck and the angle of attack. It was like putting on the glasses of someone who was nearly blind.

"You're okay. Easy as passing a camel through the eye of a needle. Make your ball call."

"Six-two-three Prowler, roger ball, state five point five

Lamont," he said, telling the landing signal officer he'd seen the vertical light indicating the descent path, and that his aircraft had 5,500 pounds of fuel.

In order to land on the moving deck, he had to strictly control his glideslope, speed and centerline. The floating city of five thousand inhabitants, lit like a child's Lite-Brite in the black sea, looked impossibly small. The fact that it was steaming away from him at thirty knots only made the ride more interesting.

Sweat tracked down between his shoulder blades, and he wondered if experienced pilots ever got used to this. Too high and he'd miss the wire and bolt off into the night again with barely enough fuel to make another pass. The slightest tip to one side risked a collision with a jet parked on the deck. A drift to the other side meant an unscheduled swim and the loss of a fifty-two-million-dollar aircraft. The LSO might wave him off two seconds before landing. If he came in too low, he'd hit the ramp and turn the plane and its crew into a fireball.

This is so cool, he thought.

His legs twitched and trembled uncontrollably on the rudder pedals. His lineup was good, or so he thought until the expressionless voice of the LSO came in through his headset. "You're low, six-two-three. Power."

Josh shoved his hand forward, overcompensating. The uncooperative nose of the aircraft reminded him that he was a rookie with fewer than fifty traps under his belt, not even a dozen at night.

"Take it easy," said the soothing voice in his ear.

Then the emergency signal sounded. The LSO's next order was not so soothing: "Red deck! Red deck! Power!" The vertical wave-off lights lit like a Christmas tree.

Josh rammed the throttles hard to the stops to firewall the engine. A red deck was closed to incoming aircraft, even those that were seconds from landing. He cut away and climbed back into the night. The plane shuddered like a live beast.

"Watch the PIO, nugget."

Pilot-induced oscillation. "Got it. Not everybody wants to be a Blue Angel." Josh concentrated on the climb, breaking the landing pattern. The plane shifted from side to side. "She's yawing," he said, flicking a glance at the instrument panel.

"The computer will correct it," said Hatch.

"What the hell happened down there?"

"Fouled deck. Wait for instructions."

A fouled deck could mean any number of things—an aircraft mishap, equipment left on deck, maybe personnel in the landing zone. For now, Josh could only worry about resuming the landing pattern and monitoring the fuel.

"Check your lineup."

Even as he followed orders, Josh could see the lights of the "angel," the carrier's rescue helicopter, hovering like a benevolent guardian over the ship. Then the helo dipped and swept into a pattern he'd never seen before. Rescuing someone?

"Quit with the PIO, already," Hatch repeated. Then, to the tower, he said, "Got a bit of a problem, Mother. How about you send a rescue helo out our way, just in case this nugget can't get us down?"

"It's not me," Josh said. "Jesus, this plane is bent." He wasn't being defensive. The computer wasn't making the proper corrections. The Prowler yawed hard to the right as though bent over a giant knee. Josh had never felt anything quite like it. The aircraft was in an uncommanded, uncontrolled, oscillating, full-rudder deflection.

He raised the gear handle and the plane pitched back to the left. That's it, then, he thought as he took himself out of the landing pattern again and ordered the lead jet in the new pattern to get away.

"Vertical speed indicator just took a dip," Hatch reported. Josh already knew this. The VSI was part of the ECMO's instrument scan, but Josh was the pilot. It was all his business.

A negative dip. That was ejection criteria. The broadcast of "Mayday, Mayday, Mayday" sounded surreal.

With the radio squawking Emergency, he tried three more cycles, one after another. "I can't control the rudders," he reported in a voice that was icily calm. They were still climbing, and every man in the cockpit understood why, though none would speak of it aloud. If they had to eject, they would need the altitude.

Fresh adrenaline burst through him. The drop in vertical speed was only part of the emergency. Any second the nose could pitch up or the aircraft could roll, and the decision would be taken away from him. They were a heartbeat away from an unscheduled carnival ride of ejection and parachute. They'd have a bird's-eye view of a very expensive fireball.

Shit. The damned thing was still flying. He'd managed to climb to ten thousand feet. He wasn't out of control. He had *no* control. He accelerated, hoping to get some more airspeed and altitude.

He could hear Hatch briefing the controller on the situation. Captain Bud Forster, the CAG LSO, came online again. In a few minutes, the whole battle group would know about the trouble.

The plane broke ten thousand feet, and the nose pitched up. Josh wrestled with it, but it kept bucking. He dampened the yaw by working the rudders opposite the cycles, but the aircraft kept canting on its own.

Nobody said what everyone was thinking: the jet couldn't make a safe landing.

The ECMOs worked feverishly through checklists—rudder failure, control malfunctions, alternate approaches—hoping to find the magic bullet. "Nothing. There's nothing applicable," Newman concluded. "Wait here. We need to pull circuit breakers until we isolate the problem. Jeez, I do this in my basement when the dishwasher quits."

When the first two were pulled, the yaw abated. "Keep going," Josh ordered. The third one created no noticeable difference. When the fourth was pulled, the controls turned to mush. "Put it back!" Josh yelled. "Put it back!"

Too late. The nose pitched up wildly. I did this, thought Josh, fighting back with the controls. I'm the pilot, and I did this. The air-navigation computer was haywire. He tried feverishly to remember if he'd shut it off when he'd aborted the landing.

Maybe the computer had engaged automatically and was overriding him. It didn't matter now. The Prowler was completely out of control.

In the cockpit, they all knew it. Four pairs of gloved hands wrapped around four ejection handles. These were Advanced Concept Ejection Seats, 128 pounds apiece, each equipped with a twenty-one-pound rocket catapult. Success rate was better than ninety percent, but for some reason, Josh felt no reassurance.

He looked out at the ice-bright stars and wished he'd worn warmer clothes under his G-suit. At the same time, he was thinking and moving as fast as he could—faster than he'd ever imagined he could—but everything seemed to slow down. Time dilation. It was a concept he'd studied in advanced physics. *Time in the moving system will be perceived by a stationary observer to be running slower....*

He was a stationary observer; the Prowler was a moving system. *The traveler measures his own proper time, since he is at the beginning and end of his trip interval.*

In the shadowy cockpit, the glow from the instrument panel cast its eerie illumination over the faces of the crew as each man braced for disaster. They were all alone up here, yet they were not alone. Four lives, four families whose fate would be decided by a broken piece of metal hanging in midair.

Josh thought, *Lauren.* Only a minute ago he'd been confused about her. Now, with the same crystal clarity with which he could see the tumbling night sky, he knew exactly what he wanted. *Lauren.* The beginning and the end of his trip interval.

He took a deep, bracing breath. Then he gave the order he knew he had to give.

"Eject! Eject! Eject!"

CHAPTER THREE

Whidbey Island, Washington
7:30 a.m.

Lauren Stanton woke up in the same state of mind she'd gone to sleep in—thinking of Josh. He had only been at sea for a few weeks, but it felt like forever.

She grabbed his pillow and hugged it, her eyes shut and her heart about to break. "Josh," she whispered into the feathery depths. Maybe it was just her imagination, but she believed it still held his scent.

She of all people should know better than to fall for a Navy guy.

Groaning in protest, she swam to the surface of the covers and got out of bed. It was one of those perfect spring days on Puget Sound when winter seemed nothing more than a soggy, unpleasant memory. The sliding glass doors of the bedroom framed a view of the sapphire water and distant Cascades, the fiery pink of sunrise painting the vanilla ice-cream peak of Mount Baker.

She pulled on her robe, lingering at the window to watch a blue heron at the edges of the bank, lifting each foot and setting it down with great deliberation. In its beak it held a wisp of grass; it was nesting season.

She made the bed, which was a simple matter. She slept neatly, disturbing no more than a small portion of the covers. When Josh stayed over, the morning-after bed looked like a rummage sale at closing time—sheets ripped from their moorings, twisted and damp, pillows tossed willy-nilly. Josh made love and slept like he did everything else, with his whole self, with total abandon, his energy boundless and infectious.

Even through the ache of missing him, she couldn't help feeling a warm spasm of remembered intimacy at the thought of their lovemaking. It was as though he had reached across the Pacific Ocean and caressed her.

"You're a sick woman," she muttered, heading into the bathroom. Josh's toothbrush was still in the holder. He'd planted it there, as though staking a claim, the first time they made love in her bed. His absolute, unwavering self-assurance had both annoyed and thrilled her. "Just so you know," he'd said. "I'll be back."

She dressed quickly for class—no shower for her until afterward—in black spandex shorts and a turquoise top. Then she checked her gym bag to make sure she had music, shoes, towel, water bottle. Everything in order. She had grown so cautious, so deliberate after Gil died. So excruciatingly neat and unobtrusive about everything she did, from sleeping without disturbing the covers to weighing the portion of organic granola she ate with yogurt every morning for breakfast. If Josh were here, he would tease her about it, threaten her with bacon and eggs, and she would start the day laughing at herself.

Ah, Josh. Whether he was in bed with her, on top of her, inside her or thousands of miles away, he dominated her life. He was the blazing sun to her moon. Even when she eclipsed him, moving in to cover his center, he was still so much bigger and brighter; he burned around the edges.

She put out fresh food for the stray cat who showed every sign of turning into a permanent resident. Then she did the breakfast dishes, such as they were—one bowl, one spoon, one juice glass—reflecting on how small her life seemed since Josh left. When he was here, breakfast tended to be an explosion of creativity and hilarity. He might carve through half a watermelon trying to make a model of a fighter plane, or use up a whole box of pancake mix, laughing at her misgivings about the calorie count.

As she wiped the kitchen counter, Lauren burst into tears.

This shouldn't be happening to her. She'd finally gotten her life on track, her emotions under control after a three-year struggle with depression after Gil died. Now along came Josh, with his burning ambition, lofty dreams and his huge, insatiable appetite for everything in life—most especially her.

"Idiot," she said, defiantly using two Kleenex to blot her cheeks. "Quit making everything into a tragedy." She marched outside, filling her lungs with the special flavor of springtime on the island. A hint of raw salt air, new grass and the light, fragrant promise of budding lilacs.

Later it would rain, she knew. The forecast promised a change in the weather, and clouds were moving in on the morning sun.

She picked up her paper, shaking the dew off the cellophane bag, and waved to Mr. Carruthers, her across-the-street neighbor who came out to get his paper the same time she did each morning. To stare at her in her spandex, Josh had pointed out.

The night before he left, he'd asked her to marry him. It was all she thought about, consuming her like a giddy fever that kept her in its relentless grip. She hadn't given him an answer to his proposal. The issue was not nearly as simple as she wished it could be.

He was not a man to settle for half measures. He wanted everything from her. She wasn't sure she could live with his intensity, with his rocket-powered ambition. She didn't know if his dreams could somehow mesh with her own.

In the wake of unbearable grief, she had fashioned a life for herself here. A small and tidy existence she happened to like very much. She had none of Josh's scenery-eating hunger for adventure, for everything. She wondered why that was—because she couldn't handle having her dreams come true, or because she was leery of wanting something too much? She couldn't decide what scared her more, marrying Josh or losing him forever.

He was everything she wasn't supposed to want, a Navy man who spent half his life at sea and the other half moving like a gypsy from place to place. He was a heartache waiting to happen.

The cheerful *brrring* of a bicycle bell sounded. She looked down the street to see Patricia Rivera peddling toward her. She was exactly what people meant when they said pregnant women bloomed. Patricia's cheeks were flushed the color of a rose. Her slick dark hair shone. Her legs were ropy with muscle as she glided to the end of the driveway and squeezed the hand brakes. Even the bruise-colored starburst of varicose veins behind her knee looked as though it belonged there, every bit as appropriate as her protruding stomach.

Lauren held the plastic-wrapped paper away from her to let it drip on the ground. "You're looking chipper this morning."

Patricia smiled and smoothed a hand down her belly, draped in a polyester top that screamed Wal-Mart but only managed to play up her fragile beauty. "I have news."

"Let me guess. You're pregnant." Lauren spoke lightly, but deep in a hidden place inside her, a terrible envy howled.

"Very funny." Patricia opened the top of her water bottle and took a swig. "Congratulate me. It's a boy. He was finally turned in the right direction during the ultrasound."

The knife twisted. Still, Lauren found a smile of genuine happiness for her friend. "Congratulations, Patricia. That's great."

"Thanks." Patricia put her water away. "The doctor says I can keep coming to fitness class so long as I take it slow. No restrictions other than common sense."

Lauren congratulated her again and watched her friend ride away. Patricia had a husband she adored and a baby on the way. She looked like Catherine Zeta-Jones, but she was impossible to dislike. She was kind and bright, and she'd been one of Lauren's favorite people since the day she'd walked into the fitness studio last fall. And she was not without her sadnesses, either. Her husband was half a world away on the same carrier as Josh, and she was bursting with the news about their baby.

Lauren looked down, startled to see that she held both hands lovingly on her stomach. She shook her head and went back inside. The phone rang as soon as she stepped into the kitchen.

She glanced at the clock over the stove. It was the middle of the night in Josh's part of the world. She picked up on the fourth ring.

"Mrs. Stanton?" A vaguely familiar female voice used her married name, which she heard so seldom that the sound of it startled her.

"That's me."

"I have Dr. Hendler on the line for you."

The receiver in her hand was suddenly drenched in sweat. It nearly slipped from her grasp. This was the call she had been awaiting with terrifying hope and dread.

She was aware of everything around her with razor-edged clarity: the pink-toothed profile of the mountains against the morning sky; the perfect flight of wheeling gulls patrolling the beach; the sound of radio music drifting from the bedroom.

"Yes?" she asked in a strange and distant voice she didn't recognize.

"Your test results are back," said the doctor.

She tried desperately to read his tone. Was it good news or bad? She stopped breathing. She wanted to stop the world. "Yes?"

"I'm afraid it's not what we'd hoped for," he said. Softly, gravely. "Lauren, I'm so sorry...."

CHAPTER FOUR

Whidbey Island, Washington
2:30 p.m.

Grace Bennett drove off the ferry from Seattle and merged onto the country highway that formed the long, crooked spine of Whidbey Island. Fat raindrops ran backward on the window, like tears blown sideways on a face pushed into the wind. It felt as though the storm was driving her home.

As she sped up the main road, the wind and rain gradually abated. By the time she pulled to the shoulder and paused to get the mail from the box, tentative slices of sunshine shone through the clouds. She turned into the driveway and sat in the car for a moment, gazing at her house. In all her years as a Navy wife, she'd lived in a lot of places, but this was the only one she'd ever loved. It was a little bungalow on a bluff with an arbor of old roses and a view of the Sound. Some would call it dated, tacky. But Grace didn't care. It was *hers*.

She couldn't believe she'd bought it without Steve. But lately, she'd done a lot of surprising things—and the person she surprised most of all was herself.

Especially today. With a pleasant shiver, she picked up her purse and the stack of mail from the seat beside her and slid out of the car. She ducked her head to avoid drops from the ancient cedar trees that arched over the drive and skirted puddles to keep from ruining her new shoes, then let herself in through the front gate. She had just bought the ensemble of expensive skirt and blazer, and a pair of kitten-heeled pumps. The only outfit that had cost her more was her wedding dress.

On the porch, she stopped to sift through the mail, finding an assortment of bills, letters to the kids from prospective colleges…the usual overabundance of junk mail.

In the past, she used to sift through the mail with fevered eagerness, looking for a familygram or precious letter from Steve. These days, no one sent letters anymore, just e-mail. What was gained in speed and frequency with the Internet came at the sacrifice of the cozy, ineffable intimacy of a handwritten letter.

In a letter, Steve's presence used to be a tangible thing. He had a charming habit of making his point with swiftly drawn strokes, an extension of his energetic personality. He used punctuation marks no one had ever heard of, yet she could practically hear his voice when he wrote, "I ♥ you 1000x more than flying, girl❣"

She used to sleep with his letters under her pillow.

And she used to spend an hour each evening writing aerograms, watching the shape of each word on the thin blue page as it appeared behind her pen. Her letter-writing was a sort of handicraft, a way to weave her love into every word she wrote. E-mail was different. Faster, to be sure, but different. And completely inadequate for fixing what was wrong between her and Steve. But after today, she had finally figured out what to do. All that remained was to tell him.

Juggling the mail, her purse and keys, she let herself in. Daisy, who had yet to grow into her paws, scrambled in to greet her, sneezing and wagging her feathery tail as though Grace had been away for a decade. A crystal vase of roses on the hall table filled the house with their soft, evocative scent. The flowers had been delivered yesterday for her fortieth birthday. They should have been sent by Steve.

But they weren't.

Her leather-soled shoes made a satisfying tapping sound on the hardwood floor. She heard the light beep of the answering machine, indicating a number of messages. She'd check them in a moment.

She went to the kitchen and let the dog out. As she shut the door, she caught a glimpse of herself in the glass.

The image startled her briefly. She was a different person, and after today, there would be more changes afoot. Her encounter with Ross Cameron was everything she had hoped it would—and would not—be.

She still couldn't believe she'd gone through with it. It was hard to get her mind around the idea of Grace McAllen Bennett doing something like that, yet she'd been heading in unexpected directions ever since a stranger named Josh Lamont had dropped like a bomb into the middle of their lives. That wake-up call had jolted her out of the life she thought she had and shoved her into unknown territory. With Steve at sea, Grace had started down a road of her own.

She set aside the stack of mail, took off her raincoat and put her keys on the counter, pausing for a minute to study the little sterling silver anchor key chain, a gift from Steve a lifetime ago. She hung it on a hook by the door. Though the house was quiet, a trail of kid clutter formed a path from the back door to the den. When they were little, it was composed of Fisher-Price pull toys and G.I. Joe action figures. Now it consisted of sports equipment and schoolbooks.

Grace glanced at the clock. They'd be home soon. She wondered if they would notice the new dress, the hair and makeup. Katie would, and she'd worry. That was Katie, the worrier. Change upset her, an unfortunate trait in a kid whose childhood consisted of moving every three years. She'd probably look at Grace and think demons had possessed her mother.

Brian would be oblivious, of course. At eighteen, he was

oblivious to everything but baseball and drawing, his two reasons for breathing. Fortunately, they were also his reasons for getting into college, so she couldn't complain. When Brian first explained his college plans, Grace had been worried about how Steve would react. But slowly, as she grew into her new self, she quit trying to turn this family into an adjunct to Steve's career.

And Emma? There were days when Grace actually thought her older daughter had slipped away somewhere, leaving a secretive stranger in her place. She and her twin brother would be leaving home soon, yet sometimes Grace had the feeling Emma had checked out months ago, not long after Grace and Steve's marriage exploded.

A terrible heat filled her, and for a moment she had trouble breathing. Even now, she thought, stunned by the powerful grip he still held on her heart. Even now. Flush from seeing Ross, she thought she finally knew her heart, but doubts kept seeping through the cracks and crevices that had appeared in the foundations of her life.

Nothing would be resolved until Steve came back and they made some sense of what had happened. She released a sigh, her breath a series of jerky exhalations.

Breathe, she reminded herself. Lauren, her trainer, had shown her how to find the deepest reaches of her breathing apparatus, capillaries only one cell thick, yet capable of sending a burst of oxygen into every panting, air-starved region of the lungs. Breathing was a learned art, so they said.

She headed into the study to check her messages. The answering machine was blinking an ominous number thirteen. She left the island for a day in the city and suddenly everyone needed her. Her e-mail box was sure to be exploding.

Sitting at the secondhand oak library desk that served as her company headquarters, she touched Play and picked up a pen.

The first few messages on the machine were strictly business. She was currently handling the relocation of three families and juggling delivery times, tonnage estimates, shipping contracts. Then came Katie: "Mom, I'm going to Melanie's tonight, okay?"

"Actually, it's not." Grace had a list of chores she'd been saving for Katie.

"Okay," said the voice on the tape. "I'll stop by after school. Bye."

Melanie. The Corpuz girl, Grace recalled. She had a Ping-Pong table and an older brother Katie considered "hot." Katie wanted a boyfriend in the worst way. It was one of the hazards, Grace supposed, of being the brainy younger sister of the prettiest girl in the school.

"It's a boy!" the answering machine blared in the vibrant voice of Patricia Rivera. "I just got back from the doctor's, and he confirmed it. Call me and talk me out of these terrible names I keep coming up with…."

Next, a crackle of static and then Steve's voice on the carrier satellite phone. "Hey, guys."

Grace's grip tightened on the pen. In spite of everything, just the sound of his voice still touched her. Still infuriated her. Still made her dizzy with memories.

"It's your old man calling from the wrong side of the international dateline. Guess what? I'm giving a tour to a reporter from *Newsweek*…."

A reporter, thought Grace. What's that about?

"Brian," continued Steve, "I guess you'll be getting word on your Naval Academy appointment any day now. I'm pulling for you, buddy.

"Emma-girl, check your e-mail. I sent you some digital photos of a pod of whales we spotted. Katydid, how'd that science project turn out? Bet you made an A-plus. And Grace…sorry I missed you on your birthday. I tried calling, but there was no answer. Hope you had a nice time. Okay, y'all give your mom a hug from me. Hug one another while you're at it, you hear? I sure do miss you. Over and out."

Grace massaged the sides of her jaw, trying to force herself to relax.

The next message was work-related. A crisis with an overseas shipment—an entire sealed container had been dropped overboard in Seattle. Someone's whole household was bobbing in the drink.

A simple matter compared to the sticky complexities of her family.

Then Lauren Stanton. She sounded congested, or maybe she'd been crying. "Grace, hi. It's Lauren. I—um—look, I canceled fitness class today and couldn't find anyone to cover for me. Sorry about that."

Grace winced at the emotional pain she heard in Lauren's tone. Josh had been gone only a few weeks, and already Lauren was falling apart.

Grace hurt for Lauren. The two of them had their ups and downs, that was for sure, but extraordinary circumstances bound them together into an uneasy sisterhood of shared hopes and fears.

She had the phone in her hand, ready to start returning calls, as the final message played. "Hello, Grace. It's Peggy from Buskirk Law Offices. I just wanted to let you know that I sent the packet over by messenger." The voice paused as though, in the midst of a routine procedure, the speaker felt the weight of it. "The papers are ready to sign. Good luck, Grace."

Good luck. Grace felt a strange sort of dread. What did she think she was doing? What *was* she doing?

She set down the phone, not quite ready to talk to Lauren—to anyone—just yet.

As she sat there, trying to make sense of everything she was feeling, teetering on the edge of taking a major step in her life, she heard the muffled sound of a car door slamming. Then another. Frowning slightly, because she wasn't expecting anyone, she stood and went to the vestibule to see who it was. As she passed the hall tree mirror, she caught another glimpse of herself and smoothed her hands down her pencil-straight, raspberry-colored skirt.

Through the antique lace panel covering the front door, she saw the wet black gleam of a Navy vehicle, a common-enough sight on base, but fairly rare beyond the confines of the Naval Air Station.

The front gate opened. Between the tall hedges of climbing roses, two men emerged.

When Grace saw them, every cell in her body came to ringing

attention. She could hear, far away in another part of the house, the sound of a faucet dripping and Daisy scratching at the back door. The scent of roses and orange-oil furniture polish hung in the air. The wispy lace covering the front door softened and distorted the features of her visitors, but even so, Grace knew exactly what she was seeing. The nightmare every military wife dreaded.

A Navy chaplain and the Casualty Assistance Calls Officer, coming up the walk.

PART TWO
POINT OF EMBARKATION

POE: *Point of Embarkation: to make a start,*
to engage, enlist, or invest in an enterprise.

CHAPTER FIVE

Nine months earlier

In the cramped, overheated dressing room of a self-consciously hip boutique called Wild Grrl, Katie Bennett's head popped through the neck opening of a green Free People sweater. "How about this one, Mom?"

Grace helped her adjust the sweater, smoothing her hand down the textured mohair knit. Moving to Washington State from Texas over the summer meant the kids needed sweaters and jackets. As she turned Katie square into the mirror, she sneaked a glance at the tag dangling from the armpit—$64.99. *Great.* "It's a good color on you," she said. "Too bad it doesn't even cover your navel."

Katie turned this way and that, lifting a mop of straight brown hair off her neck and contemplating her reflection with the hypersensitive, overcritical eye of a fourteen-year-old girl. Grace wanted to tell her daughter she would look beautiful in a gunnysack, but Katie would argue with her. Katie always argued, and she usually won.

As Grace sorted through the other outfits they'd selected, she glimpsed the back of a woman in the unforgiving three-way dressing-room mirror. Neglected hair, a double-wide backside, jiggly upper arms. Then Grace straightened up and lifted her arm over her head.

The pudgy woman did the same.

She put her arm down.

So did the woman in the mirror.

She twitched her hips from side to side.

So did—

"Mom, what are you doing?" Katie asked.

"Contemplating suicide." Grace laughed to make sure Katie knew she was kidding. She shuddered at the back view of herself in the unflattering fluorescent light. It shouldn't be such a shock. She knew she'd been getting a little wide in the beam but had managed to avoid taking a hard look in the mirror. Whose hips were those, and why were they so large? How did she get to this state? At some point—she had no idea when—gravity must have kicked in. With no prior warning, she'd turned into a not-very-attractive stranger. But there she was, in living color, the dumpy, middle-aged suburban housewife she never thought she'd become.

"Is something wrong?" Katie prodded.

Grace sighed and picked up her purse. "No, sweetie. I don't know what I was thinking when I put on these khaki shorts."

"You look fine," Katie stated.

The kids didn't need for Grace to look like anything but Mom, and she'd done a damned good job of that. When Steve did a good job, he got a medal or pin of commendation. While she got… She wondered why no one ever gave women medals for motherhood.

"I'm the one in trouble, Mom. Nothing's right." With a long-suffering sigh, Katie peeled off the green sweater and tossed it to Grace.

"What about the hip-hugger jeans?" Grace suggested. "They were cute on you."

Katie slipped a T-shirt over her head. "In order to wear hip-huggers, you have to actually have hips."

Grace patted her arm. "Trust me, you'll get them. The Lord will provide." She avoided her reflection as Katie finished dressing.

Katie didn't seem to notice her uncharacteristic silence as they went to find Emma. She was in another dressing room, where she'd put aside a stack of selections to show her mother. As blond and willowy as a prima ballerina, eighteen-year-old Emma never experienced the uncertainties that tortured her younger sister. At the moment, Emma was modeling a jersey skirt and sweater, her natural good looks magically transforming a discount outfit into a Marc Jacobs original.

Grace smiled at her older daughter. "I see you narrowed your choices down to, what, a few dozen?"

"Two skirts and three tops, and I'll kick in for half," Emma said. She worked as a lifeguard at the Island County Aquatics Center. It turned out to be the perfect place to meet people. After living here just two months, she had plenty of friends.

"Deal," Grace agreed. A little extravagance was justified, she supposed. The Navy Exchange provided the basics, but the start of the school year, in a brand-new town, called for some serious retail therapy. Back-to-school shopping usually appealed to Grace. She took a peculiar comfort in the familiar rituals of summer's end, in getting registered for school, joining the PTA, signing permission forms for sports and extracurriculars. She liked organizing their backpacks and binders, spiral-bound notebooks and bradded folders; she liked putting things in their proper place. Stowing ordnance, Steve called it.

Shouldering her bulging purse, she stepped outside and, for a moment, forgot where she was. She felt unmoored, disoriented. She had started over so many times in so many new places that she actually had to think for a second before remembering which town this was.

With Emma at the wheel of their aging station wagon, they headed down the road to a huge Rite Aid. This was Katie's indulgence. Rather than getting school supplies at the Navy Exchange, she craved the variety available at the big drugstore. Under the bluish glare of fluorescent lights, the back-to-school aisle was jammed with harried mothers and restless kids. Emma wandered over to the makeup section, leaving Grace to pick out the basic necessities. Neither of the twins had ever been picky about their school supplies.

On the other hand, Katie took the task seriously and was presently weighing the merits of disposable versus refillable mechanical pencils. Waiting at the end of the aisle, Grace held her tongue, resisting the temptation to prod. But Katie had a sixth sense; she glanced over at Grace. "I just need a few more things."

"No problem." Angling the cart to one side, Grace selected a four-pack of glue from a display rack. She held the package briefly to her face, shut her eyes and inhaled. "I love the smell of glue sticks in the morning."

"Very funny, Mom." Katie opted for the refillable pencils, tossing them into the cart. Of Grace's three kids, Katie was the only one who would actually keep the pencils long enough to refill. Then she added a chisel-tipped highlighter pen, a pack of index cards and a D-ring binder. "Okay, I'm all set."

Katie was a moving violation of the laws of birth order. She overachieved like a firstborn, worried like a middle child and, only when she didn't think anyone was looking, still played like the baby of the family. And like the baby, she was adored by everyone—except by herself.

They headed toward the checkout stand. Emma stood at the magazine display, flipping through *Cosmo*. Katie tilted her head sideways to read the shout lines. "Nine Ways to Drive Him Wild In Bed," she read aloud. "You know, if that stuff worked, we would have world peace, I bet."

"Let's go," said Grace, taking the magazine from Emma and sticking it back in the rack. Grace was no prude, and she wasn't naive enough to think a parent could hold back the urges of nature, yet she felt a little dart of resentment at these women's magazines and the glossy, seductive promises they made.

The two-for-seventy-nine-cents filler paper and multipacks of ballpoint pens that seemed so cheap in the ad circular somehow managed to multiply to a hundred dollars' worth of school supplies. Grace handed over a well-worn credit card, knowing the balance would make her wince when it came in the mail.

Glancing across to the adjacent checkout stand, she spied a young mother carefully counting out change while her two little kids swarmed the gumball machine by the exit. She was Navy, of course. After nineteen years as a Navy wife, Grace could spot one a mile away. They possessed a peculiar forbearance, and a deep strength as well. They were a special breed of women—and lately, the occasional man—to which Grace belonged. A sorority of itinerant householders.

The woman looked up, and for two seconds their gazes held. Grace offered a smile, and the woman smiled back, then resumed counting out her money.

She sent Emma and Katie out to the car with their bloated cart while she stopped at the ATM machine by the door. As she waited for the machine to cough up the cash, her gaze wandered to the community bulletin board above the drinking fountain. Yellow handwritten cards and published brochures offered everything from dog-sitting services to weatherproofing. Garage sales abounded, as they did in every Navy town. When it was time to move, you lightened your load.

There were items on the bulletin board from Welcome Wagon, Mary Kay, the usual suspects. A glossy, tri-fold brochure caught her eye, mainly because it shouted the word *free*. She took one out of the rack. One free month of unlimited classes.

The flyer was for the Totally New Totally You fitness studio down on Water Street, owned and operated by Lauren Stanton, IFA Certified.

She stuffed the brochure into her purse among ferry schedules, receipts, change-of-address forms and the kids' health records. With much greater care, she folded the bills and receipt from the ATM into her wallet. She was almost afraid to look at the bottom line.

In the parking lot, a gray-and-white seagull cried out and flew aloft, drawing her gaze upward. The sky was almost unnaturally blue, arching over a distant mountain range topped in snow, even in August. The fathomless blue of Puget Sound surrounded misty, forested islands with interesting names like Camano and Orcas. And Whidbey, of course. This was far and away the prettiest place they'd ever lived, even more dramatic than the volcano-scape of Sigonella, on Sicily. The weather here was on the cool side, unseasonably cool, locals said, and evenings warranted a sweater or light jacket.

Grace turned her face up to the dazzling sky. This was so different from other places she knew. She had been to coast-hugging barrier islands connected by causeways to the mainland—Galveston, Coronado, Padre near Corpus Christi. Sigonella was an arid rock. But Whidbey Island had its own sort of magic. Forty-five miles of rolling hills surrounded by cold blue water, Whidbey was a world unto itself, with its air of serenity and ageless beauty. Accessible only by car ferry or by a dizzying arched steel bridge spanning Deception Pass at the north end, it commanded the heart of Puget Sound.

She was going to like it here. No, she was going to love it here. That really wasn't the problem. In a couple of years, she was going to have to leave. *That* was the problem.

Exasperated with her own thoughts, she dug for her keys, which were strung on the silver anchor key chain Steve had given her the first time he went to sea, long ago.

At the car, the girls were talking to a big-shouldered boy with a neck as wide as his head. Or rather, Emma was talking while the boy hung on her every word and Katie leaned against the shopping cart, trying to act nonchalant. The boy wore a purple football jersey and a gold stud in one earlobe. He looked like every high school girl's fantasy—and he looked familiar.

"Mom, this is Cory Crowther," said Katie.

Grace smiled at him. "Hi, Cory. I remember you from your dad's change-of-command ceremony." Earlier in the summer, Cory's father, Mason Crowther, had taken command of Carrier

Air Wing 22. Mason was one rung on the ladder higher than Steve, his Deputy CAG. In a year, Steve would be eligible to take command from Crowther.

"Yes, ma'am. I remember you, too."

"But you disappeared on us," she added.

He sent her a grin worthy of a toothpaste ad. "Went to football camp, ma'am."

"I bet your mother missed you," Grace said. Allison Crowther played a key but undefined role as the CAG's wife. Grace realized her comment embarrassed Cory, so she said, "All set?" to her daughters. She pulled the cart around to the back of the car. Maybe he'd offer to help.

"Nice to see you, ma'am. I'd better be going," he said. "Practice."

So much for gallantry, thought Grace. She kept silent, though. Moving so frequently was hard on the kids, and she didn't want to sabotage any potential friendships.

He stuffed his hands in his pockets and wheeled backward, unable to take his eyes off Emma. "See you around."

"See you," said Emma.

"Bye, Cory," Katie said, her eagerness adorable to Grace but unappreciated by the boy. "Good luck at practice."

He grinned again and took off, heading for a shiny Dodge Ram pickup truck. Navy blue, of course. An array of squadron insignia decorated the rear window and bumper.

Katie sagged dramatically against the station wagon. "Good luck at practice," she mimicked herself. "God, I'm a hopeless dork."

Emma ruffled her hair. "You're not used to football gods yet."

"Don't ever get used to football gods," Grace said. "They're nothing but trouble."

"Was Dad a football god?"

"He didn't play football," Grace said. *But he was a god.*

"What did he play?" Katie asked.

"He didn't. He was already an officer when we met."

Grace opened the back of the car, and the three of them loaded the bags. She was tempted by a tube of Pringles sticking out of a sack, but quickly reminded herself of the nightmare in the mirror. She was going to have to take it easy on the Pringles.

"I'll drive," said Emma, folding her lithe form behind the steering wheel.

"You always drive," Katie said, out of sorts over the Cory encounter.

"It'll be your turn before you know it," said Emma. "Get in and buckle up. We're taking the scenic route."

They drove through Oak Harbor, a town that took its beautiful setting for granted. A blight of strip centers and prefabricated housing flanked the main road through town. But at the foot of the clustered buildings, and above their rooftops, the view was crafted by the hand of God—an intensely blue seascape, alive with white-winged sailboats, cargo ships with containers stacked like Lego blocks, ferries shuttling tourists and commuters back and forth to the San Juan Islands or the mainland. A forest fringe of slender evergreens swept up to a white mountain range.

When they'd first arrived here, Emma and Katie would occasionally burst into "The Sound of Music" when the mood struck them. Her silly, funny girls. Watching her two daughters together gave Grace an unexpected pang.

They were nearly grown, whether she was ready or not. Looking at Emma's face was like watching one of those time-lapse photographs of a flower opening. She could see her turn from a tender-faced baby into a young woman whose beauty seemed to be made equally of strength and fragility. Meanwhile, Katie grew tall and thin, and became smarter and more inquisitive every year. Grace couldn't believe how quickly time had passed, how soon they would be leaving her.

"It's beautiful here, isn't it?" she said.

"I wish we lived closer to the water," Katie said, never wanting to make the mistake of being in complete agreement with her mother. "The base isn't pretty at all."

"Bases aren't supposed to be pretty," Grace said.

"When I leave home, I'm going to live in one place and never, ever budge," Katie declared.

"Not me," said Emma. "I'm going to live everywhere."

"Just don't forget to write," said Grace. She was tempted to broach the topic of college, but decided to wait. It was hard to resist pushing, though. Emma had barely touched the stack of glossy catalogs and brochures that flooded the mailbox all summer.

"I want to live there," Grace said, speaking out before she'd fully formed the thought. She gestured at a house on the water side of the road, with a fussed-over garden and painted gingerbread trim. Like a stately tall ship, it commanded a view of the shipping lanes and mountains. It was a restored Victorian, the kind built by fishermen from Maine who'd relocated to Whidbey a hundred years ago.

"How about this one?" asked Emma. Without waiting for an answer, she pulled off the road and parked on the gravel shoulder in the shade of a huge cedar. The driveway was marked with a realtor's tent sign and a bouquet of balloons imprinted with Open House.

Automatically Grace checked her watch. By habit she was a schedule person, but on this sunny Saturday afternoon they were in no hurry.

Visiting open houses was a hobby she'd fallen into years ago. Emma and Katie shared her fascination. There was a sort of vicarious pleasure in stepping into someone else's world. It was a guilty thrill. Walking through other people's homes made Grace feel as though she was visiting a foreign country with customs and habits she barely understood. She loved to study the gardens with perennials, displays of family photographs showing generations growing up in the same place. She was intrigued by the permanence of their way of life, and she studied it like an anthropologist researching a different culture.

She wondered what it would be like to live in a place where you could plant a garden and still be around to see how it turned out.

This was definitely a girl thing. Steve and Brian couldn't stand open houses. But for Grace and her daughters, the fantasy began as soon as they stepped onto the driveway of crushed rock and shells.

The house was a disappointment, an ugly stepsister to the Victorian masterpiece down the road. Despite an impressive arbor of old roses, the garden was an uninspired mix of perennials, rhododendrons and low, leafy shrubs. Worse, someone had tried to give the place a nautical flavor by heaping driftwood in a self-conscious arrangement, creating a rope fence. A wooden seagull was perched atop the post next to the front gate. Over the door arched a driftwood sign: Welcome Aboard.

The girls walked in through the open front door, heading for a hall table laden with bakery cookies, a coffee urn, a pitcher of lemonade and some real estate flyers.

Grace hesitated before she entered the house. Unbidden, a quiet stirring occurred deep inside her. It was just a strange day, she thought, beginning with the shock of meeting her real self in the dressing-room mirror.

She could feel the fresh sea breeze rippling across the yard and stirring the tops of the trees. Murmurs of conversation drifted through the house as little knots of people inspected the unnaturally clean rooms. Her awareness of everything heightened, and for some reason, she held her breath the way she used to in church each Sunday morning, just before genuflecting.

In the blink of an eye, the peculiar moment passed. She stepped over the threshold into a stranger's house. The spongy gray carpet beneath her feet had seen better days, and the walls were an oppressive putty color. Sometime in the distant past, a smoker used to live here. Bowls of potpourri barely masked a cindery hotel room odor. But still, the plain-Jane house cast an odd and mesmerizing spell on her.

Grace smiled and greeted the listing agent, accepting an information sheet on the house. She was a looky-loo and never pretended to be otherwise. An experienced agent could see that a mile off.

Grace strolled through an outdated kitchen with harvest-gold appliances, oversize vegetables on the wallpaper, phony redbrick linoleum on the floor and Formica countertops with the classic boomerang pattern, faded in places from scrubbing. The study was the only modern segment of the house that she could see. It contained a well-designed workstation and a state-of-the-art Mac computer surrounded by scanners, printers and devices Grace couldn't identify. Clearly, this was the domain of a computer whiz.

One set of lookers was in the corner snickering over a collage made of seashells, which framed a chalkboard. Ignoring them, Grace passed through to the front room, and there, finally, she understood the magic of this place. The living room was oriented like the prow of a ship, with sliding doors leading out to a deck. The windows were covered by heavy pleated drapes, though someone had had the sense to thrust them wide apart. The view made Grace forget every unfortunate aspect of the little house on the bluff. It was a view that encompassed the length of Puget Sound, from the uneven teeth of the snowcapped Cascades to the dimpled blue peak of Mount Baker. The Sound was at its liveliest, as though every schooner and ferryboat, every barge and pleasure boat, put out to sea just for her viewing pleasure.

The girls were out on the deck, eating cookies. Grace pantomimed "five minutes" and headed for the stairs. The two bedrooms at the top of the landing were poky and nondescript. But the master bedroom commanded the same view as the living room downstairs.

Standing in this place, Grace felt a painful tightness around the heart. It was the sense of wanting something she could not possibly have.

She was about to leave when she became aware of a murmuring voice.

"But I thought the shipper wouldn't schedule me until the house sold," said a woman's tense voice. "I can't possibly be ready before then." A pause. "I understand, but—" Another pause. "And what's the charge for that? I see. Well, it's not in my budget. I don't know…"

Grace waited until she heard the bleep of the phone, followed by a shaky sigh she could relate to. Then she approached the woman, whose lower right leg was in a walking cast. She was an older lady whose pleasant face was trembling and swollen with unshed tears of frustration.

"I couldn't help overhearing," said Grace. "Sounds as though your shipper is trying to move up the date on you."

The woman nodded glumly. "Yes. It's horrible. I had an offer on the house, but the loan fell through, so it's back on the market again. Now the shipper wants to stick to the original schedule or charge me a huge extra fee." She shook her head. "You know, I can design and launch a Web site, but dealing with a moving company is totally beyond me. My name's Marcia Dunmire," she said. "I'm a digital engineer."

"Grace Bennett. I'm a Navy wife."

"Oh. Then you've done this a few times before."

"I don't mean to be nosy, but maybe I can help. Do you have a copy of your contract?"

"Right here." The pinched expression eased from Marcia's face. "I'd be grateful if you'd look it over. I've never used a moving company before, ever." She handed Grace a carbonless copy that looked very familiar.

"Some shippers move dates around if they have space in a truck that's ready to go. And unfortunately, some agents try to tag you with extra charges and kill fees." Grace glanced over the information. The estimated weight was grossly inflated—40,000 pounds. In reality, the contents of this house amounted to no more than 20,000 pounds. The inequity didn't surprise Grace but set her teeth on edge.

Paging through the boilerplate sections of the contract, she found what she was looking for. "You're okay," she said. "They can't charge you for rescheduling so long as you ship within sixty days. I've been a relocation ombudsman for the Navy for years. I could make a call for you, if you like."

Marcia handed her the phone. "Be my guest. I'd love some help."

Grace hit Redial. She and Marcia moved aside as a young couple came to the master bedroom. Like Grace, they were instantly drawn to the view from the wide front window. Go away, she wanted to tell them. This is my house. The clarity—and the absurdity—of the thought startled her.

"Yes," she said when she finally got past the receptionist. "Terry, is it? Hi, Terry. It's Grace Bennett of...Executive Relocators." She tossed out the name from a well of fantasy inside her, claimed Marcia as a client and plunged in. It took no effort at all. When Grace discussed business, a certain confidence came over her. She stood up straighter, spoke with authority.

"Thanks for the info, Terry," she said. "Then I guess I'm confused. According to Mrs. Dunmire's contract, she has sixty days to reschedule. Yes, yes, of course." From the corner of her eye, she saw the girls come in. When they spotted her with contract in hand, phone to her ear and the older lady watching with hands clasped in hope, they rolled their eyes and went somewhere else. They were used to seeing their mother in ombudsman mode.

"Let me check with my client on that, Terry." She pressed the mute button on the phone. "He says you didn't say you'd ship within sixty days."

She sniffed. "I didn't get a chance to say anything. But the extra time would solve the problem. I'm sure of it."

Grace went back to Terry. "I'm a little concerned about this weight discrepancy here, too, so maybe you should send another agent out to redo the estimate." She honestly liked doing this—sticking up for people. Whatever floats your boat, as Steve would say.

A few minutes later, she hung up the phone. "Well," she said, "that should help some."

Marcia rolled her walker toward the door. "You have no idea. Good Lord, I'm a babe in the woods. Since my husband died I'm finding new areas of incompetence every day."

"No," said Grace. "You're finding new challenges. And new ways to shine."

"You're very wise for such a young woman."

"Bless you for thinking I'm young," said Grace, remembering the dumpy housewife in the mirror. "And wise. Actually, I know there's no comparison to being widowed, but every time my husband goes to sea, I find myself having to deal with things on my own. Moving seems to be my specialty."

"Are you really an executive relocator?"

"No, I just said that on the spot, to sound more official. I've done it unofficially for years."

"You're very good at it. You should charge for your services."

"So I've been told. But my clients are all Navy families. I work pro bono. Sometimes I think about doing this professionally, though. But…"

"It's a great idea, especially for this area. Boeing, Microsoft, Starbucks, Amazon… It's the land of the high-profile multinational company."

The notion teased at Grace, but she pushed it away. "Do you need help on the stairs?"

"No, thanks," Marcia said. "I keep another walker downstairs. Blasted ankle. I broke it playing volleyball."

Grace spotted her daughters out on the lawn, pacing. "I'd better be going. The natives are getting restless."

"Of course. I didn't mean to keep you."

"It was my pleasure. I love your house."

"Do you? We bought it in the sixties when it was all we could afford. I just couldn't deal with updating it only to put it on the market. Are you planning to buy a house?"

"Some day," Grace admitted. "But it's a long way from the wish to the deed. Steve and I always said that when we were stationed in a place we liked well enough, we'd talk about buying a house." Although most Navy families did buy homes, Grace and Steve had agreed long ago that a permanent home and mortgage didn't fit their way of life. But for a while now, she'd been having second thoughts about that decision.

"I've heard people in the service are able to retire young and start a whole new life for themselves."

Grace smiled, even as she felt the terrible tension between fantasy and reality. "I've heard that, too. But not from my husband."

"Well, you could pick a worse place than this to make a permanent home. It's beautiful and peaceful, just a ferry ride to
Seattle, yet far enough from the city to feel safe and quiet."

"It's pretty ideal," Grace admitted.

"I'll tell you what," Marcia said. "Since you won't let me pay
you for your help, let me do something I'm good at."

"You don't have to—"

"What I'd like to do," Marcia said, overruling her, "is design a
Web site for you. That's what I do for a living. I'd consider it a
privilege."

"That's incredibly generous of you," Grace said. "But I don't
have the first idea of what I would do with a Web site."

"It can be for anything. Your family, your kids, your husband."

"My husband already has a site. It's called navy-dot-mil."

"Oh, my. Well, I can't really compete with that. But something
for you, personally. We can create a Web site for your hobbies—
knitting, gardening, songwriting, what have you."

"My hobbies?" Grace grinned. "Most days, that would be car-
pooling and family finance."

"Give it some thought." Marcia handed her a business card.
"Call me. It'll be fun, you'll see. I really do owe you, big-time."

Grace was quiet as they drove away. On the seat beside her lay
the various receipts and flyers she'd collected. She had two things
to show for her day. Two impossible dreams. A perfect body and
a home of her own.

CHAPTER SIX

After the day's final briefing, which was anything but brief, Steve Bennett knew the exact date and time he'd be leaving his family. Again. Sure, he was a patriot; he'd spent his career serving his country. Yet he felt alternately harried, preoccupied and distracted by his myriad duties. A part of him missed the glory days of flying, the constant brushes with danger and the heady rush of cheating death. But he was a family man now, and he'd reached the stage of his career where he was ready for his own command.

And that didn't happen without compromise. Even if it meant putting up with rule-book blowhards like Mason Crowther, his immediate superior.

When he walked through the door, he deep-sixed the burdens of the day, shutting his eyes and inhaling the smell of baking chicken. Like magic, the aromas and sounds of home lifted his spirits. Then he took off his cap and tossed it Frisbee-style to a hook on the hall tree—a little stunt that drove Crowther nuts and often prompted him to remind Steve that replacing a damaged cover would set him back two hundred bucks.

Feeling decidedly better, he went in search of his wife.

Grace stood at the counter, tossing a salad. He gave her a quick kiss on the cheek. "Smells great," he said. "Do you need some help?"

"No, thanks. We'll eat just as soon as you get washed up. The kids want to go out tonight."

He aimed a wounded look at Emma, who was setting the table. "You're ditching us?"

"It's the last Saturday night of the summer. Our last night of freedom."

He washed his hands at the sink. "Yeah? So what are you up to?"

Emma shrugged in a way that made him grit his teeth. His elder daughter was not uncommunicative, but she definitely had her own set of private signals and gestures.

"Translation, please," he said, trying to keep the edge out of his voice. He knew this was a particularly difficult move, uprooting the kids for their senior year and thrusting them into yet another "hostile environment," as they liked to call it.

Steve knew it wasn't his fault. But it sure as hell wasn't his family's, either.

"Some of the kids are going down to the beach at Mueller's Point."

"Bonfire and fireworks," Brian added, ambling into the kitchen. Without being asked, he started filling the water glasses from a chilled pitcher.

"Excellent," called Katie from the living room. "That means I can go, too."

Both Emma and Brian snapped to attention. "In your dreams, dork," Brian said. "It's bad enough I have to drag Emma along—"

"Drag Emma along?" she said with an arch look. "Hey, if it weren't for me, you wouldn't have any friends at all."

"If it weren't for me," Grace said, tapping her arm with a spatula, "you wouldn't have any dinner."

They all sat down and Steve asked the blessing and then wondered why he bothered to ask. This family was all he needed and more. *This* was what he lived for, these moments of simplicity when they sat down to share a meal. He wondered if they had any idea how much it meant to him.

"So," said Grace, passing the bread. "How was—"

"Your day, dear," Katie finished for her. "You always say that, Mom."

"Well, I always want to know. Don't you?"

"I already know. He filled out some forms, answered a zillion e-mails, had a planning meeting with the senior staff and did all the stuff Captain Crowther didn't want to deal with, because that's what the DCAG does." Katie pushed her glasses up her nose. "Right, Dad?"

"Pretty darned close, Miss Smarty-Pants." He caught Grace's eye. She looked distracted tonight, maybe a little tired. "Thanks for asking."

This was his opening to announce the upcoming trip to the Pentagon and then the deployment in November. Not now, he thought. He'd save the news for another time. With school starting Monday, everyone had enough on their minds.

But was there ever a good time to tell the family you were leaving them? He'd done so many times, but it never got easier.

He looked around the table and his heart filled up. Although he could command a squadron or air wing, he was helpless when it came to his family and helpless to know whether or not he was doing a good job at home. His background, which included more foster homes than he'd ever bothered to count, hadn't prepared him for the powerful tenderness of family life. His instincts told him how to land a plane on a carrier deck at night in a storm, but they couldn't tell him how to talk to his daughters.

Emma was so pretty she could break your heart with a single blink of those Caribbean-blue eyes. Steve ought to know—she'd broken his often enough. Every time he said goodbye to her, from the time she was old enough to understand what goodbye meant, she had broken his heart. Yet oddly, with all the moving they had done, Emma seemed to adapt the easiest. She actually liked making new friends, and found her place in school with seemingly little fuss or effort.

Brian was his trophy son, and he appeared to like playing that role, bringing home honors in track and baseball, earning decent marks in his classes. He was a prime candidate for any number of colleges, and the Naval Academy was at the top of his list.

Then there was his little Katydid, so quick you'd miss her if you didn't keep your eye on her. She read a book every day or two and was so smart she had her teachers scrambling for material, trying to stay one step ahead of her.

And Grace. The architect of it all. She built this family brick by brick, fashioned it out of hard work and a vision he hoped like hell they both shared. In the upheaval of the move this summer and taking on his new duties, he'd barely had time to sit down and talk to her about anything.

She used to make time, carving a quiet half hour out of the day so they could discuss whatever was on their minds. He'd never told her how grateful he was for that; he figured she knew. But lately, even she'd been sucked into the breakneck pace of their lives, and those half hours had fallen by the wayside. He missed their time together, but didn't know how to tell her so.

It wasn't his fault, and it sure as hell wasn't hers, but a hairline fissure had appeared in their marriage, seemingly out of nowhere. Or so he thought. He was almost afraid to mention it for fear of giving it a name and making it real. But he had to trust that things were fine, or nothing else in the world made sense. Grace was different from women who walked away from Navy men. She wasn't going to bail on him.

He stabbed his fork into a second helping of chicken. "There's a barbecue at the Crowthers' next Sunday," he said. "The whole family's invited."

"I'm busy," Katie declared.

"I've got practice," Brian said.

He noticed Emma had no objection. The Crowther boy was her age, and he'd called at the house a couple of times, looking for her. "The whole family," he repeated. "He's the CAG, and he wants everybody to have a good time."

"Then he should count us out," Katie said.

"Maybe buy us tickets to a Mariners game," Brian suggested. "That'd be a good time."

"You don't have to stay long," Grace explained in her ever-patient tone. But even she sounded a little weary of social obligations. She used to love dressing up, going to official functions and informal gatherings. "Just say hi and eat some barbecue and take notes, because—"

"Because next year, Dad's going to be the CAG," Katie finished for her.

"Such a bright child," Grace said with a wink.

"I heard Mrs. Crowther is a Grade-A, certified b— uh, pill," Katie said in a gossipy tone. "Brooke Mather says she has these horrible teas and stuff for the wives, and gets all mad if you don't come. And my friend Rose Marie says that in the winter, you can't wear a fur to any function, because Mrs. Crowther doesn't have a fur."

"Even if it's a really ugly fur?" asked Brian.

"That's enough," said Grace with a gleam of suppressed amusement. "We'll all go, and we'll be terribly polite and charming and they'll think the Bennetts are the nicest family in the Navy."

Steve had been dealing with Crowther all day, and he yearned to change the subject. He turned to Brian. "So have you had a chance to look at the admissions packet from the Academy?" he asked.

"You bet," Brian said. "I can't wait to roll up my sleeves and start filling in all those bubbles with a number-two pencil."

Steve grinned to hide a twinge of annoyance at his son's sarcasm. Brian was a star athlete with bright prospects, yet he spent every spare minute creating intricate, almost hyperrealistic drawings of some fantasy world. He claimed to be working on a graphic novel, which was beyond Steve's comprehension. Still, Brian had a serious desire to excel, and Steve hoped he'd choose to do it at the Naval Academy.

"It's a little early in the year to burn out on the application process," he pointed out.

"I looked at that stuff," Emma said. "It's not that different from a regular college application."

"Except for the blood test, urinalysis, dental X rays, physical aptitude exam…" Brian counted them off on his fingers. "Oh, and they're not going to like my tattoo and body piercings one bit."

"What tattoo and body piercings?" Katie demanded, craning her neck to study her brother.

"The ones I might get one of these days," he said. "Now that I'm eighteen, it's all up to me."

Clearly bored with her brother, Katie turned to Steve. "Can we get a dog?"

She had been asking all summer. She asked every summer, he remembered. "We've talked about this before. A family pet is—"

"One more thing to worry about," Katie interrupted, exaggerating his Texas accent.

"It's one more thing to love," said Emma.

Steve and Grace exchanged a look. Both knew better than to take the bait. The conversation was in danger of turning into a squabble that had no resolution. With characteristic skill, Grace steered the topic around to other matters and brought the meal to a successful conclusion. She did this all the time, he realized, watching her pump Katie for details on the bike trip she'd made with her two new friends today. Grace smoothed out the wrinkles, anticipating trouble before it appeared.

"I'm proud of you for making friends so quickly this summer," she told Katie.

"Like I have a choice," Katie said.

"You don't," Grace said, getting up from the table. "None of us do."

Maybe it was his imagination, but Steve sensed a subtle tension in the air. It was probably all in his head, he thought, watching Grace serve a dessert of strawberries in little glass bowls.

Sometimes he was so grateful for his family, it made his chest ache. That was the hell of having a job like his—he missed crucial moments in their lives. And even the periods of deepest contentment never lasted. But maybe, he conceded, the job made them sweeter, made him appreciate them more. Grace used to tell him so all the time, but she hadn't mentioned it lately.

After dinner, the kids got ready to go out. Steve could hear Brian and Emma upstairs arguing. The two of them shared the Bronco II, and if their plans for the evening didn't happen to coincide, they sank into one of their legendary disputes. He wondered why, after all these years, they still bothered. It was a bit like shadowboxing.

The twins were so alike, blond and athletic, with identical blue eyes. They had the sort of looks older women fussed over in grocery stores. When they were little, Grace used to push them around in the "double wide," a dual stroller she took everywhere. By the time Katie came along, that stroller had a lot of miles on it. Katie occupied a slinglike compartment in the rear of the contraption. She was such a quiet, unobtrusive little soul. One time—Grace swore it was only once—she had actually set her diaper bag on top of the baby, having forgotten until a little kitten mew of distress alerted her.

The expected squabble subsided without intervention, and Steve let out the breath he'd been holding. The twins had entered a phase of their relationship in which they were starting to like each other on a selective basis. Perhaps as the concept of leaving home became ever more real to them, they decided to explore the deep and mysterious heart of their twinship. Whatever it was, Steve would not complain. Especially since Katie, his awkward colt of a daughter, seemed to be experimenting with her own brand of rebellion here and there.

At the moment, Katie was stretched out on the sofa, reading a book. Her long, skinny legs—Olive Oyl legs, she lamented—were draped over the backrest, her head hanging off the side at an impossible angle. She read with deep concentration, seeming to inhale the story through her eyes. Steve walked over and mussed her hair playfully, earning a we-are-not-amused glare. He bent down to see what she was reading. "*Beneath the Wheel* by Hermann Hesse. The feel-good book of the year."

"At least it makes my life seem less depressing."

"Since when is your life depressing?"

"Since Brian and Emma get to go out tonight and they've already got tons of friends and not one person even cares if I exist—"

The phone rang. "I'll get it," she shrieked, flinging aside the book and clearing the coffee table in a single leap.

"She ought to go out for the track team. I'm thinking hurdles." Steve's gaze followed her as she streaked from the room. "What's this about her depressing life?"

Grace smiled as she wiped down the dining room table. "Wait five minutes. Her mood will shift."

It took less than five minutes. Portable phone in hand, Katie rushed back into the room, bursting with smiles. "I'm going to the movies with Brooke Mather," she announced. Then she locked eyes with Steve and cleared her throat. "May I go to the movies with Brooke Mather? The eight o'clock show at the Skywarrior?"

The base cinema was crowded with teens each summer and had been for decades. Steve wondered idly what it would be like to watch the decades slip by in one place.

"Who's driving you?" asked Grace.

"We can ride our bikes."

Grace threw the sponge into the sink. "Nice try, kiddo."

"We can."

"Of course you can. But you're not going to. You know the score, sweetheart. The base is—"

"I know. I know. Too crowded with clueless drivers who don't watch for bikes, especially after dark."

"Riddled with revved-up Navy guys who have only one thing on their minds," Emma chimed in, coming down the stairs.

"Yeah, Dad," Katie said, "what's with all the revved-up Navy guys? Aren't you senior officers supposed to keep discipline?"

"No," he said, "we're supposed to throw our unfledged daugh-

71

ters in their paths as virgin sacrifices. Go ahead. Ride your bikes. It'll appease the gods."

Her face fell and her cheeks ignited. Too late, Steve realized his sarcasm had been too harsh. Lately, he seemed to have an uncanny ability to make his smart daughter feel stupid.

"I'll take her," Emma said as Katie studied the floor.

"Take her where?" Brian demanded, clumping downstairs. In a rugby shirt, khaki shorts and Top-Siders, he looked more J. Crew than United States Navy. But Steve didn't say anything.

"You're going to take me to Brooke's, and then you're giving both of us a ride to the movies." Katie recovered quickly and addressed her brother in a bossy tone.

"And when it's over, you're bringing them home," Grace added. "Please." It was the system they had worked out over the summer. The twins were responsible for their sister. It was the price they paid for car privileges. Katie took full advantage of her power over them, particularly Brian. In front of her friends, she liked to sit in the back seat and direct him with a regal "Drive on, James."

The customary rush to the door ensued. Whereabouts were verified, curfews set, cell phones confirmed operational. As soon as they departed, Steve headed into the study to check his e-mail—the bane of his command these days. On the desk he found a stack of notes in Grace's handwriting. He recognized the names of shipping companies and local agencies and clubs, along with women's names and numbers. She belonged on the Navy's payroll, considering all she did for its families. That was Grace—helping, always helping. Sometimes she was so busy helping other families that the Bennetts were on autopilot.

At dinner she had seemed quieter than usual. Sometimes Grace reminded him of the calm, clear water above a reef. Placid on the surface, a lot going on underneath, invisible yet very real. But he was a flyer, not a diver. And he sure as hell wasn't a mind reader.

CHAPTER SEVEN

In the wake of the kids' departure, the house had a hollow air, as though waiting to take a breath. It was funny how houses each had their own personalities, thought Grace. This one was self-consciously cute, with Bavarian-style windows and halfhearted gingerbread trim. It was her least-favorite type of house—a meandering floor plan, boxy rooms, open hallways that amplified noise. The Navy's idea of officers' housing was that size matters.

She wandered out onto the porch to watch the kids drive away. Whidbey Island lay so far north that in summer the sun lingered late, painting the sky with deep shades of pink and gold she'd never seen anywhere else. The sight filled her with wistfulness, though she couldn't quite put her finger on the reason.

The tread of a footstep startled her briefly, and she turned to see Steve there. "Hey, sailor," she said, instantly getting over the brief moment of surprise. Every once in a while, she forgot he was around. A Navy wife either had all of her husband or none of him. There was no in-between time.

The Bronco's taillights glowed at the intersection, then disappeared around the corner. A bittersweet feeling swept over her as she watched them go. They looked so independent, heading out into the evening by themselves. She turned to Steve with a heart full of need. "I hate watching them go."

"Brian's a good driver."

"It's not that. I hate the idea that they're leaving."

"Summer's not quite over yet," Steve pointed out, clueless.

"I don't mean school," she said. "I mean for good."

"What, do you want them to stay?"

God. He didn't get it. She turned to the porch rail, planted her elbows on it and stared out across the yard, a cramped rectangle of beaten-down grass trampled by countless families that had lived here before. Far in the distance rose the mountains in a glittering robe of gold, unreachable.

"Don't get all pissed off at me, Gracie. I didn't make the rules. The point of raising kids is to prepare them to be independent, so they can leave and find their own lives."

Logic wasn't what she needed right now. She needed...she didn't know how to put it into words. "I'm not mad at you," she said.

"Then what's this?" he asked, touching her forehead with his finger, then with his lips. And just like that, her annoyance melted. "You're frowning."

She smiled up at him. "Not anymore."

"Good."

They stood on the porch together and silence lingered, punctuated by the cry of a gull and the shouts of children playing down the block.

The neighborhood was an uninspired cluster of plain but neat houses designed for wayfaring Navy families. This section was known as officers' country, housing squadron skippers, executive officers, captains and commanders, lining streets named after aircraft or astronauts. Some of the places had million-dollar views of the mountains to the west, but the Bennetts' place faced another house that looked just like it.

As they walked back inside, a few lights came on in the windows across the way. The strange wistfulness that had weighted her chest all day pressed harder now, and she felt as though she might burst. Discontent had crept up on her, entered through a side door. Everything around her was changing, and she felt compelled to change, too.

She wanted to talk to Steve, really talk, the way they never did anymore. She wished he would notice her mood, ask her what was on her mind. That would be the day, she thought. She cleared her throat. "Steve."

"Yeah?"

"When I was out shopping for school clothes with the girls, I looked in the mirror and realized that I've turned into a fat lady." She just blurted it out. It sounded so stupid, spoken aloud.

"What?" he asked.

"Fat and forty."

"Aw, Gracie," he said. "You're not fat and you're—" He paused, and she could see him doing the math in his head. "Not forty."

"Okay, a stout thirty-nine, then."

He chuckled and pulled her into his arms, burying his face in her hair and inhaling as though he'd forgotten the scent of her. And maybe he did forget, she thought, slipping her arms around the familiar muscular torso. Maybe, when he was six months at sea, he forgot the way she smelled, the texture of her hair and the way she tasted. Funny, she had never asked him.

Though she'd known him half her life, there were facets to him that remained a mystery. She pictured the carrier as an alien spacecraft that sucked up five thousand earthlings and took them away for long periods of time, doing experiments on them in the guise of training exercises. Then the earthlings were returned to their home planet, altered in subtle ways.

When he returned from a cruise, his hair was often different. He might have a faint scar from a healed-over cut. Sometimes he grew a mustache. During the first Gulf War, when he returned from a cruise that had run three months longer than scheduled, she even had the strange sense that his whole body chemistry had changed. She remembered running her fingers through his hair so thoroughly that he asked what she was doing.

"Looking for the alien probes," she had replied.

And even though she might momentarily forget he was in the house, she never, ever forgot how he smelled and tasted, what the beating of his heart sounded like when she leaned her cheek against his chest.

"Where did that come from?" he whispered, rubbing her back.

"What?"

"This forty-and-fat self-flagellation."

He made her sound so silly. She shouldn't have spoken up. He couldn't do anything about it, couldn't fix what he didn't know was broken. For that matter, she didn't know exactly what was broken.

"I told you," she said, taking another stab at explaining. "A three-way mirror in the dressing room. The kind where you see yourself from behind—and you realize you're turning into a dump truck. And I'm not flagellating myself. Although if it were a means of fat reduction, I suppose I'd give it a try." She studied his face by the dying light of the evening. He had the square-jawed, all-American look of a career officer on his way up. The lean body of a warrior. And the kind of smile that made women pause in whatever they were doing and find some reason to sidle up for a closer look.

"I don't think you can understand this," she said. "You still fit into the same size Levi's you did twenty years ago."

He cupped the palm of his hand and skimmed it down her side, as though mapping the imperfect topography of her body. "I don't understand how you can look in a mirror and not like what you see."

For the first time in their marriage, she flinched at his touch. "I'm not fishing for compliments. I swear I'm not."

"And I'm not doling out compliments. This is the truth. You're the mother of my children, Gracie," he said, bending down to kiss her. "You're beautiful to me."

And just like that, she let her troubles dissolve. He had, in addition to the physique of a deity, a certain boyish sincerity and fortunate sense of timing that made him irresistible to her. She pressed herself against him, welcoming the growing heat of intimacy. Her eyes drifted shut. She became absorbed in his embrace and in the dreamy promise created by his gently probing tongue. She knew they would make love tonight and that it would be wonderful. It was one of the things she could depend on in her marriage.

"Better?" he whispered.

She nodded, because it was easier than trying to make him understand.

He kissed the top of her head and stepped back.

"You always do that," she said.

"Do what?"

"You're always the first to let go in an embrace." He looked completely baffled, so she went on. "The first to leave the bed after we make love."

He smiled. "Let's go work on that. I had no idea you had a problem with this, Grace. I'll stay as long as you like."

He reached for her, but she moved away. "I don't have a problem," she said, wondering how she could possibly make him understand. It wasn't something obvious, but an aspect of their relationship that, over the years, had slowly and inexorably crept into her awareness. He wasn't rude about it. He probably didn't even realize he did it. He was a busy man with important duties.

"It's just that sometimes I feel like I'm one of the things on your mental list of things to do: tell the wife to get the silly fat notion out of her head, give the kids a pep talk before thrusting them into yet another new school, take command of a carrier air wing, make the world safe for democracy—"

"Jesus, Grace, what's got you so cynical all of a sudden?"

"It's not all of a sudden." She studied his face, that all-American handsome face, and saw genuine confusion in his eyes. He was the sort of man who fixed things—but if he couldn't see it, he couldn't fix it. "Never mind. I'm just stressed out. Want to rent a movie?"

"I've got a better idea." He put some music on the CD player, soft, fluttery jazz by Authentic Rhinestone. Then he slipped his arms around her, holding her so close that she disappeared, and drew her into a sexy dance.

"Yeah?" She shut her eyes as desire simmered through her. Even after so many years, he could still make her foolish with wanting him.

"Yeah." He pressed his thighs to hers. Steve was a fine dancer. He'd been advised to learn at officer training school. He was good at anything and everything that would help him advance his career, she thought, and then felt disloyal. He was a good husband and father, two things the Navy didn't require of him.

They danced all the way to the bedroom. As Grace drew the curtains shut, he came up behind her and slipped his hands along the buttons of her top, undoing them one by one and sliding the shirt down her arms. Just for a moment, she flashed on that image of herself she'd seen in the dressing room. With a will, she remembered what Steve had said—"You're beautiful to me." And he made her feel that way, with his hands and mouth as he finished undressing her and laid her down on the bed. By the time he shed his clothes and joined her, she wasn't thinking at all.

This was a different sort of dance, one of their own invention, the moves practiced and perfected over the course of years. The intimacy was deep and genuine. It was a haven for Grace, a place where she felt complete and...yes, beautiful. She lost track of the time, and was startled to see, through gaps in the curtains, that the last light of day had finally faded. Steve lay atop her, breathing slowly with contentment.

"I should ask you to dance more often," he whispered.

She smiled and held him close, their bodies still joined. Even in moments like this, she could never get close enough, could never know him completely, a dilemma that both frustrated and excited her. He was a complicated man who had overcome a brutal childhood, and no matter how much Grace loved him or how well she knew him, there was always a part of him that was a mystery to her.

It wasn't just his other life on the carrier. The same strength that had allowed him to survive his youth had made him a warrior. When she held him like this, it was hard to believe that, at his very essence, he was a machine trained to kill. The Navy had every possible term for it, but the bald fact was, that was his job. To kill and to train and lead others to kill. That was his secret side, the shadow Steve. He could hold her with the tenderness of a bridegroom. Yet if ordered to do so, he could send men and women to drop bombs on people.

He shuddered one more time, then parted from her, sliding the cool bedsheets up over them both. "You know," he said, "I think I've figured out why kids leave home."

"Hmm?" Grace sank back against the pillows. "Why is that?"

He folded his hands behind his head. "So their parents can have sex whenever they want."

"Dream on." She laughed and moved closer to him, laying her head on his chest. A pleasant sleepiness crept over her, and she could feel his muscles relax.

"I love it here," she said, her thoughts drifting to the house she'd seen.

The CD changed to an old Rolling Stones collection, and strains of "Ruby Tuesday" drifted through the house.

He slipped his hand under the cool sheet and caressed her. "I love it here, too."

"Very funny."

"I'm serious. I'm going to miss you, Grace."

She knew that tone in his voice. "You're leaving?"

"I, uh— I'm going to Washington on Tuesday. Briefing at the Pentagon. I'll be gone a week."

She tamped down a familiar welling of resentment. Of course he was leaving. That was nothing new, and a week's absence was minor. But maybe what she resented was that he'd waited until she was drowsy with sex before springing it on her. All right, she thought, that was his dream. Maybe it was time to try out hers on him.

"Well," she said, "that's your project. Here's mine."

"Where?"

She grabbed her robe and slipped it on. Despite his romantic words earlier, she felt no need to put her middle-aged body on parade. She switched on the light and found the real estate brochure on the bedside table.

"The girls and I went to an open house," she said, handing him the sheet and putting on her reading glasses. Steve didn't need glasses yet. Of course he didn't.

Heaving a long-suffering sigh, he scooted up in bed and scowled at the flyer. "Yeah?" he said. "So?"

She realized she was holding her breath. The brochure showed a reasonably flattering picture of Marcia's home basking in the sun, clear sky and blue water in the distance. But she wanted him to see what she saw, a house on a bluff, surrounded by towering trees, an apron of emerald grass and a view of the sea. She wanted him to see a place that would become theirs, a place where they might sit on the deck and hold hands, watching the stars come out at night. She bit her lip, feeling foolishly sentimental. It was just a damned house. A plain-looking house owned by a widow who had spent her entire marriage there.

He scanned the information quickly and efficiently, with total absorption. That was the pilot in him, able to suck up multiple facts in moments. In a squadron ready room before a flight, he'd be handed charts and knee-board cards. A pilot had mere seconds to memorize the code words of the day and mission specifics on a color-coded briefing card.

Yet when he lifted his gaze to her, his expression was one of total incomprehension. Clearly he needed remedial work.

Grace took the flyer from him and set it aside. She'd never understood how he could frustrate her and turn her on all at once. "Well?" she whispered, turning to nibble at his ear. "Do you like it?"

"I get the idea there's only one right answer to that question." He slipped his hand inside her robe.

"I want it," she said.

"Me, too," he agreed.

She pushed his hand away. "Really, Steve. I want to buy this house."

He fell still. "Gracie, we're only going to be here a couple of years. Three, max. Then we'll be stuck with a house here."

"You don't get stuck with a house. You own it. You live in it. It's where you go at the end of the day—"

"Not if you're transferred to the Pentagon."

His career again. She used to find it so exciting, used to look forward to each new assignment. But lately her thinking had shifted. She wanted permanence. She wanted a home. "It's time, Steve. I need something of my own for when the kids are gone. A place we can always come back to, an anchor."

"What if we have to sell it and it doesn't sell? How can we take that kind of risk?"

She couldn't help it; she laughed. "A risk-averse Navy pilot. Who knew?"

"When I'm on the job, I put myself at risk. But this could affect the whole family. The kids are going to college. Sure, Brian is headed for the Naval Academy, so there won't be any tuition for him, but…"

Grace figured it was the wrong time to set him straight about Brian and the Academy, so she bit her tongue.

"But what about the girls?" he asked. "Even with what we've set aside, it's going to be tough enough paying tuition. This isn't the time to be taking on a big mortgage."

"No, it's not the time. We should have done it years ago. The down payment can come from my grandmother's estate, and we can easily qualify for a VA loan."

He blew out a long-suffering sigh. "If you absolutely need a house, let's find something in our price range. This is waterfront property. It's twice what we can afford."

"We've been saving for years."

"Look, we had a plan, Grace. We were going to wait."

"I've changed my mind. I want this house, Steve. That's what people use their money for. It's what they save for." She held back from pointing out that everyone else their age seemed to be homeowners, many of them on their second or third home.

He scowled at the list price. "I know you're a genius with the budget, Grace. But a house—" he pushed the flyer away from him "—was something we always said we'd talk about…later. And this one is completely beyond our means."

"What if I found a way to afford it?" she asked.

"What are you talking about?"

"I could work." The idea had been simmering inside her even before her encounter with Marcia. Now a new sort of energy heated up. This was a possibility, not a daydream. Maybe she should have approached Steve differently, eased into the topic with him, but like he said, he was leaving. At the moment, he was glaring at her as though she was the enemy.

"I'm not a traitor," she said. "This is not some wacko idea I've had. And I'm not talking about a part-time clerical job on base somewhere. It finally hit me today. There's something I'm good at, and I could actually make a career out of it. I'm going to be an executive relocator."

"A what?"

"Executive relocator—someone who helps people move. In the civilian world that's worth something."

"It sounds sketchy to me."

"Don't you dare be condescending."

"I'm being practical. Setting yourself up for business is a long-term proposition."

"These days a business can be run almost entirely from the Web." She sat on the edge of the bed and hugged her knees up to her chest. "I don't need a physical location, just a virtual presence on the Web, a voice on the phone. I've been doing it for years as an ombudsman, anyway."

"I know that, Grace. You have incredible talent. Hell, I've seen you juggle schedules and plan a move like an air traffic controller. I've seen you find schools for kids with special needs, boarding kennels for dogs and parrots and drug rehab for more personnel than I care to remember. The families of the air wing need you. You're too damned busy for a regular job."

"Will you listen to yourself?" she said, incredulous.

"Grace, honey, I don't want you to have to work for a living. That's my job. I want you to be here for the kids."

"While you were out they grew up, Steve. They don't need me home twenty-four hours a day anymore."

"Maybe I need you there, Grace. Did you ever think of that?"

"My God, no. I can honestly say I never did. It's the most ridiculous thing I've ever heard."

He pulled on a pair of boxer shorts and paced the room. He always got restless when something was bugging him.

She found herself staring at his chest. Between his perfectly sculpted pecs nestled a St. Christopher medal he never took off. She'd once asked him where it came from. He said someone gave it to him just before he went to sea for the first time. Now the dark hair on his chest was sprigged in gray, which she found unaccountably sexy. Why was it that he seemed to become more attractive as he aged, while she just seemed to turn soft and faded? It wasn't fair. He didn't need his looks. He had everything else.

"It's not that we can't afford it," he said. "We can, if we're careful. But years ago, we agreed that owning a house doesn't fit our lifestyle. When I retire, we'll go anywhere you want. That was always the plan."

"Plans can change." Once upon a time, she had agreed with him about the burden of a house, given their way of life. But once upon a time was long ago.

"When did you change the rules on us?" She tried to answer, but he cut her off. "A house is a burden. A financial hemorrhage. What's the point of buying a place when we're moving in a few years?"

"What's the point? How about our future? How about doing something for us instead of the Navy for a change?"

"I thought you were on board with our long-term plans. You've raised the three best kids in the world. I'm riding high in the Navy. What can a career for you add to that?"

"I can't believe you just asked me that."

"I can't believe what you're asking of me." He opened a dresser drawer and started rummaging around. "Why now? Why this house?"

"There's something about it, Steve. It's special. At least come and see it with me."

"It's pointless, Grace. A waste of time."

"I don't need your permission to buy a house," she said.

His back stiffened. "You wouldn't do that."

She had no idea whether she would or not. He seemed a lot more sure of her than she herself was.

"We both agreed that we wouldn't get a permanent house of our own until I retire," he repeated.

"So retire, and we'll buy the house."

"Very funny, Grace."

"Maybe I wasn't joking."

He yanked a T-shirt over his head. "Yes," he said. "You were."

CHAPTER EIGHT

"It's the last official night of summer," Emma said after they dropped off Katie and Brooke at the theater.

"How's that?" Brian asked, jiggling his knee as he signaled to pull out into the road. Even while driving, he never sat still. He was always drumming, tapping or somehow moving around. It drove his teachers nuts, but his coaches appreciated all that excess energy.

"Dipshit," she said. "School Monday."

"Yippee."

"So not only is it the last night of summer, it's the last Saturday night before senior year." The last time she'd go school shopping with her mom and Katie, the last time she and Brian would head out into a clear, cool night, looking for a fitting way to mark the end of summer before they went their separate ways.

He eased out onto the road. "Yeah, so?"

"So nothing," said Emma, tucking away an old feeling of exasperation. "It was just an observation." Sometimes she wished her twin had been a girl. Brian was such a guy. So dense and literal.

"We should make the most of it, then," he said a moment later, surprising her. "Where's the party?"

"Mueller's Point," she said, "as usual." They knew all the

common rendezvous points, because they'd had the entire summer to figure out the social scene. Both twins were adept at making friends quickly and easily, wherever they went. It wasn't a gift, exactly. It was a survival skill. Moving every couple of years, you either learned to adapt and settle in fast, or you died the slow, excruciating, life-scarring death of the social outcast.

The life of a Navy brat was not for wimps. By the age of six, she and Brian had learned to reconnoiter a place, move in and make their mark in just a short time. The system wasn't flawless, but it worked pretty well. To this day, she still kept in touch with a handful of kids all over the globe, kids she'd met and brought into her heart, shared a warm but temporary bond of friendship with before moving on. It was frustrating sometimes, because every once in a while, she really clicked with someone, only to have to leave just when it felt comfortable to share her life with that person. Each time she moved away, the goodbyes were filled with heartfelt promises: I'll never forget you. I'll write every day. I'll come back to visit each year. Even though delivered with absolute sincerity, the pledges were never fulfilled. Not even once. Emma figured that was life for you, an unending strain of farewells and false promises.

"I guess it is pretty weird," Brian said as he drove toward the waterfront county park. It had a boat ramp, a dock and a fire pit on the beach. Over the summer they'd learned it was the favored hangout for a sizable group of kids. "The thought of no more school, ever."

"Except college," she reminded him.

"Right. College." His voice sounded flat and glum.

"Quit pouting," she said. "You'll be playing baseball and running track. How bad can that be?"

"Dad wants me to go to the Naval Academy."

Her brother would be offered an appointment, of course. He was a shoo-in. But getting the appointment was only the first hurdle. Getting through was the harder task. Unlike Brian, Emma had always been fascinated by the process. It took everything you had, and more. It took a willingness to give up your whole life, to surrender everything that made you unique. You had to make yourself over in the image of the Navy. A warrior with a spine of steel. And a degree in engineering.

"It's not such a bad idea, Brian."

"Geez, not you, too."

"It's a hell of a deal. You get an education and a job, guaranteed. An awesome job, by the way."

"And Dad gets his son in the Naval Academy," Brian said. "That's what it's all about, and don't pretend it isn't."

"Well, sure it is, but so what?"

"He wants it for him, not for me. He never got to go to the Academy, and he thinks sending me there will fix it."

"Do you have a better idea?"

"I could run off and join the circus."

"Right. You could call your act World's Dumbest Brother."

"Well, hell, Emma. I'm eighteen years old—"

"Really? I never would have guessed."

"Very funny. What I'm saying is, when does it get to be my life? When do I get to do all that Goethe shit about going confidently in the direction of my dreams?"

Although she had the urge to laugh at him, Emma was caught by what he said. "You should be doing that now."

He was quiet for a while as he drove. The night swished by, a streak of stars above the treetops. Finally Brian said, "I am."

"You are what?"

"Going for what I want, not what Dad wants."

"Art school, you mean." Emma felt a grudging admiration for him. He'd wanted that forever.

"I need to take my shot."

"I know. But Dad will say it's not practical, that you'll never make a living doing art. And maybe he's not so wrong, Brian." She thought about her brother's magical drawings. He created new worlds, whole universes with such clarity of vision that sometimes she believed they were real places. "But then again," she added, "maybe he just doesn't want you to be a starving artist."

"It's my choice to make it work or fail, not Dad's. Being a starving artist is a lot more appealing to me than the Navy."

Emma said nothing, but she knew one thing for sure. Brian would never go to the Naval Academy. His hero was Robert Crumb, not John Paul Jones.

"So have you told Dad yet?" she asked.

"Idiot. Of course not."

"Are you going to tell him before he goes on deployment?"

"Hey, how about worrying about your own plans for a change?" Brian asked, parking the truck.

"I don't have any plans, so I'm not worried."

He shook his head. "You'd better start playing the lottery, then." He grabbed a jumbo bag of Chee-tos—his contribution to what was loosely termed a "party"—and took off without waiting for Emma. That was fine with her. Brothers and sisters didn't go to parties together.

All their lives she and Brian had struggled with this. On their fifth birthday, they had thrown themselves into a jealous row that didn't end until Emma sank her teeth deep enough in Brian's arm to draw blood. After that year, they'd always had separate parties, one supervised by their mother, one by their father unless he was at sea. In that case, someone else would step in, usually another Navy mother.

Their rivalry was typical of twins, according to the experts. Emma knew this because her mother had read everything ever written about twins. *Parenting Twins. Educating Twins. Raising Twins as Individuals.* There was a whole body of literature out there, it seemed, to enable twins to feel normal.

It was dumb to pretend there was nothing unique about twinship, she thought, putting on lip gloss while studying her mouth in the visor mirror. Being a twin wasn't normal, but it didn't have to be a problem if you didn't feel like making it into one. Now that they were practically through high school, it wasn't such a big deal. But that still didn't mean she felt like showing up at a party with her brother.

The action was in full swing already. A group of kids sat around a big bonfire, and music roared from someone's car stereo. Bottle rockets left over from the Fourth of July whined and popped. A few grocery sacks and ice chests hinted that the foray for beer had met with success. The last of the daylight lingered on the water, flickering with the motion of the waves.

The sight of her friends gathered around a beach fire lifted her spirits. The glowing logs gave off a peculiar aroma, and the lively yellow flames illuminated about a dozen kids, mostly seniors. They were a mixture of Navy kids and locals who knew their way around.

Driftwood logs, smoothed and bleached by storms, lay like giant pickup sticks along the rack line of the beach and provided seating around the fire. Brian had already eased into the group and was sitting between two varsity cheerleaders. Girls were nuts for her brother's goofy charm, his looks and the offhand kindness that was second nature to him.

As she stepped into the circle of light Cory Crowther stood up to greet her. She liked that. He was also sports-hero handsome, with big shoulders, a great smile and probably an ego to match, but he seemed to genuinely like her. Although he'd been away most of the summer, everyone knew him—captain of the football team, son of a Carrier Air Group commander.

"Hey, Emma," he said in a good-natured drawl, perhaps elongated by a hint of beer. He patted the spot beside him. "Come sit with us. You know Darlene Cooper, right?"

"Hey, Darlene." Emma smiled at the girl beside Cory.

"Hey." Darlene was a heavyset girl in a tie-dyed T-shirt, with multiple piercings and multicolored hair. She was extremely cool, Emma thought.

Darlene pushed a cooler toward her. "Beer?"

"Thanks." Emma took a can of Rainier, even though she didn't care that much for it. She'd take a few sips and carry the can around for a while, just so they wouldn't think she was a dork.

"So are you nervous about starting school in a new place?" Cory asked.

Emma shook her head. "If I let moving freak me out, I'd have shot myself by third grade."

"I'm glad you didn't shoot yourself." His leg moved—maybe accidentally, maybe not—so that it was aligned with hers, warm and solid. She liked the feel of it and didn't move away. Maybe Cory was a bit full of himself but he was a key player around here. He was important in the small, contained, sometimes brutal world of high school, and she could do worse than win him over as an ally.

"Where are you from?" Darlene asked.

"Most recently from Corpus, on the Texas Gulf coast. How about you?"

Darlene took a big slug of beer. "All over, like you. Whenever my dad gets orders, off we go. It's just the two of us."

"Your mom's not with you?"

"Nope. She took off when I was a baby and I haven't seen her since."

Emma sensed the hurt beneath Darlene's nonchalant attitude. "So what do you do when your dad goes to sea?"

"Depends. Sometimes I stay with friends or family. One time I had to go to a foster home because there wasn't nobody." She shook back her candy-colored hair and took another sip of beer. "This year's going to be cool, though. Now that I'm eighteen, I get the apartment all to myself while he's on deployment. Our complex has hot tubs and a pool in the courtyard."

"That is so bitchin'," said Shea Hansen, who sat across the fire. "I can't wait to be out on my own."

Shea had tanned legs and wore loose nylon athletic shorts, like a runner. Her father was the minister of Trinity Lutheran Church in Oak Harbor, and Shea taught vacation Bible school there. Emma knew the whole community would be shocked by the sight of Shea sitting around and drinking beer. Adults tended to see what they wanted to see. And in hometown girls like Shea, they saw the good girl who could do no wrong.

Emma pointed out the varsity bars, divisional championship

and state finals pins on the boiled-wool front of Cory's letter jacket. "You've been at the same high school all four years," she said. "How's that work?"

He stretched his feet toward the fire. "We were transferred here five years ago, and my mom decided this was where she wanted to stay."

"So what happened when your dad got orders?"

"My mom and I stayed put. The old man spent his next two assignments as the oldest guy in the BOQ. He's back now, learning to be a family man again. He never was much good at it."

Emma braced her hand on the beach log and turned to look out at the inky water, speckled with reflected stars. She couldn't imagine her father in the bachelor officers' quarters. He'd shrivel up and die there. Everyone's family was different. She was glad her parents believed in staying together, whether the assignment was to Fallon, Nevada, or the wilds of Alaska.

"No way was my mother moving after she found her dream house over on Penn Cove," Cory explained.

"This place seems to have that effect on people," she said, thinking of how her mother had looked when they'd gone to see that funky house on the bluff.

"Must be nice, staying in one place for five whole years." Darlene opened another beer.

"No, *you've* got it nice," Cory said. "Your own apartment. As soon as they start their cruise, it'll be party central over there."

Darlene tossed a stick into the heart of the fire. She watched the flames wrap around it. "You bet."

Emma couldn't help feeling sorry for Darlene, who lived alone with her dad and had raised herself without a mother. She drank too much and didn't quite manage to hide the loneliness in her eyes.

"So do you miss Texas a lot?" Shea asked Emma. "Did you leave a boyfriend behind?"

"No, and yes." Emma grinned. "Texas weather is too hot for me. And yeah, there was a guy." She'd dated Garrett for six months, and he'd been the best boyfriend in the world. He was polite, kind and extremely cool. His father was a country club golf pro and his family had never lived anywhere but Corpus. When she left Texas, they had both cried. He promised to write, call and e-mail every day. She promised nothing of the sort. After so many partings, she knew better. But her crazy heart didn't. It always broke, no matter how hard she tried to protect it.

"You don't have a boyfriend now," Cory pointed out.

"That's right."

He lined up his leg with hers again. "Maybe you'll get lucky."

A shriek that sounded like an Indian war whoop split the air. The thud of bare feet on the wooden planks of the dock, followed by a splash, heralded the evening's festivities. Jumping off the dock into the icy Sound was a time-honored local sport of murky origin and questionable purpose. At low tide, the pilings were just tall enough to be deliciously scary, and the water still deep enough to be safe.

The first one in, a skinny kid named Theo, bobbed in the dark water, the moonlight glancing off his sleek head. "Come on in," he yelled. "Don't let me freeze out here alone."

"I'm in," said Darlene, peeling off her shirt and shorts to the swimsuit she wore underneath. More splashes erupted. Screams and shouts rang through the clear night air, and the noise held a special quality of abandon, Emma thought. Monday morning was in the back of everyone's mind. That, and maybe the thought that had been nagging at Emma lately—in just a short time, they'd all be out in the world, on their own. The prospect was exhilarating, intimidating, inevitable.

With a laugh, Shea jumped up and went to join the others. She moved like a ship in a storm, and Emma imagined she could hear the sound of beer sloshing in the girl's stomach.

"She can swim, right?" she asked Cory.

"Hell, in that condition, she can probably fly."

"How much beer did she drink?"

He grinned. "The question is, how much of this did she have?" He held up a tiny Ziploc bag containing six pills marked with a small but recognizable stemmed cherry. He slid one onto the palm of his hand. "Your turn, new girl."

Emma hated being in this position. It was not a good idea to say no to the big man on campus. However, it was an even worse idea to mess with Ecstasy. "I'll stick with beer," she said, and tipped up her can of Rainier just to make her point.

"You chicken?" he asked.

Emma looked around and realized that she and Cory were alone by the fire. Everyone had abandoned them for the dock, and the deep night beyond the circle of fire lent the moment a certain intimacy.

"No," she said with a laugh, and tossed her head. "You shouldn't, either. Aren't you applying for an appointment to the Naval Academy?"

"Hell, yes. It's a tradition among the Crowther men."

"Yeah? Last I heard, the Academy frowned on that stuff."

He put away the bag. "I'll clean up before my physical."

"No, I mean, if you're going in the military—" She broke off and waved her hand. "I'm all for personal liberty, but I'd rest easier knowing people in the military were clean and sober."

"Dream on, new girl. Some of the best drugs on the market come through the military."

She dropped the subject. She knew there was a drug problem in the Navy. Plenty of men and women in her father's command struggled with it; some of them were barely older than her. Her father ordered sailors into drug treatment or AA, probably more frequently than she knew.

"So what about you, huh?" Cory asked. "You applying for college?"

A familiar but unsettling sense of indecision prickled over her like a skin rash. There was something wrong with her. She was sure of it. Other kids had at least some idea of what they wanted to do after high school. But when Emma considered her future, she saw no clear picture of any sort of life that made sense.

She slid a glance at Cory, considering him. He was probably

one of the best-looking guys she'd ever met. But you didn't confess the secrets of your heart to a football god. He didn't even notice that she'd failed to answer his question.

"Why are you looking at me like that, new girl?"

"Why do you keep calling me new girl?"

"Would you rather be called old girl?"

"I'd rather be called Emma."

"Emma. That's a nice name."

He had a way of looking at her as though she really mattered. She couldn't tell if that charm was genuine or if it was his way of flirting. The intimate sense of aloneness seemed magnified by the fire. She could hardly see beyond the pool of light, though she could still hear her friends laughing and splashing.

"Why don't you have a girlfriend, Cory?" she asked him.

"How do you know I don't have a girlfriend?"

"You're sitting here with me on the last night of summer. If you had a girlfriend, you'd be with her."

He turned to face her, and the breeze stirred his shining dark hair. His hand came up and lightly slid across her back. "Maybe I am," he said, his eyes clearing, his all-American smile practically glowing in the dark. "Maybe I am."

She laughed softly, though she felt a thrill of attraction. "You are so full of it."

But she let him kiss her, anyway. She wanted him to. And he was good at it. He seemed to know just how to slant his mouth and circle his strong arms around her to heighten her awareness of his body. She liked a boy who understood the intricate choreography of a kiss instead of fumbling around and shoving himself at her the way some guys did. She'd missed this all summer long, missed the feel of a boy's arms around her, his lips on hers.

He pushed his tongue into her mouth. The intimacy both shocked and thrilled Emma. A part of her—the part from the Grace Bennett School of Proper Behavior—compelled her to pull away. It was trashy to make out with a boy you hardly knew.

Reluctantly she put her hands on his rock-hard upper arms and moved away. But that only made him hold her tighter, and another part of her—the wicked Emma part—indulged in the fierce sweetness of the kiss, letting sheer sensation block out common sense. She didn't care who saw her or what they thought. It was the end of summer and she was about to be the new girl for the last time. And life was good.

Until Brian interrupted. Yelling like a maniac, he raced into the circle of light cast by the fire. "Go on in," he yelled, spraying them with drops of icy water. "The water's fine."

Emma and Cory broke apart like a pair of negative charges. She straightened her shirt and glowered at her brother. Wearing only his shorts, he stood shivering beside the fire. His skin was covered in goose bumps, his hair plastered against his head and his eyelashes spiky from salt water. Darlene and another girl Emma recognized trotted along at his heels. The other girl's name was Lindy, but Emma and Katie had another name for her: the Stalker. She was crazy about Brian and had been after him all summer.

"Don't mind me," he said. "Just getting warmed up for the next round."

"So were we," said Cory, laughing but baring his teeth in annoyance.

"Do me a favor, Crowther," Brian said. "Next time you decide to grope my sister, don't do it in front of me. It skeezes me out." He gave an exaggerated shudder.

"Try minding your own business," Cory snapped, using a stick to stir up a shower of sparks in the fire.

"Hey, I know why you go out for football every year," Brian said.

"Because I'm the best there is."

"Because you're too fat and slow to make the track team," Brian said. As he spoke, he coiled into a runner's crouch.

With a growl, Cory lunged at Brian. His big angry hands grasped at empty air. Like a cartoon Road Runner, Brian took off. Even barefoot, he managed to stay ahead of Cory. He led him on a chase all over the park, dodging behind trash cans and picnic shelters, veering and feinting in and out of the shadows.

Emma watched with mixed amusement and annoyance. Brian was both pest and protector. She wanted to explore the possibility of liking Cory Crowther, but at the same time, she couldn't blame Brian for feeling protective. She felt the same way about him when some girl she didn't like threw herself at him.

"Cory'll kill him," Lindy said.

"He'll have to catch him first," Emma said.

"Brian's pretty fast, isn't he?" Lindy gave a dreamy sigh.

"Nobody's been able to beat Brian since we were in fifth grade." Her brother had always run like the wind. But for that one glorious, preadolescent year, she had grown taller and could outrun him, much to his wild envy.

She watched their silhouettes chasing around the area. The kids on the dock started egging them on. Brian eventually enticed Cory to charge like an enraged bull at him. Smaller and quicker, Brian raced down the length of the dock and kept going even when he ran out of planks.

Too late, Cory seemed to realize where they were headed. Emma laughed aloud, imagining his oh-shit expression when he couldn't stop his momentum. He caught himself at the end of the dock, wheeled his arms like a windmill, then lost his balance. His loud splash concluded the show.

Still laughing, Emma walked over to the dock. "Acme Hour is over," she called, leaning out to watch the two sputtering boys swimming to the beach.

"You son of a bitch," Cory said even as Brian guffawed. "My jacket's ruined. My wallet's soaked."

"Big mistake," Lindy said under her breath. "You should tell Brian to apologize."

"He was just goofing around," Emma said.

"Yeah, but if you piss off Crowther," Lindy warned, "he'll make your life a living hell."

"Cory?" Emma shook her head. "He seems like a great guy."

"He doesn't like to be teased."

Emma looked around to see if someone had a towel handy. It

was then that she noticed Shea's UW Huskies sweatshirt lying in a heap at her feet. Funny. She didn't see Shea amid the cheering group on the dock. The only two in the water were Brian and Cory.

"Where's Shea?" she asked.

Nobody answered for a few seconds.

"I don't see her," someone said.

"Did she go in the water?"

"I saw her jump in like ten minutes ago."

No one stayed in the fifty-four-degree water for ten minutes.

"Who's got a flashlight?" Emma demanded.

"You think she's in the water?"

"I think we'd better make sure she's not."

"I'll go check the glove box," Lindy said. "My dad keeps all kinds of gear in there."

A few of the kids who weren't reeling drunk yet scanned the water and called Shea's name. Somebody turned a car's high beams on the water and Lindy came running with a Maglite torch. Emma saw Brian and Cory emerge from the water, Brian keeping a safe distance from Cory. The two were hooting with laughter now, she noticed fleetingly. No one stayed mad at Brian for long.

But Shea was still missing.

Out on the water, the waves sloshed over the occasional floating beach log or snarl of seaweed. No Shea. Emma felt a hum of tension. It was probably nothing, but worry kept drumming at her.

"There." Lindy aimed the beam of light.

"Do you see her?" Emma asked.

The beam flickered over a buoy about fifty yards away. "Guess not." Lindy shone the light farther out.

"Make a pattern," Emma instructed. "Don't just sweep the beam randomly around." Despite the increasingly frantic calls all around her, she felt a sense of cold and focused calm. Someone suggested that Shea had passed out in a car, maybe even on the ground somewhere, but Emma kept looking. Her gaze followed the scanning flashlight beam. Without taking her eyes off the water, she slipped off her sandals, peeled her shirt over her head.

"What, are you going to jump in and go looking for her?" Lindy asked.

"No. I'm going to spot her from here," Emma explained, still scanning the water. "Then I'm going—" she grabbed Lindy's arm "—back that way," she ordered in a voice she scarcely recognized. She directed the beam to the left. Something was out there.

"Is that her?" Darlene asked.

"I can't tell." It resembled a clump of seaweed, maybe some floating debris. "Keep the light right there," she said. "I'm going to check it out."

"I think it is her," Lindy said. "God, she's not moving."

Emma dove. The water was so cold that, at first, she felt nothing at all. Then it slid over her like a forest fire, an icy burn from scalp to toes. She was already stroking hard when she broke the surface. She kept her eyes open even though the salt water stung. The light trembled and shifted but stayed trained on the indistinct shape.

In search-and-rescue training, they told you not to think about anything but the task at hand. She focused solely on finding Shea. Pretty soon she couldn't feel her fingers and toes; the water was that cold. She hoped Shea really wasn't out here.

Trying to ignore her flagging strength, Emma pushed past a floating log, terrified that she'd been misled. But then she recognized Shea's nimbus of long, dark hair and the bubble of her nylon shorts—possibly the thing that was keeping her afloat.

Training kicked in. She reached Shea and turned her faceup. She spoke her name, neither expecting nor receiving an acknowledgment. Shea's limbs were cold and unresponsive as Emma took her in a life-saving hold and struck out for shore.

She had done her training under an off-duty Navy swim instructor in Texas, and she could still hear his loud voice in her head. He was so mean that half the people in the course dropped out after the first session. Not Emma, though. His barking, his constant drills, his insistence on memorization and recitation all had a point. To save someone's life, you had to be able to perform under pressure. You had to remember procedure down to the last detail, because making a mistake could be deadly. She had stuck it out through twelve intensive sessions.

Swimming with a victim was like swimming in a bad dream—slow, laborious. The water was like mud, sucking at her stroking arm, holding her back, dragging down the victim. Adrenaline alone kept her going. She heard herself breathing, an accelerated rhythm that rose at the end of each frantic gasp. She moved stroke by stroke, breath by breath, refusing to let herself think of failure. Still, she couldn't help but picture the depths below, where it would be too dark for anyone to find her and Shea.

Her breathing came even faster, and she forced herself to kick and stroke again and again, knowing each pull brought them closer to shore. She was aware of the stars glittering, and the crescent moon glared in her eyes so brightly that it hurt. Then she realized the light came from the high beams of a car's headlamps.

Her foot scraped bottom. Thank God, she thought. Thank God.

Brian and Cory splashed down into the water to grab Shea and drag her up on the beach. Between them, her body resembled a limp, crucified corpse. Emma staggered after them, starved for air, making a hungry gasping sound with each inhalation. "Put her down," she said. "Lay her on her back."

They lowered Shea to the damp sand. Everyone from the dock came running and then stopped a few feet from Shea's unmoving form as though an invisible force field held them back. Emma dropped to her knees, straddling the victim.

In the wavering beam of a flashlight held in someone's trembling hand, Shea lay like a figure carved in stone, her skin a flat gray, her lips two colorless shadows, her eyes eerily slitted open, rolled back in her head, no pupils showing. Her hands were puffy, like bloated sponges.

"Holy shit," said Cory. "She's not breathing."

"Is she dead?" someone asked.

"She isn't breathing," someone else said. "That means she's dead, moron."

"Who's got a phone? Someone call 911," Brian said. "Hurry."

Emma knew the average response time of the local emergency medical service was thirteen minutes, assuming they could even find the remote spot. Shea might be beyond saving by then.

ABC, Emma thought, racking her brain to remember her mandatory life-saving training classes. Airway. Breathing. C…shoot. What did the *C* stand for? The procedure had been drummed into her. She knew this stuff. She knew it, but her panicked brain didn't seem to be working right. Why didn't anyone tell you the truth about this, that one day you'd actually have to revive a dead person?

When that horrifying notion struck, her hands got busy. She could do this. She had to. A broken girl lay helpless on the sand. "I have to do the Heimlich maneuver," she said.

"Isn't that for people who are choking?" someone asked.

"She's a lifeguard," said Brian.

Emma ignored the dubious murmurs of her friends and got to work. God, she wished those eyes weren't halfway open. It was creepy. A drowning victim had only a fifty-percent chance of surviving unless the airway was cleared of water before CPR. Then her chances of survival jumped to ninety-seven percent. Emma much preferred those odds. She turned Shea's head to the side, and water trickled from her mouth. She put one hand over the other and used her body weight to administer the Heimlich maneuver. More water spewed from Shea's mouth. She pressed several more times until there was no more water.

"Okay," she murmured, "airway's clear. Now start breathing." But between the noise of the surf and the babble of worried voices all around, she couldn't tell whether Shea was breathing or not. She bent over and tried to check for further airway blockage, sweeping her finger into the mouth. Hurry up, hurry up. Her heart galloped the urgent message to her brain and her hands. Emma was drenched in seawater and sweat. Shea wasn't breathing. Emma knew she had to breathe into her mouth, start her lungs functioning again.

She tried not to see those slitted, rolled-up eyes, tried not to feel the cool rubbery skin of the girl lying on the ground. She swept everything out of her mind except the task at hand.

The first resuscitation breath was awkward and ineffectual. The taste of beer and salt water filled her mouth. Her teeth clicked against Shea's, and she didn't seal her mouth completely over the other girl's. Behind her someone said, "Gross," but Emma didn't think it was gross. She didn't think anything at all. She just kept working.

"Whoa," someone else said nervously, "kinky."

"Shut up," Brian snapped again. "Go get a blanket or towel or something."

Emma checked to see if the chest was rising between breaths. In the dark, it was hard to tell. Come on, she told herself, you can do better. The next breath went where it was supposed to go. She could feel it, as though she was blowing up a rubber raft.

Shea lay unresponsive through the slow one-two-three count between breaths, but Emma kept trying. Breathe, turn to look at her chest, breathe, turn…. Everything around her fell away and she was barely aware of the noise surrounding her—girls crying, boys shuffling their feet and swearing, the waves hissing over the sand and sliding back down into darkness.

She fell into the rhythm of resuscitation—breathe, one-two-three, breathe. Her lips went numb and her head felt light from all the breathing, and stars danced behind her eyes, but she didn't break the cadence and knew she would not stop, ever. Something stronger than herself took hold and kept her going. Again and again and again. It was, for those moments, as though she had been created for precisely this purpose and no other.

She knew exactly when she felt the change. Everything turned. Desperation shifted to hope, slowly, secretively. The transformation was barely discernible. Not like in the movies when the left-for-dead victim suddenly hauled in a loud, dramatic breath. This was just a tiny buzz and a shudder, so subtle Emma thought she might have imagined it. But no. Shea twitched. With both hands, Emma rolled her to her side. Then the drama started.

Shea's body convulsed with new life. Someone screamed, but others moved in closer to see the sudden miracle on the beach.

Shea gasped and pushed her hands against the sand, sitting up as she coughed and sobbed. Emma collapsed beside her, breathless, dizzy and awestruck.

"Hey, Shea," she said, patting the girl's back. "Do you know what happened? Do you know where you are?"

Shea's eyes cleared but focused out to sea. "I'm scared. I need my mom," she whispered, pulling her knees up to her chest and shivering.

"You're supposed to lie down to minimize the shock," Emma said. She looked around at the others. "Did someone call for help?"

"I called," said Lindy.

"I'm not waiting." Shea rubbed her arms and shivered again. The knowledge that she'd almost died haunted her eyes. "I want to go home. Now," she said.

"I think you should wait," Emma advised.

"I said I'm not waiting."

Brian held out a hand and helped Shea up. Someone settled a dry towel around her shoulders. "Can you walk?" Brian asked, putting his arm around her. "Steady now."

"Take her to my truck," Cory said. "I'll drive her home."

Emma knew she ought to insist on waiting for professional help, but Shea looked so desperate and miserable that she didn't argue.

"Just get me home," Shea said. Someone handed her a wad of dry clothes, and she hugged them to her chest. She was still shivering violently, almost convulsing. "I really need to go home."

"You're going to be fine," Emma said. She was shivering, too. "But you should let your parents know what happened, maybe see a doctor."

"No way. Never," said Shea. Her eyes were two black shadows. "Will you come with me?"

"Sure," said Emma, sensing that Shea was teetering on the verge of hysteria.

"I feel so weird. So…stupid."

"Everyone's glad you're all right," Emma said. "Go wait in Cory's truck. I'll be there in a sec."

Shea hugged herself and walked up to the road.

Emma stood very still for a moment. The night had taken on a surreal quality. Thoughts streamed randomly through her head—she was supposed to help out at college night next week, which was ironic as she hadn't even picked a college. She had an appointment at the base dental facility. She was still waiting to see if she could get the work schedule she wanted at the pool.

And then all the swirling thoughts seeped away. A shudder rippled through her body as the adrenaline wore off.

Cory put his arm around her. "You did real good," he said. "You saved her life."

"Thanks," she said, but she wasn't sure what she was thanking him for.

The fire was extinguished, stray towels collected; then everyone melted into the night, heading for their cars.

"What time is it?" Emma asked.

"A little after ten."

"Brian, go pick up Katie and her friend. I'll be home after we drop off Shea."

He nodded once, then trotted to the car, throwing on his shirt as he went. Every once in a while she was grateful for Brian. In a pinch he had a knack for doing exactly what was needed.

She glanced at Cory. "Um, are you okay to drive?"

"Heck, yes. I'm wide-awake, especially after that swim." He headed for his truck. "Hey, can you grab that sack of beer?" he asked over his shoulder.

Emma picked it up and continued walking toward the road. Somewhere in the night, an aircraft headed in for a landing. She recognized the rumble and clatter of a P-3 Orion. A spy plane, the kind that could see anything from the air no matter how small. She wondered if they'd seen her rescuing Shea Hansen.

As she approached Cory's truck, a car pulled off to the side, its headlights burning into her. She squinted and shaded her eyes, nearly dropping the large paper bag.

A door slammed and a man in a horrifyingly familiar khaki uniform emerged from the sedan.

"Shit," said Emma between clenched teeth. The sack of beer in her arms suddenly felt very heavy.

"You can hold it right there, miss," said the sheriff's deputy in a firm voice. "Party's over."

CHAPTER NINE

The jarring beat of Shredded Virtue pulsed from the stereo as Josh Lamont slammed his shot glass down on the table. Across from him, the Air Force pilot named Roger Bell did the same. A horse-shoe-shaped crowd of his squadron mates and their dates surrounded the table, leaning in to see the drama unfold. With the studied solemnity of a laboratory technician, Marty Turnbull refilled their shot glasses.

"Idiots," said Rachel Willis, the CO's wife. "Give it a rest, okay? You're not a couple of fraternity boys anymore."

"We never were," said Roger, whom the Navy pilots had dubbed Tinker. The visiting Air Force pilot was Rachel's brother, which was the only reason the men of the Prowler squadron tolerated his presence. "Lamont here never made it out of *Romper Room*."

"Oooh," the others said, elbowing one another.

"Did you hear that, Lamb?"

"I can't hear," said Josh, disliking his call sign more than ever. Maverick and Iceman didn't exist in a real squadron, only in the movies. "Ms. Willis, you might as well call a taxi, because old Tinkerbell is going to be needing a ride any minute now."

Roger closed his fist around his shot glass. "Dream on," he said, his breath reeking of tequila. "Bottoms up."

Josh was too drunk to remember how he'd ended up in a drinking contest with a golf-playing Air Force flier, a breed Navy pilots held in disdain. All he knew was that as the most recent newcomer to the squadron, he was compelled to defend his honor. If he couldn't drink an Air Force guy under the table, his squadron mates would never let him hear the end of it.

Although Roger didn't seem to be moving, his image tilted in Josh's eyes. It was like trying to find the horizon at night without an instrument panel. Fucking impossible. But he was a Navy pilot, capable of the most elite and dangerous aviation in the world. He could land an airplane on the churning deck of a carrier at sea. He sure as hell could hold one more shot of tequila.

He lifted the glass, grateful that he could even find his mouth, and downed the tequila. He had lost all sense of taste at least a half hour before, so the liquor went down like water.

He and Roger slammed their glasses on the table and glared at each other. Roger's image wavered again. To keep himself focused, Josh took a deep breath and sang "Mary Ann Barnes, the Queen of All Acrobats" in a clear voice that had earned him a place as a soloist in the Naval Academy choir, not that he admitted this to anyone.

In a terrible but loud tenor, Roger bellowed the Air Force song about the wild blue yonder.

Josh's squadron mates joined in with "Mary Ann Barnes," but that only made Roger sing louder.

Rachel threw up her hands in disgust and walked away.

Roger's image seemed to list at a steeper angle, and Josh was pretty sure he felt himself sliding toward deck. Then he realized it was not him who was moving, but Roger. In the middle of the second chorus, old Tinkerbell got a dazed and blurry look on his face. Then his eyes rolled up toward the ceiling and he passed out, his forehead slamming the tabletop and knocking over the empty shot glasses.

Thank God, Josh thought.

A cheer erupted from the pilots and ECMOs gathered around the table. Hearty slaps rained down on Josh's back. He wished they wouldn't whack him like that, because he was about to puke. But he had too much pride to be seen yarking up his liquor in front of his brand-new squadron. He grinned and held it in.

"Let's finish this guy off," he said.

"Good idea." Lieutenant Becky Kent-Dobias, an ECMO from Sammamish, Washington, yanked Bell's USAF T-shirt over his head. He groaned an obscenity but didn't regain consciousness. Becky's husband Tom, a civilian, produced a can of shaving cream and a razor, handing it to Josh.

"You do the honors," he said.

"Thank you, sir." Josh hoped he wasn't so drunk he'd do permanent damage to the Air Force pilot. He studied Bell, who now lolled back in the chair, his face pointed at the ceiling. What the hell.

Josh circled his victim. Then he lathered up Roger's left eyebrow and, in one precise stroke, shaved it off.

Another cheer went up from the squadron. "It's perfect," Josh said, solemnly studying the victim's lopsided face.

"Almost." Becky came forward with a thick-tipped black permanent marker. In bold, block letters, she wrote Go Navy across his bare chest. "Now, that's perfect," she said.

Someone took a couple of Polaroid pictures of him for the squadron scrapbook. Then he was bundled, half-conscious, into a waiting taxi.

"Sorry about your brother, ma'am," Josh said to Mrs. Willis. He hoped she'd be understanding. She was married to a Prowler pilot. She had been to these parties before. He offered her his best grin, though it was probably a little off center. He couldn't feel his face anymore.

She confirmed this by tilting her head to one side and bursting into laughter. "When did you get here, Lamb?"

"Just a few days ago, ma'am." He enunciated every word, trying not to sound as drunk as he was. "I'm grateful to be training with the Sparhawks. Best squadron in the U.S. Navy."

She narrowed her eyes. "Have we met before?"

Uh-oh, thought Josh. He'd been expecting this but hadn't figured out what to say. "Why do you ask?"

"You remind me of someone."

No shit, he thought.

"Did you leave a sweetheart behind somewhere?" she asked.

"No, ma'am. Right now, my most intimate relationship is with the stick in my jet."

"Good plan," said Marty Turnbull. "You ought to keep it that way. Ma'am," he said, "we'd best be going. Luckily we came on foot and I know the way back."

Rachel made Josh promise to go out on Jet Skis with the kids some weekend. She mothered the whole squadron, especially new guys like Josh. Since he was crazy about kids, he said, "Thanks. I'll take you up on that."

"Just make sure you're sober when you do."

"Yes, ma'am."

They said goodbye to their hosts and stepped out into the cool air. Josh inhaled, hoping the late-night chill would sober him up. On the other end of the base, a plane glided in for a landing. A P-3 on night drills, probably, judging by its large size.

"You sure you know the way to the BOQ?" he asked Turnbull, who was more commonly known by his call sign, Bull.

"You bet. It's a long hike, though."

It might as well be Mount Everest, thought Josh, the distant blocky building pulsing in his blurred vision. "That's all right. I don't have anything waiting for me at home, anyway." Josh spoke without self-pity. He was getting plenty of stick time. That was what he'd come here for.

"Smart man," said Bull. "Stay away from that ball and chain."

"How come you're all soured on marriage, Bull?" Josh asked.

"Staying single keeps things nice and simple. You don't get your heart broken, and you don't hurt anybody but yourself. If you've got a wife back home, it eats you alive. It's hard to be flying missions when your mind is on what's going on at home."

"Is this the voice of experience?"

"Yeah, I had me a wife and, yeah, she was all I thought about while I was at sea. Before shipping out, I signed over my power of attorney so she could take care of business while I was gone. Turns out she used it to clean out the bank account and run off with my best friend."

Josh fished for words and came up empty. "Jesus, Bull." It was all he could think of to say. Even stone-cold sober, he wouldn't have the first idea how to respond. That kind of betrayal had to be a guy's worst nightmare.

"Whoa," said Bull, watching a car come around the corner and roll at patrol speed along the street. "It's the MPs."

"We're not doing a damned thing—" Josh broke off as the headlights of the squad car washed over a mailbox marked with stick-on reflective letters spelling the name *Bennett*.

All of a sudden the blurry euphoria of tequila resolved into painful sobriety. In the blink of an eye, Josh was as attentive as a midshipman facing inspection.

So that was Steve Bennett's home. Just knowing where he lived made him all the more real to Josh.

He and Bull slowed down to watch the dark-colored sedan pull into the Bennetts' driveway.

"Wonder what's up with that?" Bull said.

They crossed the street as the MPs exited the vehicle and opened the back door. Josh was sickly fascinated to see a teenage girl emerge. She looked both calm and defiant as she was escorted to the front door.

The porch lights blinked on and a tall silhouette loomed in the doorway. He wore pajama bottoms and a T-shirt and had bare feet, just like any guy.

My God, thought Josh, seeing him in person for the first time. *That's him.* He felt a sick lurch of his stomach and decided then and there to put off the inevitable for as long as possible. He hadn't asked for this, and wasn't looking forward to meeting Bennett.

"Well, well, what do you know?" Bull murmured, oblivious to Josh's roiling thoughts. "The DCAG's got problems."

Bull didn't know the half of it.

Seeing Bennett like this changed him in Josh's eyes. Before, Bennett had been larger than life, an icon. But right now, he looked all too human.

CHAPTER TEN

Steve didn't usually have trouble sleeping, even with the distant noise of jets on the runways, but tonight was different. He usually knew just what to do with worries and unsettling thoughts. They went into a compartment in his mind, walled off by themselves where they wouldn't bother him until he chose to deal with them. The Navy taught you that. You divided yourself—your mind, your heart, your life—into compartments and managed things one by one. The present issue was different. This spilled out and over and down, threatening to make a mess of everything.

He turned his head to look at his sleeping wife. She lay on her side, her back to him, her bare arm on top of the covers. Ordinarily he would reach out and gather her close, curve his body protectively around her until they both settled down to sleep.

But tonight wasn't ordinary. In the gray half-light, he watched her for a minute, searching for some visible sign of her discontent. She looked exactly the same to him. She looked like Grace. His wife. The glue that held the family together. Nothing made sense without her. And yet that was how he lived half his life, it seemed. Without her.

That wasn't supposed to be a problem. Navy families had to be strong. They had to make sacrifices. All the Bennetts understood that. But now, seemingly out of the blue, Grace appeared to have discovered a problem with a way of life she had helped create. All of a sudden, she wanted a mortgage and a career. She wanted to "invest" in expensive waterfront property.

A dull thud of apprehension sank in his gut. Maybe she was thinking she didn't want to move anymore. Maybe she wouldn't make the next move with him.

That was ridiculous, he told himself. For nineteen years she had followed him all over the globe, picking up the family with the ease of a vacationer on a summer picnic, packing up and moving on. It was what they did. It was who they were.

Setting down roots in this place would change everything. It had the potential to alter the course of their lives, to turn their long-standing goals upside down. He didn't know what to make of her change of heart. And maybe, he reflected, it wasn't so sudden. Maybe they just hadn't talked about it until now.

He eased himself from the bed without waking her and put on a pair of pajama bottoms. He walked out into the darkened hallway and down the stairs. In the kitchen, he looked out the window and checked the driveway. Good. The kids' car was there, which meant they were home safe.

He pulled open the refrigerator, found the orange juice and drank straight from the carton. Grace frowned on that, of course, but Grace was upstairs, sound asleep. She frowned on a lot of things lately.

After putting the juice away, he stood in the shadowy kitchen, listening to the hum of the fridge and the distant buzz of aircraft on night-training maneuvers. The Naval Air Station never slept.

He braced his fists on the counter as frustration bubbled up inside him. He didn't need trouble on the homefront. Not now. If he stayed the course, his next tour of duty would likely be a command cruise with the carrier air wing. This was what he'd been working for all his career. But now Grace was deviating from a course they'd both agreed upon, and he was supposed to simply to allow it.

Pushing back from the counter, he let out an explosive sigh of frustration. He was about to go back to bed when a white beam of headlights washed through the downstairs. A car was pulling into the driveway.

Across the street, a pair of men in civilian clothes passed by, walking none too steadily.

What the hell? He grabbed a T-shirt from behind the laundry room door and pulled it over his head.

Middle-of-the-night visitors never meant good news. His mind flipped through the possibilities. Someone had been injured, maybe one of the rookie pilots. Or an enlisted man was in trouble, perhaps. A fellow officer. Or—

He pulled open the front door.

"Sir, we're sorry to disturb you," said the MP standing at attention. "But we need to talk to you about your daughter."

Steve stared at Emma with only the most reluctant comprehension of what was going on. Who was this young woman who stared back with unflinching calm? She stood on the threshold like a stranger he'd never met before. Her blond hair was uncharacteristically stringy and dirty-looking. Her clothes were damp and hung on her frame.

The MPs explained that, at the main gate of the station, they had received her from the local authorities. The sheriffs' deputy who had picked her up at a county-park beach had made the delivery. They enumerated infractions that were the stuff of parental nightmares: drinking, risky behavior, swimming in an unauthorized area.

In a numb state of shock, Steve went through the motions like an automaton, thanking the MPs for their help, instructing Emma to apologize for the trouble she'd caused and to promise she'd never do it again. She obeyed in a flat, clear voice, exhibiting neither fear nor contrition. But apparently it was enough to mollify the MPs. Showing deference to Steve's rank, they saluted him and returned to their patrol duties.

Steve waited until their taillights disappeared before he turned to Emma. "All right, young lady—"

"Don't wake Mom," she said.

"Is that all you have to say for yourself, don't wake Mom?" Steve demanded. But in reality, the same conviction had been close to the surface in him as well.

When Emma didn't answer, he paced back and forth in the foyer. "You're soaking wet."

"Can I just go to bed?"

"Not until you explain yourself." Steve broke out in a sweat. He never knew what to say to his kids when they got into trouble. When hardened sailors were brought before him, he knew exactly what to do. He evaluated the infraction and meted out justice firmly and fairly. But with his own kids, he was at a loss.

Her shoulders sagged. "What happened was—"

"Are Brian and Katie home?"

"Yes. Now, are you going to listen?"

Privately, he admired her poise. Katie or any other girl would probably be lying in a puddle of tears by now, but Emma held herself straight and tall, and she looked him in the eye.

"I'm listening," he said.

"We all got together," she said, "to mark the end of summer. There was a fire on the beach and a bunch of people started jumping off the dock into the water—"

"Into Puget Sound? In the dark?"

"It's no big deal. It's a tradition on the island. The kids say their parents did it, and probably their parents before them. Anyway, one girl got into trouble, so I went in after her. By the time I swam out to her, she was just floating facedown, not breathing."

"You went in after her."

"That's what I said."

"Why you?"

"I'm a lifeguard. I know how to do this stuff."

"So is the girl all right?"

"Yes. Her lungs were full of water, and I had to do…mouth to mouth." For the first time, Emma's composure wavered. Her lower lip trembled. "I was so scared, Daddy. At first she wouldn't breathe. She was all cold, like she was dead or something. I was so afraid she was—"

He cut her off, pulling her awkwardly against him, her wet clothes soaking him. "You did fine, baby," he said. "You did the right thing. So did your friend go to the emergency room?"

"No." Emma spoke against his chest. "Ask Brian if you don't believe me. He saw the whole thing."

Steve felt torn between admiration and skepticism. He let go of her and stepped back. "How is it that you managed to save someone's life one minute and get hauled in for drinking the next?"

Her eyes narrowed. "Just lucky, I guess."

"Where'd you get the beer?"

"Some kid brought it."

"Which kid?"

"Just…some guy."

"I need a name, Emma. Full disclosure. Complete information."

"No, you don't," she said with infuriating calm.

"Emma, I'm warning you—"

"Fine. You really want to know? It was Cory Crowther." She thrust up her chin and glared at him. "Aren't you glad you asked?"

Crowther. Damn.

"See?" said Emma. "You were better off not knowing. Now you have to decide whether or not to rat out your superior's kid."

"You know I wouldn't do that."

"I know. I never should've said a word, not even for the sake of full disclosure."

Steve thought Cory was a good kid. From their few encounters, he had formed a positive impression of the boy. He was tall, athletic, polite and respectful. But apparently he had another side. "Look," he said, "this kid sounds like bad news. You shouldn't be hanging around with him."

"Yeah, well, when you're me, you can't exactly be choosy about your friends."

"What's that supposed to mean? When you're you?"

"When you're a Navy brat, Dad. Do I have to spell it out for you?"

"Why don't you do that? Why don't you spell it out?"

"I can't be picky about my friends because I've never stayed in one place long enough to have a lot of options. One or two years at a school, three max. That's what I've had, all my life. It doesn't exactly give me time to build perfect friendships, does it?"

His daughter was bright and funny and kind. How could she think she had to go begging for friends? "You're looking at it all wrong, Em. You kids are lucky. You are privileged. You've lived all over the world. You speak two languages. You've seen things most kids never dream of."

"But I've never had a best friend," she whispered, and her soft voice cut him like a knife.

"So you go out drinking with my commanding officer's boy."

"I didn't plan it that way."

"Did Crowther get escorted home by the MPs?"

"As if. The deputy commended him for looking after the girl who nearly drowned, and told him to be careful driving her home. I was the one holding a sack of beer, just like they told you."

"If Cory Crowther was responsible for the beer, why didn't he step in when he saw you were getting into trouble?"

"What would be the point of two of us getting in trouble? For that matter, what would that have done to your career, Dad, if we had both gotten in trouble? You know what would have happened. It would have turned out to be my fault, and you would have paid the price."

Where had she learned this stuff? There was no book explaining the intricacies of Navy politics. But his kids had understood such things since they were tiny. They'd had a graphic lesson back when the twins were in second grade. He was being considered for a tour in either northern Alaska or the Spanish Riviera. Things were looking good for Spain when Brian beat the crap out of his superior officer's boy over a baseball game.

The next week they'd been ordered to Alaska.

Apparently that lesson had sunk into Emma. She knew his fortunes were tied inexorably to his superior's whims. If Mason

Crowther decided to make his life a living hell, he'd do it. The position of Deputy CAG was precarious and Emma knew it. Emma, his daughter. His heart. He thought he knew her. But here she was, out jumping off docks and getting into trouble with boys who had more of a sense of self-preservation than honor.

"Look, Emma, your behavior matters, and not just because of my position. It matters because you need to respect yourself."

She suppressed a yawn. "Can I be excused, please?"

"All right. Look, I'm proud of you for saving your friend."

"Thanks, Dad."

"So do me a favor, okay? Keep your nose clean."

Emma pursed her lips. "I'm just going to try to survive my last year of high school." She started toward the stairs, then hesitated and turned back. "What about Mom?"

Given what was going on with him and Grace, he wasn't eager to stir juvenile delinquency into the mix. "We won't bug your mom with this. I expect you to have a great start to school. And I don't want to hear one more word of trouble with the Crowther boy. His old man is the type who looks for ways to make my job harder. Do you hear me? Not one word."

"Fine," she said in a harsh whisper. "I won't say a word."

CHAPTER ELEVEN

On the kids' first day of school, Grace got up early. She was always the first one awake, insisting on a proper breakfast and then gearing them up with backpacks and book bags, as though arming warriors for battle. She was packing three lunches when Steve came into the kitchen. She knew that, at 0800 hours, he would assemble the troops to subject them to the customary first-day-of-school pep talk. He looked wonderful, as always, fresh from the shower, his khaki uniform crisp. But on closer inspection, she saw faint lines of fatigue around his eyes.

"Didn't you sleep well last night?"

"I slept fine." He poured himself a cup of coffee and started organizing his briefcase.

Grace took a deep breath. The argument still hung between them. They were out of synch. They needed to talk more. But he was leaving for Washington, D.C., so once again, a big discussion would have to wait. "Guess who I'm meeting today?"

"Who?"

"A banker. About a commercial account for my relocation business."

"Aw, Gracie. I wish you wouldn't rush into this. You're going to need credentials, references—"

"I'm not rushing. I have stellar credentials. I'll have references coming out my ears, what with all the Navy families I've worked for over the years. Everything's falling into place, Steve. I'm applying for a business license, too."

He looked at her as though she were an alien life-form. "A business license? What the hell is that, Grace?"

"It's the first step." He wasn't getting it. She could just tell. "I even got the name of a firm to handle the incorporation."

"Grace, Incorporated?"

"My God," she said. "You're being condescending again."

"Who, Dad?" asked Katie, clumping down the stairs. "Condescending? I'm shocked."

"Hey, Miss Smarty-Pants. Give your dad a hug." While he embraced Katie, he sent Grace a look that would have to pass for an apology. They weren't finished with the discussion, not by a long shot, but without saying a word, they came to a mutual, unspoken agreement. This morning was about the kids.

Katie had risen at 6:00 a.m. She'd changed her clothes four times, spent a half hour fixing her hair and had chewed her nails to the quick. By eight o'clock, she looked exhausted.

"How about some breakfast?" Grace offered, holding out the blender pitcher. "I'll give you half my tofu smoothie."

"Since when do you drink tofu?"

"Since I heard it's more healthy than a Pop-Tart. Here, have a sip."

Katie wrinkled her nose. "I'm not hungry."

"At least drink some juice." She took a glass from the cabinet.

"Look at that," said Steve. "My own little Katydid starting high school. I remember when you started kindergarten."

"You were at sea when I started kindergarten."

"That doesn't mean I don't remember it."

Unexpectedly Grace felt a lump in her throat. Because she *did* remember. Only yesterday, it seemed, she'd been primping her little girl for the first day of school, holding back the tears as she sent her youngest child from the nest. Katie had been nervous—no, terrified. But like a resigned prisoner going to the gallows, she had bravely marched to meet her fate. She was terrified now, Grace realized, seeing the tremor in Katie's hand as she lifted the glass of orange juice to her lips. Ah, poor baby. New situations always rattled her.

Grace felt a pang of regret for all the times they'd thrust Katie into new schools, new neighborhoods, new ways of life. As soon as she settled into a place, they moved again. The process had made her daughter fragile and insecure.

She stood as though bracing herself for having the rug pulled out from under her. Just once, Grace wished they could offer Katie stability beyond her immediate family circle. What sort of person would she become, given the opportunity to attend the same school for more than three years, and have a group of friends she wouldn't be forced to leave?

"I remember your first day of first grade," Steve said, looking for concurrence. "Don't I, Gracie? I remember thinking, look out world, here comes Katie Bennett. I feel the same way now." He put his hand on top of her head and grinned at her. "This school has never seen the likes of you."

"Then they won't notice if I don't show up," Katie said.

Brian came into the kitchen, his hair damp from the shower, his duffel bag stuffed with gear. "Is he starting that whole Henry V thing about 'we few, we happy few'?"

Grace poured him a glass of juice. "I think he waited for you."

"I knew you wouldn't want to miss a word of it," Steve said.

Emma arrived, quiet and self-possessed, not showing even a hint of the nervousness that seemed to crackle and buzz around Katie like a force field. "Morning," she said. "Do we have any Pop-Tarts?"

"Breakfast of champions," Grace said, holding out a box of frosted strawberry pastries.

"Thanks."

Steve watched Emma for a moment, his expression unreadable.

She seemed to concentrate extra hard on operating the toaster. Then Brian stepped between them. "Excuse me," he said, reaching for the cupboard. He found a two-quart mixing bowl and filled it with Cheerios and milk. Then he sat down and dug in.

Grace turned away to refill her coffee mug. "Where did he learn that, anyway?"

"Learn what?" Emma set her backpack by the door and leaned toward the hall mirror to check her makeup.

"To eat like a caveman," Katie said.

"You mean like a star athlete in training," Brian said between mouthfuls. "It's a gift."

"I've got to go," said Steve, picking up his attaché case and taking his cap from the hook by the back door.

Grace could already see him pulling away, moving out of one world and into another. From breakfast and children to meetings and briefings, great matters and challenges. Like a knight from times past, he donned the trappings of his office, drawing the uniform like a shield around him. He belonged to a secret world, and although she had been privy to it for many years, she would never truly be a part of it. That was never more apparent than now, when he was on his way out the door.

"What, no 'happy band of brothers' speech?" asked Katie with mock disappointment.

"You know it by heart, anyway," said Grace. "If the school has a drama club, you're all set."

"I'm going to try out for marching band," Katie declared.

"Of course you are," Grace said. "You'll knock 'em dead with your clarinet playing."

"You say that like it's a good thing." Brian put the huge bowl to his lips and gulped it dry.

Steve kissed Grace's cheek, and she shut her eyes and inhaled his scent of shaving soap. The dispute stayed open, though, hanging between them like a chilly shadow.

She flashed on a memory of the early years of their marriage. Sometimes, in the morning, he used to laugh and make love to her with a sweeping spontaneity that took her breath away, and then he'd rush off to work.

Where had that laughter, that spontaneity gone? She didn't recall waking up one day and realizing it had fled. Instead, it seemed to have bled away like a slow, almost imperceptible leak, its effects masked by everything life heaped upon their plate: children, Steve's career, frequent moves and the simply day-to-day routine of living. Yet they were a happy family, Grace insisted to herself fiercely. She had dedicated her life to making it so, and to believe otherwise now was to call herself a failure.

But was it so bad to want something more? Steve seemed to think so.

He headed for the door. "I'll probably be late today," he said. "Public affairs meeting. Some big magazine wants to do an in-depth report on the carrier. I'll call and let you know."

"No, you won't," said Grace. He almost never did. He gave himself to his work one hundred percent. If he didn't, he wouldn't be the man she loved. Although if he did... "Killigrew will call."

"That's his job."

Grace reminded herself that he had to stay on top of all aspects of air-wing intelligence, maintenance, operations and public affairs. Homeport tasks removed him from combat, and sometimes he almost seemed like any other husband, going to the office for the day. She had to remember that no matter what his orders, he always had the heart of a warrior.

"You kids have a good day, you hear?" His smile flickered over each of them, a swift benediction. Katie met his gaze and lifted her chin in determination. Brian squared his shoulders and hefted his duffel bag. Steve and Emma shared a look Grace couldn't quite fathom. "You hear?" he repeated.

"Yes, sir," Emma said with a surprisingly convincing salute.

Once he was gone, the next wave of departures began. Brian was happy with the new school; Grace could tell. He liked his coaches and his teams—track in the fall, swimming in the winter and the all-consuming baseball in the spring—and fitting in had never been a problem for him. Emma seemed relatively untroubled as well. She took change in stride, treating each move as a new adventure. With more practicality than vanity, she used her looks to advantage. Her hair was a yard of blond silk, her smile as bright and genuine as a new coin, and she made the most of the attention they got her.

Grace wished some of that effortless *je ne sais quoi* would rub off on Katie. "How would you like me to drive you to school?" she offered, thinking it might ease her nervousness.

"No, thanks," Katie said, finishing her orange juice. "I'll ride with the twins."

Grace gave her a hug. "I want you to love high school," she said. "I know high school is going to love you—if you let it."

"Like middle school loved me?" Katie gave an exaggerated shudder.

"No. Middle school is simply survival training for anything else life dishes out. You survived it, so you're ready for anything." Grace dumped the rest of her smoothie down the sink. The hell with the diet. It was too much trouble. Defiantly she put a forbidden, sugary Pop-Tart into the toaster.

Katie picked up her backpack and clarinet case. Grace hoped she wouldn't change her mind about band tryouts this afternoon.

Out on the driveway, the kids good-naturedly endured her final hugs and bits of sunny encouragement, then piled into the Bronco. The neighborhood brimmed with similar scenes of worried mothers wearing overly cheerful smiles and dispensing advice to unnaturally silent, well-groomed children. As Brian backed out of the driveway, Grace stood alone in the yard, her hand raised in farewell until the truck turned the corner and she lost sight of them. Then she lowered her hand to her heart and held it there momentarily, lost in thought. She shook herself alert and waved to Helen Coombs across the way, and noticed Sylvia Dowd loading her young kids on a lumbering yellow school bus.

Grace turned back toward the house, feeling unsettled. The start of the school year was a new beginning, but it was always bitter-sweet for her. She was the one they left, the one who stayed behind.

Ordinarily she would throw herself into her duties as an officer's wife, organizing socials, coordinating volunteer work and support groups. But for the first time in her marriage, the incredible adventure of being part of a Navy family lacked appeal. For once, she wanted something different. The idea planted by Marcia Dunmire had taken root, and Grace wasn't about to let Steve talk her out of doing this.

But first she decided to take a walk. Exercise was more important than counting calories. Everyone knew that. She dressed in shorts and a T-shirt, put her hair in a clip. The frosted Pop-Tart clenched in her teeth, she tied on her ancient Reeboks, then strode out the door and down the driveway. Still chewing, she headed along the sidewalk, certain she'd walk off the calories in just a few blocks.

She felt perfectly virtuous until a pair of joggers passed her, their lean, muscular legs gleaming in the morning sun, their ponytails swinging rhythmically with each swift, athletic stride. Like grim sailors on parade, they held their gazes straight ahead as though reluctant to lose focus by looking at Grace.

Resolutely, she balled her hands into fists and forged on. Power walking, it was called, but she didn't feel terribly powerful. A little sweaty, maybe. But not winded yet. She passed a row of gray-painted hangars, each labeled with the squadron number and its insignia: the Gray Knights, the Lancers, the Screaming Eagles. Tough-sounding names for squadrons of men and women willing to put their lives on the line.

Pushing her chin up and trying to pretend she wasn't winded, she walked all the way to the geographic tip of the Naval Air Station. It was a perfect morning, the sea and the mountains shining with that rare clarity unique to this part of the world. She filled her lungs with the mingled scents of brine, jet exhaust and fresh air, then pivoted on her heel and headed back.

To her right, surrounded by a fringe of grass, was a monument that gave Navy families a chill of apprehension. Yet people seemed drawn to it, perhaps by some fatalistic sense of reverence. This morning, Grace noticed a young woman standing on the U-shaped walkway around the retired EA-6B Grumman Prowler.

The jet was permanently parked there and anchored to earth by stout cables of twisted steel. Off to the side was a pair of frozen bronze men, and bronze kids stood on the walkway, permanently pointing to the plaques of lost personnel in the Prowler community. The empty pilot's bubble was stabbed through by sunlight and magnified on a patch of grass. The distorted light and shadows in the cockpit created ghosts under the clear canopy. For a moment, Grace imagined she could see a doomed young pilot at the controls, but when she blinked again, the image dissolved into a bowl of reflected morning sun.

Grace stopped next to the young woman who stood there. She had thick dark hair, olive-toned skin and deep brown eyes that misted as she moved reverently along the row of granite plaques that surrounded the jet. Each plaque was chiseled with the names and call signs of men and women who had died in the service of their country. After each name was listed the aviator's shockingly short life span.

"They were younger than my husband is now." The dark-haired woman glanced up. Her delicate beauty seemed curiously piercing to Grace.

At least the woman wasn't here lamenting a lost loved one. "Does your husband fly?" she asked gently.

"No, thank goodness. He works in ordnance."

Grace decided not to point out that some of the memorial plaques were for enlisted personnel.

"I probably shouldn't be looking at this," the woman said, "but I was curious. Michael—that's my husband—says most men don't come here."

"Aviators have a lot of superstitions," Grace said. "My husband never flies without his St. Christopher medal." She smiled and stuck out her hand. "Grace Bennett."

The woman frowned. "Bennett, as in Captain Steve Bennett?"

"That's right."

"Patricia Rivera. I just got here. It's an amazing place."

"Where do you live, Patricia?"

"We're staying at the Navy Lodge until our household arrives. But these days, I tell people I'm living in a state of confusion. I can't imagine how I'm going to get everything done."

Grace smiled, filled with understanding. She still remembered the jittery young bride she'd been, full of dreams that had quickly been eclipsed by life in the military.

"Welcome to the club," she said. "Just take things one task at a time and enjoy the ride."

"Thank you, Mrs. Bennett."

"I hope you'll call me Grace."

"All right…Grace. You know, I'm the oldest of five kids. My mama worked, and I practically raised them all, so I thought I was ready for anything. But nothing prepared me for the Navy. I thought I knew what I was signing on for. I mean, Michael told me as honestly as he could what to expect, but…"

"How long have you been married?"

"Less than a month, and the first week of that was a honeymoon in Ixtapa. I thought moving to a new place would be fun, and it is. Then last night he asked me to sign a power of attorney."

"Everyone does that," Grace assured her. "We need to be able to conduct business ourselves and in their names while they're gone."

"I know, but it just hit me so hard. My husband is leaving me."

"He's going to work," Grace said. "He works because he loves you and wants to serve his country." Here she was, dispensing advice as though she knew what she was doing. For a long time she'd felt like a fraud, playing a role for an audience of one. But somewhere along the way, the unexpected happened—she became good at what she did. Good at juggling the demands of husband, home and family. Good at being a Navy wife.

They fell in step and left the memorial, walking in silence for a while. Grace thought about when she first met Steve. Their love had been so palpable, a live thing, close to the surface. She kept checking on it, the same way she used to check on her new engagement ring. She remembered waking up at night, turning on the light to see that the diamond solitaire was still there, that it still belonged to her. Mainly, she had to assure herself that Steve Bennett wanted to marry her, Grace McAllen, the unhappiest woman in Edenville, Texas. It seemed too good to be true.

Funny. She hadn't thought of that in a long time. The simplicity of their newborn love had grown and changed over the years. When she first met him, a brash junior officer in pilot training, his motivation had been as sharp and pure as his clean-shaven jaw. He wanted a job that mattered, that challenged his deep reserves of courage and skill, that satisfied his lust for adventure as well as his desire to serve the country he loved. In the early nineties, he'd flown in combat. That was when she'd seen a side to him she hadn't known existed.

Yet as the years passed, ambition to advance through the ranks narrowed his focus to the next rung on the ladder. Perversely, his world grew smaller when it should have expanded.

She knew it would not be helpful in the least to share these thoughts with Patricia, who was disconcertingly close in age to Emma.

"You're where I was nearly twenty years ago," Grace told her. "Steve's gone to sea so many times, I guess you could consider me an expert at being left by my husband."

"How do you cope when he's gone?"

"You fill your days with things that don't require his presence," said Grace. "You'd be surprised at how much that encompasses. When we were first married, I had a job as an administrative assistant for a shipping company." She smiled. "Some people think that sounds awful, but it was a great job. I was good at it."

"Having a job isn't the same as having a husband."

"True. But having a life shouldn't depend on the man you marry."

"I know." Patricia offered a shy smile. "But it does."

Her candor caused a lurch of emotion in Grace's heart. "Only if you let it," she felt compelled to say. *Like I did.*

They passed the Navy Exchange and the commissary, more rows of hangars and long, low buildings surrounding the airstrip. The runways were busy as always, this morning with the fat, gray bodies of P-C3 Orions in training exercises. They were not the sleek birds of combat aviation, but their brains were the biggest in the Navy, as their purpose was surveillance and antisubmarine warfare.

"All right." Patricia quickened her pace. "Enough whining. So, do you still have that job?"

"I gave it up when the twins came along," she said.

"Wow—twins. That must be fun."

"Never a dull moment. They're seniors in high school now. Still fun, but they don't need their mom so much. Their sister, Katie, just started ninth grade. She's getting pretty independent, too." She felt a quick dart of guilt. "Don't get me wrong, my husband and kids are great. I don't know what I'd do without them. But I'll admit, sometimes I don't know what to do *with* them. My youngest, Katie, is trying out for marching band. She plays the clarinet like a dream. But last night she got cold feet and cried for an hour."

"How old is Katie?"

"Almost fifteen."

Patricia smiled. "Then her behavior makes perfect sense. It sounds like everything's going great. We're already trying for a baby, but sometimes I get so scared, wondering if I'll be a good mother."

"I wondered the same thing. Still do. Sometimes you depend solely on instinct, and all you can do is pray you don't crash and burn. Steve always complained about flying blind, but he had a landing signal officer in his ear telling him what to do. Every once in a while, I wish I had that."

"You must be doing something right if you're still married after twenty years."

Grace sometimes suspected it was what she was not doing more than any action she'd taken. She simply followed Steve's career, looking after the children along the way, seldom stopping to wonder if she was on the right track—until lately.

She and Patricia stopped to browse through a garage sale hosted by three squadron wives preparing for their next move. "Baby things?" she suggested to Patricia.

"Not quite yet." Patricia picked up an ashtray in the shape of a baseball mitt that probably hadn't been used in ten years. "Look at all this stuff."

"You know, once I actually bought, sold and rebought the same chicken-shaped pitcher at a garage sale."

"Now, that sounds like a treasure."

Grace smiled, remembering. "When we first got married, we lived in Pensacola, and I bought this strange-looking pitcher at a neighborhood garage sale. It was so homely that it was charming. Then, a year later, we were sent to Pax River, Maryland and, honestly, I had to rethink my commitment to the chicken pitcher. I sold it at our garage sale and didn't give it another thought. A few years after that, we were transferred to Pensacola again, and I spotted that same damned pitcher at a yard sale in the same neighborhood we lived in as newlyweds."

"And you bought it again," said Patricia.

"Yep. Still have it, too." Some things in life were like that, Grace reflected. You kept them longer than you needed them, because it was easier than letting go.

She briefly touched Patricia's arm, feeling an affinity for her even though they had just met. Navy wives tended to bond quickly, knowing their time together was limited. Sometimes Grace thought her friendships with women were what kept her going through the difficult times.

"Can you join me for a cup of coffee?" she asked.

"Thanks, but no. I need to get back to the motel and shower. I have a job interview later this morning." She held up a hand. "Don't look so impressed. We're talking about waitressing at IHOP."

"They'll be lucky to get you."

"I guess."

"Why IHOP?"

"We need the money to make ends meet. IHOP works out because it's a national chain. If I keep at it, I'll earn seniority and qualify for benefits." She raked a hand through her glossy dark hair. "There's so much to do, I don't know where to start. I wish getting moved and settled in didn't seem so impossible."

"If you'd like some help with your relocation, give me a call. I might not have all the answers to being married to a Navy guy, but I do when it comes to moving."

The look of relief on Patricia's face filled her with a peculiar and satisfying warmth. It was a small thing, she told herself as they traded phone numbers and made plans to meet later. But its power was undeniable. She had a gift for helping people in very specific ways. That gift was separate from the Grace who was the officer's wife or the mother of three, the school volunteer or the purveyor of afternoon teas for Navy spouses. This talent for organizing and helping belonged to her and her alone.

As she walked home, her step felt lighter and more assured. For whole moments at a time, she managed to put out of her mind the fact that it was the first day of school, that Katie had been trembling with nervousness this morning, that she and Steve had unfinished business. She even managed to forget he was going away. That was nothing new.

What was new was the sense that something was subtly wrong. They were "having problems." She couldn't figure out when the trouble had started; it had probably been brewing for a long time. The house was not the cause. It was the line she'd drawn in the sand.

He didn't want to buy the house. He'd made that clear. He didn't want her to have a career, either. It wasn't in their plan. At some point they had been in complete accord. Early on, when being a Navy family was the ultimate adventure, they told each other that a house was a burden, a ball and chain. They might consider it one day when they could see beyond the life the Navy gave them.

Steve didn't get it. She'd been able to see beyond that life for a long time.

CHAPTER TWELVE

In the grief recovery group, they advised Lauren Stanton to prepare herself a gourmet meal at least twice a week. She was supposed to shop for herself as though for company, fix a perfect meal for one and serve it to herself on her best china and silver, along with a crystal goblet of excellent wine.

After two years of eating Froot Loops or key-lime yogurt for supper, she was willing to consider a change. It seemed pointless to go to so much trouble just for herself, but that, claimed the experienced members of the group, was the wrong way to look at things. You are the most important person in your life, they told her with earnest compassion. Treat yourself that way.

Lauren embraced the idea. Why the heck not? Since Gil died, she'd done nothing but work and…well, work. Her life had shrunk. That was it, pure and simple. If she didn't do something soon, she'd disappear.

That was why she found herself out at the mussel beds of Penn Cove in the middle of a sunny Saturday afternoon. Gil had hated seafood and found shellfish particularly offensive. It was probably due to his white-bread upbringing in South Dakota. Lauren, an island girl, adored fresh mussels and found the idea of eating something cultivated in the dark, cold depths of the ocean uniquely appealing. That made this afternoon's foray all the more personal.

Being alone is good for you, they said in the group. It is your opportunity to regain a sense of yourself as a strong person. They urged her not to canonize Gil, but to keep a realistic sense of their marriage in her heart. They cautioned her not to push into a relationship too soon, but not to wait too long, either, because that carried its own kind of risk. Sometimes a widow could become so set in her ways that her life couldn't expand to include someone new. At twenty-six, Lauren had best leave room for someone else.

Gil had been sixteen years her senior. She'd adored him, and the greatest heartache of their marriage was that she'd never had a child. His death sent her spiraling into blackness. Then she dragged herself out of the depths, bringing three life lessons with her: diet and exercise can save a failing heart, a childless couple face special challenges and it's too emotionally risky to fall in love.

She was getting better, she told herself as she headed out to Haglund's dock. From there, she'd row a dinghy to the rafts where islanders had grown the tender mussels for generations. Old Ollie Haglund sold his harvest to Puget Sound's finest restaurants, but he didn't mind surrendering a pound or two to friends and neighbors.

Backed up to Ollie's bobbing shed on the rickety floating dock, a boxy brown UPS van looked incongruous. Lauren caught Ollie's eye and waved at him. With his flat-topped hat and a pipe clenched between his teeth, he resembled the Norwegian fisherman his grandfather had been.

Mid-September was the hottest time of year on the island. The sun felt warm and strong on her bare shoulders and thighs, which she'd coated liberally with sunscreen. It was a perfect day, crisp as her white denim shorts and blue as her sleeveless midriff blouse. Wearing bleached Keds over bare feet, she felt completely at home on the water. She had grown up amid the salt marshes and forested uplands, watched over by a fond mother and doted on by the locals. Outwardly, she had changed a great deal from that insecure girl—on the outside. Inside, she was still ruled by caution and timidity.

She edged around the UPS truck. "Hey, Ollie."

"Hey yourself, young lady."

"I'm here to make a trade," she said, holding out a white plastic bucket. "My tomatoes for your mussels."

"My mussels are free," Ollie said with a wink. He turned to the UPS guy, who was loading crates into the truck and simultaneously checking out Lauren's legs. "Only to beautiful women who bring me tomatoes, so that counts you out, pal."

The buzz of an engine drowned out his reply. A maniac sped past on a Jet Ski that threw up a rainbow arc of spray in its wake. On the seat behind the driver rode two skinny children. Their shrieks of delight were barely discernible over the nasal whine of the engine. Lauren shaded her eyes and for a moment she was caught up in the sheer physical exuberance of the trio on the Jet Ski. Even from a distance she could see the simple joy of a thrilling ride across the calm water.

Not that the maniac on the Jet Ski seemed to notice the beauty of the day, she thought as the bare-chested man and shrieking boys crisscrossed the mouth of the cove.

"Probably another goddamn Navy guy," said Ollie, "you'll pardon my French."

"Hey, those Navy guys were my husband's clients," she pointed out. Gil had been a civilian contractor.

"Your Gil didn't ride his Jet Ski across my shellfish beds," Ollie pointed out.

True. Gil would never do that. Caution was his middle name, a fact that tainted his death with painful irony.

Lauren lowered her white plastic bucket to the dinghy as the Jet Ski sped past again. That was when she heard it—a wolf whistle, distinctly coming from the suntanned man.

"At least that one's got good taste," said Ollie.

A flicker of the old laughter sparked inside her, but she crushed it quickly and went about her business. "For Pete's sake," she muttered. "What a terrible example to set for those kids."

"To admire a beautiful woman is terrible?"

"It is if you're married with children."

"Ah. So you know this one."

"I'm just assuming," she said, climbing down into the boat. She'd leave it to someone else to tell the guy the Stone Age was over. Yet despite her outrage, an unexpected feeling crept over her, fiery as a schoolgirl's blush. She caught herself sneaking glances at the Jet Ski guy as she took up the oars.

She struck out for the floating platforms. The drops of water that splashed from her oars were icy cold. The idiot on the Jet Ski was going to give his kids pneumonia.

She tied up at the mussel raft and rummaged around in the hull for a pair of thick rubber gloves. The mussels grew on long, weed-bearded socks suspended from the platform. She worked happily for a while, indulging in fond memories of childhood when she and her sister Carolyn would pick mussels for their mother's cioppino.

She was hauling in a waterlogged rope when she noticed the Jet Ski plowing up to the platform.

"What are you doing?" she demanded, shading her eyes.

"Just visiting."

"I think you took a wrong turn." She tried not to stare. His chest and shoulders were polished oak, beaded with water droplets. He had dark hair, cut short, devastating blue eyes and a mouth that seemed to be on the verge of laughter. No wedding ring.

"I never make a wrong turn."

Dear God. He had a Southern accent. She adored Southern accents.

He nudged the kid behind him and put on a serious expression. "Bond," he said. "James Bond."

The kids, a pair of skinny, shivering brothers in board shorts, snickered appreciatively. They were maybe six and eight years old, the perfect audience for this clown.

"What's your name?" the little one asked her.

The stranger's experienced gaze slipped over her with shocking frankness. "I'm guessing Malibu Barbie."

For the briefest second, she felt a keen forbidden thrill. But just as quickly, she scrubbed away the feeling and invoked a little common sense. "I'm actually busy," she explained. "So if you'll excuse me—"

"What are you doing?" The younger boy was missing one lower tooth and had cowlicks all over his head. The oversize orange life vest fit him like a spongy tube, atop which sat his bright-eyed, freckled face.

"Harvesting mussels."

The kids looked at each other with wide eyes.

"Show the nice lady your muscles, guys," the hunk said.

They obeyed immediately, cocking up their fists with fierce pride. Lauren bit her lip to hold in laughter. "Wow," she said. "Double wow."

The boys giggled as only little boys can do, a sound that gave her no choice but to smile.

"Show her your muscles, Josh," the older one said.

"Show her, Josh, show her," echoed the little one.

They called him Josh, not Dad.

"Josh has giant muscles," said the little one.

"Massive," said his brother.

She grinned. "I'll take your word for it. But actually, I'm picking this kind of mussel." She hauled up a rope heavy with shining black shells.

"Yuck," said the little one.

"Cool," said the other one.

"I'm going to fix them for dinner," said Lauren.

"Eew." They reacted in unison. "Are you going to make your kids eat them?"

"I don't have kids. But you can eat some, if you want."

They clung to the hunk and writhed in disgust.

"Whoa, pardners," he said, "that's no way to reply to an invitation."

They straightened up immediately and said together, "No, thank you, ma'am."

At the same time, the hunk named Josh grinned straight at her. "I'd love to."

She nearly dropped the bucket. She meant to say, "You're not invited." Instead, she said, "I'm Lauren Stanton."

"Josh Lamont, ma'am. And these hooligans are Danny and Andrew."

Ma'am. Definitely Navy, then. Which meant he was not her type. Here on the island, she had met her share of Navy men. Some of her girlfriends from high school had dated them; a few had even married them. To Lauren's knowledge, none of those relationships had worked out. Navy men were like cotton candy, deliciously sweet while they lasted, but insubstantial and quickly gone, leaving hunger unsatisfied.

"Josh made a date," Danny said to Andrew. They giggled like munchkins.

"Be quiet," he said. "I'm not finished. Where and when?" he asked Lauren.

She looked down at the bucket's shiny black harvest. This was supposed to be her therapy. Treating herself well was an important step in grief recovery. Then she remembered that her last attempt to fix herself an elegant dinner had resulted in her polishing off the bottle of wine and falling asleep in her BCBG dress.

"My place," she said. "Seven o'clock." She pointed at the cottages and bungalows on the bluff overlooking the cove. "You can see my house from here. It's the green one with the row of sunflowers across the front."

He never took his eyes off her as he addressed the boys. "Now that, sailors, is a date."

At five minutes to seven, Lauren stood in front of the stereo, programming a few hours' worth of background music. She didn't want anything overtly sexy. Just something to fill the awkward pauses in the conversation. No Dixie Chicks—that had been one of Gil's favorites. She ruled out Dave Matthews, too, and eventually settled on an anthology her sister had sent her.

Most of the selections were neutral, inoffensive. Practically elevator music.

At exactly seven, the doorbell rang, and she jumped. Punctual to the last second.

The heels of her sandals clicked on the tiles as she went to the door. She paused at a shelf in the hall that held a photo of Gil and whispered, "I have no idea what I'm doing here. But wish me luck."

As she put her hand on the doorknob, a sweet Love Riot ballad drifted from the stereo. Oops, that wasn't elevator music but wildly suggestive. Maybe he wouldn't notice.

She pulled the door open.

"Good song," he said, smiling at her.

She felt as though she had tumbled into a dream. He was a cliché, standing there—perfectly groomed, a bottle of wine in one hand and a bouquet of flowers in the other. The only thing slightly out of place was the eggplant-colored minivan parked in the drive. Navy guys, especially single Navy guys, drove Harleys or muscle cars, not minivans. Didn't they?

"Wow," he said to Lauren. "You look terrific."

My thoughts exactly. "Thanks," she said. "Come on in."

He filled her small, excruciatingly neat house. It wasn't just his size—he was probably six foot, built like an Olympic athlete—but his energy seemed to take up space, to move in uninvited.

"I have a confession to make," he said.

Uh-oh. Wife, girlfriend, sexual orientation… The possibilities spilled through her mind. "Yes?"

"I'm a goner when it comes to a woman with short red hair."

The stale line should have put her off. But in spite of herself, she felt an absurd thrill of attraction. She ducked her head to hide the swift blush burning her cheeks, and took the flowers and wine. It was a bottle of Provence Rosé, Domain Tempier Bandol.

"Is the wine all right?" he asked.

"It's the perfect accompaniment for mussels. So you're classy, too."

"I like to think so, but I cannot tell a lie. I looked it up on the Internet."

"Well, thank you again," she said. "I'll put the flowers in water."

He scanned the room, which had cut flowers in jars and vases on every surface. "Looks like I brought coals to Newcastle."

"I love flowers," she called from the kitchen, filling a flared vase with water at the sink. "These are all from my garden."

When she came out to set the vase on the table, he was standing at the sliding glass doors, looking at the view. "Multitalented, then," he said. "She fixes mussels, grows flowers—"

"And tomatoes," she added. "Best tomatoes on Whidbey Island."

"What else do you do?" he asked without turning around.

She forgot to answer. She was staring at his butt, and was suddenly pounded by a wave of lust that nearly knocked her over.

He swung back to face her and she prayed he couldn't read the expression on her face. "Do you grow your own mussels, too?"

"My friend, Ollie Haglund, runs that outfit. It's an old family business." She smiled, trying to tamp down the lust with a mental image of Mr. Haglund.

"So should we keep playing twenty questions, or do you want to tell me all the basics?"

"I haven't played twenty questions in years."

"Okay, hometown?"

"Right here on Whidbey Island. You?"

"Atlanta, Georgia. What's your favorite carnival ride?"

"Merry-go-round," she said, slightly surprised, because she'd never really considered it before. "Yours is the roller coaster, of course."

He looked amazed. "How did you guess?"

She couldn't keep in a laugh. "It wasn't a guess. I saw how you rode that Jet Ski. So when you left Atlanta…?"

"I went to the Naval Academy. What do you do for fun around here besides grow flowers and fix mussels?"

He kept turning the subject away from himself. What a concept. Most men were their own favorite topic. "I like sports. Swimming and boating in the summer, skiing in the winter. How about you?"

"I boxed when I was younger." A proud grin lit his face. "I once took on the Venice Bomber."

"The Venice Bomber?"

"Scott Burns. I can't believe you haven't heard of him. But I hung up my gloves years ago. What I've always wanted to learn is sailing. The Jet Ski's fun enough, but it's a little noisy."

I can teach you to sail. She almost said it. But she stopped herself. It was too much of a commitment. "A sailor who doesn't know how to sail?" she asked. "Now, there's something for the taxpayers to worry about."

He sent her a look she felt all the way to her toes. "I'm a fast learner."

"New question," she said. "After the Naval Academy, what did you do?"

"I went to Pensacola for flight training. I'm doing more training here and in Nevada, and I'm also serving as an ALO—admissions liaison officer for the Naval Academy—helping local kids with their applications. I'm going to be flying the Prowler."

Great. A carrier-based pilot. Pretty much the most dangerous flying there was. "I'll just open that wine," she said, escaping to the narrow galley kitchen.

He followed her, looking around at the bright white walls, the cabinet displaying her collection of blue-and-white Delft china. She saw him poking a finger at the dessert—chocolate pots de crème in white china cups.

"Don't even think about it," she said, pushing his hand away.

He laughed and kept hold of her hand. "I'm thinking of something else entirely, ma'am."

She nearly recoiled from the unexpected heat of his touch. "It's from a recipe called Chocolate Sex."

"Sounds great, but it can't come close to the real thing."

"You haven't tasted it yet."

"Doesn't matter. Some things you just know."

His suggestive voice slipped over her like silk. His smile seemed to wrap around her heart, and she pulled her hand away.

139

"I know you're trying real hard to send out 'unavailable' signals," he said, "but I have never shied from a challenge." Ever so gently, he took the corkscrew from her. "I've got it."

She let him, knowing she wouldn't admit that she had never mastered the art of opening wine, because Gil always did the honors. Just as he always cleaned the leaves out of the gutters, balanced the checkbook, rotated the tires and figured the taxes. After he died, Lauren set herself to each task with grim determination and persisted until she mastered it. She was still a little weak in the wine-opening department.

The cork pulled free with a resounding *thwok*. She poured two glasses and handed him one. "Cheers," she said.

"Cheers, and do you have a pet?"

"Oh, we're still on the twenty questions?"

"I think we're only on number five or six. So what about a pet?"

She glanced dolefully at a flap in the back door, two little metal bowls on a rubber mat. "A cat named Ranger. He was a stray, and then he strayed again. I haven't seen him in a while. I plastered the neighborhood with signs and I change the food and water every day, just in case." She eyed him over the rim of her glass. "I bet you're a dog person. Big dogs, specifically."

He grinned.

This man's looks were wasted in the Navy. He could be modeling boxer shorts or sports cars. "Well?" she prompted him.

"And here I thought I was going to be the mysterious new man in your life. I'm so predictable."

"Spill," she said, pretending she hadn't heard the intriguing part of his comment.

"Three Chesapeake Bay retrievers. Curly, Larry and—"

"Let me guess. Moe."

"Gotcha. The third one's name was Scarlett. My mother claims I was raised by them."

"Is that like being raised by wolves?"

"Friendly wolves. They were my siblings. I was an only child. You?"

"A perfect sister who went to Georgetown and stayed in D.C. to be a lobbyist. We grew up right here with our single mom. She died five years ago and left this house to me and Gil."

"Your sister's name is Gil?"

Lauren's hand tightened painfully on the stem of her wineglass. She hadn't meant to mention him right away. After he died, she quickly discovered that the moment she mentioned she was widowed at the age of twenty-three, it tended to put a damper on any conversation.

"My late husband," she explained. "He died two years ago."

"I'm sorry," he said. "And I bet you'd be a rich woman if you had a nickel for every time someone said that to you." There was genuine kindness in his smile that took away the awkward moment. "So how are you doing?"

"Better. One day at a time, as they say in my therapy group." She picked up a knife and chopped some parsley for the broth. "At first I was taking it one minute at a time, even one breath at a time, so I've made progress." She ran water over the mussels in the colander over the sink. "Fixing this dinner was supposed to be part of my therapy, but you ruined it."

"Hey, thanks a lot."

She laughed at his phony, wounded expression. "The assignment was to treat myself to a gourmet meal. Alone."

"So I'm spoiling your evening."

She looked him straight in the eye and felt something inside her melt. He was interesting, funny, smart and kind. And suddenly he was standing so close to her she could practically touch him.

"Yes," she whispered as he brought his mouth slowly down to kiss her. "You're spoiling it."

CHAPTER THIRTEEN

Grace pulled into the driveway at 8853 Ocean View Drive, and fantasy took over. She was pulling up to her own house, listening to the crunch of crushed oyster shells beneath the tires. The old roses twining over the garden arch were blooming in generous clusters of seashell pink, the last burst of Indian summer, probably. She could pick some to float in a bowl on the dining room table. Dahlias like lollipops nodded in the breeze, and stalks of hollyhocks reached as high as the eaves. In the side yard, a pair of martins flitted around a birdhouse on a tall pole.

Was she wrong to love this house? Was it really priced beyond her reach, like Steve said? They had been arguing about it constantly. And at its heart, the dispute was not about a house or a career. It was deeper than that. There were things Grace had put on hold—willingly—that needed expression. The kids would be gone soon, and it would be just her and Steve. Sometimes she worried that he balked because he was afraid of giving up his career and finding himself alone with her.

She knocked at the door, and Marcia Dunmire answered, mild and friendly as the dahlias blooming in the yard. Since the open house, she'd replaced the walker with a four-legged cane. "Hello, Grace," she said. "It's good to see you in person again."

They had spent hours together on the phone, planning Grace's strategy. She'd found a local CPA and bookkeeper. She had developed a business plan. She had contacted other relocation services, even set up reciprocal arrangements and referral agreements with some of them. Regardless of Steve's attitude, she intended to launch her own company.

"Come on in," Marcia said. "I'm so glad you decided to go ahead with this."

"I halfway wish you'd talk me out of it," said Grace, feeling a subtle flutter of apprehension in her belly. Maybe Steve was right, she thought. Maybe this wasn't the time to start something new and risky.

"You seem nervous, dear."

"It's not every day someone offers to start a Web-based business for me."

"It's not every day someone takes on a moving company on my behalf. Coffee?" She indicated a pot on the stove. "Help yourself."

Grace took a mug from the counter and poured. The kitchen, like every other room in the house, was hopelessly outdated and gloriously oriented toward the view of the water. The sight took her out of herself, and she felt an unexpected jolt of emotion in her gut. Of all the places they'd lived, none had ever affected her like this. She belonged here. She truly did, in a way she had never belonged anywhere else.

"Mount Baker's the prettiest mountain in the world," said Marcia. "Don't you think?"

Grace nodded. The rounded, creamy summit was painted in yellow and gold by the autumn sun. A single small cloud clung to the peak like a pennon from a castle. "You've been blessed, waking up to this every morning."

"Don't I know it. I wish I'd dared to climb it when I was young, like you," Marcia said. "I always meant to, but I never got around to it." She sighed. "I wonder how many things never get done because people keep putting them off."

"Plenty." Grace reached for the cream, then she thought better of it and took the coffee black. "However, I've been busy on your behalf." She took a set of brochures and forms from her tote bag and laid them on the counter. In exchange for Marcia's design work, Grace insisted on handling every detail of her move. "These are the best seniors-only residences I could find near your daughter in Phoenix. I made a chart listing all the amenities of each, and a map with the features of each neighborhood. For instance, would you rather be closer to a bookstore or a movie theater? Is a gym important? Church? That sort of thing. You can look them over and decide which one you like best, and I'll make all the arrangements for you."

"Grace Bennett, you are a wonder," Marcia said, the slight frown easing from her brow. "These look lovely. I won't be homeless when I get to Arizona after all."

"You're going to miss this place a lot, aren't you?" asked Grace.

"Actually, I don't think I will. I'm moving closer to my daughter and grandchildren because I don't want to miss out on their lives." Marcia looked around the room, with its faded walls and old furniture. "I used to feel so trapped here when the kids were little. I couldn't wait to get out somewhere, anywhere. I always envied the Navy wives with their jet-setting lifestyle."

Grace nearly choked on her coffee. "Jet-setting?"

"That's how it looked to me."

"Well, I bet you never realized that the Navy wives envied you."

Marcia shook her head. "That's hard to imagine."

"Women like me think what a luxury it would be to plant bulbs and know you'll be around to see them come up. To give your heart to a friend and know you'll still be close in ten years. To watch your kids settle into the same school, year after year."

"It can work both ways. Staying in one little town can be very stifling."

"Moving around like a gypsy tribe isn't as romantic as it looks. You want to talk about small towns? Think of it this way, the marriage is the town. Population two. With a handful of temporary visitors known as children."

Marcia refilled her coffee mug, adding a generous splash of cream. "I never thought of it that way. Grace, I don't want to get too personal, but are you saying you feel stifled in your marriage?"

"No," Grace said quickly. "I didn't mean to sound that way. The Navy's been wonderful for us. The past twenty years have been an incredible adventure."

"But...?" Marcia raised an eyebrow.

"Am I terrible to want a different kind of adventure?"

"Heavens, no."

Grace released a breath she didn't realize she was holding. Marcia led the way to the study adjacent to the kitchen. "Here are a few of my other clients," she said, motioning Grace to a chair on rollers next to the Mac computer.

Clients, thought Grace with a sense of wonder. I'm a client.

Marcia had created impressive, functional Web sites for a florist, a law office, a finance company and a fitness studio.

"Wait a minute," Grace said. "A fitness studio? You mean I can get physically fit on the Internet?"

Marcia laughed. "Don't I wish." She clicked on the site, displaying a young woman hefting a pair of hot-pink barbells. "Lauren Stanton is a local girl. She grew up with my kids, in fact."

"Totally New Totally You," said Grace. "I picked up a brochure in the store. I've been thinking of checking it out."

"I take her senior lifetime fitness classes," said Marcia. "At least up until my injury. You're far too young for senior fitness."

Grace laughed. "I don't remember the last time someone said I was too young for anything."

"You're a baby," Marcia assured her. "Let's have a look at what I've done so far." She typed in a Web address. "This," she said, "is your domain."

"In medieval times, that meant manorial land retained for the private use of a feudal lord," said Grace.

"Well, now it means your own little corner of cyberspace. It's not running 'live' at the moment, but as soon as you tell me to launch it, you'll be all set. I put up the features we discussed on the phone."

Grace blinked at the screen. "GraceUnderPressure.org," she said. "So you like the name I picked?"

"I think it's perfect," Marcia said. "What do you think of the design?"

That was perfect, too. Against a calm blue background, the heading stood out in clean white type. A row of links down the side of the screen were marked by small, puffy clouds.

Grace looked out the window. "I can see where you get your inspiration."

"So you like it? It's not too frivolous for a woman of commerce?"

"I love it. And I don't know about the woman-of-commerce bit. It's something I've always wanted to do, but—"

"Then you should do it. No buts."

"You're a good coach." She marveled at how easy Marcia was to talk to, how simple things looked through her eyes. Grace had tried to discuss the project with Steve numerous times, but all he could see were the pitfalls and roadblocks. By contrast, Marcia made it look like a natural outgrowth of a service Grace had been performing pro bono for years.

"Well, if you're not ready to get started in business, we can turn this into anything you want. A lot of Navy families keep personal sites for pictures and reports. That way, all their friends and family can check in and keep in touch."

"Our circle of friends and family is pretty small. Relatives are in short supply. Steve grew up in foster homes, and I was an only child. My parents and grandmother are gone now."

"Dear, I'm so sorry."

"Don't be. My grandmother made me promise not to be glum about it, and I'm usually not." There was more to the story, but Grace didn't feel comfortable sharing it with Marcia. "Both Steve and I wanted a big family, and I think that's one of the reasons."

"And you've moved this whole family all over the world."

"That's right."

"Then you're definitely a professional."

Grace laughed. "I don't have any clients."

"That's the point of the Web site. Here's a form for people to put in their basic information and request a contact from you." She clicked to a new screen. "Stop looking for ways for this not to work, Grace. It's the perfect place to start. Check this out. Once you submit your banking information, you'll be able to take credit cards."

Grace's head was spinning. Launch yourself into business. Start a career. The words had been haunting her for weeks, prodding her, keeping her awake at night. She always thought she'd do well in business. And even though she'd set aside that dream long ago, it still resonated in her.

Now she sat and listened politely to Marcia's concept of a Web-based business. It sounded fantastic. It was as though Marcia had opened a door, and Grace had stepped into a world that was absolutely familiar to her in every way. With a vision as clear as a cloudless day, she could see exactly how the enterprise would work. If only she would commit to it.

She must have shown some physical sign of excitement, because Marcia looked over at her with concern. "Are you all right?"

"Yes," Grace said, and took a deep breath. "I'm ready to get started."

Marcia beamed at her. "I was hoping you'd go forward with it." They spent the morning working out the details, and the dream not only took shape, it took on a life of its own.

Hours later, a formation of jets rocketed overhead; Grace knew them by the sound. "Look at the time," she said, startled. "I'd better go."

"You can stay as long as you like."

"Actually, I need to get to the bank. And after that, I'm meeting someone who needs help with her move."

Marcia winked. "Get a letter of reference from her."

Grace was positive Patricia Rivera would offer a reference if she asked. So maybe she'd ask.

"I'll walk you to your car," said Marcia, grasping her cane.

"Oh, you don't have to—"

"Nonsense, I need the exercise." Out on the driveway, she shot a troubled look at the For Sale sign.

"No takers yet?" Grace asked.

"No. I might have to lower the price again or offer to owner-finance."

"Could you afford to do that?"

"Absolutely. I wish you'd buy it."

Grace laughed. "Am I that transparent?"

"You love this house. I could tell the first time I met you."

"I do love your house, Marcia. Somehow, it just took hold of me. I've never felt that before—about a house, at least. But we'll be moving in another two years," she said. "Maybe less."

"So live here for two years." Marcia drummed her fingers on the handle of her cane.

"That wouldn't be very practical."

"You've got to live somewhere. Why not in a place you love? Listen, the way you spend each day adds up to the way you spend your life."

The words struck Grace like soft blows. Flustered, she opened the car door. "Thanks for everything."

While she drove home, she replayed Steve's objections to the house in her head. A jumbo mortgage was a huge responsibility. It was a lot to ask him to take on just when his job was getting more complicated than ever. As an investment, it was risky. They could easily wind up with a white elephant on their hands.

"The kids have always wanted a pet," Grace said aloud.

CHAPTER FOURTEEN

Grace blinked at the Inbox icon on her computer screen. Fifty-six new messages had come through the address linked to her Web site. That couldn't be right, could it? She'd never received that many messages in a single day.

Maybe the spammers and virus spreaders had found her despite the filters and firewalls installed on her computer. Or maybe...

It couldn't be. Marcia had only launched her Web site live yesterday morning.

The project had taken longer than expected as Grace truly got down to business. She stopped daydreaming and fooling around. The kids were settled into their school routine and were busy all the time. Predeployment madness had taken over the air wing. Steve remained skeptical of her enterprise. That only made her more determined to succeed.

She placed a notice in the Yellow Pages, created a brochure and sent press releases to the local papers. She organized an office around the computer in the study. Over the years she'd amassed and cataloged information on everything from moving companies to pet-sitters. As for references, she could produce letters from Navy families across the globe. Several had, at her request, already e-mailed testimonials for posting on the site. She contacted other firms and created a list of services and prices. Yet it never felt quite real until the Web site finally went public.

The previous evening she'd tried to make the launch an auspicious event for the Bennetts, fixing a special dinner and announcing her news. But somehow the moment had fallen flat. Steve had said, "I hope you know what you're doing, honey. Once I leave, I won't be around to help you out." Brian and Emma fell into a dispute over the use of the car. Katie was preoccupied by some incident at band practice. Grace had shrugged away a tiny nudge of resentment. The fact was, even she had no idea what might happen once she hung out her virtual shingle. It could very well amount to nothing.

With an unsteady hand on the mouse, she clicked open the mailbox. A little flutter of nervousness stirred in her stomach. Then she read the first one: "Our Bulk Mail Program reaches 10 million Inboxes…" She scowled, deleted the ad and moved on to the next. "Business Opportunities on the Web…" Delete. With growing exasperation, she scrolled through promises to reduce her home mortgage, enlarge her penis and find her a Russian bride. The prime minister of a Third World nation wanted her to loan him fifty thousand dollars.

Grace was about to delete the whole Inbox when the next message caught her eye. "…Wonder if you could advise me about getting estimates from a moving company." The message seemed legit. So did a few others: "…check the rental rates for office space in San Jose…"; "…private schools in the D.C. area…" Between the ads, inquiries from real people sped past in message after message. Grace was amazed. She was in business. In business. Oh, how she loved the idea of that. People wanted her advice. Her professional opinion. And if she impressed them the right way, they would become her clients. Paying clients.

"I'm a fraud," she murmured, her confidence sinking. "A total fraud. An Internet pirate. I can't believe I did this."

She picked up the phone and called the person who had sent

the first legitimate message. A fill-in form on the site collected preliminary information and phone numbers. She got an answering machine and left a slightly breathless message. A couple of the other requests were incomplete, so she replied in e-mail. Several were dead ends. She cautioned herself not to get impatient as she punched in yet another phone number. Someone picked up before she chickened out.

"Cameron Vintages. May I help you?"

"Mr. Ross Cameron, please." Grace's request was crisp and clear, giving no hint of her nervousness. "This is Grace Bennett of, um, Grace Under Pressure Executive Relocation Services. I'm calling at his request."

After a brief hold, a male voice said, "This is Ross Cameron."

The voice made her shiver. She didn't know why. It was smooth and dark and sweet. Audible chocolate. "Mr. Cameron, thank you for taking my call. This is about the message you left at my Web site."

"Oh, yes. Your firm came up on a search."

Firm. She had a firm. "How can I help you, Mr. Cameron?"

"I'm moving my company from Chicago to Seattle. I'm a wine importer. It's a six-month project, maybe more. Does that sound like something you can help with?"

Grace took a deep breath. Good Lord, *no.* "I certainly can."

"Good, then—"

"Mr. Cameron?"

"Yes?"

"May I ask what you typed in the search engine?"

"Yeah." A smooth chuckle drifted through the wire. "Moving help—desperate."

Grace relaxed, took out a notepad and got down to work. This was her first flesh-and-blood client, and she wanted to do a good job.

"Mr. Cameron, I feel I should be completely honest with you. If we come to an agreement, you'll be my first client through the Web site."

There was a long hesitation. Butterflies beat against the walls of her stomach. "Mr. Cameron?"

"Sorry," he said. "I was just wondering if I get a free toaster or something, for being first."

"You do, actually. We're offering a free comprehensive change-of-address notification service." It had been Marcia's idea to offer the incentive. "I want you to know, though, that I've been doing this for years. I hope you'll contact some of the references listed on my site."

"I already have. So is it true you walk on water, Ms. Bennett?"

That voice. She could listen to it all day. Instead, she gave him another half hour, noting his needs and concerns, brainstorming the ways she thought she could help coordinate the move. By the end of her conversation with Mr. Cameron, she had a verbal agreement and had e-mailed him a written contract. She smiled at the tangible note of relief in his voice when she told him he could relax and let her make all the arrangements. She couldn't believe how rewarding it was to know she had the power to help someone, to hear the tension in his voice unfurl. By the time she hung up the phone, the butterflies in her stomach were gone. They had taken flight.

She stared at the computer monitor until the screen saver kicked in. This was going to work. She was not nervous anymore; she felt confident. She could do this, and do it well.

By the time she got up from the desk, she had a grand total of two potential clients and one more who promised to get back to her. A few were looking for free assistance, and although Grace was tempted, she forced herself to resist. Marcia had advised her not to open that door. If she did, she'd cheat herself out of legitimate clients. Instead, her site offered fee-based departure-and-destination services, move management, orientation and consulting.

She jumped up from the desk with a list of chores to do. She was in this for real now. She headed for the door, then hesitated. She paused in front of the hall mirror and smiled at her reflection. There was nothing different about her. She still carried a good twenty extra pounds. Still had a hairstyle that was at least five years out of date. But the look on her face transformed her.

"You go, girl," she said to her reflection. She hurried upstairs and changed into a pair of black matte jersey slacks and a breezy white blouse. It was a tad conservative, perhaps even matronly. She'd better start that diet again, and soon.

Meanwhile, she had work to do. But first she reached for the phone to call Steve. She was bursting with her news. It was a funny thing. Her new enterprise didn't feel real to her. She knew it wouldn't until she shared it with Steve.

She set the phone down. This was something she wanted to tell him in person. He was bound to be busy making the final preparations for his departure, but she only needed a few minutes of his time. She'd tell him and the kids the full story at dinner tonight.

While she gathered things into her handbag, she reflected that Steve had always been her validation, whether she was planning a tea for officers' wives or checking the kids' report cards. When he was away, everything stayed on hold until he came back. She held things in like a diver under water, and when he returned, everything came out of her in a rush of relief. It struck her that she'd been living her entire adult life to the rhythm of his duties.

Maybe her new career would give her a better sense of balance, let her breathe while he was away.

The hangar buzzed with a special energy on the eve of deployment. Lumbering transport trucks and buses clogged the parking lots. The reality of Steve's imminent departure struck hard. Oh, how she would miss him. That never changed, never got easier. But maybe this new project would make the time pass more quickly and convince him they could afford Marcia's house after all.

As she drove toward the CAG offices, she thought about the kids. Like her, they were used to deployments, but they always took them hard. She hoped they were getting along all right in school. The twins were busy seniors, and even Katie, the worrier, had settled happily enough into her classes. She had qualified for honors classes and divided her time between homework, music lessons and band practice. Unlike Brian and Emma, who loved sports, Katie was content with her books and music. She had already advanced to second lead clarinet in the marching band.

Other than the fact that Steve was going away, life was good, Grace told herself. Better than ever now.

Yet a shadow lay beneath her perception. It wasn't just the lingering dispute over the house. A weird disconnect seemed to hang in the air between them lately, and she wasn't sure of the cause. She had been meaning to talk to Steve about it, but so far she hadn't brought it up. Mainly because there was nothing to bring up. Her sense of discontent was so vague and unformed that it was probably a figment of her imagination.

Except that it felt as real as a bone-deep bruise.

She parked in a visitor slot and pulled down the visor to use the mirror. Next to her, a minivan the color of an eggplant pulled up and a door slammed. As she was refreshing her lipstick, she caught a movement in the mirror. She turned and saw a young officer walking past. The parking lot was crammed with personnel, but there was something about the stranger that captured her attention.

A funny feeling came over Grace. She could only see him from a distance and from behind, but he looked so eerily familiar that a chill slid down her spine. The narrow hips and broad shoulders were typical of a Navy man, but something in the way he carried himself, or perhaps his peculiar gait, teased at her mind.

Before she could put her finger on it, he entered the hangar, disappearing from sight.

CHAPTER FIFTEEN

The appointment window on Steve's computer screen popped up, alerting him to a meeting with someone he'd never met—Lieutenant Junior Grade Joshua James Lamont, of the VAQ 168, the air wing's Tactical Electronic Warfare Squadron. Under the purpose of the meeting it merely read "personal."

That could mean any number of things: rivalry with his squadron mates, a medical issue, troubles on the home front. But ordinarily when a pilot was having problems, he'd approach his squadron leader, not leapfrog up to the deputy commander of the air wing.

Of course, there might not be any sort of problem at all, he told himself. It was just as likely to be a fouled-up personnel transfer.

More and more lately he found himself dealing with petty annoyances, red tape and meaningless procedure. Of course, that was the chief domain of the DCAG. But on the eve of deployment, he ought to be thinking bigger. What sort of leader would he be? Would he inspire the men and women in his command and motivate them to excellence? Or would he turn into the sort of barking, punitive commander he used to despise? When he'd flown in the first Gulf War, a young hotshot looking for adventure, his CO had been a sadist the whole squadron detested.

That commander was a Rear Admiral now, with a whole battle group in his charge. He had a reputation of being one of the most respected senior officers in the Navy.

Steve reminded himself that he'd chosen this life. He wanted the big Navy career. Regular promotion was essential. An upward-bound officer was like a shark—if he didn't move forward, he'd drown and pass from existence.

But sometimes the compromises between ideals and reality frustrated him. The festering argument with Grace had the unwanted effect of making him question himself and the choices he'd made. What kind of man didn't buy his family a house?

Oh, he'd offered. He told her to find something they could afford. But she wouldn't meet him halfway, so they were at an impasse.

He scowled away the thought. Self-doubt was not supposed to be part of his makeup. From the time he'd stepped off the bus at the Great Lakes Naval Training Center, a raw recruit with nothing but ambition, he'd been focused on the job. It defined him and challenged him, gave his life shape and structure. Without the Navy, what would he be? Just another guy with a family and a mortgage.

He had no idea if he could be happy in an ordinary life as a regular Joe. Without the Navy, he didn't know who he was.

Grace used to be on board with his career plan. She was a big part of his rise through the ranks. From the first day they'd met, she'd believed in him with a sturdy faith he was never quite sure he deserved. But lately...

"Lieutenant Lamont to see you, sir," said Killigrew's voice over the intercom.

"Send him in." Steve automatically swept his desk with a cursory inspection. The Navy drummed that into you—neatness and order above all. It was that orderliness and attention to detail that could make the difference when it mattered. Besides, you always wanted to show your best side to a junior officer.

The door to his office opened and Killigrew stepped aside. "Sir, this is Lieutenant Lamont."

"Thank you." Steve stood up, as much to flex his legs as out of courtesy. Sitting behind a desk had never been his favorite activity, but it was starting to be the largest part of the job.

"You're welcome, sir."

If he'd been less preoccupied, Steve might have wondered why his assistant's voice sounded strained, why his inflection wavered as he introduced Lamont. The visitor stood at attention in the open doorway, backlit by the strong sunshine streaming in through the clerestory windows that lined the upper deck of the hangar.

Killigrew stepped away, closing the door behind him and cutting off the sunlight.

Steve stared at Lieutenant Lamont and said nothing. He could not have choked out a word under threat of death. Because he was mute with shock as he looked at a younger version of himself.

CHAPTER SIXTEEN

Grace stepped into the glaring sunlight of the upper deck of the hangar where Steve's office was located. Kevin Killigrew was not at his desk; she spotted him halfway down the hall at the water cooler, animatedly relating some story to his co-workers. People said women were gossips, she thought. Those people had probably never worked with military men.

She headed straight down the hall to Steve's office. The door was marked with a plaque engraved with his name and rank. She smiled, filled with the anticipation of sharing her news with him.

She should have done this a long time ago. Well, better late than never. She loved her life, but deep down, she wanted more. She adored her family, but she had been gradually disappearing as their needs eclipsed her own. This was his world, this place of busy offices and plaques on the wall, scurrying aides and ringing phones. Grace didn't have a world of her own, and more and more she needed that.

She had once dreamed of running her own business, building it up, looking after clients and having the satisfaction of knowing she did her job well. Until now, the Navy way of life—picking up and moving every few years—had seemed like an insurmountable obstacle to her dreams. Lately she was coming to realize it was an artificial barrier.

There was no point in psychoanalyzing herself. Her business was off the ground. She had three potential clients. And if she was a success, buying the house would no longer be a bone of contention.

It was the perfect news to share with him the day before deployment. A happiness she hadn't felt in a long time lit her like the sun. She was nervous, excited and even a bit defiant as she knocked once and then let herself in rather than obeying protocol and waiting. The heck with protocol. She was bursting with her news.

"Steve, guess what? I—" She broke off as a young officer stood, cap in hand, and turned to her in deference. Her smile disappeared.

"I'm sorry," she said. "I didn't know I was interrup…" Her voice simply died. She could do nothing but stare, frozen by shock and willful incomprehension. She took in the features one by one: clear blue eyes, clean-cut face, glossy dark hair. Broad shoulders, slim hips. Square-shaped hands with thick fingers. Every button and crease in place.

Nothing computed in her mind. She was trapped in a dream where nothing made sense. Here she stood, staring at a perfect stranger who looked exactly like Steve had when she first met him. The young Steve swam before her eyes, and the Steve who was her husband seemed to float in the background, distant as a mirage.

The mirage spoke. "Grace, this is Lieutenant Joshua Lamont. Lieutenant Lamont, my wife, Mrs. Bennett."

"How do you do, ma'am."

I have no idea. Somehow, she mechanically reached out and shook his hand. She felt her lips moving but had no idea what she was saying.

"Lieutenant, I'll take this matter under advisement," said Steve. His voice sounded distant and hollow. "You're dismissed."

"Yes, sir. Thank you, sir. Good day, ma'am." With his cap tucked under his arm, Lamont saluted, then stepped out of the office and shut the door.

Steve came around the desk and reached for her. But suddenly he was a stranger.

She stepped away from him and folded her arms. "So he's what, your long-lost nephew?" She ached for him to deny what she knew, to tell her it was a bizarre coincidence. But it was futile to hope, for Steve had no brothers or sisters. Unless he was hiding that, too.

"No. He's…mine."

For the first time she peered through the haze of shock and studied his face. He looked as pale and shaken as she felt. Because he was shocked, too? Or horrified that she'd discovered his secret?

Dear God.

"So what is this? Are you one of those guys who keeps two of everything in different parts of the world? Two women? Two sets of kids—"

"Gracie, you know better than that."

"Actually, I don't." She was numb all over, even though she knew she should be feeling the sharp heat of rage. She was like a burn victim. The damage was apparent, but had gone so deep she couldn't feel it. "I really don't know anything right now."

He shoved his hand through his hair. "Let me explain."

She should probably walk out now. Save her pride, make him come crawling to her, begging for… She had no idea what he'd beg for. Steve Bennett had never begged in his life. Besides, he was leaving in the morning, and even a marital crisis of epic proportions wouldn't stop him. There was no time for begging and crawling. Also, she wanted to hear what he had to say. A part of her was morbidly curious, like a rubbernecker at a car wreck.

She didn't dare move. If she moved, she'd collapse like a house of cards. If she said anything more, her voice would betray the welling tide of hurt and anger building inside her. Out of necessity, she stayed quiet, waiting. For what, she wasn't certain. She wondered if there was anything he could say to make this right.

"I married a girl right out of high school," he said.

She tightened her grip on herself. *Married.* He was married and she never even knew.

"Her name was Cecilia King. Cissy, everyone called her. We got married right after I finished basic training. The two of us were just kids. We were together less than six weeks, and then I got deployment orders. She promised she'd be waiting when I got back." He steepled his fingers together. Grace thought maybe his hands were shaking, but she didn't budge. She was not going to help him.

He didn't explain it very well. "She didn't last five weeks after I left," he said. "It was a lot harder to be at sea then. There was no e-mail, almost no chance to phone."

Grace remembered those days. On rare occasions, they would luck into a ham radio operator who would orchestrate a phone call. Other than that, they had to rely on paper mail and photographs.

"I got a letter," he continued, "saying she'd met someone. An orthodontist from Atlanta. She used her power of attorney to end the marriage."

She shut her eyes and pictured him as a boy alone at sea, getting a Dear John letter early in his first cruise. Her heart lurched and threatened to soften, but she wouldn't allow it.

"I signed the papers and never saw her again," Steve said, his hand going to the St. Christopher medal around his neck. "I never spoke of her or let myself think about her. There were almost no reminders. She was someone I hardly knew, and she just wasn't a part of my life. I never heard from her again and never expected to. I had no idea she was pregnant. None at all, I swear, or I would have insisted on having contact with him."

Him. Joshua Lamont, the Naval officer she'd just met was Steve's son. His firstborn.

"He said his stepfather legally adopted him at birth. He always knew he was...he'd been fathered by someone else."

Somehow, Grace dredged up her voice. "And it took him this long to find you?"

"He could've found me anytime he wanted," Steve said. "But he didn't want to. He didn't come here on a quest or spiritual journey, searching for his birth father. He learned he was probably going to be under my command. He did the right thing and sought me out."

"Can you have a—" She couldn't say it. "Can you have him under your command?"

"Absolutely."

"So why would he come to you now?"

"You saw him, Grace. It was the right thing to do. We have no legal relationship. There's no reason he cannot serve under my command."

He spoke as though he believed that was the only issue created by Joshua Lamont. Maybe he thought it was.

"I can't believe you kept this from me," she said.

"I told you, Grace, I didn't know she was pregnant."

"You knew you were married and divorced. Why on earth did you never tell me?"

He looked so mystified by her question that she wanted to smack him. "There was nothing to tell."

"There was the truth," she snapped. "Or didn't you think the truth should matter?"

"Of course it matters. But…my marriage to Cissy was a mistake, and I wasn't proud of what happened." He touched her shoulder. "I didn't want you to know I'd failed at marriage—or anything."

She pulled away. "You don't make a lifelong commitment to someone while holding back such a huge thing. You were married, Steve. I deserved to know that."

"Why would I sabotage my chances with you?" he demanded. "Jesus, Grace, I wanted you to trust me—"

"Then you shouldn't have lied to me."

"I didn't."

"Yes, you did. It's a lie by omission. You want trust, after keeping this from me for twenty years? I deserved to find out from you, not from seeing your grown son." She couldn't get the image of Joshua Lamont or the sound of his smooth Southern accent out of her head. No matter what he said about this being official business, she was certain he knew as well as she did that it was personal. He was Steve's son. Regardless of who raised him, he grew up to be a Navy flyer, not an orthodontist.

162

She thought about her own children, and her sense of horror and betrayal deepened. "What are you going to tell the kids?"

"We don't have to tell—"

"No, we don't," she said, tears burning her throat. "You do. And it had better happen tonight, because you're leaving in the morning."

"Don't tell me what to do," he said.

"I'll pretend I didn't hear that."

"It'll only upset them, Grace."

"You think?" She gave a pained laugh. "Whatever gave you that idea?"

Suddenly she couldn't look at him anymore. The sight of him took her apart. Only moments earlier, she'd rushed in to tell him her news, the news that was going to help mend the rift in their marriage. Who was she kidding? The gulf between them was wider and deeper than she'd feared.

Just a few minutes ago, she couldn't wait to see him. Now she couldn't get away fast enough.

She had her hand on the doorknob when he said, "Gracie, wait. Let's talk about this."

She turned back to him. "We should have done that twenty years ago."

"Well, we didn't. So we'll discuss it here. Now. You have to listen to me, Grace. Sit down, and we'll talk this out so we both can understand."

She wasn't sure which did it, the autocratic tone or the patronizing words. It didn't matter. All that mattered was that she needed to get away from here, to find some private place where she could think about the bomb that had been dropped into her life and figure out what to do about it.

She stepped out of the office and pulled the door shut. She could feel every eye in the office on her as she headed for the stairs.

PART THREE
COMMUNICATIONS
BLACKOUT

*Communications blackout: 1. A cessation of
communications or communications capability
caused by a lack of power to communications facility
or equipment. 2. A total lack of communications
capability caused by propogation anomalies......*

CHAPTER SEVENTEEN

When Lauren opened the door of her house, Josh didn't bother with a greeting. "I don't know what I need worse," he said, striding inside. "You, or a bottle of tequila." He grabbed the whole lovely five-foot-nine length of her, pushed her back against the wall of the entryway and kissed her. Hard. The scent of her hair filled his senses. Of all the women he'd dated, she smelled the best. He figured that had to mean something.

She gripped his upper arms and leaned back. She'd liked the kiss. He could see it in the way her eyes drifted half-shut.

"Nice to know I rate up there with a bottle of tequila," she said.

That was another thing he liked about her, she didn't let him get away with anything. Other women he'd known put up with a lot—too much—from him. When he was in pilot training, he discovered that everything he'd heard about Navy pilots was true. Women literally threw themselves at him, launching their well-endowed assets into his arms everywhere he went. Bars and honky-tonks were strung like Mardi Gras beads all along the beaches of Pensacola, and in every one, the women were waiting—and willing.

He'd loved it and had his share of fun. But after a while he discovered that he wanted more than sex out of a relationship. He kept the revelation to himself, because it made him seem like a misfit among the hard-drinking, womanizing pilots of his training wing. But he couldn't change who he was, couldn't stop wanting what he wanted—a life, not just a good time. Now, for the first time, he saw the possibility of both.

She went to the kitchen and returned with a shot glass, a lime cut into wedges and a shaker of salt. She took a bottle of El Patrón from a cabinet. "So here we are. Tequila and me."

He grabbed her again, loving the feel of her in his arms. Thanks to his training schedule, he only had time to take her out maybe once or twice a week. But each time he saw her, he became more and more convinced that they were meant to be together. Especially now. She was the exact person he needed this minute, in the aftermath of the difficult meeting with Bennett. He knew he should have called his mother immediately to let her know how things had gone, but he was learning to listen to his heart. And his heart told him Lauren was the one he wanted right now.

"So tell me," she said, drawing him over to the sofa. They sat down together and she draped her legs across his lap.

Josh shut his eyes briefly. He was falling for her so fast and so hard, he was getting vertigo. With an unexpectedly steady hand, he poured a shot of tequila and knocked it back.

"That bad, huh?" she asked.

"It's about my family."

She tilted her head to one side. "I'm listening."

He closed his eyes again, trying to pick the place to start. "My father was actually my stepfather."

She widened her eyes comically. "I'll set up a press conference."

"I'm not finished."

"I'm all ears."

"Okay. So I was raised by my mother and stepfather. No big deal, happens to lots of people. My parents told me who my biological father was as soon as I was old enough to understand. Again, no big deal."

"So what's the crisis?"

"He's never known about me and today I had to tell him." He opened his eyes to find her watching him expectantly. "You sure you want to hear this?"

"Are you kidding? And here I was going to watch reality TV shows all night."

"It's not that complicated. My mom married for the first time as soon as she got out of high school. He was a Navy guy. They divorced after just a few months and she married Grant, my stepdad, before I was born. My dad adopted me at birth, and he's the only father I've ever known or ever wanted to know."

"You're lucky," she said softly. "I always wanted a dad."

He touched her hand. "I loved him with all my heart. Turns out they couldn't have kids, so he gave me plenty of attention. A lot more than I deserved, probably."

Lauren shifted in his lap, resting her face against his shoulder. "Why couldn't they have any more children?"

"I don't know. Didn't ask for details. Grant was older than my mother. He didn't have kids from his first marriage, so I suppose I assumed the problem was his."

"Sorry. I didn't mean to be nosy."

He turned her face up to meet his gaze. "You're not nosy. I want you to know everything about me, Lauren."

For a moment, she looked panicked. He laughed and poured her a shot of tequila. Clearly that was a conversation for another time. She took a sip and grimaced. "So did you like being an only child?"

"It's not like I had a choice. But I always swore I'd have a big family when it was my turn." He touched her hand, wondering if she caught his meaning.

She studied their joined hands. "So I'll bet you're the apple of your dad's eye."

"I was. And he was everything to me. Goddamned everything." Josh looked out the window at the mountains across the Sound, pink with the sunset. *I miss you, Dad,* he thought. "He died a year ago."

"Aw, Josh." She cupped her hand along his jaw. "I'm sorry. Here I am joking around while you—"

"You're exactly what I need," he said. "Exactly." He brought her hand to his mouth and placed a kiss in her palm.

"What was he like?" she asked softly.

"Caring. Funny and smart. The whole time I was growing up, he wanted me to go into orthodontics with him. I think he and my mother dreamed of a family partnership." Josh helped himself to more tequila and remembered his father's advice: "Don't let your work define you. If you do, it'll swallow you whole." Grant had given his trademark mischievous grin. "No chance of that happening in orthodontics, son."

He was right about that. The profession was stable, respected, lucrative. As a partner in a prosperous group practice, Josh would have it all—the country club membership, the big house in Buckhead, the debutante wife, as many kids as he wanted.

He looked into Lauren's eyes and admitted the truth. "I saw all the advantages of what he was offering me, but I couldn't do it. Couldn't make it my dream."

"And you feel guilty for that?"

"Yeah, I do. Hell, the guy raised me. Gave me everything he had. All he wanted in return was for me to follow in his footsteps, and I refused to give him that."

"Oh, come on, Lamont. He loved you. I get that. He wanted you to have the life you chose, not the one he picked out for you."

"My going into the Navy was a slap in the face to him."

She shook her head. "Yeah, I'm sure he thought it was a real shame, you making it through the Naval Academy."

"Okay. All right, so I could have done worse. I just wish I could've made myself want something else instead of this." He shook his head. "I almost left the Navy to be with my mom when he died. She was pretty torn up. Still is."

"But you stayed in the Navy."

"I incurred years of service for the Academy and pilot training. But over and above that commitment, I wanted this. I convinced myself that it would've been a huge mistake to shape my own life around my mother's needs."

"I think the lady raised you right."

"She never would have asked me to quit, even though she hated the idea of me being in the Navy."

"Most mothers are proud to have a son in the Navy," Lauren said.

"Not mine. She did her best to talk me out of going to Annapolis, but she knew I wouldn't give up on it." He kept a firm hold on Lauren's hand. "She also knew it meant I was eventually going to contact my biological father."

"The Navy guy."

"Yes. He's an officer now. A pilot." Over the years, Josh had viewed Bennett from a distance, seeing his service portrait in Navy publications. He'd never felt anything but curiosity. After today, he felt something else, but he wasn't quite sure what that was.

Lauren was quiet for a long time. Then she reached for the bottle. "So, who is he?"

"Captain Steve Bennett. He's second-in-command of the air wing of the *Dominion*."

"Did you choose flying because of him?"

"I hope not. I hope I chose it because of me." He smoothed his hand over Lauren's hair. Each moment he spent with her, he felt more comfortable. He'd never been so at ease, talking with a woman. She had a way of listening that made the words come easily. "It's kind of like I've been following a ghost," he admitted, "taking after a guy I've never met, a guy who didn't mean squat to me except for his contribution to my DNA. For all I knew, he was a complete asshole."

"Gosh," she said. "Just like Luke Skywalker and Darth Vader."

"Very funny." But she was, he realized. She made him smile even when he didn't feel like it. She made the world seem lighter. He was so damned glad he'd come here.

"So you finally met him."

"I had no choice. Eventually, I'll be on the same carrier as Bennett. There were formalities to get out of the way."

"So what's Darth Vader like?"

Josh hesitated. Based on one meeting, he didn't know. Today Bennett had been a professional to the last inch of his shadow. He'd allowed himself only a moment of shock. Then he'd been all business. But there was an image stuck in Josh's head of Bennett being awakened late on a summer night by a pair of MPs, dropping off a young woman who was probably Bennett's daughter. That was an incident Josh knew he wouldn't share with anyone, not even Lauren.

He dug in his breast pocket and produced a folded page he'd torn out of the journal *Contrails.* There was a service portrait of Bennett posed next to the flag.

She stared at the photograph and caught her breath. "Are you sure he's responsible for only half your DNA? My God, you're clones."

He nodded, feeling the floating strangeness he always experienced when considering his biological father. How could someone he'd never met be so...present in him?

He told Lauren about walking through the hangar today, garnering stares and generating whispers as he passed members of Bennett's staff. The LDO in the outer office had almost pissed himself. Then, the moment Josh stepped into Bennett's office, a shimmering sense of unreality took hold.

"Sir, my name is Joshua James Lamont. I was born in Atlanta, Georgia, on April 4, 1977. My mother's name is Cecilia King Lamont."

Bennett had looked as though he'd been sucker punched, but only for a moment. Then he turned to granite. Josh had not needed to explain anything further. In the interest of full disclosure, Josh explained, he felt compelled to let Bennett know of their biological link.

Both men had shielded themselves behind a rigid mantel of military professionalism. They did all right, but the facade had nearly crumbled when Bennett's wife walked in on them.

"That poor woman," Lauren said.

"I got out of there fast after she arrived." He pictured Mrs.

Bennett's face, pale with shock. She had kind, intelligent eyes that reflected pain and confusion with pinpoint accuracy.

"So what happens next?"

He slid his hand up her thigh. "You and I make love and live happily ever after."

She shoved his hand away. "Very funny, Lamont."

"I'm serious. You knew this was coming, Lauren."

She lifted her legs off his lap and stood up. "I think you should go, Josh."

A note of fear in her voice bothered him. "I'm not going anywhere. Look, I've spent the day being brutally honest, and I'm not through yet. We're great together, Lauren. Damn it, you know we are." He got up and planted himself in front of her. "I want you. I'm falling in love with you."

She turned her face away and hugged herself. "Don't say that."

"I've been trying like hell not to. But I can't keep it to myself anymore."

"Listen, we've had a few laughs. You're a great guy, and you've had one hell of a day. I admire you for what you did. I think you're incredible. But this isn't going to work. Maybe we should both move on."

"Oh, sure. Like you've been moving on since your husband died?"

She recoiled as though he had struck her. But he kept talking. He wasn't about to back down now. "You're stuck, Lauren. If you don't let yourself go, you'll be stuck for the rest of your life. Is that what you want?"

"As opposed to the alternative you're offering?" she snapped.

"Yes."

"Why?"

"Because we can never live happily ever after, no matter what you say. We'll be happy until we break each other's hearts."

"I would never hurt you, Lauren."

"You're hurting me now," she said. "Don't you get it, Lamont? It hurts to want you this much and to know I can never have you."

"Bullshit. You've got me now."

"For how long? Until you ship out?"

That shut him up. He got it, finally. His commitment to the Navy was powerful enough to make him defy his parents. It would be powerful enough to compel him to leave the woman he loved when duty called.

"I don't have what it takes to love you," she said. "I won't subject myself to a life of saying goodbye—"

"And saying welcome home," he reminded her.

The tears in her eyes nearly took him apart. But then it hit him—the tears meant she cared.

He smiled at her gently, then closed his arms around her. "It's going to be all right, darlin'," he promised in a husky whisper. "You'll get used to it."

"How?" she asked.

"By believing in me. In us. Believing we'll live happily ever after, I swear. Starting now."

"I think you should go." Her whisper lacked conviction. And she didn't leave his embrace.

"Now, honey, there is pretty much only one thing in the world that's going to make me walk away from you tonight. And that's if you can look me in the eye and tell me I'm wrong about us."

She pressed her forehead against his chest. "You're—"

"Look me in the eye, Lauren. Or don't say it at all."

With a trembling effort, she pushed her fists against his chest and tilted her face up to his. The tears escaped, and he wanted so badly to kiss them away, to press her against him and promise everything would be all right.

That wasn't what she needed, he reminded himself. She needed to face up to the things that lay between them, no matter how much it hurt. He stared into her eyes and felt love wash over him in a heavy wave. See me, he thought. See the way I feel for you.

"Lamont," she whispered. "You're…"

God. She was going to do it after all. She was going to say he was wrong, they didn't belong together.

She bit her lip, took a deep breath, tried again. "You're… a…Navy bastard," she said.

"That's my girl," he said, and leaned down to kiss her until she ran out of protests.

Lauren woke up the next morning in a haze of sexual satisfaction. She didn't dare open her eyes for fear it was only a dream. But it wasn't. This was her life, and last night it had taken a left turn toward the unknown.

She opened her eyes slowly, wincing at the sunlight streaming through the sliding glass doors. She never, ever slept with the drapes open like that. But what the hell, she thought, pushing up on her elbows. She never slept with Navy guys, either.

Until last night.

Her lips curved into a smile, and she glanced at his side of the bed. Funny how, in a single night, she had already designated it "his" side. The bedclothes had been tossed into an untidy pile, and for a wild moment, Lauren thought he might still be in there somewhere. But no, he had warned her that he'd be slipping out in the wee hours. He had something called "Special Training" this week because the main part of his squadron would be flying aboard the *Dominion*. Josh would be leaving, too, but not until the spring.

As if there were any comfort in that, she thought, getting out of bed and slipping her arms into the sleeves of her robe. Leaving was leaving. It was what men did when they were in the Navy.

She went to get the newspaper from the front walk. She felt tingly all over, her bare skin supersensitized to the brush of the robe. She stood there for a moment, holding the paper in its damp plastic sleeve. More than anything, she wanted to talk to Josh, to describe the strange and wonderful feelings that were sweeping through her. But she couldn't reach him, of course. He'd said he would be incommunicado during special training.

There were more idiotic things than falling for a Navy guy, she supposed as she returned to the house. But at the moment, she couldn't think of a single one.

A faint mew froze her in her tracks. Chills spread over her, and she turned back to see Ranger, the wandering stray, emerge from the box hedge and leap to the porch. He was damp but plump as ever, and had a white flea collar around his neck. As though he'd been gone a few minutes rather than months, he slipped inside and headed straight for his bowl in the kitchen.

CHAPTER EIGHTEEN

Going to sea was never easy for Steve, but the worst—until now—had been leaving Grace while she was pregnant. Both times. He had never seen a child of his being born. Grace had been incredible about it, though. Back then, before e-mail, she wrote every day, stuffing the letters with photographs and loving notes, making him a part of his children's lives before he even met them.

He thanked God every day for Grace. She made this family work. She made deployment bearable.

Now he understood that Josh's arrival signaled the beginning of a profound change, one that had been brewing for longer than he cared to admit. They needed time to sort out the shock and confusion of the discovery, and more time still to dig out the discontent they'd both ignored for too long.

The problem was, they didn't have time. After she walked out of the hangar, he'd simply stood in the middle of his barren office, confused as a bombing victim. The inevitable gossip gathered force like a storm brewing at sea. One look at Lamont had set off the staff. And those who saw Grace come and go so quickly were already embellishing the tale, no doubt.

Maybe he should have gone after her, but pride held him back.

He didn't want to face all those inquisitive stares from his staff, those sudden charged pauses in conversation as he walked by. Instead, he went about his business with officious determination. He had things to do before he left. Regardless of the chaos in his personal life, nothing held back tomorrow.

Over the years the Bennett family had developed a number of predeployment rituals. They all did things to comfort themselves, to reassure themselves, to make his absence seem more bearable.

Before each departure, Steve tried to give something special to each of his children. When they were little, he might offer a jar filled with a hundred and eighty Hershey's Kisses, one for each day he was gone. Or a bank of coins, golf balls to hit, a book filled with stories. One time, when Katie was nearly hysterical over his impending departure, he'd stayed up for an entire night to write and fold one hundred and eighty little "Messages from Dad." He included random thoughts to make her smile: "You're the pepperoni on my pizza." Stupid jokes: "What has ten legs and drools?" And every once in a while, a heartfelt sentiment: "The sun's not up until it rises over you."

Now that they were older, it was harder to come up with some sort of daily dose of Dad. For the current departure, he had a project he'd been working on for a long time.

He was pretty sure the kids never realized how much it hurt to say goodbye. He didn't want them to know what it felt like to leave a crawling infant and return to a walking toddler. Or to come home to a child who screamed at the sight of him—a forgotten stranger. To celebrate his six-year-old's first lost tooth and return to a seven-year-old with a mouth full of permanent teeth. To leave his son struggling to throw a baseball and return to discover his coach had trained him to pitch no-hitters. Or to know he'd never see his daughter all dressed up for her first formal dance.

These were things Steve kept from them. He seized on the "chin up, duty calls" attitude of a career officer. Now, seated in the quiet of his office, emptied in anticipation of the move, he realized the truth. Keeping things from the people you love could not be done without cost.

Feeling both weary and unsettled, he created an envelope for each kid. The letters had been written before Lieutenant Joshua Lamont had marched into his life, but Steve decided against revising them. His sentiments had not changed.

But theirs might.

He hated that he had to tell them. But Grace would insist on it, he knew with a twinge of irritation.

When he got home for dinner, he didn't know what to expect. In the blink of an eye, everything was different. The world he had built was now crumbling.

Grace was in the kitchen, standing at the sink with its rusty fixtures. In the ugly little house, she looked like a visiting queen, out of place and unhappy about it. At the sound of his footsteps, she turned to look at him. She wore an expression he didn't recognize. Normally, he'd give her a kiss, and she'd ask about his day. But this was not a normal situation.

"Gracie, let's talk about this," he said.

"Talk about what?" asked Katie, coming into the kitchen and sitting on a stool at the breakfast bar. Her expression glowed in that special way she reserved just for him. "Hi, Daddy."

He returned the smile, but his heart turned over in his chest. What would it do to his little Katydid when he told her about Josh?

He turned to Grace, and the hurt and confusion in her eyes seemed to push all the air out of his lungs. He was not going to get any help from her. He was on his own.

He had no idea how to fix this. He could rebuild a jet engine, but matters of the heart were a mystery to him. In every sense of the word, this was his first true family. Up until Grace and the kids, he'd had no idea what a family could be. A product of the foster care system, he'd grown up without emotional ties or a permanent home. At a young age he learned to protect his heart and keep his secrets. It was the only way to survive.

He learned never to abide failure from himself. His relationship with Cissy was a failure he refused to acknowledge. He believed he was better off living his life as though the marriage had never taken place. Now he realized what most people probably knew all along—you're never truly free of the past.

"Talk about what?" Katie persisted.

"About where we're going for dinner tonight," he said. Good answer. The last thing Grace needed tonight was to cook.

"I vote for the Dutch place that thinks it's French," Katie said, bouncing up and down.

"The Kasteel Franssen?" Emma asked, coming down the stairs. "It looks like a miniature golf course, all those windmills and stuff."

"Yeah, but they have the best desserts," Katie declared. "Mountains of whipped cream, mountains! Can we go, Dad? Please?"

"We'll let your mother decide." For the girls' sake, he smiled at Grace and acted as though this was any other predeployment family dinner.

"I'll call for a reservation." She turned and picked up the phone. While she booked a table, he noticed the way she held one arm wrapped around her middle, as if she had a stomachache.

During the short drive to the restaurant, the kids filled the silence with their usual bright and unceasing talk. Katie shared gossip with unabashed delight. "I heard Cory Crowther asked Emma to homecoming," she announced.

Grace swiveled around to look at Emma. "That's news to me."

Emma elbowed her sister. "Me, too. The dance isn't until the end of November. He hasn't said a word, dork, and don't you go telling people he has."

"I'm just telling Mom and Dad," Katie said. "And he did, too, ask you. Or he's going to, any minute. His own mother practically said so. She did some lame presentation for our leadership class and Erin Clune asked her right out who Cory was taking."

In the rearview mirror, Steve saw Emma put her face in her hands. "My life is a nightmare."

"So do you want to go with him?" Brian asked.

"Of course she does," Katie piped up. "Who wouldn't?"

After the incident with the beer, Steve's opinion of Cory Crowther had slipped, even though Emma assured him Cory was no more at fault than any other kid that night. But even if the boy was perfect, Steve knew perfection wouldn't be enough. Nobody would ever be good enough for Emma.

All three kids started talking at once, each trying to be heard.

Steve had a fleeting thought of Joshua Lamont. What kind of kid had he been?

A weird, almost surreal feeling drifted over him, the aftermath of shock and the beginning of acceptance that his life had changed irrevocably. He glanced at Grace, his anchor, but she was turned toward the kids, discussing whether Brian should invite someone named Lindy or Candace to the dance.

"Hey, what about you?" Brian said to Katie, fending off her nosy questions. "You're in high school now. Who's taking you to the dance?"

"Some lucky guy, I bet," Steve interrupted while Katie turned beet red. "Remember what we talked about, Brian. While I'm away you—"

"Look out for your sisters," Katie finished for him, clearly grateful for the change of subject. "What is this, the Dark Ages? Emma and I can look out for ourselves, can't we, Em?"

"Always," Emma agreed. "But we need to give Brian a chance to feel useful."

"I'm extremely useful," Brian stated as they pulled into the restaurant parking lot. "Just remember that next time you need a ride somewhere."

All teasing and squabbling stopped once they walked into the restaurant, dimly lit and decorated with a charmless seventies elegance. His children became polite dinner guests with flawless posture and well-modulated voices.

Training was everything, thought Steve. In life, as well as in the Navy. Grace had trained these kids with a subtle but powerful hand, and now poise and manners were ingrained in them. They understood the chain of command both in the Navy and in the family.

As they were shown to their table, which was set in one of the restaurant's self-consciously cute private alcoves, Steve heard someone calling his name. Across the room, a guy in a suit waved at him.

"I'll be damned," he murmured. "Excuse me for just a minute," he said to Grace.

She nodded and went to their table with the kids. He made a detour to see an old friend.

"Joey Lord," he said as Joey stood and offered him a hearty handshake. "I swear, I'm seeing a ghost."

"Long time no see, you old dog." Joey turned to the attractive young woman who was his dinner companion. "Honey, this is Steve Bennett, a former squadron mate. Call sign Lone Wolf, wasn't it? Steve, say hello to my gorgeous wife, Haley."

As Steve greeted her, he estimated she was about half Joe's age and wore several thousand dollars' worth of jewelry. Number three, he thought. Joe had endured not one but two marriages like Steve's first one—brief and brutal. Joe had been so devastated by the second failure that he left the Navy.

The whole squadron had been shocked, because Joe's career as an officer was taking off. He had turned his back on the chance to be squadron commander. The position fell to Steve instead. Judging by Joey's radiant expression, he felt no regrets.

"So how are things in the private sector?" Steve asked.

"What can I say? I get paid to fly prototypes, and I'm home every day by six. I'm actually going to be with Haley when the baby comes. What a concept, eh?" He reached into his breast pocket and handed Steve a card. "You get in touch, you ever think about making a change."

"You bet," said Steve, slipping the card in a pocket and forgetting about it. "Thanks. I'd best get back to my family."

"Shipping out?" asked Joe.

"Yep."

"Good luck, buddy. Keep yourself safe."

Steve took a seat on one of the high-backed upholstered benches. "Sorry," he said. "Ran into Joey Lord from one of my old squadrons. He's in the private sector now."

"Whoa, a snake-oil salesman," Katie said in a scandalized whisper. That was the Navy's term for career officers who allowed themselves to be lured away by companies offering them big bucks. In the Bennett household, such an idea was unthinkable.

"I can't believe you spoke to him," Katie added.

"It's not like he did anything illegal," Brian said. "Maybe he wanted good pay and a chance to live his own life."

"He made a commitment to the Navy." Emma spoke up with surprising vehemence. "By the time you're a pilot or RIO, the Navy's invested more than two million dollars in your training."

"How do you know that?" asked Grace.

"Some recruiter came to school to talk to the seniors."

"I can't believe you went to that thing," Brian said. "It's not like we don't know what the Navy wants."

"It got me out of civics class for an hour."

"I can't wait until I'm a senior," Katie said.

School remained the chief topic of discussion during dinner. Steve noticed other families here, some of them for the same purpose as the Bennetts. Finally, as the promised mountainous desserts were being consumed, he caught Grace's eye across the table.

She gave him nothing, no support at all. He had the sensation of being in a free fall with an unknown landing. Should he tell them? Here? Now? Was the restaurant too public? Grace would know. But he was on his own with this; she'd made that clear. "OK," he said. "I need to talk about a—"

"—couple of things before I ship out," Katie said, swirling her spoon in the whipped cream. "We're all ears, Daddy-O."

Grace leaned back against the upholstered booth and folded her hands on the table. This was his show. He'd better get on with it. He produced four manila envelopes and handed them out. "First, a little something for the next few months."

They tore into the packages. "CDs," Katie said, holding up a set of three labeled discs in plastic sleeves. "Thanks, Dad."

"Did you make these yourself?" asked Brian.

"Every one of them," Steve said.

"I didn't even know you knew how to use a CD burner."

"Your old man still has a few tricks up his sleeve. I thought I'd never finish."

"Did you make these copies legally?" asked Emma.

"Of course. I did it at the base radio station. They're all made from legitimately purchased originals. I printed you each a copy of the play list," he added. "It's in the envelope."

"This is really special, Dad," said Emma. "Thanks."

Her smile more than rewarded him for the hours and hours of labor. Finding just the right songs, each one with a certain significance, had been like going on a treasure hunt. It was harder and more fun than he thought it would be. He'd recorded everything from "Rescue Me" and "Walk Like a Man" to selections by Nora Jones and the Vines.

"Pretty great, isn't it, Mom?" Katie said happily. But a shadow flickered over her face. His little girl always tried so hard to be brave when he left.

Grace scanned the list of songs and bit her lip. "I haven't heard some of these in years."

Steve wondered if she realized it was the soundtrack of their marriage. He had tried to include every song they'd enjoyed together, danced to, made love to. Every song that had been playing in the background throughout the years. Fortunately, he had a good memory for music. In some of the homes he'd been placed as a boy, music had been his refuge and his solace, and he had a healthy appreciation for its power to transport a person to a better place.

Katie leaned over and kissed his cheek. "Thank you, Daddy."

"Yeah, thanks," said Brian.

"There's a letter for each of you," he said. "But you should read that later."

"We always do," Katie said.

Writing those letters was always the hardest part of preparing to leave. No one ever said it aloud, but the fact was, he might go off on deployment and never return.

There was a lull as a waiter brought coffee refills and the check. Steve took a moment to look at each of his children before he broke the news. He took in their beloved faces, folded the images into his heart to keep during the long months to come. They adored him. He knew that. But in just a moment, he was going to alter their perception of him forever.

"I need to tell you guys something," he said.

"Are we at war?" Katie asked with terror blazing up in her eyes.

"I thought this was a WestPac cruise," Emma said.

"It's not about the cruise. It's about me." He looked down at his hands, solid and square, with the wedding band from Grace he never took off unless he was on deployment. Then he looked again at his kids' expectant faces. "I've never really had much to say about the way I grew up," he said. "I need to tell you a little more now."

All three of them sat up a little straighter in their chairs and leaned in a little closer. They knew about the abuse and neglect that had turned him into a ward of the state of Texas by the age of nine. They knew about the string of foster homes, none of them particularly welcoming to a smart, athletic boy with a giant chip on his shoulder.

"I need to level with you about something that happened to me a long time ago."

"Did you do something really bad?" asked Katie.

"Did you get arrested?" Brian wondered.

"No, nothing like that. But…" He allowed himself one final hesitation. In that moment, he was still the dad they knew and loved. What he had to say next was going to change everything. "Right out of high school, just before I went off into the Navy, I got married. And then I was divorced six months later."

Three pairs of eyes stared at him as though he'd grown antlers. Then they all looked at Grace. She turned her hands palms up. "This is your father's story, not mine."

The kids directed their attention back to Steve. "What's her name?" Katie asked. "Where is she now? How come you never told us this before?"

Emma turned to her mother. "Did you—"

"I just found out this afternoon," Grace said evenly. She betrayed nothing, sitting there, watching him unravel in front of the kids.

"I never told anyone," he said, "because it's not something I'm proud of." Even now, the stinging hot shame of his failure broke over him like a rash. "And, I suppose, because I never dwelled on the past. You kids and your mother are everything to me, and I just didn't see the point of telling you about something I did when I was young and stupid, something that was completely over by the time you guys came along." It was awkward, talking to Grace through the kids. She wasn't helping, either, sitting there as neutral as Switzerland.

"That's totally weird, Dad," said Brian. "I can't believe we never knew."

"You should have told us." Katie pushed her mountainous dessert away from her.

"No, he shouldn't have," Emma said suddenly, vehemently. "It's his own private business and it doesn't have anything to do with the way things are now."

He stared at her in surprise, and Grace did the same.

Emma sipped her water. "I just don't see why he should have to tell everyone about every single mistake he made. He should be allowed to move on and forget it ever happened."

Touched, he patted her arm. "Honey, I think you captured my feelings exactly. But it was wrong to keep this from you kids and especially from your mother. Something like this…I should have admitted the truth instead of hiding it. I wish I had."

"You never told us her name," Katie reminded him.

"It's Cecilia King—Cissy. She was as young and as ignorant as I was right out of high school. It took her no time at all to realize she wasn't cut out for Navy life."

"Where does she live?" Katie asked. "What does she look like?"

Steve held up a hand. "I never heard a word from her after the divorce. All she said was that she had met a guy in Atlanta. It turns out that as soon as the divorce was final, she married him. A civilian. A dentist or something."

"So why are you bringing it up now?" asked Emma.

"Because there's more to the story. Cissy left and remarried without telling me something really important. She was pregnant."

"By you?" Katie looked horrified.

"There's a kid?" Brian said. "Geez, Dad."

"I just met him today. Before that, I had no idea."

"A boy," Emma said in a wondering voice. Then, almost whispering, she said, "A brother."

And for the first time, the impact nailed Steve squarely between the eyes. He had a son. Another son. "His name is Joshua Lamont."

"Are you sure he's yours?" Katie demanded.

There would be those who might suggest a paternity test, but that wouldn't be necessary. Any fool with eyes in his head could see the truth.

"I'm sure. He's an officer in the Navy. A flyer. He never would have come to see me, except that he's going to be—"

"Flying in your air wing," Katie interrupted, way ahead of him. "Holy cow."

The questions came hard and fast: "Did you meet him, too, Mom?" "What's he like?" "Where does he live?" "When are we going to meet him?"

"I saw him," Grace said quietly. "Briefly. He's a Navy pilot. That's what he's like."

Steve didn't really consider Navy flyers a "type," but deep down, he knew he belonged to a brotherhood that had certain fundamental things in common.

Brian hadn't said much. He was looking at the table, lost in thought. Maybe this came as the biggest shock to him, Steve realized. In an instant, Brian went from being an only son to a little brother.

"When do we get to meet him?" Katie persisted.

"That's up to him," Steve said. "And your mom."

"Did you, like, fall over each other, crying and everything?"

Steve gave helpless laugh. "It's not like that at all. I don't consider myself his father and he doesn't consider himself my son.

He came to me because he knew our paths would cross eventually, and he wanted to get it out of the way. Look, we're strangers, and the fact that he came forward out of the blue doesn't change anything. Not for me, not for this family. I love your mother and I love you guys, and that will never change for as long as I live."

"Then you should have told us," Brian muttered, finally speaking up.

"He just did, moron." Emma elbowed her brother.

"I think we need therapy," Katie announced, brightening. Ever since she'd had a friend in fifth grade who went once a week to an art therapist, she'd longed for counseling. "Can we all go into therapy, Mom? Please?"

Steve put his arm around her. "We're going to be fine, Katydid," he said. He caught Grace's eye, looking for concurrence and finding none. "I swear, we're going to be fine," he repeated.

CHAPTER NINETEEN

Grace woke up early, aware before she opened her eyes that this day would be different from all others. Ordinarily, deployment set in motion a series of rituals, of quiet, frightened moments, of emotions rising right to the surface and then spilling over. Now she wasn't sure what to expect.

She turned on her side, scarcely breathing. Steve was still sound asleep, thanks to that enviable gift he had of emptying his mind so his body could rest. She had the urge to wake him, to carry on the terrible conversation they'd had the night before, but she tucked her hand under her pillow and resisted. There was no way to resolve this in the time they had left. In a few hours, she would be alone with this problem.

Like so many of the moments in their marriage, this one was about to be interrupted by the call of duty. Steve was going away for six months or more, leaving her to sort through the wreckage in the aftermath of a friendly-fire bombing.

The revelation about his past stirred up a storm of doubt and confusion in Grace. He had been married, for heaven's sake, and he never told her. Why? What else was he hiding? How much did she really know about the man she'd married in such open-hearted joy? This stranger. This intruder. Did he belong in her life anymore?

She had been so young when she met him. So desperate to escape the confines of Edenville, a tiny town by a lake in the Texas hill country. It was a place where she had almost drowned—not in the lake, but in the oppressive expectations of her parents, who had her life all planned out for her. They expected her to finish school, marry into the wealthiest family in town and live three blocks away from them. Against her will, they were already making plans without even consulting her.

Steve had rescued her in every sense of the word. The day she met him, she was home from college for the weekend and had gone swimming with her friends in Eagle Lake, hoping, perhaps, to wash away the latest argument with her parents. As she stood by the water's edge drying her hair, he roared in out of nowhere, straddling a purring Softail Harley.

Backlit by the setting sun and stirring up a swirl of caliche dust from the road, he planted his feet, in knee-high boots, on the ground. Then he took off his helmet.

She'd been uncharacteristically speechless and self-conscious, aware that her bikini top and cutoff shorts didn't leave a whole lot to the imagination. In the background, her sorority sisters whispered and giggled, no doubt as captivated by the stranger as Grace was.

"Howdy, ma'am," he said.

At twenty, she didn't get called ma'am very often. "Um, can I help you?"

"I'm looking for someone…" His eyes were devastating, blue and intense. "But I've forgotten who. My God, I can't even think straight. What's your name?"

She'd actually whipped a glance behind her to see if he was talking to someone else, but no, he was looking directly at her. Grace McAllen, Grace the invisible, Grace the overlooked. And now here was this young god on a Harley, looking at her with lust and fascination and something so promising that she got chills.

She didn't have him to herself for long. Her sorority sisters from

Trinity University quickly got into the act, flirting and peppering him with questions. She learned his name was Steve Bennett, that he was on a rare two-week leave from the Navy and had ridden all the way from Pensacola just because he felt like it, and because a friend from pilot training had invited him.

"Bud Plawski," he said, grinning at Grace. "That's who I came to see. Do you know him?"

Grace not only knew him, she'd grown up next door to Seymour "Buddy" Plawski. Her entire youth had been tormented by him; he was so energetic and annoying that his own mother used to shoo him outside and lock the doors. Years later, he surprised everyone by getting his act together and winning an appointment to the Naval Academy. Upon graduating, he went into pilot training. Then he returned to Edenville on leave, with wings of gold pinned to his chest, an instant hometown hero.

Grace still found him annoying. But he had excellent taste in friends.

She'd married Steve before the summer was out, managing to alienate her parents and grandmother and to escape her hometown for good, all in one stroke. If Steve hadn't rescued her, she might have sunk into unhappy obscurity.

Or maybe not.

Maybe she would have created a fabulous life for herself, all on her own.

She tried to remember if there had ever been a moment when she should have asked him about his past relationships. Had they even come close to discussing it? She'd been so relieved to find Steve that perhaps she hadn't dared to question him.

She recalled one conversation they'd had concerning the topic, and it had centered on her. Her parents were livid at the idea that she would reject their well-laid plans for her future. After she and Steve blasted out of town on his Harley, she hadn't heard from them again. Ever. Just from Gran, whose heart was softer. Grace never went home again except to attend her father's funeral. Her mother refused to speak to her and Steve; nor would Olivia

McAllen comment on Grace's belly, enormous with twins. Grace's last image of her mother was of a slender, stiff-backed woman in a black knit suit, her face stubbornly pointed away, her fury at life's disappointments snapping around her like heat lightning.

Grace had been so grateful for Steve then, and even more grateful still when she'd returned to Edenville two more times—for the funeral of her mother and, finally, just a few years ago, for Gran.

She and Steve became the family that neither of them had ever had. They went to church together, celebrated holidays with cozy intimacy, shared everything, good and bad. Grace realized that, without consciously planning to do so, she had created the sort of family she'd always wanted.

She used to consider their marriage the safest of places, the center of a circle made of love. There was nothing she wouldn't do for Steve, nothing she wouldn't share. He knew everything about her. He always had. From the first day she'd met him, she'd held nothing back. She trusted his love to hold steady through anything, even the hostility of her parents and the damage done by their refusal to give their blessing to her and Steve. She'd simply assumed he was as forthcoming as she. He didn't have a lot to say about his traumatic boyhood, but she figured that was because it hurt to speak of it, not because he was willfully keeping a secret from her.

Her name was Cissy. Grace was desperate to learn everything about her and knew this burning curiosity could easily become a sick obsession. She felt frozen in that moment of horror when she'd learned he used to be married to someone else.

She was consumed by uncertainty. It was like waking up one day and discovering the world had turned color. She wondered endlessly what Cissy was like, how she and Steve were together. Was she pretty? Judging by Joshua Lamont's looks, it was likely. Was she charming? Adventurous? Intriguing?

It wasn't such a big deal, Grace told herself again and again. Lots of people—half the population, if statistics were correct—married more than once.

But how many kept it secret?

She lay with her head pillowed on her elbow, facing Steve, aching with a sense of her world coming apart. The breakdown had started long before this, but they'd both ignored the warning signs. Now they couldn't ignore it anymore.

Eventually he woke up. The years in the Navy had eliminated any sort of between-time bridging sleep and wakefulness. His eyes opened and he was fully alert and instantly aware of her.

"Hey," he said.

"Hey."

He reached out, his strong arms enveloping her. Usually she loved to cuddle up with him in the morning; she even loved to sink easily into the mindless pleasure of half-awake sex. But this morning, everything was different. She didn't melt. She didn't sink. A Pandora's box of doubts and discontent had flown open, and she couldn't feel what she was supposed to feel for her husband, for this man to whom she had given her whole heart and half her life.

She pushed herself out of his arms and scooted up in bed. The clock read 6:05 a.m. In ninety minutes they had to be on the road to Naval Station Everett.

"Lie back down," he murmured. "I need to hold you before I go. I thought after last night—"

"We didn't settle anything last night," she said. They'd stayed up late, arguing while he finished packing. She usually hid things in his bag for him to discover when he went aboard—a love note, a package of Jelly Bellies, a picture of the kids. She didn't have anything to slip into the bag this time.

"Then let's settle it now," he said, looking at the clock. "We've got a little time."

"What, five minutes and the storm is past? I don't think so," she whispered, fighting tears.

"Then let me make love to you, Grace. At least give us that."

"I—" She pushed aside the covers and got out of bed.

"Baby, it's our last chance."

"Jesus, Steve, if I can't figure out how I feel about your first wife, I sure as hell can't make love to you."

"You don't need to feel any particular way about her."

"It's not her. It's you. Me. *Us.* I can't figure out—"

"How to feel about me?" he snapped. "How about being a little more understanding about something I did when I was a kid, no older than the twins?"

"I've always been understanding," she shot back, anger burning away the tears. "I've been understanding through nine locations, through missed birthdays and holidays, through crises that happen when you're ten thousand miles away. I've understood that you're going for your dream, and that it's my job to make sure you achieve that. To make sure my needs and this family's needs don't interfere with your career. So don't you dare tell me I'm not understanding."

"Fine. Then understand that I had a failed marriage, and I was ashamed of that and didn't want you to know."

She tied on her robe. "I understand that. I just don't understand why. You know everything about me. About my lousy parents and everything they tried to do to me—"

"You chose to tell me that stuff, Grace."

"I did not choose to. I didn't have a choice at all. My heart didn't give me a choice. There's no way I would keep things from the man I was about to marry. My past is part of who I am, and I believed you had a right to know that."

"I would have loved you no matter what happened to you in the past," he said.

"Then why didn't you trust me to do the same?" Her chest ached as she forced herself to lower her voice. "Look where I am," she said. "Right here, in the middle of my life, giving everything I've got to supporting you and your career."

"You love this career," he reminded her as he got out of bed. "Don't tell me you don't."

"I do," she said softly. "I'm grateful for all the opportunities we've had. I take pride in everything you've accomplished. But now I'm standing here questioning every choice I've ever made. Not because I found out you used to be married. This started long before that. I'm questioning myself and my life—"

"Look, I'm sorry you woke up one day and decided you don't like what you see in the mirror, Grace. I'm not responsible for your midlife crisis any more than you're responsible for my failed first marriage." He paced in agitation. "The fact that you're turning forty is not my fault," he declared. "And it's not my problem."

She wanted to slap him. She'd never slapped anyone in all her thirty-nine years. "You're right," she said. "My self-image is not your problem. Now, our marriage, that is definitely your problem."

"I don't have a problem with our marriage," he said. "Everything would be fine if you would just—"

"If I would just what?" she snapped. "Forget the wife you neglected to tell me about? Forget your twenty-six-year-old son? Forget half the base probably knows more about your past than I do? You're leaving, Steve. I have to stay here and deal with the fallout, and with the kids and all their questions. So don't ask me for understanding. Not this time."

"I was a kid. A stupid kid," he said. "I should have told you, but I didn't. Because of that one omission, you're going to declare war on me?"

"You don't get it. The early marriage is completely forgivable," she said. "I can even understand it—you were a kid, you were all alone and you married in haste. But that's not what's tearing us apart. That's only the thing that happened that made the real problem impossible to ignore."

"We had no real problem until you got all upset about this."

"Oh. I see. We never argued about me starting a career—"

"We did, but you don't give a shit about my opinion," he said. "You started that even when I asked you not to—"

"You didn't ask. You ordered."

"And you blew me off."

"And that surprises you? I don't take orders well. You know that. And about the house—"

"I thought that was settled."

"Of course you did. In your mind, it probably was."

"It was. But if you insist, we'll talk about it after this cruise."

"That's not good enough, Steve. I've been trying to talk to you about this for weeks. Months, even."

He didn't say a word as he stuck a few more pairs of socks in his bag. She couldn't help the way her gaze clung to his lean body, his jawline shadowed by morning stubble. He'd become a stranger, a man with secrets she didn't know. And he was leaving.

Before heading for the shower, he twisted off his wedding band and left it on the nightstand. Personnel were advised against wearing wedding bands even on a routine deployment, because it told potential enemies too much. But today, watching him take it off caused a special agony in Grace's chest.

She finished dressing, shaking with anger and hurt. The unmade bed mocked her; this was the first time they'd ever parted without making love. It would be the first time she'd stand on the platform without the warmth of their final embrace still lingering deep within her, knowing it would impart a memory she could hold on to in the lonely days to come. This time, he left her with nothing but cold, dry doubts.

Hidden inside her anger was the terrible knowledge that she might never see him again. It was unlikely, of course, particularly on a routine deployment, but the possibility always existed. Accidents and illnesses happened.

She went to the bathroom door and raised her fist to knock. But then she lowered it and turned away without making a sound.

In the car, the kids were alternately tense and quiet, or talking too much. Grace sensed them watching her and Steve, trying to read their moods. Steve had the option to fly one of the squadron planes aboard once the carrier was at sea, but he'd declined the offer. He'd landed hundreds of traps aboard a carrier, so the novelty had worn off, and newer pilots needed the experience.

Grace had told him goodbye in all kinds of weather, but she couldn't recall a day quite like today. The sky was a piercing blue, the mountains glaring white peaks painted with lavender shadows. On the ferry crossing to the mainland, she stood at the rail on the upper deck of the boxy white-and-green car ferry, staring at scenery so beautiful it scarcely seemed real. After a few minutes, Steve joined her, resplendent and remote in his dress uniform. He was the very picture of the career officer—square-shouldered and clean-cut, the hem of his perfectly tailored long coat swirling in the brisk wind. They spent a few minutes discussing routine things—banking and the kids' schedules, car maintenance and medical insurance. In those moments, things felt almost normal.

"Grace," he said to her, "I always felt sorry for guys who worried constantly about the home front when they were at sea. I never worry about home because you're in charge. You know how to manage the family without me."

"That's the deal we made," she said. The cold wind caused her eyes to tear up, and she brushed at her cheeks. "I look after the children, the finances, the routine of everyday life. That's not going to change."

"I'm worried now."

"Me, too." Neither of them said anything more. Hurt and anger and sadness lay between them like a fog. They couldn't begin to clear this up. With their marriage in upheaval, the separation might do real damage, and that terrified Grace.

"I'm cold," Grace said, wrapping her coat tighter around her. "I'm going back to the car."

"Wait." He reached for her, but she stepped away. "It's not like I had an affair or did something illegal. How long are you going to make me pay?"

"It's not about making you *pay*. It's about admitting we have problems."

"We do not. Unless you make it that way."

"Oh, Steve. I do wish you'd told me. And I'm sorry that woman never informed you about your…Joshua. But maybe we need to pay attention. This was a wake-up call about our marriage. It's time we made some changes."

"Damn it, now you're using this to hammer away at me about that damned house."

"Using this? You brought up the house, not me." Grace's temper heated. He didn't get it. And until he did, they'd be stuck in a holding pattern.

Someone called Steve's name. It was Mason Crowther, his commanding officer, strolling the sunny deck with his wife and son. Watching them, Grace felt a stab of unholy envy. They looked wonderful together, their smiles as bright and open as the morning sun. They were the all-American family. She was sure they didn't keep secrets from each other.

As they approached, her manners kicked into autopilot. She slipped her hand into the crook of Steve's proffered arm, pasted on a gracious smile and became a creature she had eagerly trained herself to be: the Officer's Wife.

"Steve, Grace, you remember my family," Crowther declared, motioning them over for greetings all around. "Where are those kids of yours?"

"In the snack bar, consuming their second meal of the day," Steve said.

Cory said, "May I be excused?"

Crowther chuckled. "Like we could stop you? Go on. We'll see you in the car, son."

Cory hurried inside, and his parents exchanged a look. "He's told us a lot about Emma," Allison said. "I think he might be smitten."

You all but announced as much to Katie's leadership class, thought Grace, but she held her smile in place. Somehow, they made it through five minutes of idle talk that passed for conversation at cocktail parties. Allison's gracious smile was taut with stress.

That seemed odd, since she was an experienced Navy wife. The Crowthers had been virtually separated for years, ever since Allison insisted on staying here on Whidbey while he took other assignments. A part of Grace admired the woman for her conviction. But she guessed that the role of CAG's wife was a difficult one for Allison. It would be hard for anyone. Though she carried no official title, she was in charge of keeping the air-wing spouses reassured, amused, organized, out of trouble and productive throughout the cruise. Next year, if Steve assumed command, that duty would fall to Grace. The prospect sat like a yoke across her shoulders.

"So how are you doing?" Allison asked, leaning forward and resting her hand on Grace's arm. "I know it must be so dreadfully hard…"

Grace was about to assure her that deployments were routine in her life. She'd be fine; she always was. But then the realization hit her like a blow—Allison wasn't talking about the deployment.

Grace suddenly had trouble breathing. They knew. The Crowthers knew about Joshua Lamont. Of course they did. On a military base, gossip was high-octane fuel. Allison might have even known before Grace. She cringed at the idea of people discussing the situation, speculating, making predictions about her and Steve.

Mercifully, the ferry horn blew, the sound cracking through the morning air. "I'll get the kids down to the car," she said. "Captain, good luck on the cruise. Allison, see you back at home."

Sunlight sparkled on the calm waters of the Sound. Trees clinging to the last of their autumn-bright foliage lined the roadway, and fallen leaves swirled in the ditches. The docks, pier area and secure parking lots were crammed with sailors and families, kids running wild as their parents tried to put on a brave face.

Grace looked around the familiar scene of clutching couples and crying children, and felt a jolt of panic. She was as uncertain as she had been the first time she'd seen Steve off. She was like one of the weeping brides and girlfriends surrounding them, nearly hysterical. This time, she didn't know how to say goodbye.

She steadied herself by concentrating on the kids—Katie, whose chin was already trembling. Emma, looking shockingly grown-up as she scanned the crowd, Brian acting nonchalant. For the kids' sake, Grace tried to act as though this were any other deployment, not one that cracked the foundations of a long-standing marriage.

She noticed a woman about her age, hugging a female sailor no older than Emma. Mother and daughter both wore looks of brave desperation, but then the young sailor broke down and fell sobbing into her mother's arms. Grace found herself reaching for Emma's hand as they navigated their way toward the *Dominion,* its decks already swarming, brows leading up to the carrier crammed with personnel.

The business of getting some five thousand personnel aboard an aircraft carrier was a process of controlled chaos. Grace was always mystified as to why the Navy made the whole operation seem so cumbersome. She always thought of a hundred ways to make it quicker and more efficient, but no one ever asked her, of course.

Some personnel lived on the ship, others had boarded early and pilots would fly their aircraft aboard once the *Dominion* reached open water. Everyone else was here, saying goodbye, offering promises and reassurances, advice and encouragement, pledges of love that would have to sustain families for half a year or more. Grace heard echoes of herself in the words of women all around her: I love you. Take care of yourself. Write to me every day. Be safe, please. Keep yourself safe.

She'd said all those things many times before. She had no idea what to say now.

A TV news van was parked nearby, and a camera crew was scouting around, filming the farewells. Predictably, they were drawn to the dramatic partings—the pregnant women, the burly sailors weeping as they cradled tiny infants. A blond reporter clutched a blocky mike and recited the usual blather about men who go off to sea and the brave families on the home front.

Steve took each child aside to exchange a few final words. It struck her as a shock to see that Brian, her towheaded little boy, was now as tall as his father. The two of them embraced in an awkward hug. Grace tried to imagine what Brian thought of having a half brother all of a sudden. Perhaps, in time, he'd tell her.

Emma and Steve hugged long and hard. He whispered something to her, and she offered him a brave smile and brushed a tear from her eye. Then he moved on to Katie, who sobbed openly as she pushed herself into his arms and clung to him. Steve swayed a little as though someone had hit him. His eyes closed as he pressed his cheek to the top of his daughter's head.

"Daddy, I love you so much," she said. "I don't care what happened all those years ago. I don't care one bit about that."

"Of course you don't, honey," he said. "Thank you for saying so."

The kids knew the drill by now. After their private goodbyes, they stepped back to wait at a respectful distance so Steve and Grace could spend the final moments together. She knew he wouldn't break down in front of his command. She wasn't so sure about herself.

Grace looked at her husband, with the massive bulk of the carrier rearing behind him, preparing to swallow him up. She felt confused and disoriented. She had been telling him goodbye for years; she ought to be good at it. But this occasion held a special sort of torment.

Dry-eyed, she faced a moment of clarity—about Steve, their marriage, herself. The arrival of Joshua Lamont was a mirror, as unforgiving as the dressing-room mirror with its stark lighting and inescapable angles. She was forced to see the truth: she and Steve had drifted apart long before she found out about his deception.

He hugged her tight against him, and she shut her eyes, absorbing the smell and the feel of him. He was her husband and she loved him, but now she wondered if love was powerful enough to keep them together. The thought paralyzed her.

Nothing felt right. For the first time she could remember, she was the first to step back from their embrace.

He must have noticed the shift, at least on some level, for as he gazed down at her, his eyes were troubled. "I screwed up, okay? I'm sorry," he said, echoing his words of this morning. "One thing, Grace. I screwed up on one thing."

His willful ignorance and the edge in his voice annoyed her. Did he really not get it? Didn't he ever feel the discontent seeping through their marriage? Didn't he see that she'd arrived at the middle of her life and had no idea how she'd gotten there?

She couldn't believe he thought that "one thing" was the real problem. But neither could she launch into the discussion now. There was no time to sort out all the old and painful history, or to figure out what to do about it. She hated that she had to wait, that her life had to be on hold until the end of the cruise.

She and Steve stared at each other, both hurt and damaged. The crowd began to separate as sailors headed for the boat. "Listen," said Steve, "I'll call you from the satellite phone on the boat and we can talk about this some more."

"No," she said. She couldn't explain it, but she was afraid somehow that dealing with a marital crisis from half a world away might do more harm than good. "I don't think that's such a good idea."

"What, you don't want me to call?" He looked at her as if she'd lost her mind.

"I don't know. Call the kids."

"I always call the kids. I send them e-mails every day."

"Yes."

"Gracie, don't shut me out."

"I'm not. But I'm also not going to put my life on ice until you get back."

"What's that supposed to—"

A loudspeaker ordered guests to leave the carrier, and the crowd on the pier started to thin. The announcement always startled Grace no matter how many times she heard it. The whistle meant one last hug, one last "I love you," one last look at a beloved face you wouldn't see for half a year. One last chance to battle the terrible, silent thought that hid in everyone's heart: he might never come back.

His fingers stroked her cheek. He leaned down and kissed the place where his hand had been, and then he kissed her lips. She shut her eyes and memorized that kiss.

"Bye, Gracie," he said.

"Take care of yourself," she said. This was one thing she could say and absolutely mean it. "Be safe. Please—"

The wind picked up and a warning whistle blew.

"I have to go," he said, glancing over his shoulder. Admiral McFly was waiting for the top officers to report for ceremonial farewells.

"Yes."

"Grace—"

The loudspeakers crackled a final advisory. Steve put on his cap and gloves, waved at the kids, then picked up his seabag and went to report to the Admiral.

Once that was done and McFly headed for his sleek black sedan, Steve went to the ship. He lifted one gloved hand in farewell, and for a moment his splayed fingers looked like a white star in the crisp blue sky. Then he slung his bag over his shoulder and walked across the black macadam surface of the pier. He headed for the officers' accommodation brow on the starboard side, under the towering island. The huge open mouth of the carrier waited to swallow him up.

Grace didn't dare move a muscle, because the slightest movement would cause her to melt. All around her, people wept and yelled and waved scarves and hats. A child screamed for her mother.

Grace's gaze clung to Steve. No matter how huge the mass of sailors and officers, he was always apparent to her. She recognized the wholly unique way he comported himself, the stride that belonged to him and only him. She knew just when he would pause, turn and wave his cap in the air.

Then he disappeared from view.

And somehow, Grace managed to move. "Okay?" she asked the kids.

They nodded, though Katie still wept into her sleeve, and the four of them headed toward the car.

CHAPTER TWENTY

"You're scheduled to take your physical aptitude exam for the Academy today," Emma reminded Brian as he pulled into a parking space in the high school student lot adjacent to the athletics complex. "In fifteen minutes, as a matter of fact."

"How do you know that, Miss Nosy?"

"Cory's taking his today, so I figured you'd be in the same group."

"Forget it. I'm not going." He yanked the truck into Park.

The woods surrounding the school were murky with shadows. As the year slid toward winter, the days had grown depressingly short. This far north, the sun didn't rise until after eight in the morning, and then it set before four. Today, with the rain falling thick and straight, she couldn't remember if it had risen at all.

Emma studied her brother's profile. He was scowling as he rifled through his duffel bag.

"It's part of the application procedure," she said. "You can't skip it."

"Watch me."

"What's the big deal? Are you afraid you'll flunk?" She laughed incredulously. "Cory told me what was on the test. A standing broad jump. Chin-ups, a shuttle run, some push-ups and a bas-

204

ketball throw. What's the big deal? You can do that stuff in your sleep. Shoot, I bet even I can do it."

"Then do it."

"Oh, come on, Brian. Why won't you take the test?"

"Because it's stupid. It's a waste of time. I told you, I'm not going to the Naval Academy. I've told everybody that, but no one believes me."

"I believe you," she said. "But you should finish the application. At least get the appointment so you'll have that option. You don't have to make up your mind yet."

"I've made up my mind. I'm not going and I refuse to waste my time with this stupid application."

She shook her head. "I'm not the one who scheduled the test. You did. You can't stand up your ALO."

The admissions liaison officer was in charge of guiding each candidate through the maze of application requirements. He was usually an active or retired Naval officer whose favor often made the difference between getting in and getting rejected. It was smart to stay in his good graces.

"I didn't schedule anything," Brian claimed. "I got a letter telling me to show up in the gym this afternoon with the other candidates. Big deal. He won't even notice I'm not there."

His hostility startled her. He was usually so easygoing. "Brian—"

"I'm going to be late for a Key Club meeting," he snapped, pushing open the car door. "Look, if you're so damned concerned about appointments to the Naval Academy, you go take the stupid test." He shoved a large manila envelope into her lap. "Here's all the paperwork. Go for it. Knock yourself out."

After he left, she sat for a few minutes by herself. She was supposed to be on her way to tennis practice. She was all suited up under her sweats, but didn't relish a dash through the rain across the athletics complex.

She was annoyed at Brian, but she also felt a reluctant admiration for him. At least he knew his own mind, which was more than she could say for herself.

She reached up and turned on the dome light of the truck. While the rain beat down on the hood, she studied the return address on Brian's envelope. Annapolis, Maryland. It sounded so important. So…auspicious. It was a historic site, the place where the nation's leaders were made. How could Brian not want to go there?

She took out the information booklet and application materials, and was not surprised to see that Brian had not made one single mark on anything. He hadn't bubbled in his personal information, hadn't written his responses to any of the questions. The dumb-ass. This was possibly the coolest future in the world, and he wasn't even interested.

She skimmed the letter from the ALO. It was a form letter, confirming the scheduled physical aptitude test in the gym today. In five minutes, in fact. Her gaze fell on the name of the ALO, and she dropped the packet in her lap, gasping with shock. Then she picked up the letter and stared some more.

"My God," she whispered. "No wonder he's skipping out on the test."

CHAPTER TWENTY-ONE

Totally New Totally You Fitness Studio
Client Information Form

Name:	Grace McAllen Bennett
Address:	820 Intruder Drive, Whidbey NAS, WA
Phone/Fax/E-mail:	360-555-3117 Grace@GraceUnderPressure.com
Age:	39
Sex:	not for another six months, at least
Height:	5'6"
Weight:	140
Actual Weight:	like I'd admit this
Problem Areas of Your Physique:	~~stomach thighs hips arms~~ From the neck down
Limitations:	see attached five-page memo
Goals:	

Grace glared at the pale blue form on the clipboard. Why did they need to know all this nonsense, anyway? Goals? Who were they kidding?

She sneaked a glance at the other four women in the lobby of the fitness studio. All of them were busily filling out their forms, probably with lofty and admirable goals, like increasing their bone density or running a marathon to raise funds for cancer research. They all looked fitter and thinner than Grace. The whole world was fitter and thinner than Grace.

In the weeks since Steve's deployment, she had not come to any conclusion or determination about the state of her marriage. But it occurred to her that there was one thing she could change—her life. Launching the relocation service was only the beginning. She wanted to launch her*self.*

Her secure world had turned into a dangerous place. It was up to Grace to create her own safe haven. The idea didn't seem terribly radical; women did this every day.

But for Grace it was a huge step.

The day before, she had gone for her annual physical to her new doctor on the Navy base. She'd dared to hope he'd look in her mouth like a horse trader and declare there was some mistake, that she couldn't possibly be that age. Or that weight.

Instead, he'd heartlessly put the accurate numbers on her chart—in triplicate.

His assessment confirmed the ugly truth she'd glimpsed in the dressing-room mirror that day. There was a huge difference between who she was and how she pictured herself. The way Grace saw it, she had fallen asleep about the time Katie was born, and she'd been on autopilot ever since. And somehow, without her noticing it, a dowdy, middle-aged woman had taken up residence in her body. In her life.

Panicked by the sneak attack of time and gravity, she'd been dieting for weeks, but according to the physician's atomically calibrated scales, it wasn't working. Up until recent years, she'd been lucky, favored with a cooperative metabolism and a decent level of natural fitness. But now gravity was at work, and, finally, for the first time in her life, Grace admitted that she needed help with something.

Her form was still blank in the Goals section. She had so much—an exciting life, a wonderful family—that it seemed selfish to want more. Yet she wanted so much more that it scared her. Steve's deception was a disaster, yes. But it had a curiously liberating effect on her. Instead of waiting around to see what would happen next in his career, she intended to make things happen for herself. She was joining the fitness class in hopes of finding her way back to her favorite jeans, or maybe even a swimsuit. But more than that, she wanted to find a way back to herself, to rediscover the dreams she'd put aside long ago and to find out if, after all this time, they could still come true.

She filled out the rest of the paperwork. After signing the liability disclaimer, she frowned at the paragraph of legalese. "I don't see a Do Not Resuscitate order," she muttered.

The receptionist, a teenage redhead, took the clipboard from her. "You must be new," she said.

"That's right."

The teenager glanced at the blue form. "Welcome, Grace." Her brow puckered in a frown. "Grace Bennett, is it?"

"That's me." Maybe the girl was one of the kids' classmates.

"We'll be starting in just a few minutes."

Grace wandered into the studio, a nightmare fun house of mirrors. Great. Just what she needed. A three-hundred-sixty-degree view of her flaws. A few other women were milling around, sipping water from Nalgene bottles and doing stretching exercises. They wore yoga pants or spandex bike shorts and bra tops worthy of Brandy Chastain. Grace suddenly felt self-conscious in her outdated leggings, Go Navy T-shirt and shabby Reeboks.

The women were setting up molded plastic benches with rubber tops. They weren't rude, exactly, but they had that earnest, humorless standoffishness Grace associated, rightly or wrongly, with Pacific Northwest women. "Hi," she said. "This is my first time here. I'm Grace."

"You'll need one of these benches," said one woman. "Later,

we'll get out the hand weights and resistance bands." She gestured at a shelf stuffed with medieval-looking equipment that would not be out of place in a torture chamber.

Then another woman arrived, and Grace was delighted to see a familiar face. "Patricia! How are you doing?"

Patricia beamed at her. She looked more relaxed than the uncertain, stressed-out new bride Grace had met last fall. "I'm fine. I don't know what I would have done without you, Grace. Thanks for helping me with the move."

"Thanks for the reference. I have two clients now. Not many, but it's a start."

"I'm trying my best to get used to being alone." Her hand drifted over her lower abdomen in a universal gesture that all women understood. "Or maybe I'm not so alone."

"Really? And it's okay for you to exercise?"

"Modified. The doctor encourages it, actually, since I was already active before I got pregnant."

The news of a pregnancy caught one of the other women's attention. She introduced herself as Radha Mitali. "I'm a doula," she said.

Grace wasn't sure whether she should console or congratulate her. Patricia said, "A what?"

"A doula. I give emotional support to women in labor," Radha explained.

"Really?" Patricia looked intrigued. "I wonder if my insurance covers that."

"I also teach a class in Tantric sex," Radha added.

"I wonder if *my* insurance covers that," Grace murmured.

Two other women joined them. One of them looked familiar to Grace. "Do you work for Island Realty?" she asked.

"You bet. Marilyn Audleman."

"I've seen your picture on a For Sale sign."

"I hope it didn't stay there for long. This is Arlene Kusik, my associate."

"Welcome to the class. I think you'll be glad you joined. Before you know it, you'll have arms like Demi Moore's."

"What, do you know her surgeon?"

Marilyn looked toward the door. "There you are, Stan. Come and meet Grace and Patricia." Grace was surprised to see a balding, middle-aged man in the class. He seemed a little bashful. "I'm trying to get in shape so I can dance at my daughter's wedding," he said.

"What kind of dancing requires athletic training?"

He grinned. "My tux is twenty years old, and I'm hoping to fit into it again. This is actually a surprise for my wife."

"Your wife's a lucky woman," said Grace. But then she completely lost her train of thought as another man arrived. He was a golden-haired god in nylon athletic shorts and tank top.

Grace blinked and nudged Patricia. "We're not in Kansas anymore."

"That's Dante Romano," Marilyn said, motioning him over.

He shook back his shoulder-length blond hair and offered his hand first to Patricia, then Grace. "It is an honor to meet you."

"Dante's a mountain guide," Arlene said.

"I specialize in summiting Mount Rainier," he added.

That accent, thought Grace, feeling light-headed. And that physique. His body was so tight, so smooth, he resembled a shrink-wrapped deli ham.

"This class is excellent for improving the stamina," he said.

Stamina? Grace hadn't thought about that. She had no stamina to speak of. Maybe she shouldn't have come here. Maybe she should leave. Then she checked out Dante again. Under the thin muscle shirt, his superhero pecs rippled.

Fine. She was definitely staying for the show.

"Okay, people, let's get moving." The teenage receptionist entered the studio, clapping her hands as she slipped a CD in the stereo. "I'm Lauren Stanton, and I'm here to get you motivated!" She shut the door to the studio, cutting off the escape route.

That was Lauren Stanton? Grace stared as she shuffled over to her step-up bench. With her boundless energy, playful smile and daring short red hair, Lauren didn't look any older than Emma. Her breasts were so perky they defied gravity.

She seemed to favor mediocre, beat-heavy music. "Get excited, people," she exhorted, leading the class in some basic moves. "This is your day!" She was a relentlessly cheerful instructor, calling encouragement from the front of the room.

Grace tried to follow the steps. Surprisingly, it wasn't all that hard. Hey, she thought, pleased with herself. I can do this. Right basic. Left basic. Up and down and over the top. She started thinking about what to fix for dinner. Within a couple of minutes, she felt winded but doggedly carried on, her pride keeping her from stopping. Sweat rolled down her face. Then, mercifully, Lauren slowed down and stepped side to side.

That wasn't so bad, Grace decided, proud of herself. Stamina, she thought, sneaking a glance at Dante.

Lauren lightly clapped her hands. "Okay, warm-up's over. Let's get to work."

Warm-up? That was a warm-up? Grace was already out of breath.

No one seemed to notice. Lauren pressed the remote control, the beat accelerated and the basics got more complicated. Within minutes, the simple routine became endless and confusing, filled with harrowing hazards like backward dance steps, up-and-over moves.

Grace figured she was burning twice as many calories simply by scrambling to catch up, so maybe this was working. But halfway through the routine, she started to question her sanity. What was she doing here, anyway, making a fool of herself in front of strangers and ham-boy? This was not like her at all. She was the sort of person who liked easy things. She liked books and movies that entertained her. She liked fixing dinners with three ingredients. Automatic transmission. Internet shopping.

All easy things, but this? This was going to be hard. Maybe impossible. She had not done anything deliberately physical since nailing Harvey Lindbloom in a dodgeball game in the fifth grade. Why on earth would she subject herself to this?

Lauren Stanton didn't seem to think it was hard at all. She kept going, the Energizer Bunny without the drum. "How're we all doing?" she shouted over the music.

Grace had a vision of herself surrounded by EMS technicians. *She's coding.*

"Let's take it up a notch," chirped Lauren.

Get the paddles!

The music's unrelenting drumbeat pounded in her head. The tune switched to a painful pop perversion of a Dire Straits classic.

Charge to 360. Clear!

"Let's up the intensity here, ladies and gentlemen. Let's see some power moves." She hit the remote control, launching a Spice Girls recording from a collection of Golden Oldies. Then she sprang into the air and leaped two-footed onto the bench.

Grace looked for the tunnel of light. Wasn't that what you were supposed to see when you were about to die? The light and the warmth, the purity of all-encompassing love? The only thing that encompassed Grace at the moment was sweat. Gallons of it. She was drowning in her own sweat. Who knew that innocent little step-up platform and a Backstreet Boys mix could be so lethal?

And then a miracle occurred. Lauren announced the start of "cooldown," slowing at last to an easy side-to-side step, arms swinging in rhythmic strokes.

Grace glanced at the clock. She was far from cool. Her vision swam; then she wiped the sweat out of her eyes. Forty-five minutes of aerobics, and she was still vertical.

The patient would live.

CHAPTER TWENTY-TWO

The familiar smell of floor wax and stale sweat enveloped Josh as he stepped into the high school gymnasium. He was missing an afternoon of training, but this was one duty he would not shirk. Nine years ago, an ALO from the Naval Academy had changed his life. He'd never forgotten that. The chance to help a young person appealed to him deeply. He loved the Navy, he loved kids, and he considered this a privilege.

He felt conspicuous in full uniform. Still, he knew it was important to look a certain way when meeting candidates for the Academy. Today he planned to conduct a general session and then administer the Academy's rigorous admissions physical aptitude exam to his charges.

He had six packets in his briefcase, one for each student. He had just received the briefings on his candidates and hadn't had time to read them thoroughly, but even without looking, he knew the odds were stacked against them. The Naval Academy was harder to get into than the Ivy League, and the application process was designed to eliminate all but the most promising young people.

Five of the students were waiting for him, standing around the gym with hands on hips, shuffling their feet on the gleaming floor. They were suited up in shorts and T-shirts. When they spotted him, they fell silent and snapped to attention.

All men, he saw. At least four of them appeared to be decent athletes. But Josh knew from experience that it took more than athletic skill, and he explained as much in his opening remarks. "When I was a senior like you guys," he said, "I thought I was all that. I had high grades, good test scores, letters in lacrosse and basketball. Teachers wrote glowing recommendations for me. How many of you men have all that going for you?"

One hand shot up. Three others lifted more tentatively.

"That's good. But you know what? It isn't enough. The person you are on paper is only the beginning of what the Academy is looking for. You have to want it so bad you dream about it at night. You have to be willing to go against your friends and your advisers and all those sports recruiters offering you a free ride just to play for four years."

He scanned their faces. "How'm I doing?" They nodded, so he kept going. "Good. So I'm here to make sure you all have your applications in order." He parked his briefcase on the bottom set of bleachers folded against the wall. "I'll meet with you each individually at some point after the fitness test. For now, let's get started." He glanced at his sheet. "Adams."

"Sir." A short, muscle-bound boy stepped forward. A wrestler, Josh guessed.

"Bennett." It felt strange, saying the name. He hadn't read the candidate's file yet, but he knew this would be Steve Bennett's kid. He tensed with curiosity, wondering which boy it was. But they all just looked at one another.

"Bennett's not here," said the biggest of the boys, a football player with the clean-cut looks of a recruiting-poster model.

Josh didn't know what to make of that, so he moved on. "Crowther."

"Present, sir." The recruitment poster boy squared his shoulders. He wore a gray jersey and brand-new Nikes. This was the CAG's only son. He looked the part.

Josh nodded. "Johnson."

"Sir." The slim, shy-looking black kid stepped forward.

"Lopez."

"Sir." His mother had probably dressed him, Josh observed. He was color-coordinated from sweats and jacket to high-top sneakers. Athletic ability looked to be nil.

"Pinchot," he said, nodding to the last boy, whose height and innate grace marked him as a basketball player.

"Yes, sir."

Josh checked his watch. In about thirty seconds, Bennett would be officially late. That would go on his report to the office of admissions.

"I'm glad to see you all suited up," he said, fitting a set of printed PAE forms into his clipboard. "We need to get started." He picked up Bennett's folder and checked his watch again. It was going to look bad if Bennett's son had to be cited for tardiness. But then again, how would it look if he bent the rules for the kid?

Five seconds to go. Four...

"So," he said. "It looks like Bennett's a no-show. Let's get—"

"Excuse me." A tall blond girl entered the gym.

From the corner of his eye, Josh saw the boys all straighten up.

"Miss," he said. "We're busy here—"

"I'm Emma Bennett," she blurted out, fixing him with an intense stare. Her eyes were as blue as the sea. As blue as...his. He remembered seeing the MPs bring a teenager home to Bennett's house that night at the end of summer. Could it have been this one?

Josh didn't betray a thing. He couldn't say a word, of course. Their relationship was for Steve Bennett to disclose—or not. "Bennett," he said, leveling his gaze at her. "We just about gave up on you."

"Actually, sir, I—"

"We're running late," he snapped. "Fall in."

"But I'm not here for the test. I just came to tell you—"

"Damn it, I said fall in," Josh barked, knowing in his gut he'd better treat her as he'd treat any candidate. "Or are you special?"

She froze and glared at him. Something—a challenge?—gleamed in her eyes. Then, with unhurried grace, she began to move, never taking her eyes off him. She was like a queen, he thought, dropping her backpack on the sidelines and shrugging out of her jacket. Then with an attention-getting flourish, she rolled her sweatpants down to reveal a pair of tennis shorts.

Behind Josh, one of the boys groaned softly. Josh felt an unexpected jolt of protectiveness. "Can it, men," he muttered under his breath. Louder, he said, "Hurry up, Bennett."

"The only reason I came here is to tell you—"

"Shut up and fall in."

She held her head at a haughty angle as she joined the gaping boys. Crowther whispered something to her, and she shrugged and looked away. Josh's head was spinning. What the hell was going on? He wondered how much she knew. Had Bennett told his family? Was that why this girl acted so hostile?

He forced himself to concentrate on the test. This was these kids' future, and he owed it to them to do a good job. He put them through their paces, noting their scores on the official forms that would be sent to the Academy. They had to pass a series of tests—push-ups, throwing, running, jumping. Four of the men did fine or better, especially Crowther, who didn't even break a sweat. Lopez was a problem. When he failed the third exercise, he left in a huff of fury and tears. Josh made no comment as he filled out the form.

The big surprise was Emma Bennett. She surpassed the women's standards on every test. He was about to congratulate her when he noticed that she was suspended from the high bar in the requisite flexed-arm hang, a challenging exercise that disqualified more than half of the female candidates. Her body was trembling.

"What are you doing, Bennett?" he demanded.

"Counting."

He glanced at his stopwatch. "You've been up there for almost a minute. Don't you know the standards?"

"No."

"Well, you can let go, Bennett. You only had to hang on for twelve seconds."

She let go of the bar and dropped to the mat, brushing the palms of her hands together. She rotated her shoulders, and then, with that same queenly attitude, she joined the other candidates on the sidelines. Josh thanked them all for coming and encouraged each of them to do their best on the other parts of the application.

"Any questions?" he asked.

They stood in silence.

"Good. I'll get your PAEs mailed off to the Academy, then. I'll also be scheduling an interview with each of you in the coming weeks. You'll also need to submit materials to Senators Murray and Cantwell, and to Representative Larsen because you need a nomination from a member of Congress. I remind you that this is the toughest institution in the country to get into. Forget Harvard, Stanford, Georgetown. The Academy's standards are higher, because they're looking for the whole package—intelligence, leadership qualities, athletic ability, raw talent. And commitment—that's huge." He handed out copies of their test results. "You're dismissed."

They shuffled around with book bags and backpacks. Josh caught Emma's eye. "Miss Bennett, may I speak with you a moment?"

She regarded him coolly, then shrugged and waited while the others left.

"You did a good job today, Bennett," he said. "How are you coming on the rest of the application?"

"I haven't sent anything in," she said.

"Is there a problem?"

She gave a brief, sarcastic laugh.

"What's the matter, Bennett?"

"Yeah. There's a problem. I'm not a candidate."

"Judging by your performance on the PAE, you are."

"You don't even know me. What if I have crappy grades and test scores?"

"You don't." He was bluffing, but the look on her face told him he was right. "What's your GPA?"

"I have a 3.8 grade point average."

That was well above the minimum requirement. "What about your scores?"

"They were 1425 combined on the SAT."

"So what's the trouble?"

She aimed a glare at the stack of files on the bench. "Didn't you read those?"

"I just received them this morning."

"Well, if you'd bothered to look, you'd see that I'm not a candidate."

He found the file marked Bennett and opened it. "You have a brother."

"A twin brother. He's the applicant, not me."

"So why didn't he show up today?"

"I'm his sister, not his keeper." The edge in her voice cut deep.

"Then why'd you come here?" he asked. "Why did you take the test?"

"It's not like you gave me a choice. You just kept barking at me."

"So you're saying you're not interested."

"Bingo," she said, and picked up her backpack. With a haughty toss of her head, she started toward the door.

"Why not?" he demanded loudly.

She stopped and turned back. "What?"

"Why aren't you an applicant?"

For the first time, she seemed at a loss. "I guess…I just never thought about it."

"You should think about it."

Maybe it was a trick of the light, or maybe not, but just for a moment, inspiration lit her face. Josh felt a weird connection with the belligerent girl he'd just met. It was like looking in a mirror, seeing his own hopes and fears and dreams.

Then the moment ended and open hostility burned in her eyes. "Why? So I can be just like you?" she snapped, and then rushed out of the gym.

She knew. He sprinted after her through the heavy doors of the gym. The rain had stopped, leaving a damp terrain under a sullen sky.

"Bennett," he said.

Halfway to the athletic field, she stopped and turned back, looking at him over her shoulder.

He held out a computer form. "You'll need this copy of your PAE."

She took it from him but didn't look at it. She was staring at him. The sense of shock and unreality that had gripped him ever since he saw the name on his list intensified. He used to long for brothers and sisters when he was growing up. He was convinced a sibling or two would fill the lonely days of his childhood with a sense of belonging he'd never quite found as an only child.

And here she was, a sister.

"I have to go," she said, and hurried away.

He quickened his pace and fell into step with her. "You did great, Bennett," he said. "I'm not just saying that. And I don't want you to withdraw from applying because of me."

"I told you. My brother's the candidate, not me. Brian's the one who's supposed to be applying, only he couldn't make it today. But he's a real good athlete, way better than me—"

"Did he send you to tell me that?"

She stopped walking and glared at him full on, with a gaze as steady as the horizon. "No. I think you can probably guess the reason for his absence. *Sir.*" She made the courtesy sound like an insult. "Just because you decided to show up out of the blue doesn't mean a thing. It's not his fault that woman left him and never bothered to tell him she had his son, so don't think you're going to make us feel bad about a damned thing." Her voice rose steadily through the tirade and cracked when she burst into tears.

Josh stood there at a total loss, horrified by the tears and unexpectedly moved by this stranger who was his sister. "Hey, I'm not out to make any trouble. I swear it. The only reason I went to see your father is that I'm going to be flying in his air wing."

She blotted her face with the sleeve of her sweatshirt. "I didn't think I'd be very upset about this."

"I didn't want to upset anyone. The man who raised me—he was my father, not Steve Bennett."

She was quiet for a long time. Then she said, "You look just like him."

He nodded and gazed out at the field where the football team was assembled and practicing hard, looking like ghosts in the white glow of the misty stadium lights. "I can't do much about that. Look, Emma," he said, using her given name for the first time. "My parents were great. I never felt like I needed a thing from my birth father."

"Did you join the Navy because of him?"

"No. I did it because of me."

"My dad always wanted a son in the Navy."

"I'm not his son. But you know what? I bet he'd be just as glad to have a daughter in the Navy."

She shook her head. "It's not going to happen."

"You'd make a hell of a midshipman, Emma."

"How do you know?"

"I spent four years of my life there. I know what it takes. I bet you've got that."

"What if I don't want to go into the Navy?"

"Then you won't. You don't make your commitment to service until the beginning of your third year at the Academy. Give it a shot." He could see her waver. Her big blue eyes hid nothing. "You should give yourself this option, Emma. Because you never know."

She stood still in the gathering dark. Her breath made tiny clouds in the cool air. The clash and crunch of the practicing football team, interspersed with the coach's whistle, sounded hollow in the silence.

"Emma?" he prompted.

"You have to swear you won't say anything. To anyone."

"About you applying to the Naval Academy?"

"Yes."

"Why?"

"It just seems so weird. And besides, I don't want to disappoint my parents if I don't get in."

"That's not going to happen." Josh knew in his bones that she'd make it.

"I also don't want to feel obligated to go if I'm offered an appointment."

Josh remembered the battles he had had with his parents over college when he was her age. Maybe it was that way in most families. "Okay, you have my word."

CHAPTER TWENTY-THREE

It felt strange to be calling Cissy from shipboard, Steve thought as he dialed the Atlanta number. Twenty-six years ago no sailor, not even an officer, had phone privileges. Now, thanks to satellite technology, he could contact anyone in the world.

Even his ex-wife.

He knew he had to make this call. From the moment he shoved his bag under his rack and set out the family pictures, he'd been overcome by a terrible, unsettled feeling that haunted him along with images of the son he didn't know. He fingered his St. Christopher medal through three rings.

"Hello?"

"Is this Cissy King...Lamont?"

A pause. "Stephen? Oh, my stars, you sound exactly the same." She spoke in a honeyed voice he'd never quite forgotten. He pictured her in her Atlanta tract mansion, widowed too young by a man who had given her everything, including a reason to keep Steve's son from him.

"Joshua Lamont gave me your number."

"Yes, he said the two of you met. Stephen—"

"Cissy, goddamn it. Why didn't you tell me?"

"Lord, I'd nearly forgotten that temper," she said.

"Oh. Excuse me for feeling put out that you had my child and never told me."

Another pause, so long he thought the connection might have gone bad.

"Cissy?"

"I was young and completely on my own," she confessed with disarming honesty. "Also terrified. I imagined raising a baby all alone, and I couldn't see myself doing that. I knew I needed a full-time husband."

It was a shame she hadn't made that discovery before marrying him.

"You didn't stay young and on your own forever," he pointed out. "He's twenty-six years old, Cissy. In all that time, it never occurred to you to pick up the phone?"

"I was afraid of you, Stephen," she admitted. "Afraid you would try to share custody of our child."

"Of course I would have. What's scary about a man wanting to take responsibility for his child?"

"I had already found that in Grant and would have fought giving you any rights at all. I thought it was kinder to walk away, to make a clean break of it and let both of us start new lives."

"It was a bad call," he told her. "You had no right to take the decision away from me."

"I'm sorry, Stephen. It was a terrible mistake to hide this, but Josh was such a happy child, and Grant such a good father. I can't turn back the clock any more than you can. All we can do is go on from here, support Josh and let him find his own way."

The whir and crash of the ship's catapult drowned out his reply, which was probably for the best. As underhanded as she was, she didn't deserve to be called *that*.

"...when he joins the Sparhawks squadron in your air wing," she was saying when the thunder passed.

"What?"

"He's going to be deployed before long," she said. "I guess I'm hoping you'll watch out for him."

Great. Now that he was grown and her husband was gone, Steve got a shot at the kid. "It's my job to watch out for every man and woman under my command."

A pause. "All right. That wasn't fair."

After twenty-six years, she was trying to be fair?

"And Stephen?"

"Yeah?"

"I just wanted to say…you sound good. You sound really good."

Jesus. Was she flirting with him? Was the woman completely insane?

"Goodbye, Cissy." He couldn't get off the line fast enough. It was cold on the ship, but he'd broken out in a sweat. Cissy King, his first love. She had been beautiful and passionate, bringing laughter to his days and comfort to his nights. He thought their love was strong enough to sustain them through anything life had to offer, that they'd be together forever.

Cissy's forever lasted less than six months. Everything Steve endured in basic training paled in comparison to the pain of reading her Dear John letter and seeing the divorce decree. He'd been a different man after that. More driven. Less trusting. Ruthlessly ambitious.

Grace had been an unasked-for miracle. She probably didn't know it, but she'd saved him from turning to stone. She'd softened his edges, taught him to laugh again, to love more deeply than he'd ever thought possible.

And now he was on the verge of losing her, too. In the same way he'd been oblivious to Cissy's discontent, he'd been blind to Grace's. She claimed that even before Josh arrived, she'd been unhappy, and he simply hadn't seen it. He dismissed her efforts to make some changes when he should have been discussing them with her. But instead, he chose not to notice. Why hadn't he paid closer attention? Why hadn't he listened better? That night she told him she thought she was fat, that she was worried about turning forty, he'd brushed off her concern and sweet-talked her into bed. How many other times had he done that?

Grace sat at her computer and wrote her now-customary neutral e-mail about the kids to Steve. They had their troubles, but she couldn't simply throw away the habits of a twenty-year marriage. Despite their dispute, they shared three children, a past she cherished and a problematic future. She felt obligated to keep some kind of continuity until he returned.

But what she really wanted to do was to tell him everything—about how well her business was going, about the professional association and the fitness class she'd joined, about the house she still hoped to buy.

She felt vulnerable since the impregnable fortress of her marriage had been breached. Its foundations had been eroding in unseen places. There was no ignoring the weakened state of their relationship.

She hadn't realized that the effort of shoring up the eroded places was emptying her out. She used to believe she and Steve were equally committed to their relationship. Now she realized that from the very start, it had been lopsided. She gave a hundred percent; he held things back. And in the meantime, she'd discovered that she wanted her own success, her own growth.

Seized by nervous energy, she pushed back from the computer. She needed to do something physical. Maybe it was time to tackle the bedroom closet. Since they'd moved in last summer, she hadn't gotten around to dragging out her winter clothes.

The prospect was disheartening. She resisted the act of integrating herself into this house. She didn't want to be here, didn't want this to be her closet. She didn't belong here anymore. The Navy had been her home for years. Living on base gave her a place to belong, a place of security. Now it was a bad fit, like the old outfits in her closet.

But Grace was a realist. She was a businesswoman, she had to pay attention to the way she dressed. There were probably outfits still packed away that she'd forgotten about. She had yet to find her favorite heather-gray sweater.

She dragged a step stool into the bedroom and gave the closest moving box a small tug. The box split open at the seams, and a flurry of papers and magazines poured down to the floor.

"Oh, we're off to a great start," Grace muttered under her breath. She climbed down from the stool and dropped to her knees on the floor. She spread her arms to collect the flotsam and jetsam of the past that had spilled out of the box.

At first she didn't recognize the neatly labeled files and folders, the photographs, the colorful clippings and folded articles. Then she realized what they were: a collection of dreams. Inspired by a scrapbook workshop for officers' wives, she had started the project. She'd never gotten around to creating the album, but over the years she had torn out pictures of hometowns, houses, neighbors who looked as though they'd known one another for years. She used to visualize herself as part of a picture like that.

She shuffled through photographs of herself and Steve and the kids. Time had faded the colors, but their essential significance still shone through. She found a shot of herself as a new bride, laughing as she held Steve's arm. She studied the brightness in the young woman's eyes, the strength and energy in her body. Then she looked at the soft, fatigued woman in the mirror and could not reconcile the two.

Despair bubbled up and crested, and then the phone rang. It was her business line, recently installed.

Saved by the bell. She rushed to the study and picked up. "Grace Bennett."

"I need you, Grace. Now."

She pretended not to feel a little thrill of heat. "What's the matter, Mr. Cameron?"

"Ross. I keep telling you to call me Ross."

Ross Cameron, her first and best client, occupied more and more of her time and attention lately. His frequent, unfailingly pleasant phone calls and the upbeat tone of his e-mails had become a regular part of her day. His promptness at paying for her services had made her company viable.

Transferring him, his business and staff cross-country gave her a glimpse into his world. She caught herself daydreaming about who he was, building the image from facts she gleaned in the course of her work. He was single and successful. The people who worked for him were loyal and enthusiastic. He traveled overseas, had inherited his grandmother's collection of Ludwig Moser glass, owned two kayaks, bought his shoes in Italy and drove a vintage red MG. He played amateur hockey and bought season tickets to the Cubs.

Now his warm voice on the phone brought her own discontent into sharp focus. "What can I do for you?" she asked.

"My CFO wants her kids to attend a Waldorf school." He sounded tense; maybe he was pacing the room, raking his hand through his hair. "She's making noises like she won't be moving with the company."

"Look, Mr. Cameron—"

"Ross."

"Don't worry about a thing. I have a service partner who specializes in educational consulting. She'll find the right school. I'll send you a list." She wandered with the cordless phone back to the bedroom and looked at the mess on the floor. "I'll make sure it gets done."

"Really?"

"I promise."

"Why does everything seem easier after I talk to you?"

She smiled and realized she was blushing. He intrigued her. And she could not deny that she felt a beat of forbidden attraction. To a man she'd never met. How sick was that?

"No idea," she said. "If I knew how to simplify my own life, believe me, I'd do it."

"What's the matter with your life?"

"Aside from my twins leaving home and me turning forty?" She laughed, hoping he'd think she really was joking.

"Forty." He gave a low whistle. "When's your birthday?"

"Why do you ask?"

"I need to mark my calendar so I know when the world is coming to an end."

She laughed again, but she told him the date.

"You sound frustrated."

I'm not. She tried to say the words, but they wouldn't come out. Holding the phone to her cheek, she stared at her image in the mirror. She'd lost herself in the worst possible way. She'd allowed her dreams to fade away. Here, in the middle of her life, she realized that she'd been slowly disappearing. Why had she never noticed that before?

"Grace?"

"Yes?"

"What's on your mind?"

My husband lied to me. He never told me about his first marriage. But she didn't say that, either. Because in the middle of the thought, it hit her. Steve wasn't the cause of her unhappiness, and he couldn't fix it. He just happened to break the news to her at the same time her discontent surfaced.

Ross was talking, but she scarcely heard him. The realization drummed through her. Her thoughts were focused on things she hadn't considered in years. Shaken awake, she squared her shoulders and stared directly into the mirror. And smiled at herself.

"Ross." Oh, it felt good to say his name. "I'm sorry to cut this short, but I have to go."

"So soon?"

"I just thought of something I have to do."

"This thing's still for sale?" Katie asked, peering through the windshield at the house on Ocean View Drive. "Didn't we look at this, like, last summer?"

"Yep."

"It was kind of funky," Emma said. "Ugly kitchen."

"Remember the view, though?" Grace pulled her car up next to Marilyn Audleman's and turned off the engine. The fitness class had become a close-knit group, and Grace had let her friends know what she hoped to do. She'd told Steve, too, when he phoned from the *Dominion*. His response had been predictable. "Wait until I get home and we'll talk about it some more."

"You *were* home and we didn't talk about it," she'd said. "We fought about it."

Beside her, Brian was unnaturally quiet. The girls jumped out of the back seat and went to find the real estate agent, who had already opened the house. "Okay, Bri?" Grace asked.

He shrugged. "Does it matter?"

"Of course it matters." Was there anything so fragile as a teenage boy? she wondered. He was taking Steve's absence hard this time, and he refused to talk about Joshua Lamont. That, combined with the pressures of figuring out his life after high school, was making him edgy.

"I've got a million things to do this afternoon. How long is this going to take?"

"Not long. Come on, Brian."

He pushed open the door with his shoulder and got out. Katie and Emma were already upstairs, probably picking out their rooms. Grace and Brian went inside together. She didn't need to walk through the place again, though she encouraged Brian to take a look around. She'd come here many times when Marcia lived here. The house had been empty since Marcia had moved to Arizona. Grace stayed in touch with her by e-mail, and Marcia was as good as her word, keeping Grace's Web site current. Now the house on the bluff rang with emptiness, a soulless box waiting to be filled.

Marilyn and Grace talked for a while about the offer Grace intended to make. She'd been preapproved for financing, and if Marcia was agreeable, the whole transaction could go through in a matter of weeks. Terror and excitement clamored inside her. "I can't believe I'm going to do this," she said.

"You want this house," Marilyn reminded her. "You've wanted it forever. Let me get this written up and I'll call you to go over it."

"Yes. All right." Grace felt light-headed, short of breath. She walked straight to the windows spanning the deck and looked out at the sea, iron gray under a bruised-looking sky. She would never get tired of looking at this, winter drama and summer light, year after year. "Tonight?"

"That's fine." Marilyn locked the house and left Grace standing with the kids in the yard.

"Well?" she asked Brian.

"It's fine," he said.

"It's awesome," Katie said. "Are we really moving here? Really and truly?"

"I'm pretty sure we are," Grace told her.

"I can't believe you're doing it, Mom. Just like that."

"It isn't just like that. I've wanted a house for years. I decided to quit waiting around."

"Good. I hope we get to stay here forever. I'm in band and I want to go out for track next year. If I have to leave junior year, I'll die. Completely die."

"You will not, Drama Queen," Emma said. "We move all the time, and it's fine."

"Fine for you, maybe."

"Has Dad seen this house?" Emma asked Grace.

Grace's stomach clenched as she remembered the night she'd told him she wanted the house. "Just in the brochure."

"And he's okay with this?"

"He's at sea," she said.

As an act of rebellion, buying a home didn't seem terribly radical, but for Grace, it was a declaration of independence. The day she officially qualified for the loan and set the date for the closing, she sent Steve an e-mail, asking him to call.

She didn't have to wait long. That was one of the benefits of being a senior officer. He didn't have to wait in line to buy a phone card or use the all-too-public phones in the squadron rooms.

"Is this some kind of joke?" he demanded, his voice thin and distant on the satellite phone.

So it had deteriorated to this, she thought, her heart sinking. Phone calls across half the world used to mean I-love-yous and hurried endearments. "I'm buying this house," she said, holding on to her composure.

"You said you'd wait."

"No, *you* said I'd wait. I said it's going to happen now."

"Damn it, Grace, I know you're pissed about my first marriage but this—"

"This is not about your first marriage. It's about your second. You knew I wanted this and I found a way to make it happen. It's going to be wonderful, Steve. You'll see."

"Don't do it, Grace. Just wait."

"I'm through waiting." Buying a home was supposed to be a joyous occasion for a couple, yet she felt close to tears.

"I guess I can't stop you," he said.

"Yes, you can."

"But I won't."

"Good. This is going to work out beautifully."

"How can it when I'm telling you not to do this?"

"What do you care where we live while you're at sea?"

"This is not what the power of attorney is for."

"Navy families do this all the time." She'd never thought twice about doing business in Steve's name. Military spouses signed contracts while their loved one was at sea. Every Navy wife she knew had probably bought a house or a car on her own at some point. "You'll come home to your own house, Steve. How can you not want that?"

"What I want is for you to stick to the plan."

"What are you afraid of? That you'll lose out because I decided to get a life?"

"You have a life. With me and the kids."

"I'm ready for more. Is that so hard to understand?"

"Yeah. It is. Look, Grace, I have to go," he said. "Someone's waiting for the phone. Just...quit acting so irrational about all this, okay?"

"I have to go, too. Your irrational wife has a meeting at the Officers' Spouses Club." She hung up and glanced at the clock. The call had exhausted her and filled her with doubts. Time to get dressed. She put on her good knit suit—navy with white piping, of course—and drove to the officers' club. She had done this a thousand times, it seemed. But something felt different today. The suit was a bad fit.

As she walked across the parking lot and entered through the double glass doors, she knew what she would encounter inside. Allison Crowther at the podium. Women and the occasional civilian husband, people who were eager, well-groomed, motivated, dutiful. Like Grace.

She overheard snatches of conversation as she entered the building. "The deployment's going well, isn't it?" "You must be so proud of him…."

Every spouse present knew what a military wife contributed to her husband's rise through the ranks. Grace used to love the excitement of Steve's career and she took pride in his accomplishments. Still, Grace felt queasy with apprehension at the thought of what she was doing. He alone had the power to undermine her.

But something had happened to her. She didn't want to be dutiful Grace, the disappearing wife. She didn't want to be here, in the lobby that smelled of stale cigarette smoke, facing a room full of tables draped in white linen. Anxiety built up in her chest, and her cheeks felt flushed as she started to hyperventilate.

Someone asked her if she was all right. Grace said she needed some fresh air and dashed back out the door. From her car, she made several calls on her cell phone. "I have news," she said to each of her friends. "I'm dying to celebrate. Can you meet me at the Rusty Pelican?"

Grace discarded the hated knit suit and pulled on her jeans. They didn't fit the way they used to. Too loose, she realized with a start.

She put on a crisp white shirt, left a note for the kids and headed out into the bleak, dark day. She turned up the radio and sang along with Avril Lavigne, pounding the beat on the steering wheel with the heels of her hands.

Her friends in fitness class had invited her a few times to the neighborhood watering hole, but she had declined. She'd never gone to a bar without Steve. Ever. Until now. She took a deep breath and walked inside. A thumping rock number pulsed from unseen speakers, and couples filled the dance floor. Marilyn and Arlene were waiting with Radha, Lauren and Patricia. The rainbow glow of neon bar signs illuminated the women's faces around a wobbly cocktail table. A pitcher of frozen margaritas and several glasses stood ready. As Grace took a seat, Stan and his wife, Shirley, joined them, too. She beamed, grateful for their friendship.

They had turned from acquaintances to friends after Stan's wife became suspicious about his absences and thought he was having an affair. When Lauren and the other class members assured her of the truth, Shirley booked a ballroom-dancing cruise and started attending some of the classes herself. Seeing the two of them together, Grace wondered if she and Steve had any chance at all of getting to that comfortable, settled point in their lives and their marriage.

She lifted her glass, which contained a twelve-ounce margarita, and clinked it with the others. For the first time in years, she had actual non-Navy friends. She admired Marilyn's confidence and Arlene's attention to detail. Radha was passionate about a woman's self-image, and Stan's steadfast devotion to his wife and family was downright inspirational.

"I still can't believe it's happening," Grace said.

Marilyn beamed at her. "Marcia was thrilled to sell it at last. It's a wonderful investment, Grace."

Oh, it was so much more than that. She felt terrified and elated and filled with a curious sort of power. She had survived the mountains of paperwork, the waiting on pins and needles for loan approval and the suspense of the final closing.

Patricia Rivera lifted her glass of pineapple juice. "You and Captain Bennett must be thrilled."

"I am," Grace said. She could only hope Steve would be, once he saw the place. She lifted the pitcher of margaritas and gave herself a refill. Stan and Shirley headed for the dance floor.

Three men sidled over, practically drooling at the sight of Lauren and Patricia.

"Uh-oh," said Marilyn. "Here comes trouble."

The strangers sat down at the adjacent table and slid their chairs closer. The women huddled together, closing ranks, but the men didn't seem to get the message. Instead, they scooted their chairs even closer.

"Wanna party?" one of them asked. He had big shoulders and wet lips, and poor Patricia looked terrified.

"N-no, thanks."

"How about you, babe?" he asked, turning toward Grace.

Grace looked back over her shoulder. Surely he couldn't mean her.

"Yeah, you," he said. "You're a Navy wife, arencha?"

"Brilliant deduction," Grace said, even as she felt a stab of cold panic in her chest. The others were frozen like frightened rabbits, just as stunned as she was. When he didn't back off, she mustered her dignity and said, "Do you mind?"

"I bet you're real lonely, eh, Navy wife?"

His leer set a torch to her temper. Civilians often thought women like her fooled around when their men went to sea. Grace had battled the misconception for years. It was perfectly true that, as a Navy wife, she was used to the pangs of desire that afflict women separated from their husbands. Of course, she never acted on those primal urges.

She looked at the stranger and his two friends, then put on her most seductive smile. "You know what they say about Navy wives," she purred.

"Yeah?"

She dumped her drink in his lap, all twelve ice-cold, sticky ounces of it. "We can't hold our liquor."

CHAPTER TWENTY-FOUR

The night was so clear that Emma could pick out every star in the sky. It made the perfect backdrop for the football tumbling between the goalposts the moment the final buzzer sounded.

A deafening cheer erupted from the bleachers. The Comets had won their final home game and would advance to the state championship.

Emma shot to her feet with everyone else. The band blared out a victory march. On the field, the triumphant players leaped with joy. A pair of linebackers hoisted the quarterback on their shoulders, for he had scored the winning touchdown.

Of course he had. Cory Crowther was that kind of guy.

The happy crowd poured like a mudslide down the concrete steps between the bleachers. Emma jostled her way to the field and finally reached Cory, who grinned from ear to ear while cameras flashed. He looked incredible, even after being baptized with Gatorade. When he spotted Emma, he yelled her name and beat his chest like Tarzan.

"Great game," she told him, bubbling over with happiness. "I'm so proud of you, Cory."

He put his arm around her, engulfing her in the mingled scents of sweat and Gatorade. "Hey, thanks."

Mrs. Crowther chose that moment to show up. She was smiling, but there was something ice-cold in her eyes when she glanced at Emma. With a shiver, Emma edged away from Cory. Mrs. Crowther didn't like her. Emma had never bothered to find out why. Maybe she'd heard something about the night Emma had been caught with the beer. But she'd probably never been told whose beer it was.

"Wonderful game, son," she said. "Emma."

"Hello, Mrs. Crowther." Emma wondered if Cory had told her about Emma's application to the Naval Academy. She'd sworn him to secrecy, but he might have said something to his mom. Maybe that was why Mrs. Crowther was so chilly. Could be she didn't want anyone to compete with Cory for the appointment.

Without acknowledging Emma's greeting, Mrs. Crowther beamed at Cory. "I know you're off to the locker room with your teammates," she said. "I just wanted to tell you congratulations."

"Thanks, Mom." Cory flashed his winner's smile.

She headed toward the parking lot. "I'll see you at home, dear."

Emma watched her until she disappeared into the crowd. "She hates me."

"She hates everybody."

"But why—"

"Hey, Cory." Katie came rushing up to them, still wearing her red-and-white band uniform and clutching her clarinet and music. "Congratulations."

"Thanks, kiddo."

Emma almost laughed at Katie's adoring expression.

"Who's the band geek, Crowther?" Jimmy Bates, a running back covered in grass stains and mud, knocked on the top of Katie's cylindrical hat. "Anybody home?"

Katie's cheeks turned a simmering red. "Go away," she muttered to Jimmy, a sophomore who had not yet grasped the idea that he was supposed to start growing up.

He batted at the fringe hanging from one of her epaulets. "I don't know whether I should salute you or ask you to play 'Sergeant Pepper.'"

"Back off, Bates," Cory said.

"What, you're into dorks these days?"

"Hey, the marching band comes to every single game," Emma broke in. "They play their hearts out, even if it's raining or freezing cold."

"Yeah, so don't knock it," Cory added.

Jimmy shook his head in disgust, but he kept his mouth shut as he headed for the locker room. Katie was regarding Cory with pure hero worship.

He'd be the perfect date tomorrow night, thought Emma. The incident with the beer last summer was no more than a flicker of memory—it hadn't been his fault the authorities had shown up when they did. "I'll see you later," she said, and watched him head for the locker room with his howling teammates. "Let's go find Brian, Katie."

"He's incredible," Katie said, floating as she got into the car. Brian was already at the wheel, waiting for them.

"Who's incredible?" he asked.

"Cory Crowther. He won the game, and just now, he defended my honor."

Brian pulled out of the stadium parking lot. "Yeah, he's a real prince."

Emma was mystified by her brother's dislike of Cory. The two of them had been like oil and water since the day they'd met. "He didn't let Jimmy Bates get away with calling her a band geek."

"And for that we're supposed to worship at his feet?" Brian snorted. "Bates has the hots for our little band geek here, in case you haven't noticed."

Katie sank dramatically to the floor of the back seat. "Jimmy Bates. My life is over."

CHAPTER TWENTY-FIVE

Grace walked into Katie's room to find her standing in front of the mirror affixed to the closet door. She unfastened the chin strap of her plumed helmet and her face crumpled.

"What's the matter, sweetie?" Grace asked. She stepped around the stack of moving boxes. Sunday afternoon they'd be out of here.

"I'm a total geek."

"You're a talented musician and you look adorable in that uniform." It was a classic, from the tall plumed hat with its shiny strap to the double-breasted jacket and the white leather spats.

"I look like a giant nutcracker," Katie declared, ripping off the helmet. "I don't even have a date for the dance tomorrow. I might as well stay home and help you pack boxes."

"You're going to the dance with a group of friends. That's more fun, anyway."

"I'm such a loser, Mom."

"Don't you dare say that." Grace helped her take off the uniform. Katie moved slowly and gingerly, like an accident victim. "What in the world put that idea in your head? Did someone say something?"

"Just forget it," she said glumly, shuffling toward the shower.

Grace folded the pieces of the uniform one by one, smoothing out each seam and crease, and put them in their own box. Katie had been so proud the day she was selected for the marching band. Now, seemingly out of the blue, she saw herself as a loser.

There were few tortures worse than hurting for your child, Grace reflected. Without warning, she found herself drowning in need for Steve. What she wouldn't give to sit down with him and talk about poor Katie. Or Brian's college plans, or Emma's reluctance to talk about the future. But he was away, their marriage was broken and she was left to either wait for him to come home or move on.

She didn't like any of the options she'd been left with.

The phone rang and she welcomed the interruption. It wasn't like her to indulge in frustration and self-defeat.

"Hello?"

"Um, yeah, um, hi. Is, um, Katie there?"

Grace felt a flutter of interest. "Who's calling, please?"

"This is, um, Jimmy Bates."

"Hold on," she said, and she meant it. The kid on the line sounded as though he was going to keel over from nervousness. "I'll see if she's available." Grace had just heard the shower turn off. With the cordless phone in hand, she knocked at the bathroom door. "Katie, you have a phone call."

"I just got out of the shower. If it's Melanie, tell her—"

"It's somebody named Jimmy Bates," said Grace.

The bathroom door opened immediately. Katie's cheeks were on fire as she grabbed the phone, whipped back into the steamy bathroom and shut the door.

Grace poked her head into Emma's room. "Who's Jimmy Bates? He just called for Katie."

Emma grinned. "Her Homecoming date."

CHAPTER TWENTY-SIX

Grace had the curling iron heating up for the girls as they rushed around, getting ready for Saturday night's dance. Brian and Emma squabbled over who would get the upstairs shower first. Katie had wisely used Grace's bathroom, possibly setting a record for longest shower ever taken. Her mood had improved since the day before, and she could barely hold still as Grace fixed her hair.

Emma wandered into the room wearing her dress but no shoes. She had the local paper folded back to the sports section. The lead story was, of course, about the football victory. A large photograph depicted a triumphant Cory Crowther hoisted on the shoulders of his teammates.

"So you're dating a football hero," Grace said.

"That's what they call him." Emma tossed the paper on the bed. Then she lifted her hair and turned so Grace could zip her dress, a simple sheath in royal blue velvet.

"Are you falling for him?" Grace asked Emma. Her older daughter had always been circumspect about her boyfriends. Closemouthed, even. She probably got that from her dad. Although Grace hadn't spoken to Steve about it, she suspected the idea of Emma with Cory didn't thrill him. She wasn't sure why, and with the way things were between them, she wasn't likely to find out soon.

"I don't know," she said. "Maybe."

"He's completely hot," Katie said, trying to apply mascara with her glasses on.

"Maybe you're the one falling for him," Emma teased. "I'd better warn Jimmy Bates."

That sparked a fresh round of bickering. Shaking her head, Grace went to get the camera ready. Within a few minutes, the bickering stopped, and as if by magic, three perfectly groomed young people came downstairs. They were shockingly mature, the girls beautifully made up, Brian a full head taller than his twin. And they were patient as always, posing in the foyer in their finery. Brian wore his only suit—he grew so fast she couldn't afford to buy him more than one at a time—and his shoes had been shined with military precision. Emma seemed to have walked off a modeling runway, and Katie was adorable, poised between coltish awkwardness and ladylike sophistication. Her smile glowed with bright anticipation.

Look at our kids, Steve, Grace thought with a surge of pride and affection. They're so beautiful. She desperately wanted him to see them and vowed to send the digital pictures tonight. No matter what state their marriage was in, he was a man who loved his children and deserved to see them in their finest moments. Over the years, she had trained herself not to resent his absence. He had a job to do, a country to serve…. But he'd missed so many of these fleeting, magical times.

"Oh, man," Brian said, looking at Grace. "Don't start crying, Mom."

"She can cry if she wants," Katie said. "But hurry up and get it over with before the doorbell rings."

Grace got hold of herself while she checked the settings on the camera.

Jimmy Bates arrived, blushing as deeply as Katie, his hand sweaty as he greeted Grace. She introduced herself to Jimmy's mother, who was driving them. She would have liked to chat for a few minutes, but Katie looked as though she might pass out from embarrassment, so Grace told them to have fun, took another picture and waved goodbye. A few minutes later Brian drove off to pick up his date, a ditzy but nice enough local girl named Lindy Banks.

In the front hall, Emma checked the contents of her handbag. "What are you doing tonight?"

"The last bit of packing."

Emma stiffened. "Dad doesn't want us to move."

"Did he tell you that?"

"He'd probably tell *you* that if you'd talk to him."

"We talk."

"You know what I mean. You've never given him the big chill before."

"It's not a chill, and it's not anything you should worry about. We'll work it out." But a dark little voice wondered, as it sometimes did lately, if they ever would.

Then the doorbell rang, and Emma's face lit up. She opened the door, and there stood Cory Crowther, glistening like a bridegroom. He took one look at Emma and his smile burst with wordless compliments.

"Hello, Mrs. Bennett," he said when he was finally able to tear his gaze away. "Hi, Emma. This is for you." He offered her a corsage with a white rosebud and a spray of baby's breath, fashioned to fit on her wrist.

Grace took pictures, savoring the sight of their beaming faces. They were clearly in a hurry to be on their way. She wanted to tell them to slow down and enjoy the magic, but she knew they would not understand.

"Have fun," she said. "Stay out of trouble and be home by midnight."

"Yes, ma'am. You have my word." Cory held the door open and they went outside. Grace watched the proprietary way he placed his hand at the small of Emma's back as he led her to the car. She felt a lurch of apprehension, watching her daughter go off with a young man. A football hero. She stood on the porch as they drove away, her hand raised in a wave they probably didn't see.

She went inside to fortify herself with a cup of tea and then tackle the last of the packing. She walked past the study, glancing at the floating screen saver. Steve would want to see the pictures of the kids, of course. Ordinarily she would accompany them with lengthy details, trying to recreate the moment he had missed. She had done this from the moment her newborn twins had first filled her arms. It had been her job to describe every milestone that occurred while he was gone. After all these years, recording all the moments he'd missed, she felt drained. Tonight she sent him the photos with only a subject line: high school dance. Then she broke down the computer and packed it away in boxes.

"God, I hate this," she said, heading into the kitchen to put the kettle on.

She forced herself to concentrate on the matters at hand. The paperwork was done, the transfer made. Her dream of owning the house on the bluff was a reality. All that was left was for Grace to move into her new home.

She looked around the house, the ugly military unit now cluttered with boxes and baskets heaped with their belongings. She was an expert at moving. Hell, these days she called herself a professional. Tomorrow would be a breeze.

But she was terrified. She put a spoonful of sugar into her tea and took a sip, trying to melt the thickness in her throat.

CHAPTER TWENTY-SEVEN

"Some things never change," said Lauren, watching a table full of nervous and overdressed teenagers across the dining room of the Captain's Quarters. She felt a twinge of sympathy for the harried waitress trying to create separate checks.

"How's that?" asked Josh.

"High school dates," she said, indicating with her head. "That could have been me ten years ago."

"I bet you were hot."

"Nope."

"You were, too." He brushed her leg under the table. "I wish I'd known you then, honey."

"No, you don't."

"You were twice as cute as that." He jerked his head at the table of heavily made-up girls tugging at their dresses and awkward-looking boys in ill-fitting suits.

"Nope."

"Damn, woman. You are contrary tonight."

She folded her hands on the linen tablecloth and sat forward to whisper to him. "When I said that could have been me, I didn't mean the girl in the Jessica McClintock dress. I was talking about the waitress." She saw him glance at the heavyset woman with her hair in a bun. "On homecoming night, prom night or any traditional big-date night, I was waiting tables. Right here, as a matter of fact, only back then it was called the Manor Inn."

He spread his hands. "Lots of kids worked."

She smiled at him. "Josh," she whispered, "I used to weigh over two hundred and fifty pounds."

He stared at her. His gaze moved from her face down to her cleavage. "No way."

"Way."

"I can't picture it."

"I have photographic evidence." She laughed at his expression. "Not on me. It's no big deal now, really. But the past is definitely part of who I am, and so I thought I should tell you."

"You're amazing."

"It wasn't that dramatic, or it didn't seem so at the time. I was overweight all through high school and college, and didn't get serious about my health until after I married Gil. He was...a pretty big guy, too, and that was a major factor in his heart disease. So it was kind of ironic that I was the one who got the warning. One day my doctor had a long, brutally honest talk with me about what I was doing to my health. I joined a fitness class, followed a strict diet and lost more than a hundred pounds in two years."

She pressed her hands on the tablecloth so he wouldn't see them shaking. Her heart rate had doubled. Although she claimed it was no big deal, this was huge for her. And frightening. She was making herself vulnerable in a way she never thought she would.

Even though Josh claimed he wanted to hear everything, there were some things she would not tell him, not now, perhaps never. She would not admit how unhappy she used to be. Or how pathetically grateful she was that Gil wanted to marry her, a dumpy, insecure neuroscience major. And she would not confess the reason she had gone to the doctor in the first place on that particular occasion.

But when she looked at Josh, she wanted to say everything. She wanted to tell him that sometimes she was so lonely for intimacy that she physically ached with yearning. She longed to admit that since meeting him, she felt alive again. "I was such a big dreamer back in my waitressing days," she said. "I imagined myself finally getting off this island, seeing the world. And look at me. Right back where I started." Her voice wavered and she took a sip of wine.

"You should be proud of yourself, honey. You're healthy and successful. You make me so damned happy sometimes I can't see straight."

He was constantly doing that, making simple, direct statements that took her breath away. "Not a good thing for a pilot," she said.

"You're a good thing for me." He leaned across the table. "Lauren, honey, I've got something to tell you."

Misgivings clattered through her head. He was shipping out tomorrow. He had a girlfriend in Florida. A boyfriend... "What's that?"

"See that young woman who just walked in?"

She looked over her shoulder. A dark-haired, broad-shouldered boy and a beautiful girl with blond hair, wearing a royal-blue dress, were being seated at a table across the room. Lauren's heart lurched. "Yeah?"

Josh waved at the two of them. They looked uncomfortable, but waved back and then gave their attention to the waitress. Josh leaned even closer and whispered, "That's Emma Bennett."

It was all Lauren could do not to stare. She kept sneaking looks at the blond girl. Josh's half sister. Grace's daughter.

"I think there's a family resemblance," she said. "Something about the eyes. So is everything all right between you and the Bennetts?"

"As far as I know. I've only ever met Emma, and she doesn't have a lot to say to me. I'm her ALO—admissions liaison officer—for the Naval Academy."

"Does she think that's weird?"

"No doubt."

"So do you feel any sort of...connection with her?"

"None at all."

Lauren debated with herself about whether or not to let Josh know she was acquainted with Grace. Maybe another time, she thought. She liked Grace a lot. And she'd misjudged her. When Grace had first shown up for fitness class, Lauren had seen her as a typical Naval officer's wife to the last inch of her tired, out-of-shape shadow, an unlikely prospect for success. She figured Grace would come a few times and then find herself too busy to continue. That was the way it usually worked.

But Grace had surprised Lauren. She often had more humor than stamina, but she was making progress. When she started the class, Grace had that soft, doughy look of a woman approaching her middle years. In Lauren's experience, women at that point found themselves at a curious crossroads in life. Some ignored the impact of time and gravity, and started buying pants with elasticized waistbands and tunics long enough to hide their hips. Others fought back, spending retirement nest eggs on surgeons and spas. But the women Lauren admired most were those who looked after their health and took their age in stride.

Grace's determination was paying off. Her fitness level was increasing, along with her confidence. Lauren was sometimes tempted to talk to her about being a wife when your husband was at sea, but given the odd connection between Grace and Josh, Lauren didn't go there.

Just as dessert and coffee arrived, a family of six bustled into the dining room. The hostess looked apologetic as she seated them at a nearby table. The kids were all little, adorable and extremely loud. Lauren watched Josh, half expecting to see annoyance in his face. Instead, he caught the eye of a boy of about six, wearing a plastic gun belt and cowboy boots. Josh winked at the kid, who grinned and ducked his head.

When Josh looked back at Lauren, he laughed at her expression. "Don't look so surprised. I'm nuts about kids."

Lauren felt the dull ache of an old yearning. She and Gil had never used birth control. His first wife had refused to have kids, and once he married Lauren, he was eager to start a family. They both had so much love to give to children. But there was no pregnancy.

They weren't worried the first year. By the end of the second, they were frantic. They made an appointment with a fertility specialist. There was a three-month wait to see Dr. Hendler, but they never got to meet him. Gil died on their third anniversary, two weeks before the appointment.

"I want a bunch of kids one day," said Josh.

"Hence the minivan." She tried to sound amused. "Why would you want to have kids if you're not going to be there for them?" She couldn't help it. She had to know.

"That's why the marriage is so important. In a Navy family, raising the kids is definitely a team effort. You like kids, too, don't you?"

"I adore them," she said, taken aback. "In fact, I'm adding a kids' after-school fitness class to my schedule. And I'm going to teach it myself."

"You're amazing, Lauren Stanton," said Josh. "No wonder I'm falling in love with you."

Her heart skipped a beat. "That's not funny."

At the adjacent table, two of the kids were playing hockey with oyster crackers.

"I'm not joking." He placed his hand over hers on the table. "I've been wanting to ask you something."

Lauren felt every hair on her body stand on end. This wasn't happening. It wasn't. But something in his eyes told her that what he was about to say might change her life.

She started to feel afraid. Only in movies did a handsome, buttoned-down Naval officer ask the desperately lonely woman to marry him. It didn't happen in real life. It was too terrifying.

She wanted to freeze everything, right here, right now. They had rushed into a mad fling, but suddenly it was turning into something else, almost against her will. She was losing her heart to a man who would make her quiet life a whirlwind, a man who craved the whole package—the career, the wife and kids on the home front.

"Why me?" she whispered.

"Good question," he said. "We're all wrong for each other."

All the anticipation rushed out of her like the air from a deflating balloon. It wasn't disappointment, she told herself. It was a reprieve. Some things weren't meant to be easy, she reminded herself. Maybe loving a man like Josh was one of them.

"True," she said. "I just don't think this can work."

He smiled. "But it's going to."

CHAPTER TWENTY-EIGHT

Emma teased Cory about his crown all the way across the parking lot after the dance. "Should I call you Sire or Your Highness?" she asked. "Or Ye Olde Homecoming King?"

He grinned and spun the cheap crown on one finger. "Just don't call me late for a party."

"Too bad they didn't let you keep the robe and scepter."

"Right. They'd come in handy at my next coronation."

She had no doubt that many coronations, in one form or another, awaited Cory Crowther in his life. He was talented and favored by circumstance. It had been no surprise that he'd been named Homecoming King. Of course he was the anointed one, a handsome senior who had saved yesterday's game.

Dad hadn't sounded too thrilled when she'd sent him an e-mail saying she was going to the dance with Cory. "I have no choice but to trust your judgment, Em," he'd written her, and she knew he was still thinking about the beer incident.

As they walked past other kids leaving the dance, people called out, teasing and congratulating him. Shea Hansen, Homecoming Queen, swept past on the arm of her date.

"'Night, Cory," she called. "Thanks for the dance."

"No problem." Once they'd passed by, he took his crown and settled it on Emma's head. "Should have been you. If you hadn't saved her from drowning last summer, she wouldn't even be here to wear a crown."

"Shea was the perfect choice," Emma pointed out. Shea was pretty and popular, but most of all, she was a local girl. Newcomers didn't get elected Homecoming Queen. Not even newcomers who knew CPR. People expected their queens to stick around.

They encountered Katie and Jimmy Bates heading for the bus circle to be picked up by Jimmy's mother. Katie was giggling, but when she spotted Cory, she stared at him as though he were a rock star.

"Hey, Bates. Katie," he said, winning them over with a gleaming smile. "Did you have a good time tonight?"

"Yeah, we did," Katie said, almost comically starry-eyed behind her glasses.

"We did," echoed Jimmy. "So, uh, we'll see you around."

Emma handed Katie a cellophane bag with her corsage and folder of photographs. "Take this for me, okay?" she said. "And tell Mom not to wait up."

"Good idea," Cory murmured, holding open the car door. "I've got plans."

Since Darlene Cooper's father had gone to sea, her apartment had become a gathering place for seniors who didn't care to be bothered by adult supervision. After the dance, Emma and Cory dropped in to find the lights low and the music high. An interesting mix of students and young enlisted men and women milled around the cluttered kitchen and the dining room, where the table was covered with open bags of chips and six-packs of wine coolers and beer. Sailors were absolutely forbidden to mingle with the local high school kids, but that never stopped them.

Darlene wasn't the best housekeeper in the world. Emma felt a little sorry for her as she tried to ask people to go outside to smoke, or ran around trying to clean up spills. She didn't even seem to be enjoying herself.

"I'll come over tomorrow and help you clean up," Emma said to her.

"Thanks. That'd be great." Darlene seemed to relax a little.

Shoot, thought Emma. Tomorrow was moving day. She'd have to figure out how to be two places at once. She looked around briefly for Brian, but saw no sign of him or his date.

"I say we check out the hot tub before it gets too crowded," Cory said, grabbing a six-pack of Tequiza as he walked past the table.

"Good idea."

They headed out to the courtyard, which contained a pool that had been covered for the season and three hot tubs aglow with underwater lights and foam from the jets. There was a dumpy little cabana house with bathrooms and changing rooms. Emma hurried to shuck her dress, shivering from the chill. She'd brought along a tote bag with her swimsuit, a towel and a change of clothes. She put on her bikini, laid her clothes across a bench, wrapped herself in a beach towel and went out on the deck.

Shea motioned her over, and Emma lowered herself gratefully into the hot, bubbling water.

"This is Jax," Shea said, indicating the guy next to her. "Jax, this is Emma—and Cory," she added when he joined them.

Emma didn't recognize Jax from school. Judging by his haircut and physique, she figured he was in the Navy. Over the years of observing her father's men, she had come to know that look. When raw recruits showed up at the Great Lakes Naval Training Center and spent eight weeks in basic training, something happened to them. They all came out with a certain look about them, and Jax had that look.

Hanging around with local high school girls was one of the chief taboos of a sailor's life, but it happened all the time. Neither Emma nor Cory said anything to Jax about their fathers being senior officers.

They looked at the stars and listened to the faint thump of

music from Darlene's apartment. The four of them chatted awhile, the conversation becoming more random and amusing as they finished off their bottles of Tequiza. Eventually Shea and Jax got out and melted into the shadows. Alone with Cory, Emma felt a little beat of excitement. She hadn't had an actual boyfriend since last May, and she was lonely for the kind of closeness you could only find with a certain kind of boy.

Cory reached his hand toward her. The underwater lights glowed weirdly between them as they twined their fingers together. Then Cory gave a sudden, playful tug and brought her next to him. They kissed, and then she pulled back and leaned her head on his shoulder.

"This is nice," she said.

"Mmm." His fingers slid down her back, pausing to toy with the fastening of her bikini top. "So, how does this work?" he whispered.

She grinned and slipped away in the water. She was not going to get that friendly with him. Not yet, but maybe in the future. The fact was, she liked fooling around, teasing and flirting. She was curious about sex and not ashamed to admit it. But she simply didn't feel ready. "The way it works is, you wait until I say it's okay."

"And then it magically opens like Aladdin's cave."

"Not exactly."

"So, what are you waiting for?"

Emma shrugged. "I'm not sure."

"Then how will you know when it's time?"

"I'll know." She laughed at his pained expression. "We've only gone out a few times, Cory. I think we need to spend more time together to make sure this is right."

"Of course this is right, Emma. I'm crazy about you. I think about you all the time."

She let herself float a little closer. "Really? What do you think?"

"That you're hot," he said, pulling her against him for another kiss.

She thought she could feel his erection through his swim trunks. That awareness was both weird and…intriguing. But she figured she'd better keep her distance, maybe change the subject.

She gently pushed away from him. "So how's your application going?" she asked. College apps were a constant topic of conversation among the kids in their class. Deadlines were approaching, hopes flying high.

"Fine," he said. "I might have smoked a little pot a couple of days before my physical at the Naval hospital."

"Oh, Cory. I can't believe you did that."

"It's no big deal."

"But if anything shows up, you'll be disqualified."

He leaned his head back on the concrete edge of the hot tub. "Not a problem," he said. "My dad will make it go away."

"My dad would kill me if any test I took came back positive for pot. Fortunately, my tests are done, applications in, and Senator Murray wrote me a letter of nomination. How about you?"

"I'll probably get nominated by the vice president," he said, leaning back again.

Emma nodded. The vice president selected only fifty candidates nationwide who were particularly outstanding, or particularly well connected. But she noticed Cory hadn't said he'd been selected yet.

"Why are you going through all this, anyway?" he asked, opening another Tequiza. "You don't really want to go to Annapolis, do you?"

"Maybe I do." After getting over the shock of meeting Josh Lamont, Emma had met with him several times. And each time he encouraged her more and more. She was nearly convinced that she wanted to do it. Brian knew what she was up to, but she'd sworn him to secrecy.

"It's eighty-five-percent guys," he pointed out.

"Eighty-three. I don't have a problem with guys."

"Oh, no? Then why do you keep scooting away from me?" He captured her again and gave her a long, hot kiss, tongue and everything. "Anyway," he said, "I doubt you'll make the cut."

His annoying comment broke the mood, just when she was starting to feel pretty sexy. "Doubt all you want," she said. "I'm taking my shot."

He crossed his arms behind his head, showing off his bulging muscles. "They'd make you cut off all your pretty blond hair."

She hugged her knees to her chest. "You know what I think? I think you're pissed because I've got a real chance at getting in, just like you."

"You're a cupcake."

"We'll see about that."

"Why do you want to go into the Navy, anyway? For the guys?"

"Yeah, that's it," she said with a laugh. "I just can't get enough guys."

He scooted closer to her. "All it takes is one."

She scooted away. Cory's sense of entitlement and privilege sometimes got on her nerves. "Not unless I say so."

"So what do you think you'll do at the Academy? There's no degree program in Home Ec."

That did it. She splashed water in his face. "Very funny, Cory Crowther. You watch me. I'll get in."

With a wet chuckle, he wiped his hand across his face, then propped his arms on the sides of the pool. His eyes twinkled as his gaze slipped over her. "I'll be watching, all right."

She couldn't help smiling as she hoisted herself up and out of the tub. "I'm glad you have a sense of humor about this."

"So where are you going?"

"Time to head home. It's late."

"Aw, Emma—"

"You promised my mom you'd have me home by midnight."

"She'll be fast asleep. Moms never make it to midnight."

Okay, so she couldn't expect him to be perfect. He wouldn't be the first to go back on his word to her mother. And he was definitely right about moms not making it to midnight. Emma had lost count of the times she had tiptoed in after a date, only to find her mother asleep on the sofa with the lights still on, her book turned upside down on her chest, infomercials playing on the TV.

"I still want to get home," she said. The mood was gone; he had ticked her off with his comments and she was tired.

The underwater lights flickered across his face, creating angry shadows around his eyes. Emma was momentarily taken aback, but then he smiled. "Whatever the lady wants," he said agreeably enough, and headed for the men's locker room. Emma went in the opposite door to dry off and put on the jeans and sweatshirt she had brought to put on after the party. She set them on the bench next to her gown and peeled off her wet bikini. She was just reaching for a towel when the lights went out.

"Hey, I'm still in here," she said, wrapping the towel around her.

"I know." Cory stepped into the shadowy room. He stood limned by the pale light from the courtyard outside. Wisps of steam rolled off his damp body.

Emma tucked the towel more snugly under her arms. "Wait for me outside, Cory," she said. "I'll just be a minute."

"I'm through waiting." He strode across the room and took her in his arms.

She was startled by his strong embrace, but she felt a little thrill of pleasure, too. She let him kiss her, although she kept a firm grip on the towel. She considered forgiving him for his crack about the Naval Academy.

"Emma," he said, crushing her against him, "I swear to God, I can't stop thinking about you. You're so beautiful." He kissed her again and, with his mouth locked to hers, maneuvered her down to the wooden bench.

"Hey, watch out for my dress," she protested, hearing the soft rustle of satin-lined velvet beneath their straining bodies. "You'll ruin it."

"Ruin what?" he muttered, and kissed away her reply. His hand found her thigh, fingers gently squeezing and moving upward under the towel.

The sensation took her breath away, and he pressed her down until she felt smooth velvet against her back. Between kisses he gave a helpless moan and tugged at the towel. Emma was drowning in sensation. The sharp physical need in her body, the giddy anticipation of discovery and the light brush of fear welled up in her, and she found herself struggling to think straight.

Her burning body and the Tequiza she'd had muddled her thoughts. But a little corner of her brain cleared, and she recognized that she had only seconds to make up her mind about what was bound to happen if she let him continue. Should she give in and go for it, or stop now?

She'd been thinking a lot about sex lately. She couldn't seem to avoid it. Maybe it was time to do a little exploring. But she wanted her first time to be a little more special then a make-out session in a cold locker room that smelled of mildew.

Cory brushed the towel aside and opened the fly of his trunks.

"Jeez, Cory," she said, trying to twist out from under him. "Cut it out."

She pushed at him, but he pressed down harder. The tiny flutter of fear that had felt so delicious earlier beat harder now.

"God, Emma," he murmured. His lips touched everywhere— cheeks and neck and mouth. "You are so—"

"I am *so* telling you to stop," she interrupted. The fear rose up through her now, pounding in her ears. It was the clean, unmistakable sensation of a real danger. God, how did she let herself be maneuvered into this position?

She tried to calm down. This was Cory. He was practically her boyfriend. She really shouldn't panic.

He pushed her legs apart and shoved himself down on her. She tried to clamp her legs together, but he thrust so hard that he pushed all the air out of her lungs.

She rocked her head from side to side. "Cory, no."

"Yes," he said, covering her face with kisses. He twined his fingers into her hair and held her head still. "I sure do like your blond hair, Emma. Your nice, long, blond hair." As he spoke, he pressed her legs down on opposite sides of the bench and sank himself into her.

Her body turned cold with shock. She tried to fight back, but his muscles were like iron, holding her pinned in place. His grip on her hair caused her head to throb at the temples. He kept pushing, shoving, thrusting, pressing, and it was like he didn't even know she was there anymore, didn't hear her gasps of shock and terror and humiliation, her pleas for him to stop. She was on fire, but it was not the fine burn of sensation she'd felt earlier. This was pain. Pain between her legs, in her chest, her back, her shoulders.

He thrust himself at her twice more, making a caveman sound deep in his throat. He was covered in sweat and hot chlorine water, and faint light from outside gleamed over him. He convulsed and shuddered, and then he went all loose and slumped on top of her.

"God," he whispered. "My God, that was so…oh, God."

"I feel sick," she said, twisting beneath him. "Get off me before I puke."

"What the—" He got up immediately and straightened his swim trunks. She somehow managed to yank the towel around her and hold herself upright. Her entire body was shaking. Her teeth were chattering. With the towel clamped under her arms, she managed to fumble into her sweater and jeans.

"Still feel sick?" he asked, sounding like Cory again.

She stuffed her things into the tote bag.

He leaned across the bench, angling for a kiss.

She nearly came out of her skin as she jumped away. The concrete floor chilled her bare feet. "Stay away from me," she said.

"Aw, Emma, come on. That was great."

"Great?" she echoed, incredulous. She picked up her bag and edged toward the door. "Great? You assaulted me."

"Very funny."

"I'm not joking. You messed with me, Cory. You forced me. We're both supposed to want it, but I didn't. I told you no."

"You wanted it. We were getting along great in the hot tub."

"Because you were behaving yourself there. I told you to stop, but you didn't. You pushed yourself on me. There's a word for that and it's not 'great.'"

"Yeah? What word?"

"Rape." It sounded loud and horrible in the cold, dark room. She moved even closer to the door, poised to run, to scream for help.

He laughed aloud. "Man, you are way off base. Don't even think about crying rape."

"I'll think about what I want." She turned and strode barefoot toward the door.

He moved swiftly, blocking her exit. A fresh wave of fear heaved through her, but she stood her ground.

"Move," she said. "I'm leaving."

"Don't say a word, Emma. Not a goddamned word."

"You know you went too far or you wouldn't be acting so scared about me telling."

"Who says I'm scared? We're just two kids, drinking and having a little fun on the weekend. No big deal. And you know, it just occurred to me that you're over eighteen, and that makes you a legal adult. I don't turn eighteen for two more weeks." He laughed briefly. "So technically, you committed statutory rape against me. Poor little old me."

Emma's head felt light as her stomach churned. She had planned to buy him something special for his birthday.

"But seriously, Emma," he went on, "if you try to make a federal case out of this, I'll tell the truth. We had a date, maybe drank a little and then had sex. Big deal. That's exactly what happened."

Her throat burned. "I told you no. I told you to stop."

"That's not what I heard. Christ, you're blowing this all out of proportion. Do you know what a stupid mess this could turn into if you decide to start spreading lies?"

"I'm not the one who's lying," she said, but her voice was a shamed whisper.

His eyes narrowed. "Your father's under my father's command. You don't even want to think about what would happen if you start talking smack about me. You wouldn't do that, baby. I know you wouldn't." He brushed his knuckles gently over her cheek.

His touch made her skin crawl. She jumped back. "I told you to get out of my way."

He stepped closer. "Emma, you're so pretty. I'm sorry you

didn't think it was good, but next time it'll be better. I'll go slower. I'll make it good. I was just all excited this time."

Despite the chills rolling through her, she broke out in a sweat. She opened her mouth to say something, but the sick terror inside her erupted. A fountain of puke spewed out of her, right onto Cory's feet.

"*Gross.*" He sprinted across the deck and jumped into the nearest hot tub.

She wiped her face with a corner of her towel. Drunken laughter drifted from Darlene's apartment. Emma knew she couldn't go back there. Making a split-second decision, she scooped up her bag and raced across the parking lot. Her bare feet didn't feel the cold bite of the asphalt. She just ran on and on, crossing the ball fields and skirting the hangar area of the base, then speeding up the hill.

Once she reached her destination, apprehension set in. She waited for a long time in front of the BOQ. The glow of sodium-vapor lights turned the parking lot a murky amber streaked with shadows. Now and then a car drove up, sometimes a motorcycle. She shrank into the darkness, avoiding detection.

Maybe she should go. Maybe this was a bad idea. There were lights on in the lobby of the building, and in many of the windows. The apartments were filled with men, young men. Men like Cory.

She was about to embark on the long walk home when a dark-colored minivan pulled into the lot. Too late to escape now. She was trapped. But at least she wasn't scared anymore.

"Emma?" Josh Lamont slammed the van shut and hurried over to her. "Hey, what's the matter?"

She refused to break down and cry, even though she wanted to. Needed to. So badly.

"Nothing's the matter," she said. "It's just…um, I'm sorry to bother you. I know it's late…." She struggled to keep her voice steady. She had no idea where it came from, but a spine of cold steel kept her upright. "Can I have a ride home? Please, Lieutenant Lamont?"

"No problem." His gaze flickered over her—the dress stuffed into her bag, her bare feet, her hair still damp from the hot tub. "Emma, are you sure you're all right?"

For a moment she nearly panicked. Did she smell like puke? Could Josh see what Cory had done to her? She was terrified that the truth was written like obscene graffiti all over her face. Her body, her soul.

She lowered her gaze to the ground. But at the same time, she held herself very stiff and straight because the urge to shake was almost overwhelming.

"What's going on, Emma?"

"I need a ride home. I was with a group of kids tonight and didn't bring my car."

"Let me guess," Josh said. "Your designated driver had a little too much fun."

"I suppose you could put it that way."

"Let's go." He headed for the ugly minivan, which was parked amid the Corvettes and SUVs that belonged to the other officers. In a strange way, she admired him for driving a car that was so uncool.

She hopped in and strapped on her seat belt. Her whole body ached. That was strange; she didn't remember Cory doing anything overtly violent. But she felt as though she'd just survived a beating.

"I saw you at the Captain's Quarters earlier," Josh said as he pulled out of the parking lot.

She nodded, though it seemed so long ago. The person who had sat at a linen-covered table with Cory Crowther, who had seen Josh and some woman across the room, no longer existed.

"We went to dinner before the dance," she said.

"I hope you had a good time tonight."

She could not imagine how to respond to that. He was mercifully quiet for the rest of the drive. No how's-school-how's-work chitchat for him. Emma was so grateful for his silence, because she was pretty sure that if she had to talk any more, she'd break open like a dropped coconut and everything would spill out of her.

She nearly wept with relief when he reached the intersection of her street. "Could you drop me off right here at the corner?" she said.

Josh didn't question her as he pulled over. She muttered her thanks, then made her escape, running lightly down the cold concrete sidewalk and letting herself in the back door. Her luck held as she skirted the moving boxes, tiptoed upstairs, slipped into the bathroom and turned on the shower.

She wanted to forget the whole thing. Better yet, she wished she could rewind the night back to the point where everything went bad. She wished she could just walk away at that point. Instead, the incident with Cory—the rape—played over and over again in her head. The memory clung to her like a stain she couldn't wash out, no matter how hard she tried. But she stood beneath the shower nozzle, scrubbed herself raw and vowed she would never stop trying.

CHAPTER TWENTY-NINE

Grace was listening to Katie's third account of the dance when she finally heard signs of life upstairs. It was noon, and Emma had apparently decided to get up.

When she heard the shower come on, Grace frowned.

"Something the matter, Mom?" asked Katie.

"She's taking a shower."

"Off with her head." Katie made a chopping motion with her hand.

"I don't care if she takes a shower. It's just odd. I woke up after midnight last night, and she was taking a shower then, too." Grace had gotten up, asked if Emma was okay. Emma had waved her off: *I'm fine. Go back to sleep.*

"Maybe she came home soaking wet because they were jumping off the dock at Mueller's Point again."

"This time of year? It's freezing."

"I never said she was smart."

"You wouldn't. So are you all packed, kiddo?" she asked Katie. All week long, Grace had been ferrying things over to the new place. She had a team coming this afternoon to handle the furniture and large items. She'd sent Brian ahead to supervise the crew she'd hired.

"Every scrap," Katie said. "I even brought some of the carpet fuzz."

"Very funny."

"Actually, I should check the top shelf of my closet." Katie headed for the stairs.

Grace stood alone in the empty kitchen of the house that had never been her home. A Dwelling Unit Inspection form was stuck to the fridge. By the end of the day every item would be checked off. She had stood in rooms like this, amid boxes and bundles, many times in the past, but she had never felt the emotions that engulfed her now. She'd moved without Steve's help before, but never without his support. She was elated and terrified. Although she was supposed to be an expert at relocation, this was not easy for her.

Emma finally came down, sulky and silent except for the loud stomp of her feet on the stairs. She was dressed in shapeless gray sweats, and she smelled as though she'd availed herself of every brand of soap in the house.

"Good morning, Merry Sunshine," Grace said. "Ready for moving day?"

"I guess." She looked pale, probably from lack of sleep. As she went to the fridge and took out a carton of juice, Grace noticed that she moved a little gingerly.

"All right, young lady," Grace said. "Let's hear it."

Alarm flashed in Emma's eyes. "Hear what?"

"I want to hear all about last night."

Emma's mouth moved, but no sound came out.

"No need to panic. I'm not mad about what you did."

Emma sagged back against a moving crate. "You...you're not..."

"If you want to go jumping off docks into ice-cold water, that's your business."

"Oh. Well, it won't happen again," Emma said. "I swear, it will never happen again. Ever." She left the juice on the counter and busied herself with the boxes, suddenly a productive worker bee determined to get the job done.

"Are you sure you're okay?"

"I'm fine." She hefted a box of books. "I swear, Mom."

Grace watched her thoughtfully. It wasn't easy, having her kids turn into adults before her eyes.

The rest of the day passed in a blur. Grace had fleeting glimpses of a muscle-bound crew, a fast-food lunch, multiple trips back and forth between houses. By nine that night, she stood in the new house—her home—amid a maze of boxes. She knew she ought to be dead tired, but instead she felt restless.

She wondered where all of this newfound energy came from. The old Grace tired easily and went to sleep early. Lately she couldn't wait to get out of bed, and stayed up long past *Letterman*. She was like a bulb warmed underground, bursting into bloom in springtime.

But still, sometimes she woke up in the middle of the night to find herself holding Steve's pillow against her, praying some of his smell had lingered there.

Brian and Katie were upstairs in their respective rooms, organizing their things.

Emma stood at the window, her hands cupped around her eyes so she could see the city lights at night.

"It's beautiful, isn't it?" Grace asked.

"Yeah." Her breath had left a ghostly circle on the window. "I still can't believe you went ahead and did this all by yourself."

"I do everything by myself when your dad is at sea. I always have."

"This is different. Mom, this is getting too weird."

"Oh, baby. This feels weird to me, too. When your Dad gets back, we'll sort it out."

"There's nothing to sort out. I can't believe you're pissed off because some woman didn't tell him she had his son. None of that was his fault, and it's not J—Lieutenant Lamont's, either. Lots of people I know have half brothers and stepsons, and it's no big deal."

"You're right," Grace said. "It's not. That was a shock, but... It's complicated, Em. We've had incredible adventures, but you know what? I've decided to do something different, and this is the start."

"Great," said Emma. "You're trying to be happy on your own so you won't need Daddy anymore?"

"Em, it's not like that."

"Then how come it feels like that?" Her eyes burned with anger as she headed for the stairs, picking up a box of clothes to take up. "I'm going to bed. I need to be up early."

"Emma? Is something else the matter?"

She paused at the bottom of the stairs, her shoulders stiffening. "No. Nothing."

"You didn't have much to say about the dance. How was it?"

"Okay."

"Just okay?"

She balanced the box on her knee. "I need to get busy. See you in the morning."

Grace let her go, hoping that whatever was troubling Emma would slip away in the night. When she was younger, she always got over her anger quickly. Emma missed her dad, Grace knew. Usually it was Katie who took Steve's absences the hardest. But lately, it seemed, Emma was struggling the most.

Things were different now, and Emma had clued in to that. The damage was rippling outward, touching each one of them. It was hard to believe this could happen to them. Grace and Steve used to be madly in love, there was no question about that. But as the years went by, both of them seemed to have forgotten to tend to their fragile bond. Between his demanding career and her absorption in raising three kids, they had lost each other. They hadn't paid enough attention to their marriage, hadn't nurtured their love. They'd both tacitly assumed it would thrive on neglect like a weed in the garden. The years wore away the shiny newness of their passion, etching it with scars.

She cleared a space on the sofa and sat for a long time in the dark so she could see the lights glimmering on Camano Island across the water. *I wish you'd wait,* Steve had said.

He didn't get it. That's what she'd been doing for a long time. She sighed and took a basket of linens upstairs to make up her bed.

CHAPTER THIRTY

Grace drove home from her fitness class and showered, ignoring the creaky plumbing. She was just getting dressed when she heard Brian yell, "I'm home."

Shaking her damp hair, she went downstairs. Brian stood with his elbow propped on the refrigerator door while he drank directly from the milk carton.

Grace opened her mouth to scold him, as she had for years, knowing even as she spoke that it wouldn't take effect. But something stopped her, a flash of memory so vivid and strong that she caught her breath. Here he was, a grown man who would soon be leaving home, yet she could picture exactly how he had looked as a little boy, standing in the glow of the refrigerator light as he foraged for food. She still remembered his favorite red plaid cowboy shirt and hat, the sagging holsters he used to fill with golf balls instead of guns. Each time she'd catch him helping himself to something from the fridge, he'd turn on that glorious smile and declare, "I'm the hungriest boy in the world."

He was gone, that little boy, and in his place was a tall man straining toward his own future.

When he finally noticed her, he stopped drinking and offered her that same smile. "Hey, Mom."

"Hey yourself. How about you get a glass from now on?"

He tossed the carton into the trash. "It's empty. Anyway, I need to go."

"Go where?"

He hesitated, shuffled his feet. "I've got an errand to run."

She frowned. "What errand?"

"I need to mail something." He took a deep breath, then set his jaw. He went to the dining room table and showed her a large, flat cardboard case with a handle on top. "I'm sending my portfolio to RISD today."

Grace was speechless with pride and hope. *RizDee,* he pronounced it, just like its artistic alumni. The Rhode Island School of Design. It was where he'd dreamed of going to college. "Good for you, Brian. Do you mind if I take a look?"

"Go ahead." He stood back while she studied samples of his work—dreamy pastels, precise etchings and fantastically detailed drawings in pen and ink.

"It's wonderful," she said. "I've always loved your artwork."

"Dad's going to have a cow."

She stiffened. "This is your decision. Your life."

"He'll say we can't afford it. This school doesn't even offer athletic scholarships."

Brian knew his father well. But Grace felt compelled to say, "Go ahead and get your materials in. Maybe he'll surprise you."

"Do you think he'll freak because I didn't apply to the Naval Academy?"

"Totally," said Katie, coming into the kitchen and setting her clarinet case on the counter. "Boy, I wouldn't want to be in your shoes when he gets home."

"Why don't you just—"

"Don't start," Grace warned them both.

"He's already got a son in the Navy, anyway," Brian muttered.

"Oh, Brian. He doesn't consider Lieutenant Lamont—" Grace

stopped. For a moment she thought about falling into her old habit of answering for Steve, explaining her absent husband to his children. That was what she used to do each time he was away. But no more. Steve was going to have to answer for himself from now on. It was up to him to convince Brian he wasn't losing his place in the family. "You should talk to your dad about that."

"No way."

"I talk to him about it all the time," Katie piped up. "He says he feels bad that he never knew about Lieutenant Lamont. But that can't be changed. He's glad the guy grew up with a nice dad, and that's that. But *we're* his family. And he *will* freak if you don't go to the Naval Academy."

Grace was relieved that, like her, Steve wasn't going to let their differences interfere with his relationship with the kids.

She heard a car door slam and glanced out the front window to see a stranger coming up the walk. Then she realized it wasn't a stranger at all.

"Holy crap," said Brian, and Grace didn't bother to correct him. "What did she do?"

"Don't say a word," Grace cautioned him as the front door opened. "Brian, don't you—"

"Jeez, Em, you hacked off all your hair," he said the second she stepped inside.

"Brilliant observation, genius," she murmured, putting her backpack on the stairs.

"You look—"

"Totally butch," Katie said in a scandalized whisper. "Oh, Emma—"

"Quit making such a big deal about it, already. It's just hair." Emma's cheeks were red.

"Can I...touch it?" Katie reached out and brushed her hand across the dark blond bristles.

"Back off, pest," Emma said. She went to the refrigerator and took out a carton of yogurt.

"It's absolutely great," Grace said, masking her shock. Emma's yard-long silky hair was now an inch all over, if that. She looked like a just-hatched chick.

Grace was dying to know what her daughter was thinking, but a girl's self-esteem was a fragile thing. Proceeding with caution, Grace added, "In fact, I wish I had the guts to do something daring with mine." She touched her damp hair, which hadn't changed in decades, except that now it was streaked with coarse gray threads.

"Speaking of change, I need to tell you something, Mom."

"What is it?" asked Grace. Good Lord, first Brian and now Emma.

"She wants to wear Jockey shorts," Brian said.

"Shut up, Brian. Just shut up," Emma snapped.

"Brian, disappear," Grace ordered. "Go do that errand."

He didn't need any further encouragement. He grabbed the portfolio and the car keys and headed out the door.

"Mom, what I need to tell you is that I'm dropping my PE class."

"The one you're in with Shea and Lindy and Cory?" Katie asked. "What are you, nuts as well as bald?"

"Katie, maybe you should disappear, too." Grace gave her a gentle shove toward the stairs.

"But—"

"March." Grace wanted to know what was on Emma's mind, and she knew she wouldn't find out with the other two hanging around.

"Is this about Cory?" she asked.

Emma's head came up. "I'm not seeing him anymore."

"I noticed that he's stopped calling. I was waiting for you to say something. Why, baby? Was he a jerk to you?"

A dry laugh escaped her. "He's a jerk in general."

Kill him, thought Grace. Kill him now. "Sweetheart, I'm sorry. What happened?"

Emma looked out the window. "Nothing. We called it quits, that's all. It's no big deal. I've broken up with boys before."

Grace gave Emma a hug. She smelled of soap and exotic hair dressing. "I hate to see you hurting. Is he the reason you cut your hair?"

"No way." Emma stepped back and took a bite of her yogurt. "Are you, like, really good friends with his mom these days?"

Grace thought about all the Officers' Spouses meetings she'd skipped lately. Quite likely she was not Allison Crowther's favorite person these days. "No. Don't worry about that. Is Cory giving you a hard time in PE class? Is that why you want to drop it?" she asked softly.

"I just want to drop it, okay?"

"Can you do that, so late in the year?"

"My adviser says I can as long as I add another PE class. I'm going to do independent study."

Grace stared at her daughter's pale, slender neck, the spiky hair a crown of thorns on her head. "What are you going to study?"

She scraped out the last of her yogurt. "I haven't decided."

Grace hated to see Emma looking so lost and hurt. She wanted to like the new hair, but it just looked…mutilated.

When the kids were little, Grace used to kiss their hurts and send them on their way. Helping her grown daughter was more of a challenge. "Swimming?" she suggested.

"I practically live at the pool as it is."

Grace glanced at the Totally New Totally You schedule on the refrigerator. "Come to my fitness class. That would count for independent study. There's at least one other high school girl who is taking it for credit."

"Your class?" Emma snorted. "Come on, Mom. You don't want me in your workout class."

"Sure I do. It'd be special. Just because they let old ladies like me in the class doesn't mean it's not challenging. You find your own level."

Emma shrugged. "I'll check with my adviser."

The phone rang in the study—Grace's business line. She stood where she was, still sensing that Emma needed…something. She couldn't quite put her finger on what.

"Go ahead and get it," Emma said.

"The machine will pick up."

"Just get it, Mom. I need to e-mail my adviser and schedule a meeting. I'm okay. Okay?"

Grace nodded, then hurried to beat the answering machine to the draw. "Grace Bennett."

"It's Ross Cameron."

"Hey." A smile eased across her face. "What can I do for you?"

"I have a list. But first, I want to tell you that my CFO is thrilled with the school you came up with. Thanks for that. I would have hated to lose her."

"You mean if she hadn't liked Briarwood School, she would have given up her job?"

"What can I say? I admire a woman for putting her kids first. So how are you?"

"Putting my kids first, as a matter of fact."

"I bet that's not as easy as it sounds."

He had a knack for detecting the slightest emotion in her voice. She leaned over and pulled the door to the study shut. "With three teenagers, there's always something."

"What is it this time?"

"My older daughter—"

"Emma."

She was pleased that he remembered. "She's sort of had a chip on her shoulder lately, and I can't figure out why. And today she came home with her hair all whacked off and said she was dropping her PE class." Grace eased into conversation with him, as she often did. He was a charming man with an infectious laugh and an understanding manner. Although they'd never met in person, she felt as though they knew each other well.

"Anyway," she concluded, "I don't really know what's up with her. She seems so...distant and unmotivated. I haven't seen her mail off a single application to college, and every time I remind her, she says she's taking care of it." Grace hesitated. This was probably far too personal. But somehow, his friendly, open silence invited honesty; he was like the anonymous priest behind the confessional screen. "Maybe I haven't been a good role model, being nothing but a wife and mother."

"Hey, the world turns because of wives and mothers."

"But I want her to get an education, find a life for herself."

"Which is exactly what you did," he pointed out.

"Well, yes."

"What does she want?"

"I can't tell. We've always had a terrific relationship. But sometimes I wonder…" Grace gripped the receiver and studied the framed portraits of her children on the wall.

"Wonder what?"

The silence was heavy, waiting. "Sometimes I'm afraid I'm failing with my kids." The whispered admission was torn from her.

"Of course you're afraid," he said. "It proves you're human. I've never had kids, but I've got a mother, and I know she had the same worries about me and my brothers as you do with your children."

"Sorry," she said hastily. "I didn't mean to dump my worries on you."

"You didn't," he assured her. "I asked."

CHAPTER THIRTY-ONE

In the spring, Grace got a dog. She didn't mean to, but once she saw Daisy, she lost her heart. She'd hardly slept at all the night before, tossing and turning and missing Steve so badly that she ached in her bones. At sunrise, while the kids were still sound asleep, she got up and went for a walk, savoring the chilly morning quiet of the neighborhood. Dew clung to the camellia and ligustrum hedges, and towhees flitted in and out of the verges, foraging for food. As she passed a yard fenced in chain link, a pack of dogs rushed at her. Grace jumped back, startled but not afraid. They were half-grown mongrels, stumbling over one another as they tried to get closer to Grace. Near the gate, she noticed a hand-lettered sign: Free Puppies.

A moment later a woman in a bathrobe came out of the house. At her side was a yellow dog with worn-out dugs. The four puppies veered toward them, leaping at the mother, who turned baleful eyes to her mistress.

"I didn't mean to stir up your dogs," said Grace.

"Everything stirs them up," the woman said as she let the grown dog in while holding back the pups with her leg. Deprived, the puppies fanned out across the yard, sniffing around, chewing the potted flowers on the porch. "I need to find homes for them before they drive the neighbors mad. You need a dog?"

Reflexively, Grace shook her head. Steve always said a dog was too much trouble for a Navy family.

But then it struck her. What a crock. A dog was one more thing this family had been deprived of for too long.

"On second thought," she said, "I'd love to take one of your puppies."

The woman's face lit with a grin. "Then you're my new best friend."

They introduced themselves, and Grace couldn't stop smiling. A dog. She was really getting a dog. She'd had one when she was a girl, but it had run off and her parents forbade her to get another. Now a dog seemed a perfectly natural addition to the family. Her neighbor, Carla van der Pol, told her the dogs were half yellow Lab, half white German shepherd.

"It's a lot of dog," she said apologetically, "but they're bound to be smart and great with kids."

Grace made a kissing sound with her lips and the smallest one, a female, looked up and wagged its tail. "I know which one I want," said Grace, her heart filled with a sweetness she'd been missing for far too long.

The pup had one of Carla's gerbera daisies in her mouth, so Grace didn't even have to pick a name for her. Carla provided a shot record from the vet and a length of baling wire for a leash, and in just a few minutes, Grace was on her way.

By the time she got home with the puppy, Katie was up. She took one look at Daisy and burst into tears. "Oh, Mommy," she sobbed, sinking to the floor and letting Daisy lick her face, "I've always wanted a dog."

"Me, too," Grace said, watching her daughter and Daisy falling in love instantly and irrevocably. "She's going to be a lot of work, though."

"She's going to be a lot of fun," Katie said, tickling Daisy's belly. "I can't wait to tell Dad." She grew serious for a moment. "Or do you want to tell him?"

"Why don't you send him an e-mail?" Grace suggested.

CHAPTER THIRTY-TWO

Lauren's favorite group of clients attended the four-thirty aerobics class. This particular bunch actually seemed to enjoy the workout rather than treating it as if it were a root canal. They came to the fitness studio and stuck with it. These were the women Lauren most admired, the sort she aspired to be one day—a healthy woman who accepted herself, flaws and all.

With U2 on the stereo, she added ninety more seconds to the usual cardio set. They seemed fine with the slight increases she added each week. In the mirror she glanced at Emma Bennett. The resemblance between the tall young girl and Josh was uncanny, she thought. Emma was a blond, female version of her half brother. They had the same intense eyes, the same thousand-watt smile bright enough to light up a room.

Emma didn't really smile much lately, but Lauren didn't know her well enough to ask her why. She touched the remote and slowed the beat for the next segment of the routine. "How are you doing, Patricia?" she asked after class ended. "You're taking it easy, right?"

"Absolutely." She touched her belly. "I feel fantastic. My mother and two of my sisters have already come to stay with me."

"Any word on the baby's sex?"

"It's never turned the right direction. Camera shy, I guess."

As much as Lauren liked Patricia, it was hard to look at her. Patricia was blooming with the classic glow of pregnancy. Lauren battled the sick envy she felt, but it was no use. She wanted a baby of her own so badly that sometimes her arms ached with emptiness. Even just the smell of an infant or the sound of its cooing could tie her in knots.

Falling in love with Josh only deepened her terrible yearning. Love seemed to do that to her. Wanting a baby with him was as inevitable as breathing.

She kept trying to find ways to tell him her fears, but it seemed premature to make such a confession. Presumptuous, even. The minute you started talking about babies, the relationship leaped to a new level, perhaps landing in a place she didn't want to go.

It was best to avoid a topic that could so easily tear them apart. Besides, the discussion would bring up questions to which she had no answers. The fact was, she didn't know why she hadn't conceived with Gil. After he died, there seemed to be no point in pursuing fertility tests.

She straightened up the studio and Windexed the mirrors as people gathered their things to leave. Grace and Emma were in the reception area, where Grace was writing a check for their next month's worth of classes.

"How have you been, Lauren?" asked Grace.

"Fine. Just super." Her cheerful reply sounded forced even to her own ears. "How about yourself?"

"Busy," said Grace. "I have only three clients at the moment, but they add up to a full-time job."

Emma handed Lauren her attendance sheet, and Lauren signed her name next to the date and time so Emma could qualify for school credit. "You're doing a great job, Emma," she said. "If I was grading you, that would be an A-plus."

"Thanks." Emma went to the locker area to change her shoes.

"Sorry about her," Grace murmured. "She's been a little on edge. I don't know why."

Lauren gave her a reassuring smile. "At eighteen, she doesn't need a reason."

"It might be the stress of waiting to hear from colleges."

"Where does she want to go?"

"That's the funny thing. I'm not sure, and I don't think she is, either. She doesn't want any help from me except to fill out those dreadful FAFSA forms. She sent in applications to the University of Washington, Western and Gonzaga, that I know of."

Lauren was intrigued by Emma Bennett, and not just because she was Josh's half sister. The girl who attended fitness class four times a week didn't seem like the same person Lauren had briefly glimpsed at the Captain's Quarters restaurant. That laughing, golden-haired girl had transformed herself into an intense young woman whose thoughts hid behind watchful eyes.

When Lauren was Emma's age, she'd tried on new identities, too. But no matter how she changed her hair and her clothes, she was still the Fat Girl. You can't escape who you are, she wanted to tell Emma. But at eighteen, Emma would never believe that. Perhaps girls that age had to believe they could become anything they wanted to be, leaving the past behind like childhood keepsakes forgotten in the bottom of a cedar chest. Emma didn't know yet that even though you could walk away from those things, they were still a part of you, the blood and bone of who you would become.

Lauren was certainly proof of that. The traumas of high school and college made her cautious. Timid, even. Being the Fat Girl had taught her to keep her expectations low. Losing her husband at such a young age had taught her to guard her heart.

She simply had not been prepared for Josh to burst into her life and sweep her off her feet. But that was exactly what he had done. Before Josh, she had never felt such exquisite agony, not even with Gil. Her first marriage had been based on quiet affection, mutual respect and similar life goals. In no way had it prepared Lauren for the frightening intensity of true passion or the wrenching agony of knowing their lives could not mesh without one of them sacrificing a dream.

"You all right, Lauren?" asked Grace.

"Of course," Lauren said, mystified by her question. "Why do you ask?"

"Well, for starters, you taught the whole routine with your T-shirt on inside out," Grace said with a grin.

Lauren glanced in the mirror behind the desk. Grace was right. And she was probably too polite to mention the coffee-stained spandex shorts Lauren had retrieved from the laundry basket on her way out the door this afternoon.

Lauren shook her head. "I guess I'm a little distracted lately. I have a lot on my mind."

"Care to talk about it?" Grace asked.

She was like that, Lauren thought. Grace was special. She had a way about her that drew people, made them open up to her. "Actually, there is this guy…"

"Ah," said Grace. "Is it serious?"

"I don't know. That's why I've been stressed out." Josh had gone to Fallon, Nevada, for training and would return today. Lauren was shocked by how much she missed him. Even a short absence was torture. How would she ever be able to cope with deployment?

Grace glanced in the mirror, too, and made a face. "I'm really not one to talk about clothes," she said, plucking at her pumpkin-colored T-shirt. "I should do something with my hair, like Emma did."

Emma returned then, jammed a baseball cap on her head and zipped her gym bag. "It wasn't all that hard, Mom."

"I know a great salon over in Seattle," Lauren said. She opened a drawer and took out a card. "Here's her number."

"Ivanka at the Gene Juarez salon," Grace read.

"Her specialty is the total makeover," said Lauren. "Not that you need it," she added hastily.

"Oh, I definitely need it," said Grace.

Lauren hesitated, then dug deeper in the drawer and handed Grace a photograph. "No, I was the one who needed it."

"Who's this?" Grace showed the image to Emma, who shrugged.

"That, my friends, is yours truly five years ago."

Both Grace and Emma did a double take. Watching their faces, Lauren burst out laughing.

"Wow," said Emma.

"I'm stunned," said Grace. "Is this Ivanka a surgeon?"

"No, but I call her a magician. She's terrific. After I lost the weight, she gave me the short red hair and some intensive makeup lessons and I became her fan for life."

"Lauren, I'm so impressed. I had no idea." Grace handed back the photo, but she kept Ivanka's business card.

"I don't emphasize my weight loss in the studio," Lauren explained. "My clients come here to get strong and healthy, not to get thin."

"Darn. And here I thought I was going to get thin."

"You might. I bet you're at least a size or two smaller. But some women are big and always will be, and I don't ever want them to have a problem with that. I want them to be healthy and to feel good about themselves." She put the picture back in the drawer. "I was not that type of girl. I was big for all the wrong reasons, and my size was endangering my health."

"I think you look fantastic," said Emma. "You totally changed yourself." She shifted her bag from one shoulder to the other.

"We'd better be going," said Grace. She took a windbreaker from a hook.

Watching her, Lauren hoped Grace actually would go see Ivanka. She was an attractive woman who didn't pay enough attention to herself.

She turned the Closed sign face out on the studio door. A movement outside caught her eye. Her heart began to pound. Josh was outside, heading straight for the studio.

Lauren looked around wildly. It was too late to zip down the blinds, too late to hide. Too late to turn her shirt right side out. She was trapped.

And so were Grace and Emma, who suspected nothing.

CHAPTER THIRTY-THREE

When Lauren made a funny sound, halfway between a cough and a gasp, Grace quit rummaging in her purse for the car keys. Lauren's face was red, as though she was having trouble breathing.

Then Grace saw the visitor outside the door, and she came down with the same malady. She froze, her silver anchor key chain clutched in her hand.

It was Joshua Lamont, square-shouldered and perfectly groomed, looking so much like Steve that Grace got chills. The minute he stepped inside, everyone seemed to stop breathing. Josh looked from Lauren to Emma to Grace, and then back to Lauren.

To his credit, he didn't actually say, "Oh, shit," but she could tell it definitely crossed his mind.

"Josh," Lauren said in a breathless rush. "What a surprise. I didn't expect to see you until tonight."

"I was in the neighborhood and couldn't wait to see you." He grinned, sheepish but unapologetic. Just like Steve. Then he bent and kissed Lauren's cheek.

"So I guess you've met." Lauren's cheeks were burning as she awkwardly stepped back. Her gaze darted from Josh to Grace to Emma.

Grace glanced at Emma, who was watching in rapt fascination.

He nodded politely to Grace. "Nice to see you, ma'am," he said. Then he turned. "Hello, Emma," he added.

"Hey." Emma spoke a neutral but familiar greeting.

Grace felt a stab of pure shock. Josh and Emma knew each other? When the hell had that happened?

"Well," she said before the awkwardness sent her fleeing to the car. "I guess this is a day for surprises." Grace despised secrets. She wanted to wring Emma's neck for not letting on she knew Josh.

"Have you met my other children, too?" Grace asked, trying not to show her outrage.

"No, ma'am," he said.

"You should come to dinner," Emma said suddenly. "At our house."

They all turned to stare at her. She faced them with a calm politeness that made Grace proud. "My mom's a fantastic cook. Would that be all right, Mom?"

Grace knew what Emma was doing. She wanted to bring Joshua to their turf. Grace couldn't bring herself to object. Emma was so quiet lately. This was the first overture she'd made in weeks. Maybe she saw a father figure in Josh. "I…yes. You'd both be welcome." She couldn't believe she was saying the words without gagging.

Joshua cleared his throat. "We'd be imposing—"

"No," Grace forced herself to say. "We should definitely get together." She felt Emma relax beside her.

"We'd love to," Lauren declared. "Well, I'd love to, anyway."

"Good," said Grace. "I'll make my famous lasagna."

As they firmed up their arrangements, Grace struggled to hold her poise. Inside, she was dying. Here she was in her ancient Texas Longhorns T-shirt, her hair plastered to her head by sweat, her face gleaming as though she'd applied a layer of Crisco. She felt like Delilah, offering lasagna to Steve's firstborn son.

She held her smile pasted in place by sheer force of will, and made her exit with Emma in tow. She held her silence until they reached the car, climbed in and shut the door. Then she turned to Emma. "So how long have you known that man without telling me?"

Emma stared straight ahead as Grace drove home. "I don't know. I met him in the fall, I guess. He, um, he's working with some of the seniors applying to the Naval Academy."

The information sank in. "Now I get it. So that's why Brian wouldn't even touch his Naval Academy application."

"That's part of the reason. But you know he has never wanted to go there."

"In the meantime, you're on a first-name basis with Joshua Lamont."

"So what?" Emma snapped. "It's totally weird, okay? We have the same father. I was just a little curious about that. I didn't say anything to you because I didn't want to upset you. And look at you. You're upset. That's exactly what I was trying to avoid."

Steve was a very lucky man to be half a world away at this particular moment. If he were here now, Grace would have to kill him. "What possessed you to invite them over?" she asked.

"I don't know. It's going to be all awkward no matter what. So I thought, why not get it over with?"

Grace blew out a sigh. "All right," she said, "I'm not mad. I'm not even upset. Just surprised. And you're absolutely correct about this being an awkward situation. So we'll get all the questions out of the way and move on."

"Good plan," Emma said quietly.

They drove in silence for a while. Springtime was bursting over Whidbey. Nodding daffodils lined the roadways and apple trees in white blossoms decked every yard. Grace tried to concentrate on the glorious scenery, but finally she had to ask. "So, what's he like?"

"Lieutenant—I mean, Josh? I don't really know him that well. But he's okay. I mean, I'm pretty sure he doesn't want to mess up our family or anything. He looks just like Dad, doesn't he?"

"Yes."

"Do you ever wonder about, you know…her?"

"Josh's mother, you mean." *Steve's first love. The first woman he'd married.* "Well, of course I wonder about her."

"And?"

Grace kept her eyes on the road. "I really don't have much to say about her. She was young and she made a terrible mistake."

"Just like Dad."

"Yes. Like Dad."

"So you can forgive her but not him?"

"It's not up to me to forgive her. I don't know her, and I'm sure she doesn't care about my opinion."

"Are you ever going to forgive him?"

"Emma, you've got it wrong. Forgiveness is not the issue between your dad and me. We're…struggling with some decisions about the future."

"Maybe it wouldn't be such a struggle if you'd talk to him for more than five minutes on the phone."

"Let it go, Emma. You just invited his son to dinner." Grace shuddered.

"Should I uninvite him?"

"That would be even worse."

Emma rode in silence for a while. Then she asked, "Do you think it's always unethical, keeping things hidden?"

"Sweetie, I can't make a blanket statement about that. Why do you ask?"

There was a long hesitation. A flock of Canada geese flew overhead and landed in a hayfield beside the road. Emma turned her face to the window.

"Just wondering," she said.

CHAPTER THIRTY FOUR

"So did you play sports in high school?" Katie asked Josh, her gaze worshiping him across the dinner table. She had been bombarding him with questions since he and Lauren had walked through the door.

"You bet," he said. "Lacrosse and basketball."

"Whoa. Dad played basketball in high school. Brian's sports are baseball and track. So did you like going to Annapolis?"

"It changed my life," Josh said.

Grace struggled with the idea that she was feeding dinner to her husband's firstborn child. It was incredible to realize that Josh had been in the world for twenty-six years, a mystery to the man who had fathered him. Yet Steve's presence shone through in Josh's smile, even the way he held himself.

Meeting their half brother was probably as surreal to the kids as it was to her. She sensed that in addition to being curious about him, they felt vaguely threatened. Emma showed Josh a surprising measure of deference. Katie was in awe of him. Brian didn't bother to hide his resentment as he shoveled in the food and gave monosyllabic answers only when directly prodded.

"I have to go," he announced in his longest speech of the evening. "I promised Mr. Clune I'd fill in at the shop tonight."

"There's raspberry sorbet for dessert," Katie reminded him.

"I have to get going," Brian said, not bothering to mask his eagerness to escape. He took his plate to the kitchen.

Grace excused herself, grabbing the chicken pitcher on the pretext of refilling it. "I didn't know the cycle shop was open tonight," she murmured.

"It is." He tugged a sweatshirt over his head.

She could feel resentment rolling off him. "Until when?"

"Depends. How late are they staying?" He jerked his head toward the dining room.

He'd been displaced, Grace realized, hurting for Brian. He was no longer the oldest, no longer the only son. And here he was, facing a Naval Academy graduate, an officer, a pilot. A man who was everything Steve claimed he wanted in a son.

This wasn't the time to discuss it, though. She had no idea what to do to make this work—for the kids, or for herself. Like so many issues in the Bennett family, this one had fallen into her lap with Steve gone. This was her problem to deal with. Her mess to clean up. And she had no idea where to begin.

"See you later, then," she said.

He left in a hurry, his "Nice meeting you" called out as he fled through the back door.

Grace returned to the table with the pitcher of water.

"This is the best lasagna I've ever had," Lauren declared.

"Thanks. It's actually a low-fat version. You mix tofu with the ricotta. So have all you want."

"It's delicious. Promise you'll share the recipe."

Katie turned to Lauren. "You probably don't ever have to watch what you eat."

Grace remembered the picture of the obese woman Lauren kept in her desk. "Emma," she said, intervening before Lauren could answer, "how about some help clearing the table?"

With uncharacteristic enthusiasm, Emma jumped up and gathered the dirty dishes.

"Ma'am, that was the best chow I've had in ages," Josh said.

"Glad you liked it." Grace handed Emma a stack of plates.

Josh studied a display of photos on the built-in wall shelves. In the middle stood a framed picture of Steve and the kids, taken at the beach at Mustang Island last year. He and Brian were shirtless and suntanned, each holding one end of a surfboard while the girls sat on the board between them. Grace had always liked the shot because it was so candid, his grin reflecting unadulterated joy in being with his children. He'd left his officer persona somewhere else for that moment, and he was simply a family man.

She had to wonder what Josh felt when he saw that snapshot. Regret that he'd never known Steve? Resentment? Or relief that he'd lived a different life?

"Want to see some more pictures?" Katie said. "We have tons and tons. Here, I'll show you."

Before Grace could decide whether or not it was a good idea, her youngest child dragged a stack of photo albums from a cabinet in the buffet. A look of stark curiosity crossed Josh's face. He yearned to know about his biological father, she realized. His half siblings.

Katie did a remarkably good job with the narration, proving herself to be well-informed about the family's history even before she was born. "They got married by a Navy chaplain. Check out my mom's dress. It was her grandmother's, wasn't it, Mom?"

"Yes. Yes, it was." Her memory of that day was crystal clear. She had been so deeply in love that her parents' disapproval hadn't mattered one bit. Steve had swept her off her feet in every sense of the word, making her giddy with excitement about the life they were about to begin.

"They went to Sigonella—that's in Sicily—after they were married," Katie said, turning to a page of photos depicting the arid scenery of the Mediterranean in high summer. There was a shot of Grace and Steve on motor scooters that were perfect for running around hillsides covered with goats and olive trees.

"And there's Pensacola," Katie said. The albums and her ideaalistic narrative depicted a happy family.

Grace wondered if the others could see what she saw, that Steve was a complicated man, often torn between duty and desire. That their marriage was one of dramatic and frequent changes. The photographs and memorabilia awakened a host of memories, and questions arose, too.

Did the laughing young bride understand that she was setting aside her own dreams in order to make his come true? There, in the shot of her standing on the pier saddled with a twin on either hip, was there a glint of desperation lurking behind her smile? In the Christmas portrait, taken in Guam when the kids were little, had she been too busy running the family to recognize the occasional pangs for what they were? And what about Steve? Did he give a thought to the life he'd chosen?

As they talked to Josh about the past, Grace felt the weight of her own history with Steve. Her feelings for her husband were deeper and more complex than she'd ever dreamed they could be. Duty and deception had taken their toll, but casualties couldn't be assessed until he returned.

The pictures reminded her of something else. Despite the upheaval, the agony of long absences and the constant juggling act of adjustment, she wouldn't trade the past twenty years for anything. She had done things, gone places, experienced cultures that made her see herself with new eyes. She'd encountered artwork, food, festivals and political unrest that Mrs. Joe Average couldn't begin to fathom. Every tea, every ceremony, every meeting with a dignitary, had become a part of her. Yet the irony was that the very thing she wanted to escape or change was the thing that had made her the woman she was.

"What a fabulous life," Lauren concluded as Katie finished with the final album, which took them up through last summer's Change of Command.

"I'm glad to hear you say that." Josh patted Lauren's arm, another gesture that was oddly reminiscent of Steve. Clueless but affectionate. Lauren managed to smile with delight and look terrified all at once.

"I have to go practice my clarinet," Katie said, pushing back her chair.

"Can I listen?" asked Josh with what appeared to be utter sincerity.

Katie blushed. "I guess. I'm not very good yet."

"She's incredibly good," Emma said loyally. She and Katie led the way to the den, leaving Grace and Lauren alone to finish the dishes.

A few minutes later, the strains of a Gershwin melody drifted through the house. The two women worked side by side, the rhythm of their movements curiously synchronized as Lauren rinsed and loaded while Grace wiped the counters and put away the leftovers.

"So what do you think about Navy life?" asked Grace, noticing Lauren's pensive expression. "It's a different world, isn't it?"

Lauren looked uneasy. "My late husband was a civilian contractor for the Navy."

"Late husband?" Grace was horrified. Lauren was far too young to be a widow.

"I used to be married. My husband died three years ago."

"I didn't know, Lauren. I'm terribly sorry."

"Thank you. It's…a sadness. But since I met Josh, it's not like a black cloud hanging over my days anymore."

"Then I'm glad you met him," Grace said.

They continued working, their silence unexpectedly companionable. A rhapsodic riff floated from Katie's clarinet.

"She *is* good," Lauren said.

Grace nodded. "We're very proud of our kids." Such a habit, she thought, speaking in the collective "we" as though she knew what Steve was thinking. Of course, when it came to the kids, she did know.

"Josh grew up an only child," Lauren said. "He said he always wished for brothers and sisters." She caught Grace's look and quickly added, "He isn't looking to be part of this family, believe me. He's devoted to his mother and to the memory of his father."

"I realize that," said Grace. "My kids are still getting used to the idea of him." She liked Josh, too. But his presence was a constant reminder that her marriage had gone wrong.

She noticed Lauren upending the chicken pitcher into the rack. "That doesn't go in the dishwasher," she said. "It's old, and probably irreplaceable."

"No problem." Lauren gently washed the pitcher under the nozzle. "Is it a family heirloom?"

Grace smiled at the irony of that. "No, but it has sentimental value. I bought it at a garage sale when we were first married."

Lauren's handling was almost reverent as she dried the pitcher with a tea towel. "You make this way of life look so easy."

"Do I?"

"Completely."

"I suppose it's because there really isn't an alternative. You learn to flourish on your own while your husband's deployed, or you're in for misery half your life."

Lauren nodded. "I've been on my own for a while, and I wasn't miserable. But…I wasn't really living, either." She stared out the window at the evening sky. "I wonder, if you didn't have your kids, how much harder it would be to endure the months without your husband."

"I never really thought about that. Why do you ask?"

"It's something I've been wondering about lately." Lauren bit her lip. "Can I be honest with you?"

"Of course."

"Well, I was pretty shocked by Josh's story of how his mother never told Steve she'd had his baby."

You're not the only one, thought Grace.

"But sometimes I think I can understand it. She was young and alone, and then Grant—Josh's adoptive father—came along and took care of everything. I'm not saying she did the right thing, but that I can understand why she did the wrong thing. Anyway, I was just wondering if that makes me terrible. Or…unsuitable as a Navy wife."

Grace smiled. "Has Josh asked you to marry him?"

"No."

"Do you want him to?"

"I don't know. I keep changing my mind every other minute. Sometimes I know for sure I could be like you and stay in it for the long haul. But other times, I imagine myself all alone and missing him, and it's awful."

"This life's not for everybody," Grace said. "It's a mixed blessing. When he's away at sea, the world is mine. I determine how the day is going to go. That's the way it should be. But then he comes back and everything changes. Sometimes I lie awake, too, wondering about my own choices. As time goes on, I have to wonder which life suits me most."

Lauren looked stunned. "You've got to be kidding."

Grace turned on the dishwasher. "Sometimes, not always. You have to decide for yourself if having two lives will work for you."

Lauren looked directly at Grace. "I keep wondering if I could cope with this life, but I'm afraid."

"What are you afraid of?" asked Grace.

"Disappointment. And maybe…getting what I want."

"Why is that scary?"

"Because it will hurt so much if I lose it."

PART FOUR
DUTY STATUS—
WHEREABOUTS UNKNOWN

DUSTWUN: Duty Status—Whereabouts Unknown.
A transitory casualty status, applicable only to
military personnel, that is used when the responsible
commander suspects the member may be
a casualty whose absence is involuntary,
but does not feel sufficent evidence currently exists
to make a definite determination of missing or deceased.

(MILPERSMAN 1770-020)

CHAPTER THIRTY-FIVE

Lauren awakened in Josh's arms and lay perfectly still, listening to the beat of his heart and the cadence of his breathing. It was easy to match her breathing with his, and somehow it relaxed her and made her feel even closer to him. Morning sunshine streamed through the parted curtains. On the deck outside, Ranger, the stray who'd stayed, prowled back and forth, home from his nightly wanderings.

Lauren studied the clothes heaped on the arm of a nearby chair, his flight jacket covering her yellow cotton sweater, his boots towering over her sling-back sandals. His squadron cap hung on one of the posters of her bed. He was moving into her life in every sense of the word, and she wasn't lifting a finger to stop him.

After being in the deep freeze of grief since Gil died, she had thawed out and learned to laugh again, learned to grasp life in both hands and pull herself into feelings she'd abandoned long ago— joy, passion and deep contentment. She knew she was breaking every rule in her own book because of Josh, but she'd lived without passion long enough. The lack of deep feeling was carving out a hollow ache inside her. She wanted laughter and joy again. Josh made her want it.

It was no use resisting him. No use trying to tell him she might not be the person to give him what he wanted so badly—a wife at the home front, a houseful of kids.

"You're thinking again," said a sleepy voice, rumbling against her ear.

"What's that supposed to mean?" She folded her hands on his bare chest and gazed up at him.

"You were fast asleep, and then you woke up and started thinking again," he said.

"If you're so smart, what was I thinking about?"

He took hold of her shoulders and drew her up against him, nuzzling her neck. His morning beard created a delicious prickling sensation on her skin. "You were thinking about how we should just keep this casual."

She winced; he was close to the truth. The disturbing fact she had discovered in his arms was that she was ready for more than passion. She was ready to love again, and falling in love scared her.

"What's wrong with being casual?" she asked, sliding her hand down his torso. He had an incredible body, young and taut, responsive and exciting.

"Nothing's wrong with it," he said, lifting her up so that she straddled him, "except that it's not where we are, not anymore. You know that, Lauren. You know."

She caught her breath and held on tight. Her doubts and his dreams ceased to matter when they were together like this. The air between them literally crackled. He consumed her, and she willingly offered herself.

"I dreamed about this all night and woke up thinking about it," she whispered, heating up to the boiling point. She could feel him rising toward a climax, and she bent down and whispered in his ear, "What do you have to say to that, Lieutenant?"

He hesitated, then gasped and rocked against her. Then he shuddered and whispered back: "Eject, eject, eject."

"How romantic," she said, but she was lost, as she was always lost with him, and she fell down against his bare chest, wondering how she had survived this long without these feelings.

And wondering what would happen when he left.

It was strange, she couldn't remember what she used to do with her time before Josh filled every moment. She could not recall how she spent the long, lonely hours. She embraced him with tenderness and gratitude for bringing her back to life, and in the aftermath of passion, she held him close and refused to let him leave the bed.

"Now, honey," he said, stroking her hair, "I'm going to have to get up sooner or later."

"I choose later." She snuggled close, feeling as lazy and contented as Ranger the cat.

He stirred, and she reared up, pinning his wrists to the mattress. "I'm serious, Josh. Stay with me."

"Yeah?" he said with a grin. "That's the first time you've admitted you're serious about me."

"I didn't mean—"

"Shh." He freed one hand and touched his fingers to her lips. "Sure you did, honey. I'm not letting you change your mind now. I love you, Lauren. I seriously love you, and I want a future with you."

His statement frightened her into motion. She drew back and tried to leave the bed, but he was quicker. "Don't run away yet, Lauren. I'm not finished."

"Yes, you are."

"No, I'm not. I was going to do this tonight, but I can't wait any longer. In case you haven't figured it out, Lauren Lynette Stanton, I'm popping the question here."

"Josh, my God—"

"Just hear me out, okay?" He grew solemn. "Listen, I'm new at loving you, Lauren. I swear I'll get better at it, but you need to give me the chance. This isn't easy for me."

Her throat filled with heat. She was going to cry, she just knew it. "All right," she said. "I'm listening, but—"

"Good. Because I hardly slept all night, trying to figure out how to say this. I never thought I'd be so pulled in different directions. I love you, Lauren, and I want to spend every minute of my life with you."

Even as the thrill of his declaration rolled over her, she sensed a "but" in the intake of his next breath. "Go on," she forced herself to say. The heat in her throat prickled more insistently.

"At the same time," he said, "I know I have to leave you."

"When?" was all she could ask.

"At 0600 tomorrow. I'm flying out to the *Dominion*."

She nodded. They'd been expecting this all along. It was what a Navy man did. Waited for orders, then went to sea.

Despite all her efforts, a tear escaped and tracked down her cheek. And deep inside her, rage flickered. She had allowed this to happen, knowing what was coming. He'd made her love him, and now he was going away. And he clearly expected her to be all right with this.

"I see." She offered the most neutral reply she could think of. Then, before her head could plan what to say, her heart spoke. "Josh, I want to beg you not to go, but I would never do that. I would never ask you to abandon your lifelong dream."

"Ah, Lauren." He wrapped his arms around her in a bear hug, then pulled away to gaze into her eyes. "Will you marry me, Lauren?"

She dropped her forehead to his shoulder. "I can't."

His grip on her stiffened. "I know it's a lot to ask you to wait for me, but I swear I'll write to you every day, phone you whenever I can. And when I get back, I'll make it worth the wait. I promise, honey."

"I know you'd keep that promise. But you don't have to. We wouldn't be happy together, Josh."

"We *are* happy together. Everything's so good between us. It'll only get better. Lauren, I've never felt this way about anyone before. I know I'm not your first husband, but I can—"

"Is that what you think?" she asked, incredulous. "That I'm comparing you to Gil?"

"The possibility crossed my mind."

Her heart broke as she held his face between her hands and

kissed him softly on the lips. "I've never felt this way before, either," she admitted. "Not for anyone. Not even Gil."

"Really?"

"This is all new to me, Josh. New and crazy and wonderful. But I'm giving you a chance to cut your losses now."

"Why the hell would I want to do that?"

"Because I'll disappoint you. I can't give you what you want."

"You already are," he said. "You already do. Every day."

She took a deep breath. "Josh, I can't get pregnant. If we got married, I wouldn't be having your babies."

The unguarded look of shock and disappointment on his face cut her straight to the core. He recovered with impressive speed, but in that flicker of time, she had seen his heart.

She said nothing more, but slipped from the bed, put on her robe and went to the kitchen to turn on the coffeemaker. She heard the toilet flush and then he joined her, wearing blue jeans and nothing else.

"I'm not withdrawing the proposal, if that's what you think," he said.

"You should, Josh. I mean it. From the first day we met, you said you wanted a big family, and I can't give you that."

"How can you be so sure? You and Gil were only married a few years. Maybe it was him. Have you…tried with anyone else?"

"Of course not."

He took her by the hand and sat down at the table with her. "Tell me everything, Lauren. I deserve to know."

She shut her eyes. "Yes. You do." And somehow, it was so much easier than she'd feared it would be. She explained about the first year, when their inability to conceive was just a mild concern. Then came the second year, when the doctor gave her a wake-up call about her health and she finally did something about it. But still no baby. "We made an appointment with a fertility specialist, but Gil died before we ever met her."

"He was the one who was infertile," Josh said with utter certainty. "Not you."

"I can't promise you that."

"Then let's find out for sure."

"You want to examine my teeth, too? Make sure I'm not lying about my age?"

He laughed at her. Laughed. How dare he?

"Aw, honey, you've got it all wrong. I don't want you to go to some specialist to find out whether or not you can conceive. Let's get married, get rid of the Trojans and find out the old-fashioned way."

"And what if you find out I can't have babies?"

"We'll have babies." His sturdy confidence rang through her. "So when do you want to do it?"

"Do what? Slow down, Josh."

"I don't have time to slow down. I have to go, Lauren. I don't have a choice."

"Exactly. So this is the wrong time to be talking about marriage."

"It's the only time I have."

She took his hand. "Let's make a deal."

He brought her hand to his lips and kissed it. "I have a better idea. Let's just get married."

Her heart ached with the yearning to simply say yes. But she couldn't do that. "While you're at sea, I'll go back to the specialist."

"Damn it, Lauren, I'm proposing to you, not to your reproductive system."

"There's so much more to consider. I don't know if I have what it takes to be a full-time wife to a part-time husband."

"But I know. Trust me, Lauren. Better yet, trust yourself."

This was what it was like to love a Navy man, she realized. This was the roller coaster. And she'd always preferred the merry-go-round.

Lauren felt shell-shocked the next morning when she told him goodbye in the rain. Even as she held him in her arms, pressed her cheek to his chest and whispered that she loved him, she experienced a peculiar numbness, as though she'd been hit by a truck.

"It'll be all right, honey," he promised her, inhaling deeply as he kissed her hair, her face, as if trying to draw her into him.

Didn't he know? she wondered. She already belonged to him. She shut her eyes and tried to memorize the way he felt, the shape of him and the texture of his hair, the way he tasted. "You'd better come back to me," she said fiercely. "Swear it, Josh."

"I swear, honey. And you've got to swear we'll get married—"

"Not that, Josh. One thing at a time." Her heart felt as though something was crushing it. Here he was, the man of her dreams, when she didn't even know she was dreaming of him, and he was going away. He wanted something from her she couldn't give.

She believed him when he said he wanted her with or without babies. But he didn't understand how sad that was, how much the yearning hurt. She'd seen him with children, and she knew he'd be a wonderful father. There was a particular sweetness in raising children, in going through all the joys and sorrows of life with them. She knew how it felt to watch other people's children, wanting your own. It hurt to the core. She wouldn't wish that on anyone.

"Just remember I love you," she said. "Be safe." She couldn't believe how easy it was to say. Maybe that was what a Navy wife did. Gave her love and wished him well.

"Always. Take care, Lauren. Remember how much I love you."

She cried, of course. She knew she would. But she wasn't prepared for his tears. When his grin faded and his eyes filled, she kissed him hard. Her heart fell down in pieces.

Then he was gone in a hiss of tires on wet pavement. For a few minutes she couldn't move. She looked around her garden and saw that the wisteria was budding, the forsythia hedge was in bloom and grape hyacinth lined the rain-spattered walkway.

CHAPTER THIRTY-SIX

Dear Daddy, I need to tell you about something that happened to me....

Emma stared at the pulsing cursor on the computer screen until her vision blurred. Then she did what she always did when she was tempted to spill her guts. She hit the delete key.

Delete, delete, delete. If only her memory had a delete button. She'd tried everything—pretending it hadn't happened, fantasizing about going to the police, getting revenge. Day in and day out, for weeks and now months. But nothing seemed to work. Everything, every moment, reminded her of the rape. She simply could not forget. Her brain overheated like a steam engine, and sometimes she imagined the top of her head blowing off and the truth erupting from her.

But even though her fingers ached to type the message to her father, to tell him about the pain and shame and terror, she knew she couldn't do that. That would only make things worse. If Cory had been any other kid, maybe she would have a choice. But she knew her dad. If she told, he'd take his chances regardless of the cost to his career.

She would never ask that of him. She wouldn't make him lose

everything he'd been building since before she was born. After this tour, he'd have the biggest command of his life. One word from her could destroy his chances.

She'd seen it happen before. As a freshman, she'd gone to high school with the son of a rear admiral. The boy had been caught stealing from the base commissary. Not long after that, his father had been mothballed to a low-level administrative job.

Sometimes when she saw Cory in school, she couldn't believe it had happened. He acted so…normal. If she'd dared to say anything, he would find a way to make people believe his side of the story. She knew it. He probably had it all planned out in his head, in case she spoke up.

Sometimes Emma even doubted herself. Had she overreacted? Maybe that was a typical encounter between kids who weren't very experienced. Maybe Cory was acting on signals she'd sent out. Up until the moment he'd pushed her down on the bench, she'd been attracted to him, had invited his kisses, his touches. Maybe, just maybe, she was wrong about that night.

Except that she wasn't. The terror and humiliation were real. The sense of violation and fury still lingered. When she woke up panicked and sweating at night, she knew exactly what had happened to her.

Daisy wandered in, her nails clicking on the floor. She came over to the desk and pushed her soft muzzle at Emma's hand with sweet insistence.

Emma petted her absently, her thoughts still troubled. She had no idea how to get over it. One thing was certain, she would never say a word. She'd made that decision and she intended to stick to it.

So instead of burdening her father and forcing him to sacrifice his career, she wrote a nice, safe note about Daisy. The big, laughing yellow Lab mixed-breed dog was easy to write about. She was so adorable. Thanks to Daisy, Emma finally understood the meaning of unconditional, nonjudgmental love. From the moment Mom had brought her home, she'd burrowed into everyone's hearts, curled up and stayed there, a permanent resident.

Some days she was Emma's only reason to smile.

She scratched Daisy behind the ears. The kids at school thought Emma was losing her mind, first by dumping Cory—she didn't contradict him when he told everyone he'd dumped her—and then by chopping off her hair.

She wasn't losing her mind. She was trying to keep it intact. It was hard, though. Everything Mom said tended to scare the crap out of her. The most innocent question made her worry that Mom knew. She had to be careful around her mom. Because sometimes the only thing in the world Emma wanted was to crawl into her mother's arms and sob out her agony.

She ran upstairs to take a shower. Again. In the months since the rape, she'd showered and scrubbed and shampooed herself raw, over and over again. But she could never get clean enough.

The hot needles of water beating down over her head and neck and back—this was her new excess. She couldn't help herself, though. She wanted to shampoo her brain. Treat her heart with detangling conditioner so she could comb out the memories, leaving only sleek forgetfulness behind.

Steve felt an ache of loneliness as he read his older daughter's latest e-mail. Emma always had something cheerful to say, some little anecdote to share. Today's note was about the dog. She'd attached a digital photo. The thing had grown as big as a horse.

The constant din of the carrier's power plant hummed in his ears. Every few minutes it felt like a bus ran into the wall beside him as the catapult hurled another aircraft aloft for drills. The crash and stomp reminded him that this was his world, a cold steel cocoon. But when he reread Emma's note, it all went away for a few minutes.

Thank God for e-mail. Even filtered and restricted, it was a way to stay in touch on a basic level. Emma had an instinctive sense of the best way to bolster morale. It was one of those intangible qualities of leadership so hard to find and even harder to measure. In his reply to Emma, he mentioned that. *Your note came just when I needed it. Knowing what to say and when to say it is a gift,* he typed. *It's one of those things that'll take you where you want to go.*

He hit Send, then scrolled through the rest of his new messages. Each day, he felt a lurch of nerves when he checked his mail. He never knew what he would find—a contract to buy a house, a son applying to art school, a new puppy.

A divorce.

He hadn't seen that particular message, yet the possibility haunted him. He desperately wanted to forget the past, but he had no idea what Grace was open to these days. This standoff was not going to resolve anything, but they were trapped in a holding pattern. And deep down, he had not forgiven her for the house, for making decisions without him. For building a life without him.

"Lieutenant Lamont to see you, sir," announced Lieutenant Killigrew.

"Send him in." Just recently, the toughest deployment of Steve's career had gotten tougher. Not only had the cruise been extended another eight weeks, but Lieutenant Joshua Lamont had arrived on the COD. Initially, for maybe half a second, Steve thought he might get away with acting as though Lamont was just another nugget pilot. But in the next half of the second, gossip ripped through the carrier with the speed of a lightning bolt.

He and Lamont were going to have to deal with each other. They were strangers related by blood alone. Yet Lamont's very existence shook Steve's world and there was no point pretending it didn't.

Lamont entered the office and saluted. "You wanted to see me, sir?"

Yeah. About twenty-six years ago, thought Steve. "At ease, Lieutenant. I wanted to know how you're getting along on board." Steve could have asked for a report from the CO of the squadron, but he wanted to hear directly from Lamont.

"Fine, sir. The squadron's everything I could want. Flying twice a day—man, that's a dream."

In that moment, Steve knew him, knew this stranger who looked so much like him. Lamont's face lit with the irrepressible enthusiasm of a young pilot in love with flying. Steve recognized it, because he used to feel exactly the same way.

Still, he felt an obligation to play his role as senior officer. "The Navy likes passion, but how have your landing grades been?" Each trap on the flight deck was graded by the Landing Signal Officer—"OK" being the best to hope for. A pilot's grades factored into all of his evaluations.

Lamont's gaze shifted. "I'm training hard, sir. I've got some OKs, no 5s yet, probably too many no-grades and bolters."

The unenviable record of poor grades was typical for a new pilot. "Tell me about the pattern wave-off yesterday."

"Sir, I was reacting to winds during zip-lip and I rolled out long, and then I was behind an aircraft that was too wide abeam. It cut my interval short."

"If there were no standards, we'd have lazy overall performance," Steve pointed out. Even though Lamont was squirming, the conversation felt normal to Steve. A senior officer had a duty to review and discuss pilots' performances.

"I understand, sir."

They talked business for a while longer, but finally Steve said, "What the hell's on your mind, Lamont?"

"Sir?"

"Don't play dumb with me. You're not focusing, and that's not a good thing when you're flying two missions a day. Is it me?"

"Absolutely not, sir. I realize there are…unorthodox circumstances between us, but it isn't affecting my performance."

"Something is." Steve liked to think he watched all the pilots in the air wing with equal attention, but the fact was, Lamont's record received extra scrutiny. He couldn't help it. When he looked at Lamont, he felt such mixed emotions—frustration and regret, and a dark anger that had no clear target. He'd missed his son's birth, his childhood, his coming-of-age. That led to thoughts of the other kids. He'd only been there half the time for them, and lately he wondered if that was enough.

"Tell me what's on your mind," he said.

"Before I left, I asked a girl to marry me," Lamont blurted out.

The drone of the ship's power plant filled the ensuing silence. Steve leaned back in his chair. So that was it. A girl. "You wouldn't be the first," he pointed out.

"No, sir. But…she didn't answer. It's bugging the hell out of me."

"What, the fact that she hasn't made up her mind, or the fact that you haven't?"

Lamont blinked. "But I have—"

"If you were a hundred percent sure, you would have gotten that answer out of her before you left. But you're not sure, because you know what this job is. You know what you're asking of a woman. You're asking her to hold the line while you go away for months at a time. If there are kids, she's a single mom half the time. Do you get the picture, Lamont?"

He looked a little queasy. "Maybe so."

"Thanks to deployment, we get to live two separate lives. It's a blessing and a curse. Did I miss one of my children's birthdays? Yeah, I did. But did I also miss a burst water heater? Getting the car repaired? Dragging a screaming kid to the dentist? Yeah, I missed all that, too. Some things, you're not so sorry to miss out on. And anyone who won't admit that is lying to himself."

Steve was a little shocked at himself for being so candid. But he felt compelled to be honest with Lamont. Deep down, he liked being away. He enjoyed the luxury of knowing Grace was taking care of everything. Maybe that was chickenshit, but it was the truth.

"Begging your pardon, sir, but if being married is such an ordeal, why are most of the guys on the boat family men? And women, for that matter."

Because the heart never stops hoping, thought Steve.

But he didn't say so. Josh Lamont was in love. He was finding that out for himself. Instead, Steve played devil's advocate. "Maybe the question is, why are so many divorced? Among carrier personnel, it's double the national rate." Steve could tell these thoughts had been close to the surface for a long time. "A Navy wife has to be strong and independent enough to be on her own for months at a time. The flip side of that is her way of life gives her the skills to walk away and make a new life for herself."

"Like my mother did."

Steve felt echoes of the old fury that had gripped him after Cissy left. "When you're deployed, you have to trust her or you'll make yourself nuts. When you come back, you have to learn how to get along, all over again." Fatherly advice it wasn't. But Steve was not this man's father.

"Anyway," he concluded, "being honest with yourself about the realities of this life is the best way to get your concentration back. It's okay to have second thoughts. Accept it and focus on the job. Because if your landing grades don't improve, you *will* move on, whether you like it or not."

Lamont looked a little shell-shocked as he saluted and left the office.

Out of habit, he reached for his St. Christopher medal, which customarily hung around his neck at all times. It was gone. He dug deeper around his collar, seeking the slim chain, but couldn't find it. Frowning, he looked around and under the desk, all over the floor. He tried to remember the last time he'd been aware of it, and couldn't. Damn.

It gave him a bad feeling. He'd worn the medal on every cruise since he enlisted, and now it was gone. It had been his talisman against bad luck. He knew it was just a dumb superstition, but this was the first time he'd ever been at sea without it. It was also the first time he'd left on bad terms with Grace, the first time he had a son he didn't know on the carrier, like it or not. A lot of firsts. None of them good.

But it was oddly fitting. Cissy had given him the medal. It was the only thing he kept from her. Now it was gone, but he had a far more powerful reminder of that time in his life. He had Joshua Lamont.

Steve took out a business card he'd kept tucked in his wallet ever since the eve of this deployment. It was the card given to him by Joey Lord, his former squadron mate who was happily working in the private sector. Steve opened a new message box and began to write.

CHAPTER THIRTY-SEVEN

Grace stared in disbelief at the calendar on her dressing table. Somehow she had managed to ignore her encroaching birthday. Now it hit her like a drive-by shooting.

Forty years old. She was forty years old today.

She wanted to run and hide. Instead, she threw on her sweats and put her hair in a ponytail. She had plenty of work to keep her busy. But it was hard, everything was hard. Her heart ached all the time these days. With Daisy trotting at her heels, she ran downstairs and threw a banana and some soy milk in the blender for a smoothie. The whine of the motor made her wince and probably woke the kids, but it was nearly time for them to get up, anyway.

Brian was the first to arrive, and this morning he had a special gleam in his eye. He look incredibly grown-up today and very handsome, with his sandy hair, his father's square jaw and a sense of humor all his own. Maybe he had some surprise up his sleeve for her birthday. But this was Brian, she reminded herself. He never remembered her birthday. She hid her suspicion and acted as though it was any other morning.

"You're up early," she commented.

He emptied half a box of Cheerios into the yellow mixing bowl. "Yep. Hey, Mom."

"Yes?"

"I've got a surprise for you."

Of course he did. He'd never remembered her birthday in the past, but he was a man now. Perhaps this was a sign of his new maturity. "What sort of surprise?" she asked, unable to keep from grinning.

He stood and took his backpack from a hook behind the door. Rummaging around, he pulled out a large, thick envelope. "This came in yesterday's mail."

Mystified, Grace took it from him. It was too big to be a simple birthday card. She held the parcel at arm's length— another lovely aspect of growing older was that her vision was weakening—and checked the return address. "Rhode Island School of Design," she read aloud. And then it finally hit her— this wasn't about her or her stupid fortieth birthday. It was about Brian and his dreams and his future. "Oh, Bri," she said. "Is this what I think it is?"

He grinned from ear to ear. It was the same expression he'd worn when he'd pitched his first no-hitter.

"Why didn't you tell me yesterday?"

"You weren't home after school. I had to go to work and you were already asleep when I got back. Doesn't matter, Mom. You're the first to know after me."

She beamed at him. "You did it, Brian. I knew you would." She felt stupid for being so focused on turning forty. "Son, I'm incredibly proud of you," she said. "Let's have a look at this."

Seated side by side at the kitchen table, they went through the materials that came with Brian's acceptance to college. Forms to fill out, campus maps, lists of things to do. Everything had a curious air of gravitas; it was all so important.

The good news was grants and loans would cover most of the tuition costs. Yet even as she congratulated Brian, a bittersweet awareness filled her, and her heart broke a little. This was his future, shining before him. It was his first step away from her, a huge, cross-country step.

"What?" he said when he caught her staring at him.

"I'm going to miss you, son."

"He has to go away before you can miss him," Katie pointed out, coming to the breakfast table. She looked at the papers. "Whoa. You got in. Hey, Emma, he got in." She turned to Brian. "You actually found a college that'll have you."

"Very funny," he said, but couldn't summon even a hint of annoyance.

Emma paged through the brochure of the campus. "Way to go, Brian," she said.

Grace tried to read Emma's mood. She didn't seem to be making any plans even though she'd received an acceptance from Western Washington University. During an appointment with Emma's school counselor, Grace had confessed her worries.

"It's normal," Mrs. Snyder assured her. "Lots of kids get stressed out about their college decisions. Just because she's quiet doesn't mean she's avoiding the issue. She's probably thinking about it a lot."

Shortly after breakfast, the kids headed off for school, calling out their after-school plans for the day. "Don't plan on me for dinner," Katie said. "Brooke and I are starting our final project for American Studies."

"I'm working at the pool until eight," Emma reminded her.

"Me, too," said Brian. "Working at the cycle shop until closing time."

Grace stood in the doorway next to the dog and waved goodbye. So what if they forgot her birthday; it came around every year whether she liked it or not. They were actually doing her a favor. Who needed to celebrate turning forty, anyway?

At the end of the driveway, Brian stopped the car and Emma rolled down the passenger-side window. "Hey, Mom."

Grace went to see what was the matter. Emma handed her a

glossy pink gift bag, filled with tissue paper. Katie leaned out the window. "Don't look so surprised."

"Did you think Dad would let us forget?" asked Brian. "Jeez, Mom."

Grace's heart filled up as she reached into the bag and pulled out a card and a printed sheet of paper.

"It's a certificate for a whole morning at Gene Juarez salon," Emma explained. "You're all booked for a manicure, pedicure, hair and makeup, ten o'clock tomorrow morning."

"The girls said you'd like it," Brian muttered.

"I love it," said Grace. "Thank you."

"It's from Dad, too," said Katie. "Don't forget to thank Dad."

Grace went to the study and got down to work. As usual, her e-mail box was filled with work-related messages from real estate agents, shippers, contractors, service partners and consultants. She was juggling four projects now, which amounted to a full-time job. And she loved it. She liked being busy, making phone calls, scheduling appointments, keeping a log. She almost couldn't remember how she used to fill her days.

But then something would remind her. A call or a note from Allison Crowther would clue her in. Soon Grace would be the wife of the CAG, and as such, would be consumed by duties for which the Navy would neither acknowledge nor compensate her.

When she and Steve were first married, she performed her duties as a Navy wife without a thought of the alternative. Now she constantly considered alternatives.

She worked steadily throughout the day, scarcely noticing the passage of time until the doorbell rang. Daisy erupted, her bark so deep and loud that the windowpanes shook.

"Hush now," Grace admonished her. The clock on her computer screen indicated 4:00 p.m. She pushed back from the desk, opened the front door and was greeted with an enormous flower arrangement. Daisy let loose with a loud sneeze.

A young woman peeked out from behind the forest of pink

roses, spicy carnations and lush ferns. "Delivery for Grace Bennett," she said.

"Wow," Grace said, setting the heavy glass vase on the hall table. "Thank you. I...wasn't expecting anything." She signed for the flowers, bade the delivery person goodbye and stood back, her heart racing.

Finally, she thought. Steve was going to end the impasse after all. It was one thing to give the kids a credit card number for the salon, but this was different. This was personal. Maybe it was an olive branch.

With a laugh that was almost a sob, she ran to the study to type him an e-mail. The least she could do was let him know the flowers had arrived. After that, maybe he'd reply, and maybe later he would call.

She clicked on the New Message icon, then hesitated. Her steps were slow and heavy as she returned to the foyer and searched through the bouquet for a card. She located it at last, propped on a slender plastic stick. Please be from Steve, she thought as she opened the little envelope.

The damned type was too small to read. She fished in a drawer for her reading glasses, then turned the card over.

To Grace. Many Happy Returns. And thanks for everything. Ross Cameron.

With a guilty start, she tucked the card between two books on a shelf. Then she took it out and read it once more. Then she hid it on the bookshelf again. But there was no hiding the scent of roses and carnations. Perfume filled every room of the house, intoxicating her.

"How do you suppose he knew?" she asked Daisy.

The dog thumped her tail on the floor.

"He asked me." Grace snapped her fingers, and Daisy came to attention. "I was whining to him about turning forty, and he asked me when." *So I'll know the date the world will come to an end,* he'd joked.

Lately she'd been thinking about him with embarrassing frequency. He was her first and most important client. He'd taken a chance on her and handed her a huge project. Even though they knew each other only through phone calls and e-mails, they shared a curious sort of intimacy. Due to the nature of her work, she knew the sort of home he liked, and that he wanted to live in a place with a view of the water. She knew how much his belongings weighed and what kind of coffee he drank. She knew he was generous to his employees and that he was a baseball fan.

He lived a romantic life. The wine importation and distribution business enabled him to travel the world. And not just anywhere, but to Bordeaux and Modena, Jerez and Napa and Chile. Fabulous places where he would meet with important people and make deals. Judging by his relocation budget, she surmised that it was incredibly lucrative.

She wondered what he looked like, if his face matched his easy laugh, if he looked as kind and thoughtful as he seemed.

He seemed interested in her, too. He always had time to hear about the kids and her friends, the new house and the misadventures of raising a puppy. Their conversations were never hurried, never forced, always interesting and sometimes even touching. More and more often lately, their growing friendship felt oddly forbidden. Sometimes there was a subtle tone of flirtation in their exchanges, but it was harmless. They were complete strangers.

But every time she inhaled the scent of roses, she thought of him.

A dozen times she picked up the phone and dialed his number, but never let the call go through. She wrote him a thank-you note on e-mail and then deleted it. She spent a half hour sorting through cards and stationery to find exactly the right paper to send him a handwritten note, but she couldn't sit still long enough to write anything.

There was a message from Steve with the subject line, "Happy Birthday." The message was simple: *Grace, I hope you have a happy birthday. Did the kids give you your gift? I'll try to call later. Steve.*

A chill slid over her skin. What if they couldn't fix this? What if all the ennui of the past few years, combined with Steve's deception and her independence, had caused irreparable damage? Grace finally put a name to the word that had been hanging around like a blight for the past couple of years, well before they knew about Josh.

Divorce.

The chill intensified, and she broke into action, cleaning the house with a vengeance. As she scoured the entire kitchen, she finally let herself think about the unthinkable. What would her life be like if she didn't have Steve?

She thought about how fast and how hard she'd fallen in love with him, but found herself wondering how much of her husband she'd ever really had. Even when they'd first met, his commitment to the Navy was clear. That was his dream, and as his wife, she would be along for the ride. They'd both believed his work mattered in a way that made all her own frustrations and inner yearnings seem petty.

But now they consumed her. That night, she went to bed with the scent of roses in her head and the unsettling feeling that she was forty years old and still invisible.

CHAPTER THIRTY-EIGHT

Grace drove onto the Washington State ferry at Clinton, which linked Whidbey to the mainland. Once she was parked, she made her way upstairs and ordered a latte in the onboard cafeteria.

"Grace! Hey, stranger," called a voice.

She nearly jumped out of her skin. Then she got a grip. "Hey, Stan. I hardly recognize you without that Jungle Love T-shirt you wear to fitness class."

They slid into a Naugahyde booth and sipped their coffee. "You're out bright and early," Stan said.

Stan worked at the Boeing plant in Everett, commuting by ferry. He looked dapper in a well-tailored brown suit, carrying a locking briefcase.

She glanced down at her plain cardigan sweater and jeans. On the way home, she would not be wearing them. Her frump days were numbered. That had been her vow last night, one of many vows she made.

"How's Shirley?" she asked.

"Couldn't be better. She and our daughter are getting a little stressed out about the wedding, but I think they're managing to have fun with it. So what are you up to, Grace?"

"A trip to the big city," she said. Naturally, she couldn't confess everything to Stan, but she could share a little of her plans. "It's a girl thing. I'm going shopping and then to the Gene Juarez salon. Then I'm meeting…uh, a client for lunch." Her stomach flopped over as she thought about it. But there was no turning back now. That was the thing about the ferry. It steamed forward at eighteen knots and wouldn't stop until it got to the other side.

"That's great," he said, all friendly enthusiasm. "Fantastic to see your business growing. Shirley always meant to get a little something going. She's a talented quilter, but never switched from being a hobbyist to a professional."

"Do you think she might, now that your daughter's getting married?"

"Nah. We talked about it, but Shirley likes things just as they are."

Grace swirled the foam in her latte. "You're sure about that?"

"You bet."

"How can you be so sure?"

"Easy," he said. "I ask her all the time. We ask each other, How are you doing? How are *we* doing? That sort of thing."

A wistful smile curved her mouth. "What a concept," she said.

The ferry nosed into the dock at Mukilteo and they headed off to their cars. "You have a good day in the city, Grace," said Stan.

She got to Nordstrom's at opening time. She walked past the stuffy St. John's knit collection, nearly wincing at the sight of crisp navy-and-white outfits, gold-buttoned epaulets, conservative, low-heeled pumps. Perfect for official functions. Some of her friends were already asking her what she planned to wear at Steve's Change of Command ceremony.

She felt out of place as she sorted through inappropriate little dresses in impractical fabrics and luscious spring colors. But she forged ahead, determined to change her image. She'd been invisible too long.

"May I help you?" The inevitable question came quickly from

a saleslady. She was a woman of a certain age, but attractive and perfectly groomed.

Grace tried not to feel inferior in her loose jeans and sensible shoes. "Yes," she said. "I need something special for a...business lunch."

She kept calling it that, but she knew it was something quite different. Ross Cameron had been urging her to meet with him for quite some time. He'd been in Seattle for two weeks, settling in and getting his company organized. He wanted to meet her for lunch.

But it wasn't just lunch. She sensed he was as intrigued by her as she was by him. It was strangely gratifying to be the object of a man's interest.

Last night, after ten, she had drummed up her courage and called him at home. Was the invitation still open?

Of course it was.

She expected to feel guilty and self-indulgent as she tried on expensive clothes and considered each outfit with the gravity of a constitutional judge. But when she was on ensemble number three, a raspberry-colored straight skirt with a black gabardine blazer, she realized that she was actually having fun.

She studied every angle of herself in the three-way mirror, and she wasn't horrified. She looked...good. The woman helping her must have sensed the shift in her mood, because she showed up with more suggestions—a peacock-blue silk dress, a lemon-yellow blouse, a pair of flattering slacks in a rich charcoal-gray. She also brought accessories—scarves and brooches, belts and bangles. Grace settled on the raspberry skirt and black blazer, adding a top with a plunging neckline and a silk scarf with a cubic design and a shiny clasp.

"I love it," said the saleslady. "It's perfect on you."

"Thanks, I'll take it. But I think it's mislabeled," she said, holding out an arm and showing the dangling tag. "It's marked size 10."

"No, that's no mistake. It's correct."

"I haven't been a size 10 in years."

"Well, you are now."

Grace felt almost reckless as she added to her purchases—

underwear and a bra, hose, shoes and a matching bag. Everything was going to be new today.

Buoyant, she headed off to her next appointment. The woman called Ivanka descended like an exotic bird, leading Grace from station to station—nails, hair, makeup. Grace grew alarmed as the damp locks piled up at her feet, but she said nothing. She wanted a change. Well, she was getting it. She submitted to golden streaks and blond highlights. Finally, at precisely 1:00 p.m., Ivanka swirled her chair toward the mirror.

"Take a look," she said. "What do you think?"

Think? She was supposed to think? She couldn't put a coherent thought together as she stared at the stranger in the mirror. Who was this creature? This interesting-looking woman with the shiny blond bob and flawless makeup?

"Do not weep," Ivanka warned her. "I do not want your makeup ruined."

"Don't worry," Grace said, her emotions shifting. "I'll be fine. I'm just…startled, that's all."

"You are lovely," Ivanka assured her. "Your husband, he will be so charmed by you."

Grace didn't know how to answer that, so she smiled and went to change out of the salon robe. In the curtained dressing room, she put on her new things, and when she was finished, she felt new herself. Confident, even a little defiant. She stuffed her old clothes and shoes and even the stupid discount store handbag in the shopping bag and handed it to an attendant at the elevator. "Could you please dispose of this? I won't be needing it anymore."

With her head high and her stride quick, she set off down Pine Street. She kept glancing in the shop windows she passed, astonished each time she caught a glimpse of herself. She looked fashionable, a professional woman off to lunch with a client.

Or a meeting with a mystery man.

Her pace slowed. Her confidence faltered. This was insane. She didn't belong here, lunching in the city at a trendy restaurant. She belonged…where? At home, fixing dinner for the kids, who were all going to be late because of work and band practice? In her study, taking care of correspondence and wondering about her marriage?

She squared her shoulders and walked on, pushing away her doubts. She was redefining her life. It was scary, yes. And it was hard, much harder than she'd ever imagined. But that didn't mean it wasn't worth doing.

Nothing like a marriage crisis to give a woman the courage of her convictions, she thought. No, that was cynical. She should take pride in the positive changes she'd made. She had started a business from scratch, bought a house, improved her health and fitness. Today, she had changed her image. Those were all good things, she told herself. Every last one of them.

She tried to keep her courage up as she headed to Pike Place. Brilliant arrays of flowers and fruit lined the stalls. A juggler performed for a group of schoolkids, and a blind clown offered balloon animals to passersby. Tourists gathered around a life-size brass pig to watch the City Fish workers perform their unending fish-throwing routine. "Heads up, Blondie," called a guy in a smudged rubber apron. Grace glanced at him, realizing only at the last second that he was talking to her. With a grin, he sent a whole salmon flying to his co-worker behind the counter.

Grace inhaled the smells of flowers and fish, of truck exhaust and baking bread. She joined the flow of humanity through the market like a leaf in a river current and let herself be swept along. On the middle level of the marketplace, she stepped outside to a narrow walkway leading to the bistro.

She hesitated at the door, her nerves buzzing with anxiety. What if he was horrible, a stalker or a pervert? Worse, what if he was wonderful?

She took a deep breath, stepped inside. People lingered over late lunches at tables set with crisp linens and thick white china.

She dared to look around for a single man waiting alone, but saw no one of that description.

The hostess greeted her, and Grace said, "I'm, uh, meeting someone." Doubts pounded at her even as she spoke. What am I doing here? This is insanity. She had to leave now, stand him up and make her excuses later. With an apologetic smile at the hostess, she said, "Actually, I'm afraid I'll have to lea—"

"Grace?"

A man in a dark suit turned from the bar and crossed the room. *Oh. My. God.*

"You're Grace, right?" said the man, his voice familiar from hours of phone calls. "Wow, it's great to finally meet you." He held out his hand. "Ross Cameron."

Get me out of here.

Somehow she managed to take his hand and smile. "It's good to meet you, too. Thanks for scheduling this on such short notice."

The hostess showed them to a corner table by the window. Grace sat down, set her new handbag under her chair and stared at the menu a good thirty seconds before realizing it was upside down.

Ross Cameron seemed relaxed and natural as he studied the menu, then set it down. "I'm sorry," he said. "I have no idea what I want for lunch. I just can't get over seeing you."

His disarming confession broke the ice, and she laughed. "God, I was so nervous about this."

He sat back, regarding her with both kindness and amusement. "Why nervous?"

"Well, I wasn't sure what you'd be like. On the phone and in e-mail, you've always been so great."

"Like Cyrano de Bergerac."

She sipped her water. "Not exactly." Then she laughed again. "Okay, maybe a little. But you have a very nice nose." He had a nice everything. Eyes the color of expensive whiskey. A mischievous smile. Great taste in clothes.

"You're nothing like I pictured, either," he admitted.

Uh-oh. She wasn't sure what he meant by that. "Go on."

"Your kids are nearly grown, so I kept imagining someone a little more…mature. You don't look old enough for grown kids, Grace." He lifted his water glass and clinked the rim with hers. "I'm pleased to meet you."

"Welcome to Seattle," she said. She gestured at the view of busy Elliot Bay, the ferry docks and the piers jutting out into the water. Misty islands rose in the distance, and steamers and container ships chugged out to sea.

The waiter came for their orders. The one thing Grace hadn't changed about herself was her reading glasses, and she wasn't about to take them out. "I'll have the special."

"Soup or salad?"

"Salad, please, with vinaigrette on the side."

"White or wheat?"

"Wheat, please. And a glass of house merlot."

"I'll have everything the same," said Ross. "Right down to the merlot."

When the waiter left, Ross asked her, "Do you have any idea what the special is?"

She grinned. "None at all."

"Me, neither."

The wine arrived and they toasted again. "One of your brands?" she asked.

"Unfortunately, no. But they do carry some of them. Now that I'm here, I'll make sure our labels become more visible in the area."

The lunch special turned out to be a sandwich of seared ahi with remoulade sauce. "That's a relief," Grace said, savoring a bite. "It could have been squid or geoducks."

"Gooey ducks?" He echoed her pronunciation.

"A local specialty. If you have time afterward, I'll walk through the market with you and show you what a geoduck looks like. Once you've seen one, you'll never order it for lunch."

He smiled. Devastating, just devastating. "I have plenty of time afterward. I took the rest of the day off."

"Really? Why?"

"Because I've been dying to see you, Grace. I wanted to spend as much time as possible with you."

Yikes, she thought as an undeniable thrill of attraction fluttered through her.

They talked business, and he asked her so much about Grace Under Pressure that she laughed and shook her head. "You're not really interested in my business."

"Are you kidding? I'm fascinated."

His warm personality was positively magnetic. He was interested in every aspect of her. He wanted to know what she liked, what she thought of things, what her goals were. There was no question in his mind that she was good at what she did, and that she would succeed. His faith and confidence in her abilities filled a place inside her.

"It's a small home-based business. How interesting can it be?" she said.

"Completely interesting," he assured her.

"I'm not used to having people find me interesting," she blurted out. She was so surprised by the admission that she grabbed her wine and drank quickly, sneaking a look at Ross. It had been a long time since she'd felt someone's belief in her. She wondered if he knew he exceeded all her expectations for him. Every last one of them.

A part of her had hoped the prince would actually turn out to be a toad, because then she could go home with the knowledge that the chemistry was driven by commerce alone.

No such luck. He was as wonderful as she'd feared he would be. Handsome, caring, genuinely interested in her. Honest, good-humored and undeniably drawn to her. Not bad for a first impression.

He was the first man to respond to the "new" Grace, and she reveled in the thought that she looked good to him.

She let him talk her into crème brûlée for dessert, and it came with little pansy blossoms as a garnish. "They're edible," the waiter assured her.

She smiled across the table at Ross. "I've never eaten flowers before."

They fought good-naturedly over the check, and in the end, Grace prevailed, because he was her client, after all. She paid with her Grace Under Pressure credit card and left a generous tip. As promised, she took him for a stroll through Pike Place Market, stopping at her favorite stalls and showing him the startling sight of a raw geoduck. "I see what you mean," he admitted, studying the thick, fleshy tube protruding from a hand-size clam shell. "It looks a little too...familiar to order for lunch."

She showed him a stall with twelve flavors of honey for sale. "Hard to believe there's a difference between clover and fireweed," he said, accepting a sample on a tiny plastic spoon. Before she figured out what he was doing, he touched it to her lips. "What do you think?"

She tasted that honey right down to her toes. "It's delicious," she said. "Irresistible. You try it." She felt bold and reckless as he sampled it.

"Mmm," he said. "I need to take this home with me."

They emerged at a tiny park at the end of the market. Ross was laden with purchases. As they strolled along, he reached into his pocket to find a dollar for a jaded-looking panhandler.

They sat down on a bench looking out over the water. He rested his arms along the back of the bench. Technically, he didn't have an arm around her, Grace rationalized, just behind her on the bench. A strange energy clamored inside her.

"My new hometown," he said easily, looking out at the sapphire water with the big sky above. "I'm going to like it here. Thanks for making it possible, Grace."

She looked up at him. "Thanks for taking a chance on me."

"It's kind of cool, being your first client."

"I certainly thought so. If I hadn't needed the money so badly, I would have framed the first check you sent me."

"I should have sent you something to commemorate our beginning."

"You did. Those flowers you sent are just gorgeous."

"No, I meant something you'd keep. Something that would last."

She caught herself studying his mouth. "Now you're making me all sentimental about a business relationship."

His arm moved from the back of the bench to the back of Grace. "It's more than that."

She had known it from the moment she saw him. In a heartbeat's time, her perception of him—and of herself—had shifted. As seagulls cried and hawkers called out, she could feel him drawing closer.

"I have a great idea," he said. "Why don't I take you to see my new condo."

"I looked at the virtual tour on the Internet. It's a great condo."

"It's even better in person. It's just up the street, in Belltown."

She knew exactly where it was. She was the one who had sent him the listing. This was business, she told herself. She had relocated this man. There was no harm in taking the final step, in seeing where he'd ended up.

"All right," she said, light-headed with defiance. The world seemed shrouded in a diffuse haze.

They stood, and in her nervousness, she dropped her purse. It emptied with a thud on the pavement in front of the bench. Her first thought was to hope nothing humiliating had spilled out.

"I've got it." Ross stooped down and handed her the little sack of makeup she'd bought at Gene Juarez. A tin of Altoids. Her phone and wallet. A date book—she hadn't graduated to a PDA yet. A book of ferry tickets.

"Thanks," she said, stuffing the things into her purse.

He bent down to check under the bench. "We almost missed something," he said. He stood up and dropped the heavy cluster of keys into her hand. "You won't get far without that."

Instead of shoving it in her handbag, Grace stared at the key chain. She'd had it for years and years. It was attached to a small silver anchor. Steve had given it to her on their first Christmas together.

For nearly twenty years, she had kept it to remind her that no matter where he went, she anchored him home.

She closed her fist around the key chain, grateful to feel the cold metal press into her hand. The world came back into sharp focus as she smiled up at Ross Cameron. A light wind played with his long, wavy hair, and the sunlight danced in his eyes. It was true that she wanted the admiration she saw in those eyes. She wanted the flutter of desire she was feeling. But now it was crystal clear— she wanted those things with Steve.

"I won't be able to come with you after all," she said, her heart nearly coming out of her chest. "You understand, I can't."

He didn't look shocked or hurt. Disappointed, perhaps. "I'll walk you to your car."

"No need. I'd rather walk by myself."

"All right. See you, Grace. Thanks for lunch. Thanks for everything."

"No, thank *you*." He would never know how grateful she was to him. She hurried across the street, turned and waved before heading to the parking garage. But he didn't see her wave. He was already striding away, garnering the admiration of every woman he passed.

CHAPTER THIRTY-NINE

Steve wasn't fooled by reporter Francine Atwater's doe-eyed admiration as she looked around his office. She was trolling for a story, and she was a pro. "You've had an incredible career," she said, going over his bio. She pressed a button on a handheld microrecorder. "But I'm more interested in finding out about the real Steve Bennett, not what the Navy publishes about you."

"Ma'am, that's about all there is to it."

"It says here you were born and raised in Texas. Are your folks still there?"

"They're deceased." He was sure about his mother. With his father, it was a wishful assumption.

"I'm sorry. That must make your own family all that much more important to you."

"That's true." Steve considered her a slippery little thing. He knew damned well that Miss Congeniality, with her concerned questions about his family life, would turn into a barracuda once she sat down to write her piece. You could make one little innocent remark that, when quoted out of context, made you sound like Attila the Hun.

"About how much are you away from them?" she asked, studying the framed photo of Grace and the kids on Mustang Island.

"Too damned long," he said incautiously. It just came out, un-censored. Normally he was more circumspect with the press. "About half the time," he clarified.

"So the other half of you belongs to the Navy."

"That's correct, ma'am."

"What role does your wife play in your rise through the ranks?"

The question caught him off guard. "She doesn't just play a role. That makes her sound less important than she is. An officer is like the visible top of an iceberg. An officer's spouse is the seventy-five percent of it that's unseen and underwater, propping up the whole structure. Someone else might tell you otherwise, but that's the way I see it, anyway."

"How do you justify the time away from your family?"

He knew the stock answer to that. He had made a commit-ment to serve his country. A career Naval officer concerned himself with issues that were larger and more important than the individual. Yet when he spoke, he heard himself say, "There's really no justification for it, ma'am. Time away from those you love is time you can never get back. It can have a devastating impact on a family."

To her credit, she kept her cool, though her eyes widened slightly. "Sir, may I quote you on that?"

He knew he could ask her to take his remarks off the record. The Navy frowned on its personnel questioning their own priorities.

"It's your job to publish the truth. And the truth is, an officer is only human. I won't speak for anyone but myself, but I can tell you this. In all likelihood, I'll become the next CAG. It's what I've worked for all these years. As CAG of Carrier Air Group 16, I'll become the leader I always knew I could be. But I'd be lying if I said I wasn't thinking long and hard about what this command will do to my personal life."

She clutched her small recording device to her chest as though it was the Holy Grail. Steve felt no regrets for being so frank—yet. He was putting his lifelong dream at risk, but it didn't feel that way. Saying aloud the things that had been on his mind for so long felt curiously liberating. It wasn't that hard to admit that there was no comparison between the job and the sight of his babies for the first time, or the look on his wife's face when she welcomed him home.

The young journalist proved to be a demanding customer in more ways than one. Taking civilians to the flight deck was never a great idea, but Higher Authority had granted her special clearance to see night ops. Up close.

Steve helped her gear up for the tour—boots, a cranial, goggles, a white float coat stenciled VIP. Then he took her to the tower, introduced her around and showed her a vantage point for getting a good view of the deck. She was practically giddy with excitement, and despite his mood, Steve found himself remembering what it was like to experience the overwhelming sights, smells and sounds of a flight deck.

In the recovery phase of the exercise, jets returned one after another to the carrier. As each steel bird came screaming home to roost, the crew raced out to prepare for the next landing. When Steve took Ms. Atwater to the dim lower level of the tower, they encountered her photographer, videographer, an assistant and a Public Affairs Officer. As they were making introductions, Aviation Ordnanceman Airman Michael Rivera stepped inside, reporting a slight problem with some decoy flares.

Steve and the PAO let Rivera visit with Atwater. They'd get a different story out of Rivera, a young man bursting with enthusiasm, completely devoted to his role on the carrier. Steve stepped away and stared through a narrow viewing pane.

He wasn't looking for anything in particular—a distraction, a place to focus that was outside himself—but he saw…something. A peculiar energy had seized the crew charged with recovering the next aircraft, very subtle, but enough to compel Steve to return to the bridge. The CAG LSO, Bud Forster, spoke quickly into his headset. "Prowler six-two-three," he said, and the look on his face made Steve's gut twist.

Lamont was driving the Prowler, and if Forster was handling

the situation rather than the squadron LSO, that meant trouble. Steve thought about Lamont, a pilot with potential but not nearly enough experience. Since their discussion, Lamont's landing grades had steadily improved. But if there was trouble, would he know what to do?

Lamont was a stranger, but he was also his son, and Steve felt the mysterious pull of their common blood. Everything inside him clamored to take some sort of action. But Josh didn't need Steve now, any more than he'd needed him for the past twenty-six years. Josh needed the Air Boss and the LSO and his own skill and sense. It was late in the cruise and the planes had been ridden hard. No matter how diligent the maintenance crews were, a loose bolt or wire was common, particularly on the frequently used Prowlers.

Steve spotted Francine Atwater and the others outside, heading toward the bomb farm. With a possible situation outside, the tour was over, even though they didn't know it yet. He'd have to go round them up and send them below. It was not simply a matter of yelling at them from the tower. He swore under his breath as he ran outside. If anything happened to the civilian reporter, he'd be to blame. She was his responsibility.

The flight deck roared with noise. Artificial light blazed across the runways. There was a flare dispenser on deck behind Rivera and the civilians. Steve thought he saw sparks shooting from the container. A cold spike of terror shot through him. At this distance, they'd never hear his warning. But he yelled out, anyway.

At first, Rivera didn't seem to see the problem. Then he turned and picked up the burning cylinder and ran. A sound like a strike of thunder penetrated the noise of the deck. A fount of sparks and billows of smoke swallowed Rivera until a gust of wind swept the deck. Then Rivera rolled free of the smoke. His sleeve was on fire, a huge torch casting eerie light over the horrified civilians. Steve was the first to reach him. He already had his float coat off as he leaped forward, smothering the flames with the thick fabric. The flames were out, but Rivera lay shuddering violently on the deck.

From the corner of his eye, Steve saw the flare dispenser. It was still smoking.

Sailors were almost there with the fire extinguishers, but the internal units were already burning.

If it smokes, get rid of it.

The handle of the dispenser was so hot that it set Steve's glove on fire. He yelped with pain but didn't let go. The cylinder was too heavy to lift, but somehow he got it to the edge of the deck. Hoping momentum would carry the burning cylinder far, he swung hard. Smoke and flames drew an arc through the night sky.

He came up off his feet and felt a violent blast. Alarms shrieked from the bridge.

Sparks shot from the top of the canister, stinging his face and illuminating the surreal sight of the carrier's hull speeding past on his long fall into the dark water.

CHAPTER FORTY

Grace drove a little too fast to the ferry terminal, and on the boat, she sat and stared out the window at the sudden squall of rain. Her heart was full, and she felt exhausted and exhilarated as she exited the ferry and headed home.

As she sped up the main road, the wind and rain gradually abated. By the time she pulled to the shoulder of the wet road to get the mail, tentative slices of sunshine shone through the clouds. She turned into the driveway and sat in the car for a moment, gazing at her house. She'd lived in a lot of places, but this was the only one she'd ever loved. The only one she owned.

So much had changed since Steve had gone away. But perhaps, Grace realized, the biggest change was within her.

She picked up her purse and the stack of mail from the seat beside her and slid out of the car. Ducking her head to avoid drops from the ancient cedar trees that arched over the drive, she skirted puddles to keep from ruining her new shoes and let herself in through the front gate.

Juggling the mail, her purse and keys, she let herself in. Daisy lumbered into the foyer to greet her, snuffling and wagging her tail. The flowers from Ross still stood on the hall table, their scent heavy and rich.

She went to the kitchen, catching a glimpse of herself in the hall mirror. The image startled her yet again. What a day it had been. Her encounter with Ross Cameron was everything she hoped it would—and would not—be.

She let Daisy out and put her keys on the counter, pausing for a minute to study the little sterling silver anchor key chain again. Then she checked the time. The kids would be home soon. She wondered if they would notice the new outfit, the hair. She wondered if Steve would, when he came back.

For a moment she had trouble breathing. Even now, she thought, stunned by the powerful grip he still held on her heart. Even now. And despite the decision she'd made today, doubts kept seeping through the cracks and crevices that had appeared in the foundations of her life.

Nothing would be resolved fully until Steve came back.

She headed into the study to check her messages. But first she paused to send one simple e-mail to Steve: *We need to talk. Love, Grace.*

The answering machine signaled thirteen messages. She touched Play and picked up a pen.

The first few messages on the machine were strictly business, related to delivery times, tonnage estimates, shipping contracts. Then came Katie: "Mom, I'm going to Melanie's tonight, okay?"

Next, a message from Patricia and then Steve's voice. "Hey, guys." Grace's grip tightened on the pen. "It's your old man calling from the wrong side of the international dateline. Guess what? I'm giving a tour to a reporter from *Newsweek....*"

Grace massaged the sides of her jaw, trying to force herself to relax as the next messages played: trouble with an overseas shipment. Lauren Stanton, sounding upset about canceling the evening fitness class; she was taking Josh's absence so hard. The final message was from Grace's lawyer, announcing that her incorporation papers were ready to sign. Soon, she would be Grace Under Pressure, Inc.

She glanced at the computer screen to see that the server was rejecting messages. Odd, she thought, but then she was distracted by the muffled sound of a car door slamming. Then another. She wasn't expecting anyone. She stood and went to see who it was.

A black Navy sedan was parked in front. Between the tall hedges of climbing roses, two men emerged.

When Grace saw them, her insides and all of her bones turned to liquid, yet somehow she managed to hold herself upright. It was happening, then. This was the nightmare every Navy wife dreaded.

A chaplain and the Casualty Assistance Calls Officer, coming up the walk.

She thought, If I don't open the door and let them in, they'll go away. They won't be real. This won't be happening. But she knew she had to.

Her life was now cleanly divided down the middle, cut with the precision of a surgeon's scalpel. And this exact moment was the dividing line. Everything on her side of the door belonged Before. Everything on the other side of the door would be After.

She wished she had loved the "before" portion more. She wished she hadn't waited for "after" to discover the precious lessons life offered. Before and after. Life and death. Love and loss.

Somehow she managed to open the door and step outside, waiting on the porch with her back pressed to the glass.

The CACO and the chaplain both wore full dress uniform. Their faces were as white as their gloves. The moment they reached the top of the porch steps, they removed their caps and tucked them properly under their arms.

"Mrs. Bennett?"

She nodded. Who else would she be? She was Mrs. Bennett. Mrs. Stephen Kyle Bennett. It was all she had ever wanted to be, all she could conceive of being. My God, she thought, what have I done?

She had dreamed of being a lot of other things, but she was just lying to herself. At her core, at her very heart and soul, she was Steve's wife, and something was terribly wrong.

"Ma'am," said the captain. "May we come inside?"

No. No. No.

She wanted to cover her ears, run and hide, turn back the clock. But instead, she opened the door and let them in.

CHAPTER FORTY-ONE

In flight school, ejection criteria had been drummed into Josh's head, but at the moment, only one factor mattered—the pilot's judgment. His safety and that of the crew was the ultimate goal, but ditching the taxpayers' high-tech airplane in the drink was not done lightly. Still, when you were losing altitude at a hundred feet per second, you didn't have time to debate the matter. No amount of training could prepare you to come to the ultimate decision so quickly.

It was every aviator's nightmare. He hadn't lost control; he had no control. It was a subtle difference and one that was pushing him fast toward the inevitable decision. The key to survival was to make sure they could all reach their handles before everything got away from them. He could feel Newman, Turnbull and Hatch waiting for his command. He thought he could smell their adrenaline in the air of the cockpit.

He and the others were strapped to Advanced Concept Ejection Seats, 128 pounds of equipment with a twenty-one-pound rocket catapult. They had to take it on faith that the crew chiefs had strapped them in properly so they wouldn't fall out of their seats on ejection. They had to trust that the chute packers had stowed the parachutes correctly. One mistake made the difference between survival and death.

As he reviewed the ejection-process checklist, time turned to nothing: The blink of an eye. The turn of a rotor. The oscillation of the rudder he couldn't control. Or the most fleeting thing of all—the thought of Lauren. She'd sent him an e-mail note, asking him to call her. And he hadn't called. He was going to wait until after the mission. What an idiot. You don't hold back when you're in love.

I love you, Lauren.

He poured his whole heart into the thought. He imagined the ring safely zipped in his pocket. Then he assumed the position, pressing against the backrest, bracing his legs and neck. Finally, he gave the order he knew he had to give.

"Eject! Eject! Eject!"

The moment he yanked the handle, he detonated a sequence of violent events. The four seats were timed to launch at close intervals to avoid midair collisions. One, two, three… He heard the loud bangs of the crews' seats in quick succession. The sharp upper edge of the first seat back breaker bar shattered the canopy. A mosaic of safety glass showered down on Josh. A tempest raged inside the cockpit, ripping his aerial charts into the atmosphere. The last rocket motor burned out, and there was an eerie breath of silence.

Josh's seat didn't move. Panic knocked in his chest as he grabbed for the yellow handle again. At that instant, the seat fired. It was a carnival ride, courtesy of the solid-rocket propellant motor that blasted him along the rails. Josh shot out of the cockpit, the trajectory automatically propelling him away from the aircraft to avoid hitting the stabilizer at the tail. His blood, eyeballs and innards were compressed by acceleration equivalent to fourteen times the weight of gravity. The icy wind ripped at him. The noise shrieked in his ears. He felt a blast of cold and a tearing sensation. A twist of fabric snaked past with a flutter like a flock of birds. Please God, let it work.

A second charge fired, this one programmed to shoot the seat away as the silk canopy popped open. Something hit him so hard he couldn't breathe, strangled by the harness around his waist. Then a giant hand swooped him up into the night sky, lifting him to a quiet place he'd never been before. And finally…nothing. A pure silence, as cold and black as a vacuum. A few seconds later, he dared to look up and saw that he was under the chute.

He laced his gloved fingers into the riser cords as he floated in the cold dark. Was it only moments ago that he'd seen two shooting stars, that he'd told Lauren he loved her?

He forced away the random thoughts and focused on survival. His whole body felt numb from the trauma of ejection. Even behind his goggles, his eyes watered. He tasted blood from biting his tongue. His crotch had been savagely yanked by safety cords. His neck ached, but he didn't think it was broken. He'd probably been snapped out of ejection position by the G-force of acceleration.

He saw no sign of his crew's parachutes—not yet, anyway. A thousand things could have gone wrong for the crew members— incomplete ejection, fouled chutes, failed rockets. Please God…

He dared to look down, but couldn't see where the Prowler had crashed. There was a glimmer of light on the water far below. Please let it be the ships of the battle group. He tried steering his parachute toward it, but the wind ran in the opposite direction in a raging, invisible current. He thought about how cold the water would be— fifty-five degrees, according to the latest briefing from the ship's meteorologist. Inside the leather gloves, his hands felt like ice.

He deployed the ejection seat survival kit, and a small life raft dropped from the lower section, inflating instantly. His feet dipped into the water, dragged for a few feet, rose and then dipped again. "Show time," he said through chattering teeth.

He disengaged from the parachute as quickly as possible to avoid being pulled underwater by the weight of the fabric. At the same moment, his vest inflated on contact with the water. The meteorologist had also reported "moderate seas"—ten-foot swells and the occasional breaker.

SUSAN WIGGS

"Moderate my ass," he choked out as a swell ripped at him.

He swore, earning a mouthful of seawater. Shit, it was cold. His flight suit had antiexposure features. He supposed it was keeping him dry. But as he fought the waves in the dark, he felt a cold dampness seeping in places that were supposed to stay warm. His initial notion that he was in a survivable situation slipped a notch.

"Get over, you son of a bitch," he said, kicking his leg up. The half-inflated raft was too soft, and it filled with water. A constant stream of swearing issued from Josh. He couldn't tell if it had quit inflating, or if it wasn't done yet. "Come on, come on," he said, his ice-cold hands feeling the bladders. Lying back in the raft, Josh bobbed for a minute, panting with exhaustion, his head flung back, his eyes turned to the sky.

He'd undergone hours of survival training, but that was in a swimming pool. Emma had been at one of the training sessions, trying not to laugh as fully geared-up pilots struggled to stay afloat. Emma, his sister. His friend. He'd been encouraging her to choose this path. Now he wondered if he was wrong. He wouldn't wish this shit on anybody.

It was out of his hands, though. She'd made up her mind weeks ago. She was even starting to look like a warrior princess, with that hacked-off hair and fire in her eye.

He jettisoned his helmet and donned the rubber cap from his survival kit. He exchanged the useless leather gloves for rubber ones and pinpointed his location on his Garmin GPS locator. Then he found what he needed most—a VHF survival radio. He sent out a call for aircraft on the international military survival frequency. No response. Either that or the thing wasn't working. Next, he set off a flare, a blinding green-white flash followed by a plume of smoke.

Water seeped into his survival suit. He had to keep bailing. His teeth were chattering violently. That was a good sign, he told himself. It meant his body was still responsive to the cold. He wondered how long that would last. He called repeatedly on the

342

radio and looked constantly for the others, but there was nothing. Only the cold, and the endless sea, and the darkness.

A rhythmic thud broke the silence. Josh came to full alert, recognizing the pulse of rotor blades. White beams swept over the water, illuminating the churning swells.

The stars held a peculiar brilliance, and some of them pulsed in the blackness. A strange and quiet sense of reverence overtook Josh, and he didn't know who he was talking to when he said, "Thank you. *Thank you.*"

The rescuers arrived on a tempest induced by the swirling blades of the chopper. As strong arms buckled Josh into a harness, he used the last of his energy to shout at them, "My crew— Newman, Hatch and Turnbull. Are they okay?"

"Yes, sir. They're back aboard the ship."

The good news infused him like a shot of warm saline. "Injuries?"

"Nothing major, sir."

Josh surrendered then, going limp as the rescuers signaled to the chopper. His eyes stung with salt water and tears of gratitude, and then a long nothingness overtook him. He had no memory of being hoisted to the helo, but returned to pulsing awareness as he felt a solid surface under his back and heard the crackle and beep of radios.

Slowly an oxygen mask lowered over his nose and mouth, and a needle stabbed into the crook of his arm. With his free hand, he unzipped the smallest compartment of his G-suit, his numb fingers probing until he found what he sought—the delicate diamond ring.

Still there.

CHAPTER FORTY-TWO

Grace stood on the front porch after the Navy officials departed. She held the CACO call card in her hand, but she didn't read it. They had wanted to stay, of course, or to call someone to come and be with her. But she had looked at the men and lied. "I'll be all right." They promised to be in constant communication with her.

The kids would be home from school any minute now. She would have to tell them.

A mishap, the Navy was calling it. A *mishap.*

They might have lost their dad. How would Grace tell them that?

Be honest. Don't hold back. Keep the explanation simple and avoid speculating or making promises. She had learned the next-of-kin notification procedure in a Casualty Assistance Support training class.

She had no idea how it was possible that she could be standing here, feeling the sun on her face and hearing the twitter of nesting birds, while Steve was missing an ocean away.

She knew that in a moment the phone would start ringing. It would do so without stopping for hours, maybe days on end. When something bad happened, everyone in the community heard in a matter of minutes despite all official efforts to control the situation. Information seeped out into the world like a chemical leak.

Springtime flavored the light breeze that blew across the empty yard—lilacs and cut grass, the warm promise of summer. A rusty creak drew her attention. The front gate under its arch of climbing roses had swung free of its latch. Her eyes followed the lazy movement of the old gate, and the numbness of unreality suddenly let go. The mishap was not an abstraction. It took hold of her heart and she felt the sharp, breath-stealing physical pain of terror.

"Steve." She spoke his name, whispered it once. She wondered if he was hurting somewhere, if he was cold. Her mind raced with all the terrible possibilities of what might have happened to him. She nearly doubled over in agony, but forced herself to stand tall. She had to focus on the children. They would need her to be strong for them.

She waited. Daisy pawed at the door and Grace let her out. The dog must have sensed something because she wouldn't leave Grace's side even when Grace paced back and forth on the porch. Some of the older houses along the shore had a widow's walk. Today, she deeply understood that the structure was not a simple decoration. She felt the pain of every woman who had ever waited for a man gone to sea, and the restlessness that drove her to pace the walkway while awaiting ill news while her mind filled with memories.

She only had to shut her eyes and she could see her whole marriage in a collage of images—their wedding in the chapel at Pensacola NAS, how handsome and proud he looked in uniform. Their first home together, a modest bungalow one block from the beach where they'd made love like overheated teenagers. The way he smiled at her when she opened her eyes in the morning. The misery of fighting with him, the bliss of making up. The excitement of arriving in a new place together—Italy, Texas, San Diego, Guam. Their wonderful, funny, difficult children who meant the world to them both.

I almost threw that all away.

She gasped aloud at the thought and forced herself to breathe and resist the urge to scream. She barely had herself under control by the time the Bronco turned into the drive, the stereo thumping out "Paint It Black," which was on one of the CDs Steve had made before his deployment. Brian was at the wheel. Katie jumped out of the back seat. "Wow!" she said, her eyes practically bugging out. "What happened?"

Grace dragged in a deep breath. "Well, I—"

"You look great, Mom," Emma said.

"Fan*tas*tic," Katie added. "You're so…*blond*."

"You look totally different," Brian stated. "I've never seen you with short hair before."

Grace took a second to regroup and force herself to remember the way her day had started out. She looked down distractedly at the new outfit and said, "Thanks. Come on inside, guys. I need to tell you something. There's been a mishap on Dad's ship."

They were Navy kids. They understood what the word "mishap" meant. To civilians, it was a bit of bad luck. To Navy families, it meant nothing would ever be the same. But the children didn't get hysterical. They didn't interrupt or bombard her with questions. They simply sat on the sofa in front of Grace's view of the sea and listened while the tears rolled down their faces.

"Is Dad okay?" Emma asked.

"We're waiting to find out."

"What happened?"

"There was an explosion and fire on the flight deck. It had something to do with a flare. Your dad saw that a fire was starting, so he threw the flare container overboard to prevent an explosion and a chain reaction on the bomb farm. If the ordnance had caught fire, explosions could have caused huge casualties." She looked at their dear, pale faces and went on. "He, um…oh, God. He fell—or was blown—overboard."

Katie covered her face with her hands and whispered, "Daddy."

"Did the safety net catch him?" asked Brian.

"I'm afraid not."

"But his float coat would save him," Katie said, looking up. "They'll use the transmitter to find him."

"According to the report, he wasn't wearing his float coat."

"No way," Emma snapped. "He would never be on the flight deck without it."

"They said he used it to put out a fire." Grace's temples pounded. "There was…another man was on fire."

"Who?" asked Emma.

"We don't know. I'm sure his family is waiting like we are."

"When will we hear something?" Brian demanded. "When?"

"No one knows. There's…a lot going on. They were in the middle of a landing sequence on the carrier. The incident caused a wave-off, and four men were ejected from their aircraft. Five men are Status Unknown—your father and a Prowler crew. For the time being, a communications blackout has been ordered."

"So where *is* he?" Brian asked. "Why haven't they found him?"

"It's dark. The search-and-rescue team is looking, and we'll get a call as soon as they find him."

"*If* they find him," Katie whispered.

"Shut up, dipshit," Emma said. She glared at Grace. "This wouldn't have happened if you and Dad hadn't been fighting."

Grace felt the blood drop from her face. "What?"

"Maybe Dad took unnecessary chances because you're dumping him."

"I can't believe you said that, Emma."

"You shut up," Katie yelled. "You're wacko, Emma." She drew back her hand to slap her sister. Brian caught it in midair.

Grace sent him a grateful look. "Listen to us," she said. "Dad would want us to be good to one another." She caught Emma's eye. "Wouldn't he?"

Emma nodded. "Yeah. All right."

With nothing to do but wait, Grace gathered her children close and braced herself.

★ ★ ★

It was Allison Crowther who disclosed the names of the others, though there was no further news about Steve. She sounded terrible on the phone, her voice heavy with the terrible weight of dread. A whole Prowler crew, she said. A crew of four.

Grace shut her eyes and pictured the memorial on the windy tip of the Naval Air Station. All those blank tiles waiting to be inscribed.

Then Allison read their names from a list, and the name of the burn victim. She invited Grace to wait with her and the squadron families.

"Thank you, Allison. There's something I need to do right away." She hung up and found the kids glued to the TV.

"Nothing yet," said Emma.

"I need to go see Patricia," said Grace.

Comprehension broke over Emma's face. "Oh, Mom."

"And then I need to see Lauren," Grace concluded.

"Josh," said Katie. Her face turned pale. "But we only just found him."

Grace asked the kids to monitor the phone and computer, then grabbed her cell phone and headed for the door. Before leaving, she paused and looked back at her children.

"It's okay, Mom. We'll call you the second we hear anything," Brian said.

"Promise," Emma added, and Katie confirmed this with a nod.

Grace's heart filled up. Her children were almost adults, and their steady courage humbled her. "I love you," she said. "I'll be home soon."

She drove straight to Patricia's and found the chaplain already there, along with the wife of Rivera's commander. Patricia lay on the sofa, lost in terror and grief. A cordless phone receiver was perched atop her extremely pregnant belly.

Murmuring in Spanish, Patricia's mother and sisters surrounded her like a flock of angels. They had come for the baby's birth, but she needed them in a different way now.

"It's a boy," she said to Grace in a dull voice. "I found out this morning."

Grace sank down beside her friend. "Oh, Patricia—"

"Michael didn't make it," Patricia said, letting the phone slide to the floor.

Grace felt sick, but she refused to let it show as she turned to Captain Prudhomme.

"He gave his life saving others," the chaplain said. "He took it upon himself to dispose of an incendiary flare. Captain Bennett went to his aid, but Aviation Ordnanceman Airman Rivera sustained grave and extensive injuries. The medical team did their best to save him, but he died."

Grace took Patricia in her arms. Patricia sobbed with the peculiar rough gasps of heart-deep grief. It was a sound Grace had heard only a few times, and its eerie quality never quite left her. She wondered if Steve knew the man he'd tried to save had died. *Oh, Steve.*

"I sent Michael an e-mail, telling him about the baby," Patricia said. "I'll never know if he saw it."

"He loved you and the baby so much." Grace felt helpless. Patricia wasn't the first young wife she'd tried to console, but Grace would never, ever get used to it. Every woman's grief had a depth and cadence all its own. "He knows you and the baby will always be together, to comfort each other."

After a while, she took Patricia's hands. "I have to go see Lauren," she said.

Patricia made the sign of the cross. She had not been a Navy wife for long, but she knew what that meant.

"I'll call you tomorrow."

Grace left in a hurry and fell apart in the car, convulsed by fear and rage and sadness. Maybe Steve was dead, too. She couldn't stop herself from thinking it. Maybe he was dead, and she didn't know it yet.

Regrets welled up, pounding at her. Why had she been so uncommunicative during this deployment? Why had she been the first to stop hugging on the day he left? It seemed horrible and petty now. "I'm so sorry. I'm so sorry," she said over and over again. But it didn't matter how sorry she was. It didn't matter that, in walking away from Ross Cameron and all he represented, she had embraced the task of finding her way back to Steve. Now she might never get the chance.

Tormented by the thought, she phoned home as she drove to Lauren's house. No word, Emma reported.

As she pulled up at Lauren's, Grace forced herself to get a grip. No one would have told Lauren yet. She might be the love of Josh's life, but she was not his next of kin. The first word of the mishap would have to come from Grace. She knocked and waited, then noticed that she still gripped the cell phone in her sweating hand. Ring, she prayed. Tell me he's all right.

Lauren's appearance shocked Grace. She looked terrible, pale and puffy-eyed and immeasurably depressed. Dear God, had she heard something?

"Can I come in?" asked Grace.

Lauren nodded and stepped aside. A well-fed gray tabby cat slipped out the door as Grace stepped inside. The house was small and excruciatingly neat. It had a perfect view of Penn Cove. Evening light lay across the water, turning it to a mirror of pink and gold. Grace remembered a distressed-sounding message from Lauren on her answering machine. A hundred years ago, she'd been standing unsuspecting in her house, playing back her voice mail.

Steve's voice was on that message tape.

She touched Lauren's shoulder. "You don't look so good."

"I heard from the doctor today," she said. "It's…the worst." She sank down into a chair and clutched a throw pillow to her middle.

No, thought Grace. It's not the worst.

CHAPTER FORTY-THREE

"Lieutenant? Lieutenant, can you hear me?"

The voice thundered in Josh's ears. The glare of a blue-white light stabbed into his eyeball and he turned his head away. "Jesus," he said, "I'm okay. I just fell asleep for a minute." He looked up at the doctor and was almost afraid to ask. "What time is it, sir?"

The doctor tucked his penlight away and checked his watch. "It's 0500."

"Damn." He'd been asleep longer than he thought.

The doctor scribbled on a chart. "I'm ordering a thorough checkup, X rays and enough blood samples to make you cry." He clicked his pen. "How's your neck?"

Josh swiveled his head, feeling a hot twinge but masking his reaction. "Fine. Sir."

Josh spotted Lieutenant Martin Turnbull, who was sitting up in the bed across from him, eating a plate of scrambled eggs. They gave each other the thumbs-up sign. Hatch and Newman lay sleeping. Josh felt half dizzy with relief. Every man in his crew had survived the ejection. People would say they got lucky, but Josh knew it was more than that. It was a testament to the seat and to every minute of training and discipline they had undergone.

He'd been pleading to God a lot, too. Josh was not about to dismiss that.

"I need to use a phone," he told the doctor.

"We're way ahead of you. We've sent for one."

Bull threw a whole-wheat roll to Josh, who gratefully took a bite. The last thing he remembered as the chopper landed on deck was the shriek of alarms, announcements over the PA, people running every which way. He'd managed to stagger to the battle-dressing station under his own steam, but he remembered nothing after that. "What happened?" he asked. "Why were we waved off?"

"There was a mishap last night."

"I know there was a mishap, you knucklehead. I want to know what happened." Josh could tell Bull was holding out on him. "Bull—"

"Okay." He pushed his breakfast tray aside. "I heard there was an explosion. Aviation Ordnanceman Airman Rivera died."

Bull shifted his gaze in a way that made Josh stop eating. "What else?"

"Captain Bennett was present during the incident. He spotted a canister of burning flares and jettisoned it. There was another explosion and...he went overboard. I'm sorry, Lamb. He's Status Unknown."

Josh sank back against the pillows. He felt as though someone had hit him on the head with a sledgehammer. Bull and everyone on the ship knew of his relationship to Bennett. It wasn't a big deal. But at the moment, it felt huge. "How can he be Status Unknown? Didn't they get him out?"

"Not that I know of. He, uh, he didn't have a float coat."

Josh shut his eyes. Bennett was out there without a flotation device, in the cold waters of the Pacific. Right now, he might be floating away in the dark, an invisible speck against the swells and breakers. "Why haven't they found him?" he demanded.

"There were five of us in the water at different locations. Maybe they didn't have enough personnel and equipment to chase everyone down."

"That's bullshit. They train for this every damned day."

"Yeah, but the thing about a mishap is that every one is different. We train for fire mishaps and ejections, but both at once?" Bull shook his head. "The whole battle group's on alert. The Japanese sent out choppers from Chitose Air Base on Hokkaido, too. Maybe they've already got him and we just haven't heard."

Josh shut his eyes hard. He tried not to think about how cold the water felt, and how big the seas were, turning a grown man into a bobbing cork.

"You want to hear something weird?" Bull said. "They got it all on film."

"What?"

"The mishap. You know that magazine and video crew that came aboard? They were present during the mishap, and apparently they had cameras rolling, video and still photos."

"Of a guy burning on the deck."

"And Bennett beating out the flames and then taking the flare dispenser overboard. I bet it's fucking amazing."

"No, what will be amazing is when they get him out of the water," Josh said. "That's what I'm waiting for."

Captain Bud Forster came to see them. He had no further information about Bennett, but he had a phone. He kept it in his hand and looked Josh in the eye. "The doctor says you'll be up and about in a couple of days."

"I'm looking forward to getting back to flying, sir."

Forster's face was stony. "There'll be a Board of Inquiry to determine the cause of the incident. And a safety stand-down. Until then, you're grounded."

"Yes, sir." Josh understood the implication. If it turned out the aircraft wasn't malfunctioning and pilot error was to blame, there'd be hell to pay. Just like that, his dream would be snuffed out.

He dictated the number to Forster, then took the handset from him and put it to his ear. Damn. His mother wasn't home. Here he'd ditched his plane, and his mother wasn't home to hear about it. He told her answering machine that he was all right and would call her later. Without hesitation, he dialed another number. She picked up on the first ring. The sound of her voice brought his first smile since he'd pulled that ejection handle.

"Lauren?" he said. "Hey, honey..."

Something awakened Josh from a fitful doze. The hospital was a bad place to sleep. His first thought was of Lauren. She'd nearly blasted his ear out, screaming into the phone when she heard his voice. It turned out she had heard about the ejection from Grace Bennett and was waiting on pins and needles. His call, she told him, made the world right again.

"What's going on with Steve Bennett?" she asked.

"Status Unknown. I swear, that's all I can tell you at this point."

Despite the sweetness of hearing her voice, he couldn't stop worrying about Bennett. Now something was going on in the trauma bay. Lights glared and a team in survival suits came in, followed by medics with a stretcher.

Josh got out of bed, ignoring the twinge in his neck. In the resuscitation bay, Steve Bennett looked like a corpse. It was a shock to see his face, so like the face Josh saw in the mirror every day, sapped of color and unmoving, like a wax effigy. "Is he alive?" he asked the medics.

"Move aside, sir, and let us do our work."

Josh watched the trauma team work, the doctor calling out a stream of orders, monitors whining, a respirator puffing like a locomotive. After ninety minutes in a raft, Josh had been half-dead. Bennett had been out there the whole night, in the water.

Josh couldn't quite tell what was going on. The docs' dialogue was laced with technical jargon and it didn't sound good. As an aide went to get a satellite phone, Bennett still lay motionless on the table.

CHAPTER FORTY-FOUR

Grace bargained with God. She would give up every bit of the new life she'd built, if only Steve was all right. She would close down Grace Under Pressure, give up the new house and strap every lost pound back onto her body. She would become the best wife in the Navy, if only the phone would ring and she'd hear his voice. The offerings were too paltry, though. The miracle she needed was too vast.

Nervous energy flooded through her as the hours stretched out, and there was no word from Steve. Her cell phone was an adjunct. She kept it in her pocket and took it everywhere she went—to the garden to pick a rose, to the bathroom, to the car. She did a load of laundry, baked a batch of cookies for Patricia and washed down the deck as the sun set. Maybe the gutters needed cleaning. She was thinking of detailing the car later.

Still, her nonstop activity could not block out crippling terror and regret. Steve had left as their marriage was cracking apart. Now she might never see him again.

"Mom!" Brian yelled from the den. "Mom, come look at the TV!" He'd been parked there for hours, surfing the news channels and the Internet, desperate for information.

At the same time, the phone rang. Grace's heart leaped, but she let one of the girls answer. It was never the call Grace wanted, the one she yearned and prayed for with every bit of her heart.

Emma spoke to someone, then ran into the den with Katie close at her heels and the phone in hand. "Darlene says to turn on CNN."

Brian already had it on. The small TV in the kitchen was set to Fox News. "There's going to be a report about the mishap on the *Dominion,*" he said. "Exclusive footage."

"So much for the communications blackout," Emma said.

The anchor attributed the visuals to a team from *Newsweek,* with someone named Francine Atwater providing voice-over commentary. Suddenly Grace was there, on the deck with nothing but blackness in the distance. "On a night of routine training missions aboard the *Dominion,* they did everything right," the woman narrated, then paused dramatically. "But something went wrong. Terribly wrong."

Dear God. Grace reached for the remote control. The kids didn't need to see this.

Brian was quicker. "Leave it, Mom."

She didn't argue, because suddenly, like millions of other viewers, she was mesmerized by the images on the screen. An ordie in a red shirt was gesturing to someone. Even his cranial and goggles couldn't obscure his brilliantly handsome smile.

"…Michael Rivera, who was the first to notice the burning flares," the reporter said.

Something must have jarred the camera, because it turned cockeyed and blurred. By the time it righted itself, Rivera was rushing away with a large metal container that had smoke billowing from the top. Then there was a flash and more smoke, obscuring everything. The camera swung away, and a bleep censored the cameraman's comment. A moment later, a man in a white shirt rushed into view.

"It's Dad," said Brian. "There's Dad."

"Daddy," whispered Katie, then pressed her hands to her mouth.

He was so real to Grace in that moment, so strong and vital as he stripped off his vest to put out the flames. The voice-over narration had stopped; there was no need to explain what anyone with eyes could see. The boom and hiss of the flight deck roared from the speakers, and alarms shrieked as Steve picked up the big steel object.

The camera showed him racing toward darkness. And then the cameraman must have laid it on its side, for it showed only blackness.

"In an act of selfless heroism, Captain Bennett jettisoned the burning flares—"

The phone rang, and Grace's chest lurched in anticipation.

Katie pounced on the receiver like a cat on a grasshopper. "Bennett residence."

Her back was turned, but her posture stiffened as though someone had poked her. Oh, no, thought Grace. Brian and Emma moved to their sister's side, pressing close.

The reporter on TV now stood in daylight. "Only moments ago…"

Grace shut her eyes. *No. Oh, please, no.*

Katie gave a loud gasp and then shrieked, "Daddeee!"

CHAPTER FORTY-FIVE

Steve had only a few minutes to talk to his family, but the sound of their voices flooded him with strength. He knew how to get better without all the high-tech medical interventions. That phone call was all he needed. Grace had always been his home port. She never bailed out on him.

He shut his eyes, a smile lingering on his face. *Grace*. Her years of constant devotion held him fast; he was convinced that she was the reason he'd survived so long in the water. While the rest of the world might swirl in confusion, she held him steady. He wanted to tell her so, to fix the things that were wrong, but that would have to wait. In that first call, he had time only for the crucial information: I'm okay. I love you. I'm coming home.

The trauma took its toll. He fell dead asleep for a time, even with medics still swarming around him. Hours later, he awakened and ate three meals in succession, clumsily, with his left hand. His right hand was severely burned, covered with a Teflon dressing and immobilized. Then he voluntarily dictated a statement for the press. He gave a narrative of the mishap from his perspective. To beat out the flames engulfing Rivera, he had removed his float coat with its transmitter, air bladders, survival kit, fluorescent dye and navigation devices. He took it upon himself to avert disaster and in so doing, went overboard. Through the skill of the battle group's search-and-rescue operations, he was found, hoisted into a helicopter and transported safely home to the *Dominion*.

The worst moments of Steve's ordeal would remain private—the burning of his hand through his glove, the bone-jarring impact when he hit water, the endless hours of cold and half-consciousness. The deadly cylinder almost dragged him underwater, but he wrenched his hand free, then took off his boots, praying through clenched teeth the whole time. But strangely, not for himself. For Grace and the children, who were so much more important. He prayed they would be all right, that their lives would be filled with love, that they wouldn't be miserable with missing him.

He remembered seeing the ice-white glare of search-and-rescue lights crisscrossing over the churning water. He knew they were working hard to find him. But without any survival equipment, he couldn't help. He used his shirt to create an air bubble, which kept him barely afloat. Waves broke over him, choked him until his nose and throat stung. Out of nowhere came a memory of Emma the night she had saved a girl from drowning and been caught with beer. He wished he'd praised her more for the rescue, rather than yelling at her about the beer. "Rescue Me…" The song stuck in his head.

In survival training, he had studied every aspect of hypothermia and drowning, and he kept himself conscious by tracking his own inexorable deterioration.

It happened swiftly. The water was cold, the waves brutal and the current strong. He slipped under more and more frequently, expecting each plunge to be his last. Then his nemesis—the flare dispenser—popped to the surface and bobbed like a cork. Steve managed to throw his arm over it, and he lay there, half-dead of exhaustion, listening to the rhythm of chopper blades beating the water and hearing the far-off whine of engines. They would not stop looking for him, but at some point, search and rescue would turn to search and recovery. They'd be looking for remains.

He thought he remembered daybreak, but that might have been a flash caused by his brain shutting down. He knew he was getting close to the end when the only image he could conjure in his mind was Grace, his beautiful Grace who had given him the very best of herself for two decades. The only warmth he knew in that moment came from the tears on his face. She had never seen him cry. He'd hidden so much from her.

Then his brain woke up just enough to puzzle over a new sensation of heat emanating from the flare dispenser.

A wild hope brought him back to life. If he could manage to find a live flare, he would either burn himself to ash or alert the searchers. The flares were no good, but some emitted smoke, which would be visible to the rescuers just as dawn touched the sky. Minutes later, a UH-60J helicopter swooped overhead, creating a well of wind in the water. A pair of rescuers jumped from the helicopter and swam to Steve. He thought he remembered the transport, but a long blankness blotted out the rest until he became aware of glaring lights, the smell of antiseptic, the clink of instruments and a doctor giving orders. Warm saline slipped through his veins.

They said it was a miracle that he'd survived so long. It would surely be discussed at length at the safety stand-down. But Steve knew better now. It was no miracle. He had unfinished business with Grace, and nothing could keep him from seeing her again.

"Captain Bennett." Lieutenant Lamont stood beside Steve's bed. He was in uniform, freshly shaven, every hair in place, a cervical collar around his neck, his cap in his hand. "I'm sorry to wake you."

Steve had slept again. He didn't know whether it was day or night. "Lieutenant." He held up his good hand, reached for a plastic bottle with a straw and took a long drink of water. "What is it?"

"I wanted to thank you, sir. I know you'll get a medal for this, but I wanted to thank you personally. Sir."

Steve's heart ached. He wished he'd known this young man, wished he could have watched him grow up. "I appreciate that, Lieutenant."

"I have to go now, sir. I just wanted to stop in before— I just wanted to stop in."

"What happened to your neck?" Steve asked.

"Sir," said Lamont, "we had to eject."

"Jesus. Is everyone all right?"

"Yes, sir. One of the ECMOs broke an arm, and I have a minor neck injury. I'm on my way to a preliminary board of inquiry."

He had a vague memory of some trouble with Lamont's Prowler. Lamont looked scared. Steve could tell, because he had seen that look before. In the mirror.

"I ditched a plane," Lamont said incredulously. "Jesus."

"Planes are replaceable. People are not."

"Yes, sir."

Steve could see Lamont's frustration, even though he tried to hide it. And he understood it—both as a pilot, and perhaps even as a father. Flying out here on the edge forced a man to look at himself with new eyes. Maybe Lamont had finally caught a glimpse of the man he wanted to be, and maybe he liked what he saw. And now, if he was found to be in error, that might be taken away from him.

Steve thought about what the Navy meant to him back when he was that age. Losing it then would have been the end of the world. "What caused the ejection, Lamont?" he asked.

"Equipment failure, sir. When I was waved off, the Stability Augmentation System went haywire during the climb. I believe it kept sensing yaw and pitch that weren't there and overcorrecting. The Air Navigation Computer kept overriding me."

"The system's not to be turned on prior to a thousand feet," Steve said.

"I'm aware of that, sir, but in this case, I believe a blown fuse caused it to engage with weight-off wheels. Lieutenant Hatch started pulling fuses to see which one was bad." Lamont nearly crushed the frame of his cap in his hand. "Sir, this squadron has the best air crew coordination in the Navy. I did the preflight with the plane captain, signed off on everything. I looked the preflight documentation and checklists over and over. Can't see where we missed a thing."

Steve focused on Lamont's grip on the cap. "If you're that confident, you have nothing to worry about."

"Except a ruling of pilot error." He took a step back. "If you'll excuse me, sir."

"Dismissed."

Lamont left the sick bay, moving with a measured, ceremonial gait. Steve recognized that walk. It was the posture of a man who was in pain and scared shitless.

Steve sent for Killigrew immediately. "Tell Francine Atwater I need to review the video of the Prowler preflight. And for Chrissakes, get me out of here."

Over the objections of his doctor, he was dressed and waiting outside the conference room when the preliminary inquiry concluded. His hand felt like it was still on fire, and he wobbled on his feet, but he refused to send Killigrew for a chair. The door opened and people streamed out. Josh Lamont spotted Steve and hurried over to him. "It was the equipment, sir," he said, barely able to contain his excitement. "The video showed the error. During preflight, someone installed the wrong fuse. It belonged in an EC-2, not a Prowler. That's why it kept shorting out." Josh visibly tried to contain himself.

Steve grinned. "Congratulations, Lieutenant."

"Thank you, sir," said Josh.

"It was all on the video." In ordering every frame to be studied, Steve had felt the dedication of an officer to another in his command. But he'd also felt something else, something surprising— the fierce protectiveness of a father for his flesh-and-blood son. He smiled, filled with the happiness of simply knowing Lamont was here in this world, that he was a fellow officer and a good man.

Finally he said it, putting his heart out there as much as he was able for this young man. "I'm proud of you, sailor."

Josh held out his hand. In his open, honest expression, Steve recognized things he wouldn't say, might never say. But his joy spilled over into a jubilant grin as he said, "I'm glad I found you."

PART FIVE
ACTIVE HOMING

Active homing: A homing (guidance) method where the missile provides its own signal (typically either radar or sonar) transmissions and homes in on the energy reflected off the target.

(NAVAPS 1022.020)

CHAPTER FORTY-SIX

Grace felt like a bride on her wedding day. No, this was worse. At least a bride could look forward to a happy ending. Grace's expectations, her hopes and fears, were much more complicated than that. There were some similarities, though—the agony of waiting, the excited crowds, the cameras, the red carpet. Only, this carpet led to a restricted airfield rather than an altar.

The kids stayed close to her as they waited in the viewing area, demarcated by heavy ropes. Outside the airfield, news vans disgorged crews and equipment, and reporters jockeyed for position along the chain-link fence. Grace knew that whatever happened on the tarmac out there would be preserved on film and broadcast worldwide.

She always wondered what she would do in this situation, how she would ever show her gratitude for the miracle of her husband's survival. She doubted she'd look as dignified and calm as the wives in movies or staged events. Steve's survival overwhelmed her with joy, and she meant to show it.

In her pocket, she had his wedding band. He always left it behind when he went on deployment. She always made a small ceremony of giving him back his ring each time he came home. The night following his return was always a honeymoon.

She had no idea what was in store for them tonight.

An escort told them apologetically that the transport wasn't expected for another hour. He motioned them into a waiting area designated for families only. A long table was set up with fruit punch and an enormous cake decorated with squadron insignia. It was quieter here, and Grace tried to force herself to relax and be patient. One of the greatest lessons the Navy had taught her was that big events and ceremonies took time.

The kids looked wonderful, carefully groomed and dressed up. It was the first time she'd seen Emma in a skirt in months. Her Emma, who used to be the fashionista of the family, had abandoned pretty clothes just as Grace rediscovered them. Brian couldn't stand still; he walked back and forth, pausing to look out the window, and then resuming his pacing. Katie had used a small gold safety pin to repair her glasses this morning. She held a bouquet of yellow roses and wore a smile that outshone the sun.

Watching her, Grace was infected by that smile. Her youngest child had survived her first year of high school and was blossoming fast. Her body was rounding out and her face had taken on that ineffable air of mystery that surrounded teenage girls. Katie was such a jumble of contradictions these days. She'd spend hours writing deep, "angsty" poetry in her journal, and then, every once in a great while, she'd take out her Barbies. Grace touched Katie's shining hair. "Any time now."

"Thank God." She tore her gaze from the runway and turned to Grace. "This isn't like other homecomings, is it?"

"Well, no. Usually your dad comes home with the ship, or at least with his squadron."

"I don't mean that."

Grace knew that, of course. She also knew she was walking a thin line. She wanted this day to be a celebration of Steve's survival and homecoming, his heroism and pride. At the same time, she didn't want to mislead the kids into thinking life would go on exactly the same as it had before. "Today is your dad's day," she said. "He's the miracle man."

"What about tomorrow?"

"Tomorrow, we sleep in."

"Mom—"

"Whoa," said Brian in a low voice, and they all turned to look.

Lauren had arrived, looking radiant in a cherry-colored suit. Already she had the scrubbed, attentive look of a Navy wife, but that wasn't what had captured Brian's notice. It was the woman next to her.

"Whoa is right," whispered Katie.

They all knew who it was; they'd been expecting this. But Grace hadn't expected her to look exactly like Kim Basinger. She caught herself holding her breath as Lauren and the woman worked their way toward them, passing the families of the Prowler crew.

"Cissy Lamont," said Kim Basinger. "It's a pleasure to finally meet you."

She spoke in a delicious, honeyed drawl. She was perfectly dressed in a Chanel suit, Prada pumps and a flawless manicure.

Bravely, Grace stuck out her hand to the gorgeous blonde. "I'm Grace. And these are my children, Emma, Katie and Brian."

Cissy Lamont's hand trembled in Grace's. "My goodness," Cissy said. "It's an honor to meet you all."

Grace felt like Quasimodo, towering over Steve's movie-star-gorgeous first wife. Cissy was nothing like the trashy, immature woman Grace had conjured in her mind. Grace had pictured Anna Nicole Smith dressed in tight, overpriced clothes, pretending to belong to the country club set. Instead, Cissy was lovely, stylish and mourning her lost husband, a character straight out of a Danielle Steel novel. And worst of all, she laid claim to a part of Steve that Grace could never have. Cissy was his first love. She had known him in the wild flush of youthful passion. He must have been reckless then, and filled with a sense of possibility and excitement.

By the time Grace had met him, he was already an officer and a pilot, a man with duties to perform. She had no doubt that he was a better man than the boy Cissy had married, but Grace couldn't help wishing she'd known that boy, too.

"I'm sorry we're meeting under such terrible circumstances," Cissy said. "But I'm happy for us all that Josh and Stephen are coming home in one piece."

Stephen. No one called him Stephen.

In the awkward silence that followed, Cissy nervously snapped and unsnapped the clasp of her handbag. She appeared calm, but a delicate blood vessel in her temple leaped visibly. "I'm sure you all think what I did was awful," she said.

Lauren put a hand on her arm. "Cissy—"

"No, I should say this. Who knows when I'll get another chance?"

Brian shuffled his feet and looked longingly through the glass at the open field outside. Grace looked right along with him.

"I'm not making excuses for myself," Cissy said. "But I didn't think things through before heading off to a wedding chapel. No one explained the realities of Navy life to me, and then one day the man I'd just married was gone for good. I couldn't see him or speak to him or touch him. It felt like someone had died." She sent a quick glance at Lauren. "I had no family, no support system at all, just a group of other Navy wives who were as young and as scared as I was."

"So you up and left," Katie said bluntly.

Cissy nodded. "I cried for weeks. But, right or wrong, I truly believed that never contacting your father again, never telling him about Josh, was the kindest thing to do. I worried that if he knew there was a child, he'd feel torn. I couldn't bring myself to torture him like that."

Grace was shocked to feel a pulse of sympathy for Cissy. And perhaps a small, grudging respect. Cissy had demanded more for herself than a half-time husband. She'd gotten out as soon as she discovered the consuming nature of Steve's career. Ah, but look what she'd missed, Grace thought.

"I'm not without my regrets," Cissy admitted. "Even when

Grant was alive, I sometimes caught myself wondering about what I'd tossed away so long ago, what my life would have been like if I'd stayed the course." She looked Grace in the eye. "After meeting you, I don't feel those regrets anymore. Your family is wonderful. I can tell that already. Things were meant to happen this way." She rummaged in her handbag and took out a copy of *Newsweek*. "The new issue just came out. I bought every copy I could find at the airport," she said.

"We haven't seen it yet," Emma said, gaping at the cover.

The reporter, a woman with a flat, East Coast accent, had phoned Grace for comments, but she had not returned her call. It seemed a little surreal, though, seeing her husband's face on the cover of a national magazine. It was one of those shots that revealed much. Taken just hours after he'd been plucked from the ocean, it showed a man nearly flattened by the effects of trauma, fatigue and triumph. A small inset showed the Prowler crew and Rivera, looking so young that the sight brought tears to Grace's eyes. The headline read Heroics: All In A Day's Work.

While the kids gathered around Cissy, Grace gave Lauren's hand a squeeze. Her fingers were ice-cold. She seemed fragile, as though she were the survivor of an accident, too. This was her first experience of having a loved one at sea. The difficulty of her ordeal was written in the lines of strain on her brow and around her mouth. "Are you all right?"

"I'm holding up. This is so hard, Grace. I don't know how you've been able to do it all these years."

"When you see Josh again, you'll know."

A protocol officer came to say the plane would be landing soon, and the buzz of excitement heightened. The homecoming would be highly ritualized, and everyone had a part to play. From the Secretary of the Navy, who would emerge from a secure limo when the transport plane touched down, to the color guard and brass band, this would be a formal hero's welcome for a man who had saved an aircraft carrier from blowing up.

The AC-2 Greyhound appeared in the sky, and everyone

rushed forward. There was a prescribed order for the families to file out in, and Grace was at the lead with her children. She could feel the energy of anticipation shimmering through the lobby. A sailor stood at the door, arms folded behind his back as he awaited the order to proceed.

Grace waited, too. She caught a glimpse of her reflection in the glass double door. She was wearing a navy-blue suit she hadn't been able to get into in years. Now it fit her perfectly, and last night Allison had stopped by to give her a Hermès scarf because, as Allison pointed out, "You're going to be on national TV, after all."

Like the best of Navy wives, Allison was good in a crisis. She'd been there for the wives of the Sparhawks squadron since the mishap occurred. "And how is Emma these days?" Allison had asked.

"She's fine."

"Are you sure?"

"Of course I'm sure. We were all horrified by the mishap, but now that Steve's coming home, we're fine."

"I'm…glad she's all right."

Fortunately, Emma hadn't been around. It would have been awkward for her to see her ex-boyfriend's mother.

The plane taxied to the terminal and stopped. A truck with a staircase coupled with the hatch. Sailors rushed forward with the carpet and velvet ropes.

Grace walked through the door with the children as the hatch popped. An aide stepped out and came to attention. And then there was Steve, blinking at the sun, tall and straight as an oak tree. His uniform hung looser on him, and his arm was in a sling. Even so, to Grace he looked the same as he had on the day they married, and she vowed to love him forever.

She and the kids were told to wait until instructed to proceed.

Steve's searching gaze found her, and both of them froze for a moment, locked up with terror.

Grace didn't wait for instructions. She broke free and rushed to the plane, meeting him in a near collision as his foot touched the ground. His good arm went around her, and they kissed with a fierce gratitude that made them oblivious to the commotion around them. "You're home," she whispered, kissing his face. "Thank God you're home…." He was thin and his skin felt hot, and a medicinal smell clung to him. But he was home safe at last, and she wanted to melt right into him, or to absorb him into her, to turn the two of them into one unbreakable whole.

She stepped away in time for Katie to go flying into his embrace, and then Brian and Emma followed, laughing and crying, shouting over the noise of the airfield. She watched the children hugging him as though they'd never let go, and wondered how she ever could have put all of this at risk.

Cameras recorded the homecoming. Grace suspected the photo of Steve, surrounded by his jubilant children, would be one of the defining images of the day. He smiled at her over Brian's shoulder, and then he did a double take. How different she must look to him. Like a stranger.

"Sir," an aide said, "we need you over here."

Steve reluctantly disengaged himself from the children and headed for the official receiving line, the Secretary of the Navy at its head. The Prowler crew came next. Steve spoke briefly to the Secretary of the Navy, but Grace couldn't hear the words they exchanged.

She fingered the wedding band in her pocket, then looked at his arm in the sling. She'd never felt prouder of her husband, yet a curious distance still hung between them. She reminded herself that today was about Steve. This was a day of joy and celebration.

He scanned the crowd, barely able to sit still. Then she saw him sit up straighter. He'd spotted Cissy.

The two of them locked eyes across the crowd. His face didn't change when she put her hand to her heart. How beautiful she looked, how filled with regrets. Cissy was at a crossroads, a widow still young and attractive enough to have a new life, a woman with a past who made no secret of her regrets and who was clearly filled with curiosity about her first, lost love.

The connection was severed as Joshua Lamont greeted his mother with a hug. Then he grabbed Lauren, bending her backward over his arm for a prolonged and passionate kiss. Cameras went off everywhere and a collective sigh rose from the crowd. When Lauren stepped away, she looked dazed and weepy.

At the podium, the Secretary of the Navy briefly welcomed everyone, and brought Steve and the Prowler crew to answer questions from the press. Steve spoke the simple truth: He didn't consider himself a hero. He was a Naval officer, and his ordeal was all in a day's work. Good training and a positive attitude had kept despair at bay. "Dying simply wasn't an option," he said in response to someone's question. He flashed a grin as he gestured at Grace and the kids. "Look what I had waiting for me at home."

CHAPTER FORTY-SEVEN

"So this is our new house, Dad," Katie said excitedly. "What do you think?"

Steve felt like a tourist at a new destination. He recognized the house and gardens from the flyer Grace had shown him, the flyer he'd thrust aside, telling her it was a bad idea. Seeing the real thing was strange.

"It's great," he said as Brian parked in front of a two-car garage.

"It is great," Katie sang. "You can see eagles and ferries and mountains. The best view is from yours and Mom's room."

Poor kid. Clearly she felt compelled to fill any possible silence with chatter. He wanted to tell her to slow down, let him take it all in. He got out of the car and headed up the walk.

Grace took his good hand, her touch oddly tentative. His head was still spinning from finding her so different. She was not the Grace he had left behind. He had always loved the way Grace looked, but he realized now that it was because he loved her. Her new way of dressing and doing her hair made her beauty apparent to anyone.

He wanted to grab her and hold her next to his heart, right here and now. Still, he waited. There was a lot going on inside her—inside him, too, for that matter—that would have to wait until all the hoopla of his arrival subsided and they could find some time alone. He had a million things to say to her and no idea where to start.

Emma went to unlock the door. Of the three kids, she had changed the most, which surprised him. She was always his sunny, constant Emma. She seemed more somber now, more mature. That was reflected in the haircut, he supposed. She was on the brink of going out into the world to find her life. Maybe that was it. Everything was starting to feel very real to her.

She opened the front door and a large dog bounded out. Daisy. She approached him, head down, tail stiff, and made a great show of checking him out. When he reached down to pat her on the head, she snuffled and sidled close, her tail swishing. He used to think a family pet was a bad idea, too. He'd never had a dog.

"She's wonderful," Grace said. "I can't imagine being without her." She darted a glance at Steve. "Since the day I adopted her, she's slept on a dog bed in the bedroom. She snores, but it doesn't bother me. At least I don't toss and turn in bed so much." She flushed and looked away.

He squeezed her hand. "Then she won't bother me, either."

"Watch this, Dad, watch." Katie ran Daisy through a series of tricks—sit, heel, speak. "She's the smartest dog ever."

"Sure she is." His arm hurt like it was still on fire, but he kept smiling.

"Let's go inside," said Grace.

He stepped over the threshold, and it hit him. Grace had built a world for herself while he was away. He'd said no house, no pets, no career. And here she had all three.

On the front hall table, he noticed a legal-size envelope with the return address of a law firm. He wanted to ask her about it, but the rest of the day was filled with official functions that kept them busy, and kept them apart.

After dinner the kids made themselves scarce earlier than usual, Grace noticed. The girls had MTV turned up loud, and Brian was on the computer, absorbed in some incomprehensible quest game. Grace felt wedding-night nervous as she took Steve's hand. "Let's go upstairs."

He offered her a slow smile, weary but ripe with meaning. "Yeah."

She led the way, her stomach churning. "What do you think?"

"It's got a bed. It's got you. That's all I need." He stripped off his tie one-handed, then kissed her, and a sweet rush of desire swept through her. She let go of the things that were pressing at them, and for a few moments simply reveled in his embrace and in the contours of his body against hers.

The careening emotions of a busy day made her feel vulnerable. She pulled back and looked up at him. "I'm so glad you're all right," she whispered. "When you were missing, I asked for a miracle. And I got it."

"Grace—"

"Steve—"

They laughed at the awkward interruption, but the fact was, she felt nervous, and she could tell he felt so, too. They had stood at the brink of falling apart. Now they had to find their way back to each other.

She kept thinking about the miracle she had begged for, bargained for. In exchange for his survival, she'd vowed to change back into her former self. Would she? Could she?

"You first," she said.

"Honey, I asked for a miracle, too. I had to come back to you. The docs couldn't understand how I survived so long in the water, but it's no mystery to me."

He swayed against her, and she slid her arms around him, burying her face in his shoulder to hide her alarm.

"You need to lie down."

"Yeah, okay."

He didn't even bother with the tough-guy routine she'd expected. She helped him to the bed and gently undid the buttons of his shirt.

"Now, that's a move in the right direction," he murmured.

She touched his cheek, then drew back her hand. "You're burning up."

"It's from the arm. I'm not contagious, Gracie, I swear."

"Oh, for Pete's sake. I'm calling the doctor."

"Don't." He intercepted her hand as she reached for the phone. "I missed a dose of my antibiotics," he said. "That's all."

She hurried to the bathroom for a glass of water and his bag of toiletries. "I still want to call the doctor."

"Come on, Grace. I'm not spending tonight in the hospital."

She found several brown plastic vials of pills. "You have a whole pharmacy in here." Chills ran over her skin. "You're in bad shape. Why didn't you tell me?"

"I'm fine," he said. "Just give me a hand with these pills."

She made him take his antibiotics and anti-inflammatories, followed by a powerful painkiller. "Does that bandage need changing?"

"Don't worry about it, Grace."

She touched his cheek. "You don't have to be a tough guy around me."

"What, you're tough enough for both of us?" His eyes took on a glazed quality. The meds were kicking in fast.

"I always have been." She helped him remove his shirt. Layers of high-tech bandaging concealed his arm, but the sight of it made her wince. She went to his bag to find a pair of pajama bottoms and came across a familiar typed form. "Travel documents?" she said.

"I have to go to Washington." He paused, shut his eyes, then opened them again. "Tomorrow, after I go see Mrs. Rivera. I tried to get them to postpone it, but there's no way. After the debriefing, I'm supposed to meet the president, Grace. Imagine that."

She felt light-headed with pride in him, and yet, at the same time, a too-familiar sinking feeling weighed her down. "You've always been my hero," she said, battling tears as she handed him his pajamas. "Now you're everyone's."

He touched her hand. "I hate that I'm leaving so soon."

Love and pride collided painfully inside her. It was selfish to want him all to herself, but how could she keep him from being the man he was? "Don't worry. It's not every day you get to meet the president."

He settled back against the pillows. His unfocused smile told her the painkiller was taking effect. Grace stroked his cheek as she watched him. Though she'd known him for two decades, she had the sense that she had only just begun to understand him. And there was another person she was just beginning to understand—herself.

"I believe this belongs to you," she said, and took his wedding band from her jacket pocket.

"I believe you're right." He couldn't seem to lift his left hand. The tips of his fingers peeked out, swollen and discolored. "I'll wear it on the other hand for now."

She slipped it on the ring finger of his right hand. "That'll do."

He held his hand up, studying the ring. "So we're all right."

It wasn't a question. She was sort of relieved about that, because she wasn't sure she knew the answer. She stretched out beside him, praying the fever would subside.

"I should be making love to you," he mumbled.

"Hush," she whispered, stroking his cheek. "You are."

The next day, Steve had an official call to make, and Grace went with him. Their footsteps rang on the polished tile floor of the Naval hospital. They didn't talk, and Steve sensed her sadness as they approached the lounge where Patricia Rivera would be waiting. In his gloved hands, he carried a burden a thousand times heavier than its actual weight. It was a zippered bag containing Rivera's most treasured possessions—a pocket-size photo album with pictures of his wife, a sterling silver cross, his wallet, a logbook of his scribbled thoughts about everything, including lists of baby names and what Rivera expected of himself as a father.

The lounge was filled with people by the time Steve and Grace arrived. Most were probably relatives. When they spotted Steve, they fell quiet and moved aside. A small, pretty woman sat on a green Naugahyde sofa. She wore a plain cotton gown and slippers, and a hospital bracelet around her wrist.

Steve offered a crisp salute. "Ma'am, I'm Captain Steve Bennett."

"I know." Patricia said. "You tried to save my husband. I'm grateful for that."

"I'm so sorry I failed, ma'am," he said. "Airman Rivera was among the finest sailors I was ever privileged to know. He performed his duties with skill, honor and courage." Steve swallowed, moved by the sadness in her eyes. He'd brought Rivera's effects, he'd said his piece, but he wanted—please God, somehow—to leave her with more.

"Ma'am," he said, "I just want you to know how proud Michael was of you. He'd just received word that the baby's a boy, and he was so happy he couldn't stop smiling."

She stared up at him, and for a second Steve thought he'd said the wrong thing, that he'd offended her somehow. But then she smiled, a deep serenity radiating from her grief. A single tear tracked down her cheek.

"I didn't know if he ever got that message," she said.

"He did, I promise you that, ma'am. And he was on top of the world." Steve held out the package. "These are some of his belongings," he said. "The contents of his locker will be sent later."

"Thank you." For the first time, she made an attempt to smile. "Would you like to see my little boy?"

"Ma'am, I'd be honored."

A nurse wheeled in a clear plastic bassinet. The relatives closed in, clucking like hens. The infant was swaddled in a blue blanket and wore a hand-knit cap with a Stars and Stripes design. Michael Eduardo Rivera had come into the world after the man who had fathered him was gone. The sight of the little dark-haired bundle stabbed Steve in a vulnerable spot. The Riveras were living every Navy man's worst nightmare.

Steve watched Grace with Mrs. Rivera. Their quiet tears tore at his heart. It would be said that Rivera paid the ultimate price in the service of his country. No one would say that of Rivera's wife and child, though. But it was true of them as well.

Steve's thoughts were splitting him in two. He'd already had to decline a twenty-day leave—there was no time for that. In a month, there would be a change of command.

It was the next step; the path was crystal clear to him. He had built his world around setting ambitious goals and fulfilling them. He had an obligation to the men and women who served under him, and this would be the biggest shot of his career.

But now the Navy's expectations were running up against the urges of the heart and the needs of the people who mattered most. Steve had nearly died out there. You didn't walk away from something like that unscathed.

Josh's girlfriend, Lauren, arrived with Cissy. Steve looked at his ex-wife and felt a dull, hollow sense of failure. When she looked back at him, her smile wobbled and she quickly turned away. That was Cissy for you, he figured. She hadn't changed.

More crying, more cooing over the baby ensued. Surrounded by the women, Patricia seemed to grow a little stronger. The baby had the opposite effect on Lauren, though. She stared at the little thing and turned away to hide the slow slide of tears on her cheeks.

Grace hugged Patricia one more time. "We have to go. Steve's leaving for D.C. I'll be back tomorrow."

Thank God, thought Steve. Sleeping newborns and weeping women were tough company. As he and Grace headed for the car, he felt her watching him. "How'd I do?" he asked her.

"With Patricia? Fine." Her eyes softened a little. "That was particularly kind of you to let her know Michael got message about the baby."

"It was true. He was a good man." As they crossed the parking lot, he studied her, trying to figure out what was on her mind.

"What?" she asked, eyeing him suspiciously.

"You're upset about something," he ventured.

She tilted her chin up. "I'm not. But…I can't help but wonder what it's like for you to see Cissy again."

"It's weird."

"Just weird?"

"I don't know, Gracie. It's hard to describe. She's like someone I once knew who fell off my Christmas card list. Someone I didn't much care about finding again." He slowed his pace, wanting to finish the conversation before they got into the black sedan waiting for them. He knew better than to discuss personal matters with a driver in the front seat. He didn't need to explain that to Grace; she walked even slower.

"But you know," he added, "now I wonder if having that attitude cost me the chance to know Josh."

"What?"

"If I'd hunted Cissy down, I would have known about Josh."

Grace let out a soft gasp. "So you're having regrets?"

"How can I not?" he said, raw emotion breaking his voice. "He's my own flesh and blood. I missed watching him grow, seeing him become a man. I had no say in that, none at all."

She stopped walking altogether. "And just what," she asked, "do you suppose you can do about that?"

"Not a damned thing," he said, frustration burning in his chest.

"Well, you'd better figure out a way to be all right with it, because you can't change what happened." She started walking again. "You should talk to Josh."

"What?"

"You heard me."

"And that's okay with you?"

She glanced over at him, her silk scarf fluttering in the wind. "Of course it is."

"He doesn't need a father," Steve pointed out.

"And he doesn't need any more commanding officers," she said. "How about being his friend? Do you think you could manage that?"

He grinned at her. He wanted to swoop her up in his arms, but the sling got in the way. Besides, there was the driver, holding open the door of the black sedan, waiting to take them to the airfield.

CHAPTER FORTY-EIGHT

On her way to meet Josh in the hospital lobby, Lauren stopped in the ladies' room to wash away the effects of crying. Visiting Patricia and her baby had been both joyous and devastating. She ached for Patricia and the life she faced without Michael. But seeing the baby had reminded Lauren in the most concrete way that she would never give birth.

Her fertility counselor had advised her to take it easy on herself, but she was still wallowing. She was barren. An incomplete woman. A maiden aunt. And she had no idea how she was going to break the news to Josh.

She still felt tender, on the verge of tears, as she met him in the glassed-in foyer. "Where's your mother?"

"She went home." Josh sent her a penetrating look. "I told her I needed to be alone with you. I'm getting tired of waiting to see you."

Her heart filled up with warmth, and she willed herself not to cry again. This was it, she thought, the part Grace had told her about. You didn't break down and cry when duty called.

They walked hand in hand to his van. "So how are you and Mother getting along?" he asked.

"Fine," she said, too quickly. But the single word was inadequate to encompass the charged relationship between her and Cissy. Lauren had vowed to make a good impression. "I wasn't even nervous about meeting her," she added.

"I'm glad." He pulled away from the parking lot. "You bit off all your fingernails," he said.

"You rat. You're not supposed to notice." Lauren rolled down the window and let the air rush over her face. "*Nervous* doesn't begin to describe the way I felt about meeting her," she admitted. "I was terrified. This matters so much, Josh. It means everything." She swallowed hard. "Because you mean everything."

"Oh, honey. You don't have a thing to worry about. She already loves you. I can tell."

She settled back as they drove onto the base, stopping at the entrance checkpoint. But instead of heading toward his quarters, he went straight, pulling off beside a Prowler parked on a swath of grass.

"What are you doing?" she asked.

He went around and opened the door for her. It took only a moment to recognize what this was. "Oh, my God." She approached the memorial plaques with reverence and dread. Name after name had been engraved in the seemingly endless row of granite plaques surrounding the jet.

"I'm bringing you here because I don't want to lie to you. What your friend Patricia's going through, it happens. It's a rare occurrence. There are only fifty names here, because this doesn't usually happen. We try everything in the world to prevent mishaps, but it's a fact of life in the Navy."

She eyed the polished plaques glinting in the sun, each representing a life given to a cause she was only beginning to understand. She took a long, deep breath. "I get the point," she said.

"And?"

"And…I'm not afraid of this, Josh. Living scared never did a thing for me."

"I love that you said that. This is a sacred place to me, Lauren. I'm not afraid of it, either." Beads of sweat stood out on his upper lip as he sank to one knee.

At first, she thought he was having a fainting spell or something. Then he reached into his pocket. "I kept this next to my heart every time I went flying. Now I want to give it to you, with my promise to love you until the end of time." He paused, and a glint of mischief appeared in his eyes. "How'm I doing? Better than last time?" As he spoke, he slipped the ring on her finger and kissed her hand. Then he stood up. "Well?"

"I love you, too," she said in broken whisper. "But—"

"I take it that's a yes?"

"Josh. It's not that simple." She felt a special kind of pain. It was bittersweet, knowing she'd have to disappoint him. "I want so badly to say yes to you."

"Then say yes. Say it. Y-E—"

"Hear me out." She laced her fingers with his and gazed up at him. "When you left, I went out of my mind. I felt lost and abandoned. Grace says it's normal for a Navy wife to feel that way, that you get used to the feelings and learn to cope, if I had to ask myself if I could learn to cope, if I could stand to go through what we've just been through—getting a report of a mishap, waiting for news. I'm telling you, Josh, you're asking a lot."

"I know I am. But I have so much to give you, Lauren. I'll make it be enough."

"That's true. That's why, in my heart, I know I could be a Navy wife. I'd be good at it, Josh. I'd learn to love this lifestyle as much as you do."

"Thank God—"

"I'm not finished."

"Jeez, Lauren, you are one tough woman to propose to."

"Because I want us to be clear on what we're getting into. I've been busy while you were gone, Josh. I've had so many fertility tests I feel like a lab rat."

"Damn it, I told you, that doesn't matter to me."

"You might not think so now, but it's huge. You've always wanted a big family. You're the only pilot in the history of the Navy to drive a minivan." She tried to stay calm, but her voice kept trembling. "I can't give you that. In time, the fact that I can't have babies is going to drive a wedge between us. If you marry me, you're not going to get what you've always wanted. I can't ask you to give up your dreams."

"That's exactly what I'd be doing if I let you go. I knew it was true when I was floating through the night sky under a parachute. There's nothing like an ejection to clear your head. I know exactly what I want from this relationship."

"You want a family, too. You said so the first day we met."

"Sure, I want kids. But we don't have to make babies in order to have babies. We'll adopt. You'll give your whole heart to a child you didn't give birth to. Big deal, it's easy. Grant Lamont could not have loved me more if he'd been my biological father. Honey, you and I will be great parents."

She shut her eyes and saw a clear picture of them together. Children were a part of that picture. "I know," she said.

He hugged her close and lowered his voice. "Sweetheart, love and loss are a part of life. You and I both know that. Chances can slip away while you're looking for guarantees. It doesn't work in flying, and it doesn't work in life. You're my chance, Lauren. You're my best chance. And I'm yours."

The monument behind him was a watercolor smear, blurred by tears. "You are," she said.

"Now did I get you to yes?"

She threw back her head and laughed through her tears. "Oh, Josh, I can't wait."

CHAPTER FORTY-NINE

"We really need to talk about your college plans." Mom set a stack of five plates on the table.

Emma concentrated on distributing the plates, centering each one with military precision. Dad had just arrived home from Washington, and Mom had fixed his favorite meal—roast beef, garlic mashed potatoes and green bean casserole. That was a good sign, at least.

"I don't want to rush it," Emma said.

"You don't want to miss your shot, either," Mom pointed out. "You've been accepted to UW and Western. I just don't know what you're waiting for."

Emma knew, but she wasn't saying. Everyone would find out soon enough. Her silence was a protective cocoon. She had learned that if you told your dreams to people, you were putting them out there to get shot down. Annapolis was her dream, and she didn't want to put it in jeopardy or jinx herself by announcing her intentions. Brian, who knew what she was up to, was amazingly keeping his mouth shut about it.

"I'm still working on my decision," she told her mother. "I'll let you know when my plans are set."

"Fine, I won't push. But I doubt your father will be terribly patient about this, Em."

She grasped at the chance to change the subject. "He was great when Brian told him he's going to art school."

"Yes," Mom agreed. "He was great, wasn't he?"

"So what's up with you and Dad?" She folded each paper napkin carefully, running her thumbnail along the edge.

Mom looked flustered. She probably didn't even know that her hand touched her heart. "We've barely had five minutes to sit down together," she said. "It's hard, being married to a hero. When things settle down, we'll work out what comes next."

That used to be a no-brainer. What came next was Dad's next assignment. "He's going to be the CAG."

"That's right. But we have to look beyond the next eighteen months. You only get one shot at your life, Em. After what happened to your dad, that's never been more apparent."

"So when his next assignment takes him to the Pentagon…?"

"I'm sure that will come under discussion."

"You sound like a PAO," Emma said. "You're not telling me a darned thing."

"But I'm doing it so well." Mom put the last fork in place. "Come on. Let's get dinner on."

Emma noticed that her dad wasn't his usual teasing self. He'd been to Washington, he'd met the president, but he hadn't really settled in at home. He was superpolite, and he kept watching Mom like she was a pot about to boil over.

Mom looked really good, Emma thought. She'd totally changed herself. But that wasn't why everything felt different. It was much more than that. They were in a house their mom had bought, their dad had survived a mishap, and they were still trying to figure out if they could survive each other.

"Katie, supper," Mom called out.

"Coming," Katie replied, clomping down the stairs.

Emma was shocked when she saw Katie. "What the hell are you wearing?" she demanded.

"You said 'hell.' Mom, she said 'hell.'" When Katie realized no one cared, she grew defensive. "I found the dress all wadded up in the bottom of your closet, so I had it dry-cleaned," she said. "I didn't think you'd care."

The sight of the blue-velvet dress from Homecoming night made Emma want to puke. "You don't want to wear that."

"Sure I do." She twirled into the dining room. "It fits just right. There's a dance tonight, and I have a date."

"Jimmy Bates?" asked Mom.

"Him? He's *so* yesterday."

"Then who are you going with?" Mom asked.

Katie sat up very straight in her chair. She looked so pretty, Emma realized with a pang. So happy. Stay that way, Katie, she thought. Never change.

"Well?" Dad prompted her.

"Cory Crowther asked me," Katie announced, her voice soft with wonder.

Emma's blood chilled. "Oh, no, you're not."

"He asked me, and I said yes. I promise I'll stick to the rules. Eleven o'clock curfew."

"He's three years older than you," Dad pointed out.

"I can do the math."

"You're not going out with him." Emma breathed through her nose, but nausea kept bubbling up in her.

"You said you were totally over him months ago, so you shouldn't care if I go out with him."

"I care a lot. I won't let you go near him, Katie. I swear, I won't."

"You're just ticked because the dress looks good on me."

"It's not the dress. Don't let her go out with him. Dad, tell her." She wished her dad would remember how pissed he was about Cory last summer. She wished she'd understood back then what kind of person Cory was. She wished she'd walked away from him that long-ago night.

Dad spread his hands, palms up. "If it was up to me, I wouldn't let anyone date either of you, ever."

"What about me?" Katie demanded. "I made straight A's in school this year. I deserve a chance to make my own friends. I'll never see Cory after graduation. It's just for fun."

"You're not doing it." Emma's blood was boiling now. She should have spoken up, should have denounced Cory. The price of her silence would be paid by other girls, innocent girls, like Katie. Because Emma had refused to take responsibility for what had happened to her, Cory was free to attack the next victim. For all Emma knew, he already had.

"I swear, you are such a spaz," Katie said, exasperated. "I just don't see what the big deal is."

"The big deal is he raped me," Emma blurted out.

Stunned silence greeted the comment. She had never meant to say anything, to bring her family down this path, but now she understood that even though the rape had happened to her, it affected everyone she loved. She looked from Katie's stricken face to her mother's, her father's, Brian's. Emma burst into tears.

"Baby, oh, my poor sweet baby." Her mother's arms went around her, cradling her as though she were a small child.

That made Emma cry all the harder. "Oh, Mommy, I wanted to tell you so bad," she sobbed. "It was horrible, but I was afraid to say anything."

"You have to, Em," Mom whispered. "Please, we need to know. Are you injured? Do you need to see a doctor?"

A strange and remarkable calm settled over Emma. "No. It wasn't like that. It was…awful, but not violent. Not in the way you're thinking." She drew a deep breath. And finally, in a flood of confession, she told about the events of that night. She spoke up right in front of Katie, because Katie needed to hear this. She told them about the attack, about her confusion and pain and shame, Cory's insistence that he hadn't forced her, his threats about the consequences of telling, the vow of silence she took, the terror she had carried around inside her ever since.

"That's why you cut your hair off, isn't it?" Katie asked in a frightened voice.

"Yeah, I guess." She wiped her face with a napkin.

"And why you switched out of PE and started dressing all weird."

"I shouldn't have done that," Emma admitted. "I shouldn't have let him affect me at all, but I did, and that was stupid. I'm finished, though. I'm not going to be scared anymore." Emma could feel her old self glimmering in the shadows. It was amazing. She was finally coming back.

Brian shot up from the table and headed for the door.

"Where are you going?" Dad demanded.

"You know."

"Wait. This is about me. I'm the one who's going," Emma said, giving her mom a last squeeze and then disengaging herself. She couldn't believe how simple this was, what a relief it was to finally cry out her pain and heartbreak to her family. She felt cleansed inside and out, clean and strong and powerful.

Her mom took her hand. "Brian, you're staying here with Katie. Your father and I will go with Emma."

Steve burned. They said the flares he'd jettisoned burned at 1600 degrees, but this felt hotter, and it went all the way to the bone. He stayed quiet, though. He was trying not to lose it in front of Emma. Oh, God. *Emma.*

They talked to her in the car. Grace drove, because his arm was still giving him trouble.

"Baby, I have to know. Why didn't you tell us?" Grace asked. Steve could hear the ache in her voice.

"I was confused. Cory didn't think he did anything wrong. We were, you know, kind of kissing and getting close..." Her chin trembled, but she didn't start to cry again. "He told me I'd be nuts to make a big issue of it. And since his father's your CO, I knew it would cause you trouble, Dad."

He crushed his teeth together to hold in the anger and sadness at the sacrifice she'd made. And he knew that her decision to keep silent was partly his fault. Over the years, she'd seen him suck it up, hold things in to avoid making waves, all for the sake of the job.

"Ah, Emma," he said, reaching back to cradle her cheek in his good hand, "the Navy's my job. But you, oh, honey, you're my heart."

She offered a tiny smile like a benediction. "I get it, Dad."

"You're sure you want to do this?" Grace asked. "We can hand the matter over to Sheriff Hawley, you know."

"Not unless he turns down Dad's plan."

Steve wanted the little bastard in R.E.S.P.E.C.T., a voluntary rehabilitation program designed for violators in the military. Over the years, Steve had sent a few of his men to the facility in Montana.

The Crowthers' home had a view of the water and fussed-over gardens. After he rang the doorbell, Steve glanced at Grace and Emma, and was struck hard by the resemblance he saw in their determined faces. "I love you," he said.

"I know," said Emma.

When Allison Crowther opened the door, her face lit with a perfect hostess's smile. "Steve and Grace," she said. "What a surprise. Please, come in." Then she hesitated, and her eyes widened. "Hello, Emma."

Steve felt a little sorry for her. Mason Crowther was still on the carrier, and his wife would have to deal with this alone. "Allison. We need to speak to your son. Is he here?"

"Of course. Make yourself at home." She went out to the back deck and called out. Then Cory appeared, a pair of pruning shears in one hand.

The boy spotted Emma and froze.

In that moment Steve knew that Emma was wrong about one thing—Cory knew damned well he'd done something wrong. Guilt was written all over his face.

"Allison, I'm afraid we've got a problem here," Steve said.

"Actually," Grace added, "Cory has some bad news for you."

"He's got something to tell you about the night of Homecoming last winter."

"Aw, come on," Cory said. He turned to his mother. "She's still all mad because I broke up with her."

Emma's eyes turned fierce. "You raped me that night, Cory. You can tell your mother all the chickenshit stories you want, but that's what happened."

Allison swayed and held on to the door frame.

"It's all bull, Mom," Cory said. "I can't believe these people are here, telling you this shit while Dad's on deployment." He glared at Steve. "We were on a date, *sir*. She wanted to be with me. I don't have to force girls. I never have."

"You crossed the line, Crowther," Steve said. "You need help, and if you refuse that, we're handing the matter over to the sheriff."

Cory's eyes narrowed with hate. "You might not like it, but it's no crime to pork your slutty daughter."

Steve balled his uninjured hand into a fist. After the mishap, he had thought the fight had gone out of him, that he'd become a peaceful and gentle man. Now he knew there were some things he would never stop fighting for, even if it meant decking the CAG's son.

But Grace stepped in front of him, probably aware of the damage Steve was capable of in his present mood. Her arm flashed out like a lightning bolt, her hand cracking against the kid's cheek. The blow was so loud that they all flinched. The gardening shears clattered to the floor. Shocked silence froze everybody in place for a moment.

"Jesus." Cory stepped back, clutching his cheek.

Grace stared him down like a queen. And Emma regarded her mother as though she'd grown a foot taller.

"My husband will not be provoked," Grace announced.

Even in his fury, Steve felt a wave of admiration for her. Although the most apparent changes she'd made were outward, the most dramatic were within. The new Grace was cold and formidable as she turned to Allison. "Steve has a plan for Cory's rehabilitation," she said. "If you agree to it, he'll be able to take responsibility for what he did, and this can stay…between our families."

Allison wept, but her resolve didn't waver as she looked at Emma. "I never liked you. I never wanted you to date my son."

Emma glared back, every bit her mother's daughter. "Mrs. Crowther, this is not about your opinion of me. It's about something Cory did that was wrong, that was a perverted, criminal act. I was wrong, too. I never should have stayed quiet about it—"

"Did I hurt you?" Cory demanded. "Did I hit you? No. You were all over me. Everybody saw us—"

"Not when you stalked me to the women's locker room. I told you to stop. I *begged* you to stop. The only reason I kept quiet was that you said your dad would ruin my dad's career."

"And he will, you can count on it. He has before—" He snapped his mouth shut.

Allison gasped and pressed the back of her hand to her mouth.

Grace looked as though she wanted to hit her, too. "You knew. That day you asked me about Emma, you *knew.*"

Allison shook her head. "I swear, I didn't realize…I mean, I suspected something happened that night but—"

"That's nuts, Mom." Cory crossed his arms over his chest. "I'm not agreeing to a damn—"

"Be quiet, Cory," Allison said in a sharp tone. She stood up straight and drilled him with a glare. Steve saw the steel backbone every Navy wife seemed to possess, and he expected a she-wolf defense of her cub. But her next words shocked him. "This is not the first time a girl's parents have come to me," she said. "I want to hear about this plan."

CHAPTER FIFTY

Grace was the first one up, as usual. She made coffee and took her mug into the study to finish the kids' graduation gifts. Her e-mail box looked like Grand Central Station, but e-mail would wait. Everything would wait until Emma got better.

The pain and guilt of learning what her precious daughter had endured haunted Grace, and she knew Steve was tortured by guilt. They talked about it in broken whispers in the dark: Why hadn't she come to them? Had they somehow led her to believe it was better to keep silent about a rape?

There were no answers, of course.

Emma had agreed to intensive counseling, but Grace saw her healing begin the moment she confessed her secret. Walking away from the Crowthers', she seemed a little more like her old self. Yet she was a new person, too, possessed of a strength and depth that could only come from suffering and then surviving. Perhaps she'd finally decide on what she wanted to do with her life. Grace suspected her indecision had been related to the rape.

Now, at last, things would have a chance to settle down.

Or maybe not. There were two baskets of correspondence in the study, one for her and one for Steve.

She picked up the name bar the kids had given her for Mother's Day. They'd had it engraved Grace M. Bennett, CEO, and it was one of her most treasured possessions. She'd explained to Steve that she had created a corporation. She was so proud of it, but he didn't share her excitement. He seemed distracted by it all.

A staff psychologist had set up pre- and post-homecoming meetings, and those sessions would continue, with the family and separately, to help them process what had happened to Steve. He was at risk for the symptoms of post-traumatic stress disorder, which could affect the whole family. Distraction and detachment were part of that syndrome.

Grace shuddered, realizing she would never know everything about the trauma he had survived, just as she would never know all the details of Emma's ordeal. Grace was trying to make peace with the fact that it was not her job to absorb every single bump and bruise for her loved ones. Surviving something terrible was a personal journey, and doing the work on one's own was the surest path to healing.

She stared at the painfully familiar thick envelope on Steve's stack of paper. It had arrived yesterday. She'd seen that envelope many times over the years. *Honey, we've got orders.*

She parked her coffee mug on top of the envelope. Then she turned her attention to the kids' graduation gifts. She'd created a photo collage for each of them. The pictures were in chronological order, beginning with a shot of two perfect newborns, one swaddled in pink, the other in blue. Right from the start they'd asserted their own personalities. Gregarious Brian saw all of life as an adventure. There were photos of him white-water rafting and stealing home, building snow forts in Alaska and sand castles in Hawaii. Emma was their social butterfly, presiding over tea parties and birthdays, dances and Christmas pageants.

Standing on tiptoe, she put a couple of photo albums on a high shelf. A book fell to the floor, bringing with it a small florist's card, the one that had come with Ross Cameron's flowers. She looked at it for a moment, shut her eyes and let something soft and unformed fade away. Then she dropped the card into the trash can and got busy again.

As she gathered up the photos she'd sorted through, she was struck by those images, and all of a sudden she was crying. What happened to her little girl, her Emma who used to love so open-heartedly? Now she was a grown woman, struggling to heal from an unspeakable assault. Where was that laughing, blue-eyed boy who used to curl up in her lap at the end of the day? Brian was a man now, with plans of his own.

Did I appreciate my years with them enough? Grace wondered. *Did I really see these children?*

She used the hem of her nightshirt to dry her cheeks. The photo boxes weighed a ton. Judging by the number of pictures she'd taken, and the even greater number of memories in her heart, she knew the answer was yes.

Grace and Steve sat together in the bleachers overlooking the football field. She'd dressed for the unseasonable heat in a new sleeveless linen tank dress that had made Steve do a double take when he saw her in it.

The deep emerald green of the grass and the dazzling blue of the sky created a vivid backdrop for the three hundred folding chairs facing a podium draped in bunting. Down on the field, the band stood at attention, all eyes on the conductor's baton. Even from a distance, Grace could see Katie licking her clarinet reed in nervousness. She was soon to be an only child.

Draped in cameras, parents of the other graduates waited with the same sense of pride and expectation Grace was feeling. Every so often she felt an inquisitive stare. Steve was a local celebrity, with his picture on the cover of a national magazine.

But Grace knew that some of the curiosity had to do with Cory Crowther, too. The news had flown at the speed of heat—Cory, the football hero, would not be graduating with his class.

Grace slipped her hand into Steve's as the first nasal strains of "Pomp and Circumstance" drifted from the band. Then the blue-gowned graduates filed in, and they spotted the twins right away. Brian was unmistakable; with Day-Glo paints, he'd turned his mortarboard into an artistic statement. Next to him, Emma walked like a queen and took a seat, her eyes trained forward. A gold cord from the National Honor Society was draped around her neck, and Grace smiled. Emma was a proud and gifted young woman. She would do more than survive Cory's attack. She would thrive. "That's the best revenge I can think of," she'd told Grace while getting dressed this morning.

The teachers and school officials filed out and took their places on the raised platform around the podium. Grace nudged Steve. "What's Joshua Lamont doing down there?"

Lieutenant Lamont looked resplendent in dress uniform. He took a seat at the end of a row of teachers and gave his full attention to the school board president, who stood to introduce the first speaker.

"He's the admissions liaison officer for the Naval Academy," Steve whispered. "He confers the official appointment."

"I heard the only appointee was Crowther. Maybe Lieutenant Lamont didn't get the word that Cory's been withdrawn from the pool of appointees."

"Maybe there's an alternate," Steve said.

While the class valedictorian spoke, Grace studied her husband. It had always been a given that Brian would go to Annapolis. Even after Brian declared he didn't want to join the Navy, it was still a given in Steve's mind. Grace had expected him to mount a final assault on Brian's artistic aspirations. Instead, Steve had surprised them all. Even when Brian explained that RISD didn't have a baseball team, Steve hadn't blinked. "Some other family will get their Annapolis grad," he'd said last night.

Each graduate went to the podium for the traditional diploma and handshake. Principal Ellick pronounced each name with appropriate gravity: "Sarah-Marie-Adams." Burst of applause from her family. "Stefan-Amundsen." "Lawrence-Avery-Baker." Some graduates received additional distinctions—an associate certificate from the local community college, a special scholarship or award. "Brian-James-Bennett."

Grace hooted and clapped while Steve snapped a picture.

"Emma-Jean-Bennett."

More clapping, another picture.

"There is a special distinction for Miss Bennett," the principal said. "Lieutenant Joshua Lamont is here to present it."

Josh walked up to the podium. "On behalf of the United States Navy, I hereby appoint Miss Emma Jean Bennett the rank of Midshipman Fourth Class of the United States Naval Academy."

Pride and shock collided, stealing all rational thought from Grace. "Am I really seeing this?" she asked Steve, groping for his hand.

"Yeah," he said, looking dazed. "You really are."

The rest of the ceremony passed in a blur. Then, while the band played "Louis Louis," a shout went up from the graduates. Three hundred caps sailed into the blue sky. Steve and Grace jostled their way down to the field amid tearful relatives and jubilant grads. Grace hugged Brian, congratulating him. Then she turned to Emma. Her daughter had never looked more proud—or more vulnerable—to her.

"I can't believe you did that," Grace said.

"I wanted to surprise you."

Grace and Steve exchanged a look. "Well, it worked."

"How did you pull it off?" Grace asked.

"After I turned eighteen, I didn't need parental signatures on anything." She looked from Grace to Steve. "But I'll always need you guys."

The Navy is taking my daughter, thought Grace. They're damned lucky to get her.

Katie came rushing to meet them, pulling Josh along behind her. "That was the coolest," she said.

Josh offered his hand to Brian. "Congratulations."

Brian hesitated, his eyes narrowing in suspicion. Then he grinned and shook hands. "Thanks."

"There's a barbecue at our house this afternoon," Katie piped up. "You should come."

Grace fumbled through momentary shock, then said, "Absolutely. We'd love to have you."

"Thank you, ma'am. But I have plans with Lauren and—"

"Bring her along, of course."

He cleared his throat. "And my mother, too."

"She's welcome," Grace heard herself say. "All three of you are. I insist." It was a week for firsts, the first time she had nearly broken her hand smacking a boy across the face and the first time she had invited her husband's ex-wife to her home.

CHAPTER FIFTY-ONE

"Where are the kids?" Grace asked as she fastened her seat belt.

"They're going with Josh to pick up Cissy and Lauren." Steve started the engine. "You're sure that's okay, Cissy Lamont coming to the house?"

She turned and regarded him steadily. At one time, the idea of Steve's ex and his natural son coming to her house for a party would have driven her around the bend. But now she understood what the past was—and what it wasn't. "It's fine."

He smiled. "You're amazing. Amazing Grace."

She smiled back, but in a small, cold corner of her mind, she wondered what lay at the heart of his manner toward her. Was he reacting to the way she'd changed her looks, or to the reminder of failure Cissy had brought all these years later? What if he wanted to stay together simply to avoid failing again?

Not now, she told herself.

The relief and joy of his homecoming were powerful forces, but the unasked questions hovered in the back of her mind.

The deck was ready for a party, with paper streamers and napkins printed with caps and gowns, balloons sailing from the deck rail and a swag across the front window with the message

Congratulations Brian and Emma. There were ice chests of soft drinks and charcoal piled in the grill, ready to be ignited. The fridge was filled with hamburger patties, marinating salmon and a huge bowl of potato salad, and the freezer with five kinds of ice cream. A sheet cake decorated with a mortarboard had arrived from the bakery that morning.

Grace headed for the kitchen to start on the last-minute preparations. But when she set her purse and graduation program on the counter, Steve grabbed her wrist. "Not so fast," he murmured, bending to kiss her.

Despite the quick dart of heat she felt, she pushed back from him. "Your arm—"

"I've been practicing one-handed push-ups."

She bit her lip, delighting in the temptation. "I've got work to do. In a little while, the house is going to be crammed with people."

"Then we'll be quick." He gave her no more time to object, but kissed her again and walked her backward out of the kitchen. "You look hot in that dress, Grace," he said. "Is it new?"

"I…yes…" She felt him press her against the wall at the bottom of the stairs, and a helpless sense of need slid through her.

"I've been wondering all day," he said, his hand lifting the hem, "what you're wearing underneath it."

They barely made it up the stairs, and were out of their clothes by the time they hit the bed in a tangle of limbs. His hands found places that had not been touched since before his deployment, and she gave an involuntary whimper.

"We're going to get caught for sure," she said, mildly shocked and deeply turned on.

"Nah," he said. "I gave Brian twenty bucks to take the long way home."

"Then I suppose," she whispered, winding her arms around his neck, "we had better get busy." Her heart opened like a flower as she relearned the taste of his lips and the shape of his body. A passion that felt both familiar and brand-new rose up inside her. They strained together with urgency, trying to span the endless months of absence, the anger and fear, the uncertainty that hovered like shadows in the corners of the room.

He lay back and she straddled him, noting in passing that he'd grown thinner, paler during the deployment. She leaned down and gently kissed him while his hands and lips caressed her with a slow reverence that brought her to a state of searing anticipation that was almost painful in its intensity. For a while, there was only Steve, and the deep joy of rejoining her body with his. Heat shimmered over her skin and all through her, and even his most familiar caress and the rhythm of his kisses felt exotic. She shut her eyes and surrendered, the way she used to, the way she always did, with a blinding crash of sensation.

Sometimes, she thought, sinking down against him, they made love and that was all there was to it, and it was enough. But other times, like now, it was a revelation. They reclaimed the love that used to be, and Grace remembered all the ways they were so good together. This was no flutter of new love, no obsessive and dizzying first romance. This was the grand passion of her life. Steve, her husband. It seemed incredible to her now that she'd ever doubted that this was exactly where she belonged, no matter what the price.

They lay together, listening to each other's breathing and to the muted sounds of ships' horns and the wind in the trees. Grace circled her arms around him, wishing they could stay like this forever.

"That wasn't supposed to make you cry," he said, kissing the tear that slipped down her cheek.

"I was so scared," she confessed. "We lost ourselves, Steve. We lost each other."

"That's nuts."

"No, it's true. I used to think it could never happen to us. We're not bad people. This is a good marriage. But we started falling apart, and I realized no couple is immune. No matter how much we love each other, we're not impervious to damage. What's the Navy's term for it? A mishap."

"An unplanned or unexpected event resulting in injury, loss or damage."

"Can you honestly say you weren't worried about us?"

"All right. I was worried. The Cissy thing…I'm so sorry about that, Grace. I wanted to be…perfect for you."

"I don't need for you to be perfect. We're perfect together."

"Then why all these changes?"

She touched her fingers to his lips. "That was something I had to do. The day I walked into this house, I wanted it so badly that it hurt. Not because it's such a great house or anything, but because of what it represents. I didn't have the guts to go for it until you and I started falling apart. After that, I felt…entitled. Determined to succeed. I hated being separated from you, but it forced me to take a look at myself and make some changes."

He brushed the tears from her face. "I shouldn't have stood in your way. The staff psychologist I talked to after the mishap thinks I didn't want you having a life of your own because it meant I wasn't enough for you. And maybe there's something to that. Look at all you've done." He gestured at the room around them. "You don't even need me."

She lifted herself up on her elbow to look at him. "Idiot."

"That's what the shrink said."

She offered a last, luxurious kiss, ripe with promise, before she slipped from the bed. "We'd better get dressed. Everybody's going to be here any minute."

He protested with a groan, but got up and started putting on his clothes. "Gracie, the promotion board results are in…."

She fastened her bra and stepped into her dress. "What about it?"

"Turns out the Crowther kid made an empty threat." He paused, and his eyes shone. "Grace, I've been offered my own command."

"Oh, Steve." Her heart soared and sank at the same time. She was proud of him. How could she not be? Yet her heart seized with apprehension as she braced herself, waiting for him to instruct her that very soon she would have to abandon her home, take Katie away… "You've worked so hard for this. You've waited so long."

He looked at his bandaged hand. "I still have nightmares about the mishap, Grace. If I hadn't been there, if I hadn't done what I did, more people would have died. Maybe a whole lot more." He spoke matter-of-factly, without pride. "When it comes to saving lives, the Navy needs me every once in a while. But you—you and the kids—need me every day."

She stopped with her zipper halfway up her back. "What are you saying?"

"I've had an offer from Boeing. It's a permanent position as an aerospace consultant."

She fell still, not even breathing for a few moments. For her own part, she knew what she wanted. It was what she'd always wanted, to spend the rest of her life with the man she loved. The trouble was, life was complicated; Navy life doubly so. They had some hard choices to make. "When did this happen?"

"I made some inquiries when I was at sea. Then the offer came in a couple of days ago. I've been waiting for the right time to tell you." He paused. "It's a tough call."

She pictured him as a man in the private sector, taking the ferry to work and getting home in time for dinner every day of the year. It would mean giving up a dream he'd worked for all his life. "I'm not making the call for you—"

"And I wouldn't ask you to."

"—but you can't give up the Navy. It's your life." She was shocked by her own words. She was shocked that she meant them. Here he was, offering to surrender everything to her, and she couldn't bear to let him do it.

"Do you hear yourself? Last fall you were practically begging me to get out."

"A lot has happened since last fall. You can't sacrifice every-thing you've worked for," she said.

"Watch me." He stepped behind her and finished zipping her dress. His good hand rested on her shoulder, its solid warm weight holding her still.

"Steve, when you give up a dream, there's a price to pay. Trust me on this. Don't do this because you think it's what I want."

"I was dying out there in the ocean, Grace. And all I could think about was you and the kids. This is my second chance," he said, turning her to face him. "I've spent my whole adult life serving my country. I want to spend the rest of my life with my family. I want to get to know my kids better, help Emma with what's ahead. I want to fall in love with you all over again."

Even as her hopes soared, she had to ask, "Are you sure?"

"Hell, no, I'm not sure. But why should that stop me?" He chuckled at her expression. "I'm sure about one thing, Gracie—about us."

"Yeah," she said. "Me, too." As she bent to straighten the bed-spread, Grace couldn't feel the floor beneath her feet. She honestly couldn't.

Steve picked up their wedding photo from the dressing table and held it at arm's length. "Who are those people?" he asked. "I barely recognize them."

How wide-eyed she looked in the old photo, next to her handsome officer, how excited she'd been about the years to come. She smiled at that young Navy wife and felt a rush of grati-tude for her. She was deeply, profoundly thankful for that life. But now it was time to move on.

"There's one thing that hasn't changed," she said, turning toward him, her heart in her eyes. "And it never will."

They stood at the window, looking out at the calm blue water against a backdrop of eternally white mountain peaks. Ferryboats crisscrossed the Sound, and in the distance, a haze-gray destroyer steamed out to sea. Steve slipped his arms around her from behind and bent to kiss her neck.

She pictured the two of them here, in the house on the bluff, watching the shipping lanes from the deck, year after year. The image filled her with a sense of contentment so deep that she sighed aloud.

The sound of rowdy laughter and car doors slamming drifted from below. Steve stepped back and straightened his tie. "Ready?" he asked her.

"Ready," she said, taking his hand.

They went downstairs together, and opened the door wide.

★ ★ ★ ★ ★

ACKNOWLEDGMENTS

Thanks to my friends "in fitness and in health" at Island Fitness and Gym at the Pavilion. As always, I'm grateful to my first readers: Joyce, Rose Marie, Lois, Susan, Anjali, Kate and Sheila. Thanks to P.J. and Alice for insightful comments. I'm grateful to MIRA Books, and, as always, to the irrepressible Meg Ruley and her gifted associates at the Jane Rotrosen Agency. Island County Sheriff Mike Hawley provided answers about local details.

I've taken dramatic liberties with my fictional carrier, squadrons and military base, but through it all my goal has been an honest depiction of this unique way of life. To bring authenticity to this story, I relied on the generosity of Captain Joe Bradley, HM3 Owen Keifer and Public Affairs Officer Nancy McMullen. I'm also deeply indebted to the personnel and families of the Whidbey Naval Air Station, especially Geri Krotow and Captain Steve Krotow. I've written many books, and doing research is always a part of the process, but dramatizing the background for this novel presented unique challenges. Thank you for opening your very special world to me. Thank you for the sacrifices you make and the duties you undertake to keep us all safe. We are humbled by your bravery at home and abroad. I wish you peace and joy, every day.

READERS' GUIDE

1. Have you ever parted on bad terms with a loved one? Did you feel regrets about it or was it justified? Should Grace and Steve have tried to put their differences aside when he shipped out?

2. How much input should a parent get when it comes to advising kids what to do after high school? Did Brian and Emma make good choices? What were other choices they might have explored? Does Steve's job make it easier or harder for the kids to plan their futures?

3. How did you feel about Steve's decision to hide the past from his present family? When is it all right to keep something in the past a secret from your loved ones?

4. What's missing from Lauren Stanton's life? How do you think she and Josh will fare in the future? Is happiness possible for this couple?

5. How does the life of a Navy wife differ from the life of a civilian woman? Does it seem exciting to you, or would it be a nightmare? Would you like or dislike moving every three years? What are the advantages and disadvantages of doing this?

6. What did you think about Emma's ordeal? Was her decision to keep silent understandable? Did you agree or disagree with her parents' reaction when they found out the truth?

7. Steve's decision in the end was a bombshell. How do you think this will play out for the family? Have you ever made

a life-changing decision without being sure of the outcome? How did it work out for you?

8. This quote is featured on the author's Web site: "One advantage of marriage, it seems to me, is that when you fall out of love with him, or he falls out of love with you, it keeps you together until you maybe fall in again." (Judith Viorst, "What Is This Thing Called Love?" *Redbook,* Feb. '75). What's your opinion of that? How does it apply to the characters in *The Ocean Between Us?* Is this a factor in your own life?

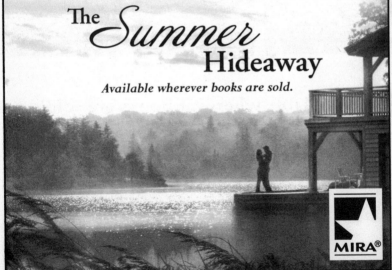